SILKS

DICK FRANCIS

AND
FELIX FRANCIS

SILKS

PAN BOOKS

First published 2008 by Michael Joseph,
an imprint of Penguin Books, London

This edition published 2009 by Pan Books
an imprint of Pan Macmillan, a division of Macmillan Publishers Limited
Pan Macmillan, 20 New Wharf Road, London N1 9RR
Basingstoke and Oxford
Associated companies throughout the world
www.panmacmillan.com

ISBN 978-0-330-51926-7

1 3 5 7 9 8 6 4 2

A CIP catalogue record for this book is available from
the British Library.

Typeset by SetSystems Ltd, Saffron Walden, Essex
Printed in the UK by CPI Mackays, Chatham ME5 8TD

Visit **www.panmacmillan.com** to read more about all our books
and to buy them. You will also find features, author interviews and
news of any author events, and you can sign up for e-newsletters
so that you're always first to hear about our new releases.

Our thanks to

Miles Bennett, barrister

Guy Ladenburg, barrister

David Whitehouse QC

PROLOGUE

MARCH 2008

'Guilty.'

I watched the foreman of the jury as he gave the verdicts. He was wearing a light-coloured tweed jacket over a blue and white striped shirt. At the start of the trial he had also regularly sported a sober striped tie but perhaps, as time had dragged on, the ultra-casual dress of the other eleven had eventually made him feel uncomfortably formal and his shirt was now open at the neck. Unlike most of them, he was grey haired and upright in his stance. Maybe that was why he had been selected as their foreman. I imagined that he was a retired schoolmaster, well used to taking charge and keeping discipline in a classroom full of unruly youth.

'Guilty,' he said again rather nervously, but with a strong deep voice. He kept his eyes firmly on the robed and bewigged judge sitting slightly above him to his left. Not once did he look at the young man in the dock, who also sat slightly above him, but to his right. We were in number 3 court at the Old Bailey, which was one of the older, Victorian-built courtrooms of the Central Criminal Court, designed at a time when the process of the law was intended to be intimidating to the wrongdoer and a deterrent to others. However, for all its formality, the courtroom was small, no larger than a reasonably sized drawing room. The judge, sitting up high behind his long bench, dominated the space and all the other participants, defendant, counsel and jury were so close together that they would have been able to lean forward and touch one another, provided, of course, they had wanted to.

In all, the schoolmasterly foreman repeated the same word eight times before sitting back down with, I sensed, a small sigh of relief that the ordeal was finally over.

The jury had found the young man guilty on all eight counts, four of them for assault occasioning actual bodily harm, three of inflicting grievous bodily harm, and one of attempted murder.

I wasn't really surprised. I was also certain that the young man was guilty, and I was his defence counsel.

Why, I asked myself, had I wasted my most favourite days of the whole year sitting in the Old Bailey trying to save such an undeserving character from a lengthy stretch in the slammer?

Well, for the money, I supposed. But I would much rather have been at Cheltenham for the racing festival. Especially as, this afternoon, I had been expecting to ride my own twelve-year-old bay gelding in the Foxhunter Chase, also known as the Gold Cup for amateur riders.

British justice has, for the past five hundred years, held that a man is innocent until proven guilty. The courtesies of courtroom etiquette are maintained with the accused being referred to simply as the defendant. He is not required to prove his innocence, rather just to defend himself against allegations, allegations that have to be proven beyond a reasonable doubt. The defendant is addressed using the title Mister, Doctor or Sir, or My Lord, or even Reverend or, dare I say, Right Reverend or Your Grace, as is appropriate. However, once the jury has pronounced his guilt, the defendant instantly becomes 'the offender' and loses the right to such niceties. The mood changes from one of polite discovery and laying bare of the pertinent facts, to one of punishment and retribution for misdeeds now proven.

Almost before the foreman settled again in his seat, the prosecution counsel rose to inform the court of the previous convictions of the offender. And previous there were. Four times before he had been convicted of violent offences including two of malicious wounding. On two occasions the young man had been detained for periods in a young-offenders' institution.

I watched the members of the jury as they absorbed the information. They had spent nearly a week in deliberations before delivering their verdicts. Now some of them were visibly shocked to discover the true character of t' smartly dressed twenty-three-year-old young man in the dock who looked as if butter wouldn't melt in his mouth.

I again wondered what I was doing here. Why, I asked myself for the umpteenth time, had I taken on such a hopeless case? I knew the answer. Because I had been urged to do so by a friend of a friend of the young man's parents. They had all pleaded with me to take him on, promising that he was innocent and that the charges were the result of mistaken identity. And, of course, because they were paying me handsomely.

However, I had soon discovered that the only thing mistaken in this case was the unshakeable belief of his parents that their little angel couldn't possibly have done such a nasty thing as to attack a family with a baseball bat. The only motive for the attack was that the father of the family had complained to the police about the young man using the road outside their house as a drag-racing strip each night until two or three in the morning.

The more I had learned about my client the more I had realized my error in accepting the brief. So clear was it to me that he was guilty as charged that I thought the trial would be over nice and quickly and I would be able to go to Cheltenham races with a light heart and a heavy wallet. That the jury had inexplicably taken so long to reach a conclusion of the bleeding obvious was just one of those things.

I had thought about bunking off to the races, claiming sickness, but the judge was a racing man and he had only ~e previous evening commiserated with me that I would be unable to ride in the Foxhunters. To have feigned sickness and then ridden in the race would likely have put me up before him on contempt charges, and then I could kiss goodbye any aspirations I might have of promotion to QC, a Queen's Counsel – a silk.

'There will always be next year,' the judge had said with an irritating smile.

But one didn't just enter a horse in the Foxhunters, one had to qualify by winning other races, and this was the first time I had managed to do so in ten years of trying. Next year both horse and rider would be another year older and neither of us was in the first flush of youth. There might never be another chance for us together.

I looked at my watch. The race was due off in half an hour. My horse would still run, of course, but there would be another jockey on board and I hated the thought of it. I had played out the race so often in my head and now someone else would be taking my place. I should be in the Cheltenham changing room right now, pulling on the lightweight racing breeches and the brightly coloured silks, not sat here in pinstripe suit, gown and wig, far from the cheering crowd, in depression rather than anticipation.

'Mr Mason,' repeated the judge, bringing me back from my daydreaming. 'I asked you if the defence wishes to say anything before sentence.'

'No, Your Honour,' I said, half standing and then returning to my seat. As far as I could see there were no mitigating circumstances that I wanted to bring to the court's attention. I couldn't claim the young man was the product of a deprived or broken background, nor could I try to excuse his behaviour by reference to some past abuse. In fact quite the reverse was true. His parents were loving both of him and of each other, and he had been educated at one of the country's leading private schools, or at least he had until he was seventeen, when he had been expelled for bullying the younger boys and then threatening the headmaster with a broken bottle while being reprimanded for it.

'The prisoner will stand,' announced the court clerk.

The young man rose to his feet slowly, almost smugly. I stood up too.

'Julian Trent,' the judge addressed him, 'you have been found guilty by this court of perpetrating a violent and unprovoked attack on an innocent family including a charge of attempted murder. You have shown little or no remorse for your actions and I consider you a danger to society. You have previous convictions for violence and you seem unable or unwilling to learn the errors of your ways. I am conscious of my duty to protect the public. Therefore, you will go to prison for eight years. Take him down.'

Julian Trent simply shrugged his shoulders and was ushered down the stairs from the dock to the cells beneath by two burly prison officers. Mrs Trent in the public gallery burst into tears and was comforted by her ever-present husband. I wondered if a week of listening to the damning evidence in the case had made any changes to their rosy opinion of their little boy.

SILKS

I had quietly hoped that the judge would lock young Julian up for life and throw away the key. I knew that in spite of the eight-year prison sentence it would be, in fact, only half of that before he was back on the streets, arrogantly using his baseball bat to threaten and beat some other poor soul who crossed his path.

Little did I realize at the time that it would be a good deal sooner than four years, and that it would be me on the receiving end.

PART ONE

MURDER, ARREST
AND REMAND

NOVEMBER 2008

CHAPTER ONE

'Hi, Perry. How're you doing?'

'Fine, thanks,' I replied, waving a hand. My name isn't actually Perry, it's Geoffrey, but I have long since given up expecting the other jockeys in the changing room to use it. When one is a lawyer, a barrister even, with the surname Mason, one has to expect it. It's like being a White in the forces: invariably the nickname Chalky is added.

I was secretly quite pleased that I was addressed at all by the professionals with whom I occasionally shared a moment's contact. They were together, day in and day out, going about their daily work at the many racecourses around the country, while I averaged only a dozen or so rides a year, almost always on my own horse. An 'amateur rider', as I was officially defined, was tolerated, just, as long as he knew his place, which was next to the door of the changing room where it was always coldest and where clothes and towels were regularly trampled when the jockeys were called to the paddock by an official.

A few of the older changing rooms still had v

11

burning stoves in a corner to provide comfort when it was wet and freezing outside. Woe betide some eager young amateur rider who took a seat near the heat, however early he might have arrived at the racecourse. Such comforts had to be earned and were the privilege of the senior jocks.

'Any juicy cases, Perry?' asked a voice from up the far end.

I looked up. Steve Mitchell was one of the elite, constantly vying over the past few seasons with two others for the steeplechase champion jockey's crown. He was currently the reigning champion, having won more races in the previous year than any other, and he was lying third in the present campaign.

'Just the usual,' I said. 'Kidnap, rape and murder.'

'Don't know how you do it,' he said, pulling a white roll-neck sweater over his head.

'It's a job,' I said. 'And it's safer than yours.'

'Yeah, suppose so. But some guy's life depends on you.' He pulled on his breeches.

'They don't hang murderers any more, you know,' I said. More's the pity, I thought, for some of them.

'No,' said Steve. 'But if you mess up, someone might go to jail for years.'

'They may go to jail because they deserve to, no matter what I do,' I said.

'that make you a failure?' he said, buttoning up te hooped jacket.

'Ha,' I laughed. 'When I win I take some of the credit. When I lose I say that justice takes its course.'

'Not me,' he laughed back, throwing his arms open wide. 'When I win I take all the credit, and when I lose I blame the horse.'

'Or the trainer,' piped in another.

Everyone laughed. Changing-room banter was the antidote to danger. Five or six times a day, every day, these guys put their lives on the line, riding more than half a ton of horse over five-foot fences at thirty miles an hour with no seat belt, no air-bag, and precious little protection.

'Unless you stopped it.' The voice had a distinctive Scottish accent. The laughter died instantly. Scot Barlow was, it was safe to say, not the most popular regular in the jockeys' room. That comment from anyone else would have been the cause for renewed mirth but from Scot Barlow it had menace.

Like Steve Mitchell, Barlow was one of the big three and he currently led the title race by the odd winner or two. But the reason Scot Barlow was not the most popular of colleagues was not because he was successful, but because he had a reputation, rightly or wrongly, of bleating to the authorities about his fellow jockeys if they transgressed the rules. As Reno Clemens, the third of the big three, had once said to me by way of a warning, 'Barlow is a snitch, so keep your betting slips out of his reach.'

Professional jockeys were not allowed to bet on horses.

It expressly said so in the terms of their riding licences. Some of them did, of course, and it was reliably reported to me that Scot Barlow had been known to go through his fellow jockeys' pockets to find the illicit betting slips to give to the stewards. Whether he had or not, I didn't know, it was hearsay evidence only and might be inadmissible in court, but the others believed it absolutely.

Somewhat strangely, as an amateur rider, I was allowed to bet, and I did so regularly, but usually only on myself to win. Always the optimist.

We were in the jockeys' changing room at Sandown Park racecourse, in Surrey, and I was riding in the fifth race, a three-mile chase reserved for amateur riders. It was a rare treat for me to be part of a big-race Saturday. Races for amateurs were rare these days, especially at the weekends, and I usually had to confine myself to such races as my weight had inexorably risen to what was considered natural for someone nearing his thirty-sixth birthday and standing five foot ten and a half in his socks. I tried my best to keep it down and regularly starved myself through the winter months to ride at the amateur riders' days in the spring. At least the races reserved for the likes of me tended to have higher weights than those in which I would compete with the pros. There was no chance of me seeing ten stone again and the lowest riding weight I could now seriously consider was eleven stone seven, as it included not only my expanding body, but also my clothes, my riding boots and my saddle.

The jockeys were called for the third race, the main

event of the afternoon, and there was the usual lack of a mad rush for the door. Jockeys are generally very superstitious and many of them like to be the last one to leave the changing room for luck, while others simply don't want to spend any time making small talk in the parade ring with the owner and trainer of the horse they are riding. Some even hang around polishing and re-polishing their already clean goggles until the get-mounted bell has already been rung and the officials are having palpitations trying to get them out. I had grabbed all my stuff from off the floor and I now held it close to my chest to protect it until even the last of the tardy bunch had exited, then I put my tweed jacket over my silks and went out to watch the contest on the weighing-room televisions.

The blue and white hooped colours flashed past the post to win by a head in a tight finish. Steve Mitchell had closed the gap on Barlow and Clemens with one more win.

I went back into the jockeys' inner sanctum to begin my mental preparation for the fifth race. I had discovered that I increasingly needed to get myself into the right frame of mind. If I wasn't properly prepared, the whole thing would seemingly pass me by, and be over before I was even ready for it to start. As I knew that my racing days were numbered, I didn't want to waste any of them.

I sat on the bench that ran all round the room, and went through again in my head where I wanted to be as the tapes went up, where I would be as we approache the first fence and where I hoped to be as we approached the last. Of course, in my mind's eye we would win the race and my apprehension would turn to joy. And that wouldn't be all that unexpected. My bay gelding and I would start as favourite. His win in the Foxhunters at the Cheltenham Festival in March would make sure of that.

Steve Mitchell came waltzing back into the changing room with a grin on his face wider than the eight-lane highway down the road.

'What about that then, Perry?' he said, slapping me on the back, bringing me out of my trance. 'Bloody marvellous. And I beat that bastard Barlow. You should have seen his face. Furious, he was.' He laughed expansively. 'Serves him bloody well right.'

'What for?' I asked innocently.

He stood still for a moment and looked at me inquisitively. 'For being a bastard,' he said, and turned away towards his peg.

'And is he?' I asked his back.

He turned round to face me. 'Is he what?'

'A bastard.'

There was a pause.

'You're a funny bloke, Perry,' he said, irritated. 'What bloody difference does it make whether he's a real bastard or not.'

I was beginning to wish I hadn't got into this conversation. Being a barrister didn't always help one to make friends.

'Well done anyway,' I said to him, but the moment

had passed and he just waved a dismissive hand and turned his back on me once again.

'Jockeys!' An official put his head round the changing-room door and called the group of nineteen of us amateurs to the parade ring.

My heart rate rose a notch. It always did. Adrenalin pumped through my veins and I positively jumped up and dived through the doorway. No superstitious last one out of the changing room for me, I wanted to savour every moment. It felt like my feet were hardly touching the ground.

I adored this feeling. This was why I loved to ride in races. This was my fix, my drug. It was arguably less safe than sniffing cocaine and certainly more expensive, but it was a need in me, a compulsion, an addiction. Thoughts of heavy falls, of mortal danger, of broken bones and bruised bodies were banished simply by the thrill and the anticipation of the coming race. Such was the feeling on every occasion, undiminished by time and familiarity. I often told myself that I would hang up my saddle for good only when that emotion ceased to accompany the official's call for 'jockeys'.

I made it to the parade ring without floating away altogether and stood excited on the tightly mowed grass with my trainer, Paul Newington.

When I acquired my first horse some fifteen years ago, Paul had been thought of as the 'bright young up-and-coming trainer' in the sport. Now he was considered to be the man who never quite fulfilled his potential. He was originally from Yorkshire but had moved south in his late twenties, headhunted to take over from one of the grand old men of racing who had been forced into retirement by illness. Far from being up-and-coming, he was now in danger of becoming down-and-going, struggling to fill his expansive training establishment in Great Milton, just to the east of Oxford.

But I liked him, and my own experience of his skills had been nothing but positive. Over the years he had bought for me a succession of sound hunter-chasers that had carried me, for the most part, safely over hundreds of miles and thousands of fences. Mostly they had been steady rather than spectacular, but that had been my brief to him when buying. I wanted to be in one piece more than I wanted to win.

'I think you should beat this lot,' Paul said, loosely waving a hand at the other groups in the parade ring. 'Fairly jumping out of his skin, he is.'

I didn't like being expected to win. Even when defending in court I was generally pessimistic about my clients' chances. That way, winning was unexpected and joyful while losing wasn't too much of a disappointment.

'Hope so,' I replied. My apprehension grew as an official rang the bell and called for the jockeys to get mounted.

Paul gave me a leg-up onto my current pride and joy. Sandeman was the best horse I had ever owned by a long way. Paul had bought him for me as an eight-year-old with a mixed history of fairly moderate results in hurdle races. Paul had reckoned that Sandeman was too big a horse to run over hurdles and that he would be much better as a chaser and he had been right. The horse had quickly learned the skill of jumping the bigger obstacles and was soon shooting up the handicap. So far we had won eight races together and he had won five others without me in the saddle, including that victory in the Foxhunter Chase at Cheltenham.

This was his first run since the summer layoff. He would be thirteen on the first of January and, consequently, he was close to the twilight of his career. Paul and I had planned that he would race just twice before the Cheltenham Festival, before what we hoped would be a repeat victory in the Foxhunters.

I had first been introduced to steeplechase racing by my uncle Bill when I was twelve. Uncle Bill was my mother's younger brother and he was still in his early twenties when he had been delegated to take me out for the day and keep me out of mischief. I had been staying with him and his parents, my grandparents, while my own mother and father were away together on holiday in South America.

I had clambered eagerly into the passenger seat of his beloved open-topped MG Midget and we had set out for the south coast and the planned day at Worthing in West Sussex.

Unbeknown to me, or to his somewhat austere p‌

Uncle Bill had no intention of spending the day dragging his young nephew across Worthing's steep pebble beach or along its elegant Victorian pier so I could be entertained by the amusement arcades. Instead he drove us about fifteen miles further to the west to Fontwell Park racecourse, and my abiding passion for jump racing was born.

At almost every British racecourse it is possible for the spectators to stand next to a fence, to experience the thrill of being so close up as half-ton horses soar over and through the tightly bound birch, to hear the horses' hooves thumping the turf, to feel the earth tremble, and to sense the excitement of being part of the race. But at Fontwell the steeplechase course is a figure of eight and one can run between the jumps that are near to the cross-over point and be close to the action twice on each circuit, six times in all during a three-mile chase.

Uncle Bill and I spent much of the afternoon running across the grass from fence to fence, and by the end of the day I knew for certain that I wanted to be one of those brave young men in their bright coloured silks fearlessly kicking and urging his mount into the air at thirty miles an hour with hope in his heart, trusting that the spindly legs of the thoroughbred racehorse beneath him would save them both from crashing to the ground on the other side.

Such was my conviction that I could think of nothing for weeks and I begged my uncle to take me with him to the races whenever I could get away from more mundane things like school and studying.

I enrolled at a local riding stables and soon mastered the art, not of dressage as they would have preferred, but of riding at speed over jumps. My teacher tried in vain to get me to sit upright in the saddle with my heels down. However, I was determined to stand in the stirrups crouching over the animal's withers just as I had seen the jockeys do.

By the time I was seventeen and learning to drive a car, I could navigate my way around the country not by the positions of the major cities but by the locations of the racecourses. Maybe I couldn't find my way to Birmingham, or to Manchester or to Leeds, but I knew unerringly the quickest route from Cheltenham to Bangor-on-Dee, or from Market Rasen to Aintree.

Sadly, by then I had come to terms with the fact that I was never going to earn my living from race riding. For a start, despite my best efforts in refusing my school dinners, I had grown too tall and was already showing signs of becoming too heavy to be a professional jockey. Coupled with that was an apparent gift for academic success, and the fact that my future career in the law had been planned out to the nth degree by my father. He had decided that I would follow him to his old college at London University, then, like him, to the College of Law in Guildford and, finally, into the same firm of high-street solicitors that he himself had joined some thirty years previously. I would spend my life, like his, conveyancing property from seller to buyer, drawing up last wills and testaments, and untying the knots of failed marriages in south-west London suburbia. The promised boredom of it all had filled me with horror.

I had been twenty-one and in my third year of a Bachelor of Laws degree at UCL when my darling mother had finally lost her long battle against leukaemia. Her death wasn't a surprise to me, in fact she had lived far longer than any of the family had expected, but, perhaps for the first time, it brought home to me the fallibility and transitory nature of the human state. She died on her forty-ninth birthday. There had been no cutting of cake with blown-out candles, no singing of 'Happy Birthday to You'. Just despair and tears. Lots and lots of tears.

The experience made me resolve to do what I really wanted and not what everyone else expected of me. Life, I suddenly decided, was too short to waste.

I had duly completed my degree, as it had somehow seemed a mistake to give it all up at such a late stage, but I had absolutely no intention of becoming a solicitor like my father. I had written to the College of Law to withdraw my application for the Legal Practice Course, the next step on the solicitors' ladder, and, much to my remaining parent's horror and anger, had arranged instead to go to Lambourn as an unpaid assistant and amateur jockey with a mid-ranking racehorse trainer.

'But how will you afford to live?' my father had demanded in exasperation.

'I will use the legacy that Mum left me,' I'd replied.

'But . . .' he had blustered. 'That was meant to be for the down payment on a house.'

'She didn't say so in her will,' I had said rather tactlessly, sending my father into a tirade about how the young these days had no sense of responsibility. This was not an uncommon rant in our household, and I was well used to ignoring it.

So I had graduated in June and gone to Lambourn in July, and had used my mother's legacy not only to pay my living expenses but also to acquire a seven-year-old bay gelding that I could ride in races, having correctly supposed that I was unlikely to get any rides on anyone else's horses.

I didn't tell my father.

August had mostly been spent getting fit. Each morning I would ride my horse in the stable string to the gallops on the hills above the village and then, each afternoon, I would run the same route on foot. By mid September both horse and jockey were showing signs of being ready for the racecourse.

Quite by chance, or was it fate, my first ride in a proper race had been at Fontwell in early October that year. The whole experience had seemed to pass me by in a blur with everything happening at once. Such was my naivety and nervousness that I nearly forgot to weigh out, had been unprepared and badly left at the start, had struggled for a full circuit to get back to the other runners before fading badly due to my own lack of stamina towards the end. We had finished eleventh out of thirteen, and one of the two I had beaten only because he had fallen in front of me at the last. It had not been an auspicious beginning. However the trainer had seemed relatively satisfied.

'At least you didn't fall off,' he had said on our way home in his car.

I had taken it as a compliment.

My horse and I had raced together five more times that year and on each occasion we had fared slightly better than the time before, finishing a close second in an amateur riders' steeplechase at Towcester races the week before Christmas.

By the following March I had ridden over fences a total of nine times and I had also had my first racing fall, at Stratford. However, it had been my ego that had been more bruised than my body. My horse and I had been well in front with just one fence left to negotiate when the excitement of the moment had become too much for me and I had made a complete hash of it, asking my mount for a mighty leap while he had decided to put in an extra stride. The result was that we had ploughed through the top of the fence, ending up in a crumpled heap on the ground watching ruefully as the others had sailed past us to the finish.

In spite of this disaster, and even though I had not yet ridden a winner, I still loved the excitement of the actual races, but I had begun to be rather bored by the time between them. I was missing the intellectual stimulation that I had so enjoyed during my time at university. And my mother's legacy had started to show major signs of exhaustion. It was time to put my fantasy back in its box and earn myself a living. But as what? I remained steadfast in my aversion to being a solicitor, but what else could I do with my law degree?

Not all lawyers are solicitors, I remembered one of my tutors saying during my first weeks at university. *There are barristers as well.*

To someone who was expecting, and expected, to become a general practice high-street solicitor, the world of the barrister was mysterious and unknown. My choice of optional study topics in my degree had concentrated on those areas I could mostly expect to encounter: conveyancing, family, employment and contract law. I had tended to avoid advocacy, criminal law and jurisprudence as much as possible.

I had researched the differences between barristers and solicitors in the local library in Hungerford and had learned that barristers were advocates, standing up and arguing, while solicitors generally did the legal paperwork in the background. Barristers tended to spar verbally across courtrooms with other barristers, while solicitors drew up contracts and litigation alone in quiet offices.

All of a sudden the prospect of becoming a stand-up-and-argue barrister had excited me hugely and I had eagerly applied for a return to legal matters.

So here I was some fourteen years later, well established in the world of horsehair wigs, silk gowns and courtroom protocol, but still trying to master this racing lark.

'Jockeys! Walk in.' The starter's call brought me back to the matter in hand. How careless, I thought, to be daydreaming at such a time. Concentrate! I told myself sharply.

The nineteen of us walked up slowly in a straggly line, the starter pushed the lever, the tape flew up and we were off. Not that it was easy to tell as no one seemed keen to make the running. The pack slowly went from walk to trot, and then to canter as the race began in almost sedentary style.

The three-mile start at Sandown is on the side of the course just after the bend at the end of the home straight, so the horses have to complete almost two full circuits, jumping a total of twenty-two fences. The first, which comes up very soon after the start, looks fairly innocuous but has caught out many an amateur and professional rider in its time. The landing side is some way below the take-off point and the drop tends to pitch horses forward onto their noses. The slow initial pace of this race, however, gave even the most inexperienced jockey, riding the world's worst jumper, time to haul on the reins to keep the animal's head up. So all nineteen runners were still standing as the pace picked up and we turned right-handed into the back straight to face the most famous seven-fence combination in steeplechasing. Two plain fences and an open-ditch fairly close together, then a slight gap to the water-jump, then the famous Railway fences – three plain fences very close together, closer than any others in British racing. It is always said that if you jump the first one well then all will be fine, but make a hash of the first and then horse and rider will be lucky to get to the far end intact.

Three miles is a long way, especially in November mud after a wet autumn, and none of us was making the mistake of going too fast too early. Consequently all nineteen runners were still standing and fairly closely bunched as we swung out of the back straight and round the long curve to the Pond fence and then up in front of the watching crowds for the first time.

The thing that struck me most when I started riding in races was the apparent isolation in which the participants find themselves. There may be thousands and thousands of eager gamblers in the grandstands, each shouting on their choices, but, for all the jockeys can tell, the stands may as well be empty and deserted. The sound of horses' hooves striking the turf, the same sound that had so excited me as a boy that first day at Fontwell Park, was the main noise that filled the senses. And obviously, unlike for the stationary spectator for whom it comes and goes, the noise travels along with the horses. There are other sounds too: the slap of the reins or whip, the clicking together of hooves, the shouts of the jockeys and the clatter of hoof or horseflesh on birch and wood as the animals brush through the top few inches of each fence. All of these together make the race a noisy place to b and they exclude any utterances from outside this bu

No word of encouragement can penetrate, not a single phrase of commentary can enter. Quite often, afterwards, the jockeys are the least informed about the triumphs and disasters of others. If it occurs behind them, they will have no idea that, say, the red-hot favourite has fallen, or a loose horse has caused mayhem in the pack. Unlike Formula 1 there are no team radios or pit-boards to inform and enlighten.

The pace quickened again noticeably as we turned away from the stands and went downhill past our starting point. The race was suddenly on in earnest.

Sandeman and I had been keeping to the shortest way round, hugging the inside rail, following the leading trio by a couple of lengths or so. Now, the horse immediately ahead of me began to tire slightly and I was concerned that I would be forced to slow with him as, with others alongside me, I had nowhere to go.

'Give me some damn room,' I shouted at the jockey ahead, more in hope than expectation. Amazingly, he pulled slightly away from the rail and I sailed up on his inside.

'Thanks,' I called to him as I drew alongside him on his right. Afresh faced, big eyed young amateur grimaced back at me. That was the difference, I thought, between how I was when I started and how I was now. These days I would never give a rival room even if he shouted at me ᵊᵈ day. Racing was all about winning and one didn't win often by being too courteous to the opposition. Not that I would purposefully baulk someone by cutting across them, although I had often been so treated by several of my colleagues. Some jockeys could be sweetness and light in the changing room both before and after the race, but vicious and ruthless in between. It was their job. Amateurs, in particular, should expect no favours from professionals.

Two horses fell at the next fence, the one with the drop. Both animals pitched forward on landing, going down on their knees and sending their riders sprawling onto the grass. One of the jockeys was the young man who had given me room up his inside. Phew, I thought, that was close. Thank goodness he hadn't fallen right in front of me. Being 'brought down' by tripping over another already prostrate horse was one of the worst ways of losing.

The remaining seventeen of us were becoming well spread out as we turned into the back straight for the second and last time. Sandeman was still going well beneath me and I kicked on hard into the first of the seven fences. He positively flew across the birch and gained at least a length on the two still in front.

'Come on, boy,' I shouted at him.

The tempo had now really quickened to a full-out gallop and I could hear some of those behind having problems keeping up.

'Pick up your effing feet,' shouted one jockey at his horse as it dropped its back legs into the water.

'Tell your sodding horse to jump straight,' shouted another as he was almost put through the wings of the first of the Railway fences.

We swung into the final long sweeping turn with just four having a realistic chance. I was still on the inside next to the white plastic rail and so the others had to go further to get round me. Kick, push, kick, push, my hands and heels were working overtime as we straightened for the Pond fence. Sandeman was just in front and another great leap from him took the others briefly out of sight behind me.

'Come on, boy,' I shouted at him again, this time with diminished breath. 'Come on.'

We were tiring but so were the others. Three miles in bottomless going is a huge test of stamina. But who would tire the most? Me, I feared. My fatigued legs would no longer provide the necessary kicks to Sandeman's belly and I could barely summon up the energy to give him a slap of encouragement with my whip.

We still had our nose just in front as we took off at the second last but Sandeman hit the top of the fence and landed almost stationary on all four feet at once. Bugger. Two other horses came past us as if we were going backwards and I thought all was lost. But Sandeman had other ideas and set off in pursuit. By the last fence we were back alongside the others and the three of us jumped it line abreast.

Even though the three horses landed over the last ~ether, both the others made it to the winning post ahead of us, their jockeys riding determined finishes while I was so tired that hanging on was about as much as I could do. We finished third, which was more to do with my lack of stamina rather than Sandeman's. I had clearly been spending too much of my time sitting on my backside in courtrooms and it showed. Three miles through the undulating Sandown mud had been just a bit too far. My pre-race apprehension hadn't turned to joy, more to exhaustion.

I slithered off Sandeman's back in the unsaddling enclosure and nearly sat down on the grass, so jelly-like were my legs.

'Are you all right?' Paul, the trainer, asked, concerned.

'Fine,' I said, trying to undo the girths. 'Just a little out of puff.'

'I need to get you up on the gallops too,' he said. 'No good having a fit horse if the damn jockey sits there like a sack of potatoes.' It was a harsh assessment but probably fair. Paul had invested heavily on Sandeman to win in more ways than one. He gently brushed me aside, undid the buckle with ease and passed me the saddle.

'Sorry,' I mumbled. It was a good job I was paying the training fees.

Somehow I made it to the scales to be weighed in, and then back into the jockeys' changing room, where I sat down heavily on the bench and wondered if it was time to call it a day. Time to give up this race-riding malarkey before I did myself a proper injury. To date I had been very lucky, with only a few bumps and bruises plus one

DICK FRANCIS AND FELIX FRANCIS

broken collarbone in fourteen years of racing. But, I thought, if I were to continue for another year I would have to become fitter than this or I might come to some serious harm. I leaned back wearily against the cream-painted wall and closed my eyes.

Only when the valets began to pack up the equipment into their large wicker baskets did I realize that the last race had already been run and I was almost alone in the changing room, and still I was not changed.

I stood up slowly and peeled off my lightweight riding strip, picked up my towel and went into the showers.

Scot Barlow was half sitting, half lying on the tiled floor, leaning up against the wall with a stream of water falling from the shower head onto his legs. He had a small trickle of blood coming from his right nostril and his eyes were puffy and closed.

'Are you all right?' I asked going over to him and touching his shoulder.

His eyes opened a little and he looked up at me but with no warmth in his expression.

'Sod off,' he said.

Charming, I thought. 'Just trying to help,' I said.

'Bloody amateurs,' he replied. 'Take away our liveli-hoods, you do.'

I ignored him and washed my hair.

'Do you hear me?' he shouted in full Scottish lilt. 'I

said people like you take away my livelihood. I should be paid to let the likes of you ride races.'

I thought of trying to tell him that I had ridden in a race reserved only for amateurs and he wouldn't have been allowed to ride in it anyway. But it would probably have been a waste of time and he clearly wasn't in the mood for serious debate. I went on ignoring him and finished my shower, the warmth helping to return some strength to my aching muscles. Barlow continued to sit where he was. The bleeding from his nose had gradually stopped and the blood was washed away by the water.

I went back into the main changing room, dressed and packed up my stuff. The professional jockeys all used the valets to look after their equipment. Each night their riding clothes were washed and dried, their riding boots polished and their saddles soaped ready for the next day's racing. For me, who rode only about once a fortnight and often more infrequently than that, the services of a valet were unnecessary and counter-productive. I stuffed my dirty things in a bag ready to take home to the washer-drier in the corner of my kitchen.

I was soon ready to go and there was still no sign of Scot Barlow. Everyone else had gone home so I went and again looked into the showers. He was still sitting there, in the same place as before.

'Do you need any help?' I asked. I assumed he must have had a fall during the afternoon and that his face was sore from using it on the ground as a brake.

'Sod off,' he said again. 'I don't need your help. You're as bad as he is.'

'Bad as who is?' I asked.

'Your bloody friend,' he said.

'What friend?' I asked him.

'Steve bloody Mitchell, of course,' he said. 'Who else do you think did this?' He held a hand up to his face.

'What?' I said, astounded. 'Steve Mitchell did this to you? But why?'

'You'd better ask him that,' he said. 'And not the first time, either.'

'You should tell someone,' I said, but I could see that he couldn't. Not with his reputation.

'Don't be daft,' he said. 'Now you piss off home like a good little amateur. And keep your bloody mouth shut.' He turned away from me and wiped a hand over his face.

I wondered what I should do. Should I tell the few officials left in the weighing room that he was there so they didn't lock him in? Should I go and fetch one of the ambulance staff? Or should I go and find a policeman to report an assault?

In the end I did nothing, except collect my gear and go home.

CHAPTER TWO

'I don't fucking believe it,' someone said loudly in the clerks' room as I walked in on Monday morning.

Such language in chambers was rare, and rarer still was such language from Sir James Horley QC, the Head of Chambers, and therefore nominally my boss. Sir James was standing in front of the clerks' desks reading from a piece of paper.

'What don't you . . . believe?' I asked him, deciding at the last moment not to repeat his profanity.

'This,' he said, waving the paper towards me.

I walked over and took the paper. It was a printout of an e-mail. It was headed CASE COLLAPSES AGAINST JULIAN TRENT.

Oh fuck indeed, I thought. I didn't believe it either.

'You defended him the first time round,' Sir James said. It was a statement rather than a question.

'Yes,' I said. I remembered it all too well. 'Open-and-shut case. Guilty as sin. How he got a retrial on appeal I'll never know.'

'That damn solicitor,' said Sir James. 'And now he'<

got off completely.' He took back the piece of paper and reread the short passage on it. 'Case dismissed for lack of evidence, it says here.'

More like for lack of witnesses prepared to give their evidence, I thought. They were afraid of getting beaten up.

I had taken a special interest in the appeal against Julian Trent's conviction in spite of no longer acting for the little thug. That damn solicitor, as Sir James had called him, was one of the Crown Prosecution team who had admitted cajoling members of the original trial jury to produce a guilty verdict. Three members of the jury had been to the police to report the incident, and all three had subsequently given evidence at the appeal hearing stating that they had been approached independently by the same solicitor. Why he'd done it, I couldn't understand, as the evidence in the case had been overwhelming. But the Appeal Court judges had had little choice but to order a retrial.

The episode had cost the solicitor his job, his reputation and, ultimately, his professional qualification to practise. There had been a minor scandal in the corridors of the Law Society. But at least the appeal judges had had the good sense to keep young Julian remanded in jail pending the new proceedings.

Now, it seemed, he would be walking free, his conviction and lengthy prison sentence being mere distant memories.

I recalled the last thing he had said to me in the cells

under the Old Bailey courtroom last March. It was not a happy memory. It was customary for defence counsel to visit their client after the verdict, win or lose, but this had not been a normal visit.

'I'll get even with you, you spineless bastard,' he'd shouted at me with venom as I had entered the cell.

I presumed he thought that his conviction was my fault because I had refused to threaten the witnesses with violence as he had wanted me to do.

'You'd better watch your back,' he'd gone on menacingly. 'One day soon I'll creep up on you and you'll never see it coming.'

The hairs on the back of my neck now rose up and I instinctively turned round as if to find him right here in chambers. At the time of his conviction I had been exceedingly thankful to leave him in the custody of the prison officers and I deeply wished he still was. Over the years I had been threatened by some others of my less affable clients, but there was something about Julian Trent that frightened me badly, very badly indeed.

'Are you all right?' Sir James was looking at me with his head slightly inclined.

'Fine,' I said with a slightly croaky voice. I cleared my throat. 'Perfectly fine, thank you, Sir James.'

'You look like you've seen a ghost,' he said.

Perhaps I had. Was it me? Would I be a ghost when Julian Trent came a-calling?

I shook my head. 'Just remembering the original trial,' I said.

'The whole thing is fishy if you ask me,' he said in his rather pompous manner.

'And is anyone asking you?' I said.

'What do you mean?' said Sir James.

'You seem well acquainted with the case, and the result is clearly important to you.' Sir James had never sworn before in my hearing. 'I didn't realize that anyone from these chambers was acting.'

'They aren't,' he said.

Sir James Horley QC, as Head of Chambers, had his finger on all that was going on within these walls. He knew about every case in which barristers from 'his' chambers were acting, whether on the prosecution side or the defence. He had a reputation for it. But equally, he knew nothing, nor cared little, about cases where 'his' team were not involved. At least, that was the impression he usually wanted to give.

'So why the interest in this case?' I asked.

'Do I need a reason?' he asked, somewhat defensively.

'No,' I said. 'You don't need a reason, but my question remains, why the interest?'

'Don't you cross-examine me,' he retorted.

Sir James had a bit of a reputation amongst the junior barristers for enjoying throwing his superior status around. The position of Head of Chambers was not quite what it might appear. It was mostly an honorary title often held by the most senior member, the QC of longest standing rather than necessarily the most eminent. All of the forty-five or so barristers in these chambers were self-employed.

The main purpose of us coming together in chambers was to allow us to pool those services we all needed, the clerks, the offices, the library, meeting rooms and so on. Each of us remained responsible for acquiring our own work from our own clients, although the clerks were important in the allocation of a new client to someone with the appropriate expertise. But one thing our Head of Chambers certainly did not do was to share out the work amongst his juniors, Sir James had never been known to share anything if he could keep it all to himself.

'It doesn't matter,' I said as a way of finishing the discussion on the matter. He would tell me if he wanted to, or not if that was his choice. My questioning would not sway the matter one way or another. Sir James was like the most unhelpful courtroom witness who has his own agenda about what evidence he will give and the direction of counsel's questioning will make no difference. Perhaps it takes an obdurate man to break down another of similar character, which was why Sir James Horley was one of the greatest advocates in the land.

'I was advising the judge in the case,' he said. So he did want to tell me after all. He was now showing off, I thought ungraciously.

'Oh,' I said noncommittally. I, too, could play his little game. I turned away to collect some letters from the pigeonhole behind me marked MR G. MASON. It was one of an array of wooden boxes each about twelve inches square lining one wall of the clerks' room. There were ten such spaces in each of six horizontal rows, open to the front, with each having a neatly printed label in a brass surround at the top showing the owner's name. They were not, of course, arranged in alphabetical order, which would have made finding someone else's box nice and easy; they were arranged in order of seniority, with Sir James's pigeonhole at the top right nearest the door. Consequently, our clutch of QCs had their boxes at eye-level while the juniors were below, even if the 'junior' had been called to the Bar long before the most recent QC and was easily old enough to be his father. Those juniors most recently called and those doing pupillage had almost to prostrate themselves on the floor to see what had been deposited in the deeper recesses of their boxes. I assumed that the whole plan was aimed at ensuring that the juniors did not forget their place. No doubt, if and when I myself made it to the lofty heights of being a QC, I would think that the system was ideal. Becoming a Queen's Counsel implied real status and was meant to be reserved for only the very best of the profession. Every barrister wanted to be a QC, but only ten per cent or so actually made it.

'The case hung on the question of intimidation,' Sir James said to my back, continuing our conversation.

It didn't surprise me. Julian Trent had intimidated me. I lifted a pile of papers from my box and turned back.

'The judge in the case and I were at law school together,' he went on. 'Known each other for forty years.' He gazed up as if remembering his lost youth. 'Anyway,' he said, looking back down at me, 'the problem with the

40

new trial was that the prosecution witnesses now either refused to give evidence at all or said something completely opposite to what they had said before. It was clear that they had been intimidated.'

Intimidation in the legal system was rife and a major obstacle to criminal justice. We all had to deal with it on a day-to-day basis.

I stood patiently and waited through a silence as Sir James appeared to decide if he would continue or not. Having decided in the affirmative, he went on 'So the judge wanted some advice as to whether the initial statements from witnesses taken by the police at the time of the incident could be read out in court as evidence without the prosecution calling the individuals concerned.'

I knew that Sir James had been a recorder for many years and that meant he sat as a Crown Court judge for up to thirty days per year. It was the first step to becoming a full-time judge and most senior practising QCs were or had been recorders. It was not uncommon for sitting judges to seek advice from them, and vice versa.

'And what advice did you give him?' I asked him.

'Her, actually,' he said. 'Dorothy McGee. I advised her that such evidence could be admissible provided the witness was called, even if the witness was now declared as being hostile to the Crown's case. However, it seemed that all the witnesses in the case had changed their tune, including the victim of the beating and his family, who now claimed that the event didn't happen in the first place and that the injuries were due to him falling down some stairs. Do they really think we are stupid or something?' He was getting quite cross. 'I advised her to press on with the case. I told her that it is essential to justice that such intimidation cannot be seen to succeed and I was sure the jury would agree and convict.'

'Trent probably intimidated the jury as well,' I said. I wondered if he had intimidated the three jurors who had come forward at the appeal.

'We'll never know,' he said. 'This note says the case has collapsed so it probably never went to the jury. I suspect that in the face of no witnesses to the event, except those denying that it ever occurred, the CPS, or maybe it was Dorothy, they just gave up. What an absolute disgrace.' He suddenly turned on his heel and walked away, back towards his room down the hall. My audience was over.

'Morning, Mr Mason,' said the Chief Clerk suddenly, making me jump. He had been sitting impassive and silent at his desk during my exchange with Sir James and I had not noticed him behind the computer monitors.

'Morning, Arthur,' I replied, moving to see him more clearly. He was a smallish man but only in stature, not in personality. I presumed he was now in his late fifties or early sixties as he often claimed to have worked in these chambers for more than forty years. He had already been a well-established Chief Clerk when I had first arrived twelve years before and he didn't seem to have changed one bit in the interim, apart from the appearance of a little grey in a full head of thick black curly hair.

'Bit late this morning, sir?' He phrased it as a question but it was meant more as a statement.

I glanced up at the clock on the wall above his head. Half past eleven. I had to agree that it was not a particularly prompt start to the working week.

'I've been busy elsewhere,' I said to him. Busy in bed, asleep.

'Are you misleading the court?' he asked accusingly, but with a smile. Misleading the court was the most heinous of crimes for a barrister.

The Chief Clerk was supposed to work for the members of chambers but somehow no one had ever told Arthur that. He clearly presumed that the reverse was true. If a junior or pupil misdemeanoured in some way, either through their bad behaviour or their poor work, then it was usually the Chief Clerk rather than the Head of Chambers who dealt out the admonishment. Each member of chambers paid a proportion of their fees to provide for the services we enjoyed and to pay for the team of clerks who were our secretariat, our minders and our chaperones. It was rumoured that in some chambers, with many high-earning barristers, the Chief Clerk was earning more than any of the masters he served. Arthur may have been nominally subservient to me but, as a junior who had aspirations of becoming a silk, I would be a fool to cross him.

'Sorry, Arthur,' I said, trying to look as apologetic as possible. 'Any messages for me?'

'Only those already in your box,' he said, nodding

towards the papers in my hand. Fortunately for me his telephone rang at this point and I scampered for the safety of my desk while he answered it. Why, I mused, did I always feel like a naughty schoolboy when in Arthur's company. Maybe it was because he instinctively knew when I was not where I should be at any given time, usually because I was on a racecourse somewhere having more fun.

Perhaps my nervousness was the result of a guilty conscience. On more than one occasion during my early years I had been forced to sit and listen to Arthur deliver a warning about my conduct, no doubt passed down from my more senior colleagues. Even though each of us was self-employed, the level of our billing was relevant to the smooth running of chambers and no one would be carried as a passenger if their fees were below par. Fortunately for me, in spite of taking days away to ride in races, my fee base was strong and none of my colleagues could ever accuse me of not pulling my weight, which had been eleven stone three, stripped, at Sandown Park races on the previous Saturday.

I sat at my desk and looked out of the window at the Gray's Inn Gardens, an oasis of calm in the centre of the great bustling metropolis of London. The lines of plane trees, which in summer gave shade to the hundreds of office workers who came to eat their lunchtime sandwiches, were now bare of their leaves and stood forlornly pointing skywards.

They reflected my mood. If our legal system couldn't

lock away dangerous brutes like Julian Trent because they frightened people away from telling the truth, then we were all in trouble.

Al Capone in 1920s Chicago was untouchable by the police. No witnesses to his many crimes of murder or assault would ever give evidence against him. It would have been a death sentence to have done so. Capone was so bold as to make public appearances for the media and was something of a celebrity around town, so sure was he that no one would bear witness against him. In the end the evidence that convicted him was a crude accounting ledger, allegedly in his own handwriting, showing his vast unlawful income, which had been discovered in a desk during a routine police raid on an illicit liquor warehouse. United States law made it clear that even illegal earnings were subject to federal income tax, so he was found guilty, not of murder and mayhem but of tax evasion. Capone's middle name was Gabriel but he was certainly no angel. The jury for his trial was changed on the day of the proceedings to frustrate attempts to bribe or threaten the original panel, and still he was convicted on only five of twenty-two charges. But it was enough. A brave judge threw out the plea bargain and sentenced America's Public Enemy No. 1 to eleven years in jail. Justice had triumphed over intimidation.

As Sir James Horley had said, it was an absolute disgrace it hadn't done so in the Trent case.

I leaned back in my chair and yawned. Contrary to what Arthur might think, the reason I had arrived late was not that I was lazy, but because at five in the morning I had been still reading the case notes for a trial in which I was currently leading for the prosecution. The court was not sitting on this particular Monday and I could have spent the whole day in bed if I had been so inclined, but I needed to use the library.

The case was against a pair of brothers who had been accused of conspiracy. Such cases were always difficult to prosecute. When does dreaming about robbing a bank become conspiracy to do so? The brothers were accused of conspiring to defraud an insurance company through a loophole in their motoring policy. The brothers had claimed in court, and under oath, that they were only seeing if the scheme was possible in order that they could then tell the company so its security could be tightened, and that they had no intention of carrying through their plans and keeping the illegal payment.

This might have been perfectly believable, except that the brothers had twice before been convicted together of fraud and were suspected of many more. The question I had been spending so long researching, and for which I needed the chambers' detailed index of trial records, was whether these facts could or could not be used in court. English law relies heavily on precedent to determine whether something can occur. If it has been allowed before then, by definition, it can be again. If it hasn't happened in the past then it might be cause for appeal right up to the House of Lords for a ruling. The trial judge would make the decision, but counsel had to provide arguments first. In this instance, as the prosecutor, I needed to find similar circumstances from the past that would strengthen my case to have the brothers' previous convictions revealed to the jury to show pattern of behaviour as evidence of their guilt.

Not all the work of a barrister is as exciting as that depicted in TV trial dramas.

Consequently, I spent the rest of the day with my nose in leather bound volumes of trial records and then in front of my computer screen searching on the internet. At least, for the most part, my search was fairly restricted. Prior to 2004 evidence of previous convictions was excluded from trials completely except in very special circumstances.

The fact that someone has committed a crime before is not, in itself, evidence that they have done so again. In many cases, quite rightly, former misdeeds should not be used to sway a jury to produce another guilty verdict. Each case should be tried on the current facts rather than on those of previous incidents. Even the most prosecution minded of judges could often believe that allowing previous guilty verdicts to be disclosed to the jury might be prejudicial to a fair trial, and hence grounds for a successful appeal. There is little worse for a barrister's ego than to win a case for the prosecution in the Crown Court only for the verdict to be overturned on appeal. All those late nights of work, all those missed social engagements, all that effort and for what? For nothing.

Well, I suppose there was the fee, of course, but for me, as in racing, it was the winning that was far more important than the money.

By seven thirty I'd had enough of ploughing through past judgments, but at least, by then, I had produced an all too short but fairly comprehensive list of precedents to further my argument. I packed everything I needed into a box ready for the morning and slipped out into the night.

I lived in Barnes, south of the Thames in west London, where my wife, Angela, and I had bought half of an early Edwardian detached house in Ranelagh Avenue over-looking Barnes Common. Typical of its time, the house had been built with a lower ground floor with high-up windows where the servants had performed their duties cooking, washing, and generally looking after the family above, but it had since been modernized and converted into two homes. Angela and I had acquired the top half, the upper two floors with views over the treetops from the dormer windows of the bedrooms. Our neighbours below occupied the original ground floor of the property with its grand rooms, together with the old servants' area below.

Angela and I had loved it. It had been the first home that we had owned together and we had lavished more time and money than was prudent on decorating the place and getting everything ready for the birth of our first child, a son, due six months after we had moved in. That ad been seven years ago.

As usual, I walked home across the common from Barnes station. It was almost completely dark, with just a few beams of light filtering through the leafless trees from distant street lights, but I knew every step of the route. I was about half way when I remembered Julian Trent and his baseball bat. Perhaps it wasn't such a good idea to walk alone across Barnes Common in the dark, but I had always felt more threatened when sticking to the roads with their meagre lighting. I stopped to listen for anyone behind me and I did turn round a few times to check, but I made it safely to my door without incident.

The house was lit up, but, as was normally the case, it was only the bottom half of the house that was bright. The upper floors were in darkness where I'd turned off the lights as I had left that morning.

I let myself in through my front door and went upstairs into the dark.

Angela wasn't there, but I knew she wouldn't be. Angela was dead.

I wondered if I would ever get used to coming home to an empty house. Perhaps I should have moved away long ago, but those first few months here had been the happiest of my life and, somehow, early on, I hadn't wanted to abandon the memories, they were all I had left.

Angela had died suddenly of a massive pulmonary embolism just four weeks before our baby was due. She had kissed me goodbye on that fateful Monday morning as happy as I had ever known her. It had been the first day of her maternity leave and she had still been in her dressing gown and slippers as I had left for work. All her life she had longed to have a child and now she was so close to fulfilling her dream. I had tried to call her several times during the day without any success but I had thought nothing was amiss until I had arrived home to find the place in darkness. Angela had always hated the dark, and she would have left lights on in the house even if she had gone out.

I had found her lying on the sitting-room floor, slightly curled as if she were asleep. But she had been so cold, and had obviously been dead for hours. Our son was dead too, inside her.

There had been no warning and no pre-existing condition. Regular checks at the clinic had revealed no hypertension, no pre-eclampsia. She had gone from healthy and happy to dead in the space of a few moments. So sad, the doctors had said, but it was the most common cause of sudden death during pregnancy. They also told me it would have been very quick and that she was likely unaware, losing consciousness almost instantaneously. Surprisingly, it was something of a comfort to know that she hadn't suffered, that she hadn't seen the void coming.

Everyone had been so kind. Friends had rallied round to make the necessary arrangements, my father had come to stay so I wouldn't be alone, and even the judge in the trial I had been prosecuting had adjourned the proceedings until after Angela's funeral. I could remember feeling like

I was living in a time warp. There had been so much rushing around going on by others, while I had sat still and alone in my grief while the hours and days had dragged by.

Gradually, over the next few months, my life had sorted itself out. I had gone back to work and my father had returned home. Friends had come round less often with ready cooked meals, and they had stopped speaking in hushed tones. Invitations began again to arrive, and people began to say things to each other like, 'He's still young enough to find somebody else.'

Now it was seven years later and I had not found somebody else. I didn't really want to because I was still in love with Angela. Not that I was foolish enough to think that she would come back from the dead or anything odd like that. I just wasn't ready to find anybody else. Not yet. Maybe not ever.

I turned on the lights in the kitchen and looked in the fridge for something to eat. I was hungry, having missed my lunch, so I decided on salmon with penne pasta and pesto sauce. Since Angela died I had become quite a dab hand at cooking for one.

I had just sat down to eat in front of the television news when the phone rang. Typical, I thought, damn thing always goes at the wrong moment. Reluctantly I put my tray to one side, leaned over and picked up the receiver.

'Hello,' I said.

'Perry?' said a voice.

'Yes,' I replied slowly. After all, I'm not really Perry. I'm Geoffrey.

'Thank God you're there,' said the voice. 'This is Steve Mitchell.'

I thought back to our strange conversation in the Sandown jockeys' changing room two days before.

'How did you get my number?' I asked him.

'Oh,' he said, as if distracted. 'From Paul Newington. Look, Perry,' he went on in a rush, 'I'm in a bit of trouble and I badly need your help.'

'What bit of trouble?' I asked him.

'Well, actually it could be rather a lot of trouble,' he said. 'That bastard Scot Barlow has got himself murdered and the bloody police have arrested me for doing it.'

CHAPTER THREE

'And did you?' I asked.

'Did I what?' Steve replied.

'Murder Scot Barlow?' I said.

'No,' he said. 'Of course I bloody didn't.'

'Have the police interviewed you?' I asked him.

'Not yet,' he said in a somewhat resigned tone. 'But I think they plan to. I asked to call my lawyer. So I called you.'

'I'm hardly your lawyer,' I said to him.

'Look, Perry,' he said, 'you're the only lawyer I know.' He was beginning to sound a little desperate.

'You need a solicitor not a barrister,' I said.

'Solicitors, barristers, what's the difference? You are a bloody lawyer, aren't you? Will you help me or not?'

'Calm down,' I said, trying to sound reassuring. 'Where are you exactly?'

'Newbury,' he said. 'Newbury police station.'

'How long have you been there?' I asked.

'About ten minutes, I think. They came to my house about an hour ago.'

I looked at my watch. It was ten past ten. Which solicitors did I know in Newbury that could be roused at such an hour? None.

'Steve,' I said. 'I can't act in this matter as at the moment you need a solicitor, not a barrister. I will see what I can do to get you a solicitor I know to come to Newbury but it won't be for a few hours at least.'

'Oh God,' he almost cried. 'Can't you come?'

'No,' I said. 'It would be like asking a brain surgeon to remove your teeth. Much better for you if you get a dentist.' I was sure that, as analogies go, and with more time, I could have done better. And not many solicitors I know would have been happy to be called a dentist, not least by some brain-surgeon barrister.

'When will this bloody solicitor arrive?' he asked, again sounding resigned.

'As soon as I can arrange it,' I said.

'The police have told me that, if I want, I can talk to the duty solicitor, whoever that is,' Steve said.

'Well, you can,' I replied. 'And for free, but I wouldn't if I were you.'

'Why not?' he asked.

'At this time of night he's likely to be a recently qualified young solicitor, or else one that can get no other work,' I said. 'You are facing a serious charge and I'd wait for someone with more experience if I were you.'

There was a long, quiet pause from the other end of the line.

'OK, I'll wait,' he said.

'Fine,' I replied. 'I'll get someone there as soon as possible.'

'Thanks,' he said.

'And Steve,' I said earnestly, 'listen to me. You don't have to answer any questions until he arrives. Do you understand?'

'Yes,' he said with a yawn in his voice.

'What time did you get up this morning?' I asked him.

'Usual time,' he said. 'Ten to six. I was riding out at seven.'

'Tell the police that you are tired and need to sleep. Tell them that you have been awake for nearly seventeen hours and you are entitled to have a rest before being interviewed.' Strictly, it may not have been true, but it was worth a try.

'Right,' he said.

'And when the solicitor does arrive, take his advice absolutely.'

'OK,' he said rather flatly. 'I will.'

Did he, I wondered, sound like a guilty man resigned to his fate?

I called a solicitor I knew in Oxford and asked him. 'Sorry, mate,' he replied in his Australian accent, he was too busy teaching some gorgeous young university student the joys of sleeping with an older man. I had learned from experience not to ask him if the gorgeous young student was male or female. However, he did rouse himself sufficiently to give me the name of a firm in Newbury that he could recommend, together with one of their partners' mobile phone number.

Sure, said the partner when I called, he would go. Steve Mitchell was quite famous in those parts, and representing a celebrity client accused of murder was every local solicitor's dream. To say nothing of the potential size of the fee.

I returned to my, now cold, pasta and thought again about last Saturday at Sandown. I went over in my mind everything that had been said, and particularly I recalled the strange encounter with the battered Scot Barlow in the showers.

It was not unknown for barristers to represent their friends and even members of their own families. Some senior QCs, it was said, had such a wide circle of friends that they spent their whole lives defending them against criminal or civil proceedings. Personally, I tried to avoid getting myself into such a position. Friendships to me were too important to place in jeopardy by having to lay bare all one's secrets and emotions. The truth, the whole truth and nothing but the truth is rare even amongst the closest of chums, and a friend would far more resent being asked a question he didn't want to answer by me than if a complete stranger had done it. Victory in court may cause the friendship to founder anyway due to too much intimate knowledge, and if one lost the case then one lost the friend for sure.

So I usually invented some little ruse to avoid the

situation. I would often say that so-and-so in my chambers was much better qualified or experienced to accept the brief, or that I was too busy with other cases and that so-and-so could devote more time to preparing the defence case. I always promised to keep abreast of the facts in the case, and sometimes I even managed to.

However, this time I didn't need to invent an excuse. I couldn't act for Steve Mitchell because I was privy to some material evidence and was far more likely to be called to testify for the prosecution than to be one of the defence counsel. But, I thought, there had been no other witness to the exchange between Barlow and me in the Sandown showers, and now Barlow was dead. To whom, I thought, should I volunteer the information? And when?

The murder of top jump jockey Scot Barlow was the number one item on the eight o'clock television news bulletin the following morning. A reporter, standing outside the property, claimed that Barlow had been found lying in a pool of blood in the kitchen of his home with a five-foot-long, two-pronged pitchfork embedded in his chest. The reporter also stated that someone was helping the police with their enquiries. He didn't say that the someone was Steve Mitchell, but he didn't say it wasn't. My mobile phone rang as I was buttering a slice of toast.

'Hello,' I said, picking it up.

'Is that Geoffrey Mason?' asked a very quiet well-spoken male voice in a whisper.

'Yes,' I replied.

'Do as you are told,' said the voice, very quietly, but very distinctly.

'What did you say?' I asked, surprised.

'Do as you are told,' the voice repeated in the same manner.

'Who is this?' I demanded, but, in response, the caller simply hung up.

I looked at the phone in my hand as if it would tell me.

Do as I was told, the man had said. But he hadn't told me what I had to do, or when. It couldn't have been a wrong number; he had asked me my name. How very odd, I thought.

I checked through the list of received calls but, as I expected, the caller had withheld his number.

The phone in my hand rang again suddenly, making me jump and drop it onto the kitchen counter. I grabbed at it and pushed the button.

'Hello?' I said rather tentatively.

'Is that Geoffrey Mason?' asked a male voice, a different male voice.

'Yes,' I replied, cautiously. 'Who is this?'

'Bruce Lygon,' said the voice.

'Oh,' I said, relieved. Bruce Lygon was the solicitor from Newbury I had called the night before.

'Are you all right?' he asked.

'Fine,' I said. 'I thought you might be someone else.'

'Your friend seems to be in a bit of a hole here,' he

said. 'The cops think there's not much doubt he did it. That's clear from their questions. We've been at it since six this morning. We're just having a short break while the detectives have a conference.'

'What's the evidence?' I asked him.

'They haven't revealed much as yet but I gather that the victim was stabbed with some sort of fork.'

'They reported that on the television,' I said.

'Did they indeed?' he said. 'Well, it appears that the fork belongs to Mr Mitchell.'

'Oh,' I said.

'Yeah, and that's not all,' he said. 'As well as Mr Barlow, there were some betting slips also impaled on the fork and they belonged to Mr Mitchell as well. They had his name on them.'

'Oh,' I said again.

'And,' he went on, 'there was a text message received yesterday afternoon on Barlow's mobile from Mitchell saying that he was going to, and I quote, "come round and sort you out properly you sneaking little bastard".'

'And what does Mitchell have to say?' I asked.

'Nothing,' said Bruce. 'But then again, I told him not to. He just sits there looking pale and scared.'

'But what has he said to you privately?' I asked.

'He mumbled something about being framed,' Bruce replied, but I could tell from his tone that he didn't believe it. 'Do you want me to stay here?'

'It's not my decision,' I said. 'Steve Mitchell is your client, not me. Ask him.'

'I have,' he said. 'He told me to call you and to do whatever you said.'

Bugger, I thought. I just could not get involved with this case. I knew too much about it for a start, and it looked like it was pretty much a foregone conclusion, and that was another good reason for not getting involved. Acquiring a reputation in chambers for having too many courtroom losses wouldn't help my potential QC credentials either.

'You had better stay then,' I said, 'but remind Mr Mitchell that it's you and not me who's acting for him, and I can't make those decisions. Have they charged him yet?'

'No,' he replied. 'More questioning first. And I know they are searching his place. They told him so. There will be more questions from that, I expect.'

Under English law, the police could only question a suspect prior to charging.

'When's their time up?' I asked him. The police had a maximum of thirty-six hours from when he first arrived at the police station before they either charged Steve, brought him before a magistrate to ask for more time, or released him.

'According to the record, he was arrested at eight fifty-three last night and arrived at the police station at nine fifty-seven,' he said. 'So far they haven't asked for more time and I think it's unlikely they will. I don't think they need his answers. Their body language says that they have enough to charge without them.'

'So you'll stay until he's charged?' I asked.

'Only if they charge him before six,' he said. 'After that I'm taking my wife out to dinner for her birthday, and I'd rather face the Law Society than fail to do that.' There was laughter in his voice. Steve Mitchell might be facing the toughest contest of his sporting life, but it was still just a job to Bruce Lygon. 'But don't worry, there'll be someone here from my firm if I'm not.'

'Great,' I said. 'Please keep me informed, but I'm not actually representing him.' But, like everybody else, I was curious about murder, especially as I also knew the victim.

'I will if I can, but only if he says so.'

He was right, of course, client confidentiality and all that.

Steve Mitchell's arrest was the front-page story on the midday edition of the *Evening Standard*. I grabbed a copy as I dodged the rain outside Blackfriars Crown Court on my way to a local café for some lunch. 'TOP JOCK HELD FOR MURDER', shouted the banner headline alongside a library picture of a smiling Scot Barlow. The story gave little more detail than I already knew, but the report speculated that the murder had been in revenge for Barlow giving the racing authorities details of Mitchell's illegal gambling activities.

I turned on my mobile phone. There was one voicemail message but it wasn't from Bruce Lygon. It was from the quiet, well-spoken male whisperer. 'Remember,' he said menacingly, 'do exactly as you are told.'

I sat in the window of the café eating a cheese and pickle sandwich, trying to work out what on earth it was all about. No one had told me to do anything, so how could I do it? I would have dismissed it as mistaken identity except that the caller this morning had asked if I was Geoffrey Mason. And, indeed, I was. But were there two Geoffrey Masons? There must be, but there was only one with my phone number.

I decided to ignore that problem and concentrate on the matter currently in hand. The judge that morning had not been very helpful and he had not been greatly swayed by my arguments concerning the admissibility of prior convictions in the conspiracy-to-defraud trial of the brothers. It made the case more difficult to prosecute, but not impossible. After all, the brothers had admitted having done it. All we had to do was convince the jury they had done it for gain.

I called Bruce Lygon.

'Any news?' I asked him.

'No.' He sounded bored. 'They are apparently waiting for the results of some forensics. From his clothes and shoes, I think. And his car.'

'How is he?' I said.

'Pretty fed up,' he said. 'Keeps saying he should be riding at Huntingdon races. Asks when he can go home. I don't think he fully realizes the extent of the mess he's in.'

'So you think he will definitely be charged?' I asked.

'Oh yeah, no question. They haven't even bothered to question him for the past four hours. They're sure he did it. One of them said as much to him and asked whether he wanted to confess and save them all a lot of trouble.'

'What did he say?' I asked.

'Told them to get lost, or words to that effect.' I smiled. I could imagine the actual exchange. Steve didn't talk to anyone without at least a few bloodys sprinkled in.

'Well, for your sake, I hope they charge him by six,' I said, thinking of his wife's birthday dinner. 'Will it be you that goes with him to the magistrate's court in the morning?'

'Will I? Are you kidding?' he said. 'It's not every day I get a case that leads on the lunchtime news. Even the wife says to stay here all night if I have to. Don't let him out of your sight, she said, just in case he finds himself another solicitor '

Maybe it was more than just a job to Bruce, after all. But if he thought representing a guilty but popular and celebrated client would bring him any respect he was much mistaken. Two years before I had been dramatically unsuccessful in defending a much-loved middle-aged comedy TV actress from a charge of deliberate shoplifting and the subsequent assault of the store detective. She had committed the crimes but it had been me who had been universally denounced in the press for failing to get her off. Everyone knows it was George Carmen QC, who, in the face of overwhelming evidence, secured an acquittal for Ken Dodd for tax evasion, but no one remembers the counsel who failed to keep Lester Piggott out of jail on the same charge. Such as it is in life, and such as it is in racing. Winning is all. Coming second is a disaster, even if it's by the slightest margin, the shortest of short heads.

The afternoon was little better than the morning had been. The judge in the case seemed determined to be as unhelpful as possible, continually interrupting my questioning as I tried to cross-examine one of the defendants. In true Perry Mason style I was trying to trap him in a lie but, every time I thought I was getting close, the judge stopped me and asked if my line of questioning was relevant. This gave the defendant time to recover and recoup. He simply smiled at me and went on telling the jury his lies. I knew they were lies, and he knew they were lies. But, from their facial expressions, I realized that the jury were believing them. It was very frustrating.

I was beginning to think that I was about to notch up another courtroom loss when the elder of the brothers carelessly stated in response to my questions that you couldn't believe what a previous witness for the prosecution had said because, he claimed, the witness was a convicted felon and a proven liar. On such things do trials turn. Because the defendant had called into question the character of a witness against him, we, the prosecution, were now entitled to call his character into question as well, and all his previous convictions were suddenly admissible into court. Hurrah. The poor defending barrister sat there with his head in his hands. He had done so well to keep the information from the jury through the judge's earlier ruling, only for his own client to mortally hole the defence below the water line. A sinking was now inevitable.

The judge adjourned proceedings for the day soon after four o'clock with the prosecution well on top. Perhaps I would actually win the case.

I took a taxi back to chambers with my box of papers and my laptop. It had been a miserably wet autumnal November day in London and the daylight had fully gone by the time I paid off the cabbie on Theobald's Road near the gated entrance to Raymond Buildings.

Julian Trent was waiting for me between two rows of parked cars. Whereas, the previous evening, I had been somewhat wary crossing Barnes Common, I hadn't really been seriously concerned that I would be attacked. I had dismissed Trent's post-trial threats as mere bravado, a lashing-out reaction to losing the case. And why would he want revenge from me when he had got off anyway? But here he was, with his trusted baseball bat, oozing menace and danger.

I didn't actually see him until I had walked beyond his hiding place because I was concentrating on hunching my body to keep my computer dry as I balanced it on the box of papers. My peripheral vision detected a movement to my right and I turned in time to glimpse his face just before he hit me. He was smiling.

The baseball bat caught me across the back of both legs about half way up my thighs. The blow caused my knees to buckle and I was sent sprawling to the ground, my box of papers spilling out in front of me. The suddenness of the strike left me gasping for breath. Far from leaping to my feet to defend myself, I lay face down, immobile on the wet tarmac. Strangely there was no pain. My legs felt numb and somehow detached from the rest of my body. I used my arms to roll myself over onto my back. I was determined that he wouldn't be able to knock my brains out without me seeing it coming.

He stood above me, swinging the bat from side to side. There was no one else about in the private road but he seemed not to care anyway. He was clearly enjoying himself.

'Hello, Mister Clever-Dick Lawyer,' he said with a curl to his upper lip. 'Not so clever now, are we?'

I didn't reply, not out of some feeling of defiance but because I couldn't think of anything to say.

He raised the bat to have another swing and I felt sure that my time was up. I put my arms up around my head to protect myself, closed my eyes and waited for the crunch. I wondered if I would die here with my head beaten to a pulp. I also wondered if Angela would be waiting for me on the other side. Maybe it wouldn't be so bad after all.

The bat landed with a sickening thud but not on my head, not even on my arms or hands. Trent hit my unprotected laptop computer with all his might and it obligingly disintegrated into several parts that scattered noisily across the road.

I opened my eyes and looked at him.

'Next time,' he said, 'I'll smash your head.'

Next time! Dear God, I didn't want there to be a next time.

He then stepped forward and trod hard on my genitals, putting all his weight on his right foot and crushing my manhood between his boot and the road. This time there was pain, a shooting, stabbing, excruciating pain. I moaned and rolled away sideways and he thankfully released the pressure.

'And next time,' he said, 'I'll cut your balls right off. Understand?'

I lay there silently looking at him.

'Do you fucking understand?' he repeated staring back at me.

I nodded ever so slightly.

'Good,' he said. 'Now you be a good little lawyer.'

Then he suddenly turned and walked away, leaving me lying in a puddle, curled up like a baby to lessen the ongoing agony between my legs. Could this really have happened in central London just yards from hundreds of respectable high-earning fellow professionals? This was the sort of thing that happened to some of my clients, not to me.

I was shaking and I didn't know whether it was from fear, from shock or from the cold. Tears had come quite easily to me over the past seven years since Angela h died and I cried now. I couldn't help it. It was mostly due to the relief of still being alive when I had been sure that I would die. It was the body's natural reaction to intense emotion, and I had been frightened more than at any time in my life.

Only a few minutes had elapsed in real time since I had stepped out of the taxi but my life had changed from one of discipline and order to one of chaos and fear. How easily I had been castrated of my courtroom authority. How fearful I had so quickly become of castration of another kind.

In my line of work one encountered fear and intimidation on an almost daily basis. How self-righteous and condescending I imagined I must have been to potential witnesses too fearful to give evidence. 'We will look after you,' I would say to them. 'We will protect you from the bullies,' I would promise, 'but you must do what is right.' Only now did I appreciate their predicament. I should have told Julian Trent to go to hell but, in fact, I would have licked his boots if he had so asked, and I hated myself for it.

Eventually the intensity of the pain in my groin diminished, only to be replaced by a dull ache from the backs of my thighs where the baseball bat had first caught me. The shaking also gradually abated and I was able to roll over onto my knees. It didn't seem to help much but at least I was looking at the world the right way up. My computer was well beyond repair and all my previously neatly ordered court papers were blowing along the road in the rain, hiding beneath parked cars and flying up into the branches of the leafless trees. My gown and wig, which had also been in the box, were soaking up the water from another puddle. But I didn't really care. It was as much as I could manage to stand approximately upright and stagger the few yards to the door of my chambers. And still nobody appeared.

I leaned up against the board with all the barristers' names painted on it and looked at the blue front door. I couldn't remember the code for the security lock. I had worked in these chambers for almost thirteen years and the code hadn't been changed once in all that time, but still I couldn't recall it now. So I pushed the bell and was rewarded with Arthur's friendly voice from a small speaker.

'Yes,' he said. 'Who is it?'

'Geoffrey,' I croaked. 'Geoffrey Mason. Can you come and help?'

'Mr Mason?' Arthur asked back through the speaker. 'Are you all right?'

'No,' I said.

Almost immediately the door opened and Arthur, my rather tardy Good Samaritan, at last came to my rescue, half carrying me through the hallway into the clerks' room. He pulled up a desk chair and I gratefully sat down, but carefully so as not to further inflame the problems below.

I must have been quite a sight. I was soaked through and both the knees of my pinstripe suit were torn where I had landed on the rough tarmac. My once starched white shirt clung like a wet rag to my chest and my hair dripped rainwater down my forehead. It is surprising how quickly one becomes wet from lying in persistent rain.

'Goodness gracious,' said Arthur. 'What on earth happened to you?'

I hadn't expected Arthur to be a 'goodness gracious' sort of chap, but he did spend his working life in close proximity to barristers who acted like they lived in the eighteenth or nineteenth centuries, and some of it must have rubbed off.

'I was mugged,' I said.

'Where?' he asked.

'Outside,' I said. 'My stuff is still on the road.'

Arthur turned and rushed outside.

'Be careful,' I shouted after him, but I didn't really expect Julian Trent still to be there. It was me he had been after, not my clerk.

Arthur returned with my gown in one hand and my wig in the other, both dripping onto the light green carpet. He had just a few of my sopping papers stuck under his arm, and I suspected that most of the others had flown with the wind.

'Is that your computer?' he asked, nodding his head towards the door.

'What's left of it,' I agreed.

'Funny,' he said. 'Muggers normally steal things, not break them. Is anything missing?'

'No, I don't think so,' I said patting myself down. I

could feel both my wallet and my mobile in the soggy pockets of my jacket.

'I'm calling the police,' said Arthur, moving round the desk and lifting the phone. 'Do you need an ambulance?' he asked me.

'No,' I said. 'But a change of clothes would be good.'

Arthur spoke to the police, who promised to send someone round as soon as possible, though it might be some time.

While we waited I changed out of my sodden clothes into a track suit that Arthur found in one of my colleagues' rooms, and then I tried to make some sort of order from the saturated paperwork. After a second attempt, Arthur had recovered about half of what had been in the box and I spent some time laying the sheets out all over my room to dry. I couldn't reprint them as nearly all the files had only been on my computer.

I thought that calling the police would be a waste of time and so it turned out. Two uniformed constables arrived about forty minutes after the call and they took a statement from me while I sat in the clerks' room with Arthur hovering close by.

'Did you see the mugger?' one of them asked me.

'Not at first,' I said. 'He hit me from behind with a baseball bat.'

'How do you know it was a baseball bat?' he asked.

'I saw it later,' I said. 'I assumed it was what he hit me with.'

'Whereabouts did he hit you?'

'On the back of my legs,' I said.

They insisted that I show them. Embarrassed, I lowered the track-suit trousers to reveal two rapidly bruising red marks half way up the backs of my thighs. Arthur's eyes were almost out on stalks.

'Funny place to hit someone,' said the other policeman.

'It knocked me over,' I said.

'Yeah, it would,' he agreed. 'But most muggers would have hit you on the head. Did you get a look at his face?'

'Not really,' I said. 'It was dark.' Why, I thought, had I not told them that it had been Julian Trent who had attacked me? What was I doing? Did I not stand up for justice and right? Tell them, I told myself, tell them the truth.

'Would you know him again?' the policeman asked.

'I doubt it,' I heard myself say. *Next time, I'll smash your head*, Trent had said. *Next time, I'll cut your balls right off.* I had no wish for there to be a next time. 'It was all a bit of a blur,' I said. 'I was looking mostly at the bat.'

'But you were sure it was a man?' he asked.

'I think so,' I said.

'Black or white?' he asked.

'I couldn't say.' Even to my ears, it sounded pathetic. I hated myself, again.

They asked me if I wanted hospital treatment for my injuries but I declined. I'd had bruising worse than this due to an easy fall in a steeplechase, and I had ridden again in the very next race. However, there was a big difference this time. Racing falls were accidents and, although the laws of chance might imply that they were inevitable, the injuries produced were not premeditated, or man made.

The two policemen clearly thought that I was not a helpful witness and I could sense from their attitude that they, too, thought that the process was a waste of time and that another mugging would go unsolved, just another statistic in the long list of unsolved street crimes in the capital.

'Well, at least you didn't have anything stolen,' said one, clearly bringing the interview to a close. He snapped shut his notebook. 'If you call the station later they'll give you a crime number. You'll need one for any insurance claim on your computer.'

'Oh,' I said. 'Thanks. Which station?'

'We're from Charing Cross,' said one.

'Right,' I said. 'I'll call there.'

'Good,' said the other, turning for the door.

And with that, they were gone, no doubt to interview some other victim, on another street.

'You weren't much help,' said Arthur, rather accusingly. 'Are you sure you didn't see who it was?'

'I'd have told them if I had,' I said quite sharply, but I wasn't sure he completely believed me. Arthur knew me too well, I thought, and I hated myself again for deceiving him more than anyone. But I really didn't want a 'next time', and I had been frightened, very frightened indeed by my confrontation with young Mr Julian Trent. T' time, I was alive and not badly damaged. And I intended to keep it that way.

I sat at my desk for a while trying to recover some of my confidence. 'Be a good little lawyer,' Trent had said. What had that meant? I wondered. If I really had been a good little lawyer I would have told the police exactly who had attacked me and where to find him. Even now, he would be under arrest and locked up. But for how long? He wouldn't get any jail time for hitting me once on the back of the legs and smashing my computer. I had no broken bones, not even a cut, no concussion or damaged organs, just a couple of tears in my trousers and a rain-spoilt barrister's wig. A fine, or maybe some community service, would be all he'd get. And then he'd be free to visit me again for 'next time'. No thanks. And was he anything to do with the 'do as you are told' whispered phone message? I couldn't imagine so, but why else would he attack me? Something very strange was going on.

Arthur knocked on my open door and came in, closing it behind him.

'Mr Mason,' he said.

'Yes, Arthur,' I replied.

'May I say something?' he said.

'Of course, Arthur,' I replied, not actually wanting him to say anything just at the moment. But there would be stopping him now, not if his mind was made up.

'I think it is most unlike you to be so vague as you were with those policemen,' he said, standing full-square in front of my paper-covered desk. 'Most unlike you indeed.' He paused briefly. I said nothing. 'You are the brightest and sharpest junior we have in these chambers and you miss nothing, nothing at all. Do I make myself clear?'

I was flattered by his comments and I was trying to think what to say back to him when he went on.

'Are you in any trouble?' he asked.

'No, of course not,' I said. 'What sort of trouble do you mean?'

'Any sort of trouble,' he said. 'Maybe some woman trouble?'

Did he think I'd been attacked by a jealous husband?

'No, Arthur, no trouble at all. I promise.'

'You could always come to me if you were,' he said. 'I like to think I look after my barristers.'

'Thank you, Arthur,' I said. 'I would most definitely tell you if I was in any sort of trouble.' I looked him straight in the eye and wondered if he knew I was lying.

He nodded, turned on his heel and walked to the door. As he opened it he turned round. 'Oh yes,' he said. 'This came for you earlier.' He walked back to the desk and handed me an A5-sized white envelope with my name printed on the front of it, with *By Hand* written on the top right-hand corner.

'Thank you,' I said, taking it. 'Do you know who delivered it?'

'No,' he said. 'It was pushed through the letter box in the front door.'

He waited but I made no move to open the envelope, and he eventually walked over to the door and went out.

I sat looking at the envelope for a few moments. I told myself that it was probably a note from a colleague in other chambers about some case or other. But, of course, it wasn't.

It contained two items. Asingle piece of white paper folded over and a photograph. It was another message and, this time, it left me in no doubt at all that the whispered telephone calls and Julian Trent's visit had both been connected.

Four lines of printed bold capitals ran across the centre of the paper:

BE A GOOD LITTLE LAWYER,
TAKE THE STEVE MITCHELL CASE – AND LOSE IT.
DO AS YOU ARE TOLD
NEXT TIME, SOMEONE WILL GET BADLY HURT.

The photograph was of my seventy-eight-year-old father standing outside his home in Northamptonshire.

CHAPTER FOUR

An Englishman's house is his castle, at least so they say. So I sat in my castle with the drawbridge pulled up and thought about what was happening to me.

I had decided against my usual walk through Gray's Inn to the bus stop in High Holborn, the ride on a number 521 to Waterloo and a crowded commuter train to Barnes, followed by the hike across the common. Instead, I had ordered a taxi that had come right to the front door of chambers to collect me, and had then delivered me safe and sound to Ranelagh Avenue, to my home, my castle.

Now I sat on a bar stool at my kitchen counter and looked again and again at the sheet of white paper. TAKE THE STEVE MITCHELL CASE – AND LOSE IT. From what I had heard from Bruce Lygon there wouldn't be much trouble in losing the case. All the evidence seemed to point that way. But why was someone so keen to be sure that it was lost? Was Steve correct when he said he'd been framed?

DO AS YOU ARE TOLD. Did that just mean that I must take the case and lose it, or were there other things well that I would be told to do? And how was the attack by Julian Trent connected? *Next time, I'll smash your head,* he'd said. *Next time, I'll cut your balls right off.* Maybe being beaten up had absolutely nothing to do with Trent's trial last March. Perhaps it was all to do with Steve Mitchell's trial in the future.

But why?

I had once had a client, a rather unsavoury individual, who had told me that the only thing better than getting away with doing a crime was to get someone else convicted for having done it. That way, he'd explained, the police aren't even looking any more.

'Don't you have any conscience about some poor soul doing jail time for something you did?' I had asked him.

'Don't be stupid,' he'd said. 'It makes me laugh. I don't care about anyone else.' There really was no such thing as honour amongst thieves.

Was that what was going on here? Stitch up Steve Mitchell for Scot Barlow's murder and, hey presto, the crime is solved but the real murderer is safe and well and living in clover.

I called my father.

'Hello,' he said in his usual rather formal tone. I could imagine him sitting in front of the television in his bungalow watching the early evening news.

'Hello, Dad,' I said.

'Ah, Geoff,' he said. 'How are things in the Smoke?'

'Fine, thanks. How are things with you?' It was a

ritual. We spoke on the telephone about once a week and, every time, we exchanged these pleasantries. Sadly, these days we had little else to say to one another. We lived in different worlds. We had never been particularly close and he had moved to the village of Kings Sutton, near Banbury, from his native urban Surrey after my mother had died. I had thought that it had been a strange choice but perhaps, unlike me, he had needed to escape his memories.

'Much the same,' he said.

'Dad,' I said. 'I know this is a strange question, but what have you been wearing today?'

'Clothes,' he said, amused. 'Same as always. Why?'

'What clothes?' I asked.

'Why do you need to know?' he demanded suspiciously. We both knew that I was apt to criticize my father's rather ageing wardrobe, and he didn't like it.

'I just do,' I said. 'Please.'

'Fawn corduroy trousers and a yellow shirt under a green pullover,' he said.

'Does the pullover have any holes in it?' I asked.

'None of your business,' he said sharply.

'Does it have a hole in the left elbow?' I persisted.

'Only a small one,' he said defensively. 'It's perfectly all right to wear around the house. Now what is this all about?'

'Nothing,' I said lightly. 'Forget it. Forget I asked.'

'You're a strange boy,' he said. He often said it. I thought he was a strange father, but I kept that to myself.

'I'll call you on Sunday then,' I said to him. I often called on Sundays.

'Right. Bye for now then.' He put down the receiver at his end. He'd never liked talking on the phone and he was habitually eager to finish a conversation as soon as it had started. Today we had been briefer than usual.

I sat and stared at the photograph in my hand, the photograph that had accompanied the note in the white envelope. It showed my father outside the front door of his bungalow wearing fawn-coloured trousers, a yellow shirt and a green pullover with a small hole clearly visible on the left elbow, the yellow of the shirt beneath contrasting with the dark green of the wool. The photo had to have been taken today. For all his reluctance to buy new clothes, my father could never be accused of wearing dirty ones, and he always put on a clean shirt crisp from the local laundry every morning. I suppose he might have had more than one yellow shirt, but I doubted it.

But how, I thought, had they, whoever they were, managed to get a photograph of my father so quickly? Julian Trent had been released from custody only on Friday, and Scot Barlow murdered only yesterday. I wondered if the one had been dependent on the other.

Bruce Lygon still hadn't called me, so I didn't even know if Steve Mitchell had yet been charged with murder, but here I was, already being told to make sure he was convicted.

As if on cue, my telephone rang.

'Hello,' I said, picking it up.

'Geoffrey?' said a now familiar voice.

'Bruce,' I replied. 'What news?'

'I'm on my way to have dinner with my wife,' he said. 'They charged Mitchell with murder at six this evening and he'll be in court tomorrow at ten.'

'Which court?' I asked.

'Newbury magistrates,' he said. 'He's sure to be remanded. No provincial magistrate would ever give bail on a murder charge. I'll apply, of course, but it will have to go before a judge for there to be any chance, and I think it's most unlikely, considering the cause of death. Very nasty.'

'Yes,' I replied. 'I agree, but you never know when there is a bit of celebrity factor.' Under English law the granting of bail was a basic right for all accused and there had to be a good reason for refusing it. In this case the reason given might be that the ferociousness of the attack provided reasonable grounds to believe that the accused might do it again, or that, owing to the seriousness of the charge, he might abscond. Either way, I would bet my year's pay that Steve Mitchell would find himself locked up on remand the following day.

'Mr Mitchell is very insistent that you should defend him,' Bruce Lygon went on.

How ironic, I thought. Did Steve also want me to lose?

'I'm only a junior,' I said. 'Someone of Steve Mitchell's standing would expect a silk.'

'He seems determined that it should be you,' he replied.

But even if I had wanted to lead the defence, the trial judge would be likely to ask some telling questions about how I intended to strengthen the defence team, especially at the front. It would be a coded recommendation to get a QC to lead.

The best I might expect was to be appointed as a silk's junior in the case. As such I might be responsible for doing most of the work. But I would get little of the credit for obtaining an acquittal, while shouldering most of the blame if our client were convicted. Such was the life of a junior.

What was I even thinking about? I told myself. I could not act in this case. The law wouldn't let me.

Do as you are told.

Next time, I'll smash your head.

I'll cut your balls right off.

Someone will get badly hurt.

Oh hell. What do I do?

'Are you still there?' Bruce asked.

'Sorry,' I said. 'I was thinking.'

'I'll contact your clerk in due course, then, I've got the number,' he said.

'Fine,' I replied. Was I mad? 'But Bruce,' I went on. 'Will you call me tomorrow and tell me what happens. And where Mitchell is sent. I'd like to go and talk with him.'

'OK,' he said, slowly. 'I suppose that will be all right.' I could tell from his tone that he didn't like it.

What a cheek, I thought It had been me that had given him his celebrity client and now he was becoming protective of his position.

'Look, Bruce,' I said. 'I'm not trying to steal your client, whom, you might recall, I gave you in the first place. But I need to speak to Steve Mitchell and may need to do so more than once. If he chooses, and I have no intention of convincing him otherwise, you can act for him throughout, including at trial. All I ask of you is that you engage a brief from my chambers, whether it be me or not. Is that fair?'

'Oh, absolutely,' he replied, backtracking a little. Perhaps he too had suddenly worked out that Steve Mitchell was my friend and would, on my say-so, drop Mr Bruce Lygon quicker than a red-hot coal. Bruce needed me, not vice versa.

'Good,' I said. 'Then you will call me?'

'You bet,' he said. 'Straight after the hearing.'

'Fine,' I said. 'Now go and enjoy your dinner. Say happy birthday to your wife.'

'I will,' he said. 'I will.'

As expected, Steve Mitchell was remanded in custody at the brief hearing at Newbury magistrates' court at ten the following morning. According to the report on the lunchtime news, he had spoken only to confirm his name and address. No plea had been entered, and none asked for.

The report concluded with the fact that Mitchell had been remanded to Bullingdon Prison, near Bicester, to appear again at Oxford Crown Court in seven days' time.

I was watching the TV in one of the conference rooms in chambers. My conspiracy-to-defraud trial had ended abruptly and unexpectedly when the court had resumed at ten thirty that morning. Accepting the inevitable, the brothers had changed their pleas to guilty in the hope and expectation of getting a lesser sentence. The judge, caught slightly unawares, and having promptly thanked and dismissed the jury, ordered reports on the two men and then adjourned the case for sixteen days. We would reassemble for sentencing two weeks on Friday at ten.

I was pleased. Any victory is good, but one where the defendants change their plea is particularly gratifying as it means that, even though I would never know if I had actually persuaded the jury of their guilt, the defendants themselves were convinced that I had. So, now believing they had no chance of acquittal, they had jumped before they were pushed. And best of all, it also meant that I had two clear weeks that I had expected to spend at Blackfriars Crown Court now available for other things. And that was rare. Trials tended to overrun, not finish early. It felt like the end of term at school.

Arthur had not been around when I had arrived back from court but he was in the clerks' room when I went through from the conference room and back to my desk.

'Arthur,' I said. 'You might expect a call from a Mr

Bruce Lygon. He's a solicitor in Newbury. He's acting for Steve Mitchell.'

'The jockey?' Arthur asked.

'One and the same,' I said. 'Apparently Mr Mitchell wants me as his counsel.'

'I'm sure we can find him a silk,' said Arthur. He wasn't being discourteous, just realistic.

'That's what I told Mr Lygon,' I said.

Arthur nodded and made a note. 'I'll be ready when he calls.'

'Thanks,' I said, and went on through to my room.

I called Bruce Lygon. He had left a message after the magistrates' hearing but I needed him to do more.

'Bruce,' I said when he answered. 'I want to visit the crime scene. Can you fix it with the police?' The lawyers for the accused were entitled to have access to the scene but at the discretion of the police, and not prior to the collection of forensic evidence.

'With or without me?' he asked.

'As you like,' I said. 'But as soon as possible, please.'

'Does this mean you will act for him?' he asked.

'No, it doesn't,' I said. 'Not yet. It might help me make up my mind.'

'But only his representatives have access,' he said.

I knew. 'If you don't tell the police,' I said, 'then they will never know.'

'Right,' he said slowly. I felt that he was confused. He was not the only one.

'And can you arrange an interview for me with Mitchell at Bullingdon?'

'But you're not . . .' he tailed off. 'I suppose it might be possible,' he said finally.

'Good,' I said. 'Tomorrow would be great.'

'Right,' he said again. 'I'll get back to you then.'

Bruce had been a lucky choice. He was so keen to be representing his celebrity client that he seemed happy to overlook a few departures from proper procedure, to bend the rules just a little. I decided not to tell Arthur what was going on. He wouldn't have been the least bit flexible.

Steve Mitchell was very agitated when I met him at noon the following day at Bullingdon Prison. I currently didn't own a car as I found it an unnecessary expense, especially with the congestion charge and the ever-rising cost of parking in London. However, I probably spent at least half of what I saved on hiring cars from the Hertz office on Fulham Palace Road. This time they had provided me with a bronze-coloured Ford Mondeo that had easily swallowed up the fifty or so miles to Oxfordshire.

'God, Perry,' Steve said as he came into the stark prison interview room reserved for lawyers to meet with their clients. 'Get me out of this bloody place.'

'I'll try,' I said, not wishing to dash his hopes too quickly.

He marched round the room. 'I didn't bloody do it,' he said. 'I swear to you I never did it.'

'Just sit down,' I said, Reluctantly, he ceased his pacing and sat on a grey steel stool beside the grey steel table and I sat on a similar stool opposite him. These functional items, along with two more identical stools, were securely fastened with bolts to the bare grey concrete floor. The room was about eight foot square with sickly cream walls. The only light came from a large, energy-efficient fluorescent bulb surrounded by a wire cage in the centre of the white ceiling. Absolutely no expense had been wasted on comfort.

'I didn't do it,' he said again. 'I tell you, I'm being framed.'

As it happened, I believed him. In the past I'd had clients who had sworn blind that they were innocent and were being framed, and experience had taught me not to believe most of them. One client had once sworn to me on his mother's life that he was innocent of setting fire to his own house for the insurance money, only for the said mother to confess that she and her son had planned it together. When she gave evidence against him in court, he had shouted from the dock that he'd kill her. So much for her life.

However, in Steve's case I had other reasons for believing him.

'Who's framing you?' I asked him.

'I've got no bloody idea,' he said. 'That's for you to find out.'

'Who is Julian Trent?' I asked him calmly.

'Who?' he said.

'Julian Trent,' I repeated.

'Never heard of him,' Steve said. Not a flicker in his eyes, not a fraction of hesitation in his voice. Asking questions for a living, I believed I was a reasonable judge of when someone was lying. But I was not infallible. Over the years I had frequently believed people who were telling me lies, but it was not often that I discovered that someone I thought was lying was actually being truthful. Either Steve was being straight with me, or he was fairly good at lying.

'Who is he?' Steve asked.

'No one important,' I said. It was my turn to lie. 'I just wondered if you knew him.'

'Should I?' he asked.

'No reason you should,' I said. I decided to change the subject. 'So why do the police think you killed Scot Barlow?'

'Because they just do,' he answered unhelpfully.

'But they must have some evidence,' I said.

'It seems that it was my bloody pitchfork stuck into the little bastard.' I could imagine that Steve referring to Barlow as 'the little bastard' hadn't gone down too well with the police. 'And would I be so stupid to have killed the little bastard with my own pitchfork? At least I would have then taken the bloody thing home again.'

'What else do they have?' I asked him.

'Something about spots of his blood and some of his hairs being found in my car, and his blood being on my boots. It's all bloody nonsense. I was never in his house.'

'So where exactly were you when he was killed?' I asked him.

'I don't know,' he said. 'They haven't told me when he actually died. But they did ask me what I was doing between one and six on Monday afternoon. I told them I was riding at Ludlow races. But I wasn't. The meeting was abandoned due to the bloody course being water-logged.'

That was really stupid, I thought. Lying wouldn't have exactly endeared him to the police, and it was so easy for them to check.

'So where were you?' I asked him again.

He seemed reluctant to tell me, so I sat and waited in silence.

'At home,' he said eventually.

'On your own?' I pressed him.

'Yes,' he said. 'I was alone reading all afternoon.'

Now he was lying. I was sure of it and I didn't like it.

'That's a shame,' I said. 'If someone was with you, they would be able to give you an alibi.'

He sat silently.

'Do you know what the word "alibi" means?' I asked him. He shook his head. 'It's Latin. It means "somewhere else". An unshakeable alibi is proof of innocence.' I tried to lighten the atmosphere. 'And even you, Steve, couldn't be in two places at once. Are you sure you were alone all afternoon?'

'Absolutely,' he said, affronted. 'Are you saying I'm a liar?' He stood up and looked at me.

'No, of course not,' I said. But he was. 'I'm just trying to make sure you remembered correctly.'

I rather hoped he would sit down again but he paced round the room like a caged tiger.

'I'll tell you what I do remember,' he said to my back. 'I remember that I've never been in Scot Barlow's house. Not on Monday. Not ever. I didn't even know where the little bastard lived.'

'What about the text message?' I said. 'The one saying you were coming round to sort him out.'

'I didn't send any bloody text message,' he replied. 'And certainly not to him.'

Surely, I thought, the police must have the phone records.

He walked around in front of me and sat down again.

'It doesn't look too good, does it?' he said.

'No, Steve, it doesn't.' We sat there in silence for a few moments. 'Who would gain from Barlow's death?' I asked him.

'Reno Clemens must be laughing all the way to the winning post,' he said. 'With Barlow dead and me in here, he's got rid of both of us.'

I thought it unlikely that Clemens would go to the extent of murder and a frame-up to simply get rid of his racing rivals. But hadn't someone once tried to break the leg of a skating rival for that very reason?

'I didn't do it, you know.' He looked up at me. 'Not that I'm sorry he's dead.'

'What was there between you two?' I asked. 'Why did you hate him so much?' I thought that I wouldn't ask him about the incident in the showers at Sandown. Not yet. Much better, at the moment, if absolutely no one knew I had seen Barlow lying in the shower, and what he had said to me.

'I hated him because he was a sneaky little bastard,' Steve said.

'But just how was he sneaky?' I asked.

'He just was.'

'Look, Steve,' I said. 'If you want me to help you, you will have to tell me everything. Now why was he sneaky?'

'He would sneak to the stewards if anyone did anything wrong.'

'How do you know?' I asked. 'Did he ever sneak on you?'

'What, to the stewards?'

'Yes,' I said, imploring. 'To the stewards.'

'Well, no,' he said. 'Not on me to the stewards, but he was a bastard nevertheless.'

'But why?' I almost shouted at him, spreading my arms and hands open wide.

He stood up again and turned away from me. 'Because,' he said in a rush, 'he told my bloody wife I was having an affair.'

Ah, I thought. That would account for the hatred. Steve went on without turning round. 'Then she left me and took my kids away.'

Ah, again.

'How did Barlow know you were having an affair?' I asked.

'I was having it with his sister,' he said.

'Do the police know about this?'

'I bleeding well hope not,' he said, turning round. 'Now that would give me a bloody motive, wouldn't it?'

'When did all this happen?' I asked him.

'Years ago,' he said.

'Are you still having the affair with Barlow's sister?' I asked.

'Nah, it was just a fling,' he said. 'Finished right there and then, but Natalie, that's my wife, she wouldn't come home. Went and married some bloody Australian and they now live in Sydney. With my kids. I ask you, how am I meant to see them when they're half the world away? It's all that bastard Barlow's fault.'

I thought that a jury would not necessarily agree with his assessment.

'And what about the betting slips found on the prongs of the fork?' I said.

'Nothing to do with me,' Steve said.

'But they had your name on them,' I said.

'Yeah, and would I be so stupid as to leave them stuck on the bloody fork if I had planted it in Barlow's chest? Don't be bloody daft. It's obviously a sodding stitch-up. Surely you can see that?'

It did seem to me that the police must think Steve to be very stupid indeed if they were so certain he had done

92

it based on that. Or perhaps they had forensic evidence that we didn't yet know about. We would discover in due course, during pre-trial disclosure but, for the time being, we could only guess. Either way, it would be worth pursuing the matter at trial.

'Were they, in fact, your betting slips?' I asked him. We both knew that gambling on horses was against the terms of his riding licence.

'They may have been,' he said. 'But then they wouldn't have had my name on them. I'm not that bloody stupid.' He laughed. 'Least of my worries now, I suppose.'

'Is it true that Barlow used to go through other jocks' pockets looking for betting slips?' I said.

'I don't know,' he said. 'I doubt it. It was probably me that started that rumour.' He grinned at me. 'I'd have said anything to get at him.'

In truth, it was Steve Mitchell, and not Scot Barlow, who had been the sneaky little bastard.

'I hope it wasn't that rumour that got him killed,' I said.

Steve looked at me. 'Bloody hell,' he said.

CHAPTER FIVE

On Thursday night I stayed with my trainer, Paul Newington, at Great Milton.

I had left Steve Mitchell feeling very sorry for himself
at Bullingdon Prison.

'When can you get me out of here?' he'd asked me as
we had shaken hands.

'I really don't know, Steve,' I'd said. 'It is most
unlikely that you would get bail on a murder charge.'

'But I didn't do it,' he had repeated yet again.

'The police don't see it like that,' I'd said. 'And I'm
afraid the court will take more notice of them than of
you.'

'But you will try?' he had implored.

I had privately thought it would be a complete waste
of my time.

'I'll get Bruce Lygon to make another application,' I'd
told him.

'I want you to do it,' he had demanded.

But I knew it wasn't always a good idea for a barrister
to appear at a bail hearing. It was seen as overkill. In

some eyes, it tended to make the accused look guilty. Sometimes that very fact could swing the decision against the award. And anyway, bail in murder cases was as rare as hen's teeth.

'I don't really think it would make any difference,' I'd told him.

'So when can I expect to get out?' he had asked in near desperation.

'Steve,' I'd said. 'I think you had better prepare yourself for quite a lengthy stretch in here. The trial date will likely not be set for at least six months and it could be as long as a year away.'

'A year!' he'd exclaimed, going white. 'Oh my God. I'll go mad.'

'I'll see what I can do to get you out sooner, but I don't want to build your hopes up too much.'

I had looked at him standing there with drooping shoulders, appearing much shorter than his five foot six. He may have been an arrogant ego maniac who annoyed most of those he encountered, but there was no doubt that he was one of the best in his chosen tough and physically demanding profession. He was basically a harmless victim and I was sure he was no murderer. And he didn't deserve to have been thrust into this nightmare.

I had thought he was going to cry. Perhaps for the first time he had appreciated the real fix he was in and he was far from pleased about it.

I hadn't liked leaving Steve in that state. Over the years I'd left clients in prison on remand in states emotion that varied from utter rage to complete collapse. It was never easy, but this was the first time I'd felt real anger in tandem with my client. Hold on a minute, I thought suddenly, he's not my client and, what's more, he couldn't be.

It was always an escape from my usual work to go to Paul Newington's place. He was so different from the people I dealt with on a day-to-day basis. For a start, I don't think I had ever seen him in a tie, and almost never in a jacket. When he was at home he habitually wore blue denim jeans with scuffed knees and frayed legs, and, on this occasion, he sported a black sweatshirt with 'Motorhead' emblazoned across its chest in lightning-strike letters. Perhaps it would not have been my choice of garb when entertaining one of his owners.

But I think that was why I liked him so much. He used to say that the horses didn't care if he was in his dressing gown so why should their owners. I tactfully didn't point out to him that it wasn't the horses that were paying him for their board and lodging. It was one of the reasons why he had never quite broken into the big time. Rich owners want to be appreciated and, in their eyes, afforded due reverence by their trainers. And rich owners buy the best horses.

Paul's richest owners had continually been wooed away by other trainers more willing to bow and scrape to their whims. I had resisted two such approaches myself because I liked the relaxed atmosphere of his stable. It was in such contrast to the old-fashioned formality I was all too familiar with in the courts.

Paul and I walked round the stables as his staff were busy mucking out and giving their charges food and water for the night. Sandeman looked wonderful in his box with his shining golden tan coat and showing no apparent ill effects from his race at Sandown the previous Saturday.

I walked over and slapped his neck.

'Good boy,' I said to him calmly. 'Who's a good boy?'

He blew through his nostrils and shifted his bulk, turning his head to see if I had a titbit for him. I never came to Paul's without some apples in my pocket and today was no exception. Sandeman gratefully munched his way noisily through a Granny Smith, dripping saliva and apple bits into his bedding. It was a satisfactory encounter for us both and I took my leave of him with a slap on his neck which caused him to lift and lower his head as if he were agreeing with me.

'See you in the morning, my boy,' I called to him as I left his box. I often wondered if our equine partners had any notion of the depth of our devotion for them.

Laura, Paul's wife, cooked us supper and, as always, we sat round the bleached-pine kitchen table, eating her best macaroni cheese with onions. It wasn't long before the conversation turned to the hot topic in racing circles.

'So, do you think he did it?' said Paul between mouthfuls.

'Who? Steve Mitchell?' I said.

'Umm,' he said while ladling another spoonful of the pasta into his mouth.

'The evidence seems to suggest it,' I said.

'What is the world coming to?' Paul said. 'When I used to ride there was always greater camaraderie than there is nowadays.'

I thought that Paul was wearing rose-tinted spectacles in his memory of how things used to be. Rivalry amongst jockeys had always been alive and well, and certainly had been in the nineteenth century, in the time of the great Fred Archer, when causing your rival to miss his steam train to the next meeting was as legitimate a tactic as outriding him in a close finish.

'Well, do *you* think he did it?' I asked Paul.

'I don't know, you're the lawyer,' he replied.

'He would have to have been incredibly stupid to have left all those clues,' I said. 'The murder weapon left sticking in the victim belonged to him. And he supposedly texted a message to Barlow that afternoon saying he was coming round to sort him out.'

'I thought Steve Mitchell had more sense,' said Paul, shaking his head. He had clearly convicted the accused before any defence witnesses had been called.

'I'm not so sure,' I said. 'There are many questions that need answering in this case.'

'But who else would have done it?' asked Paul.

'Everyone knew that Mitchell hated Barlow's guts. You could cut the atmosphere between them with a knife.'

'Reno Clemens has done well with both of them being out of the way,' I said.

'Oh come on,' Paul said. 'Reno might be a damn good jockey but he's hardly a murderer. He hasn't got the brains.'

'He may have others around him who have,' I said.

Paul waved a dismissive hand and refilled our wine glasses.

'Do you know anyone called Julian Trent?' I asked into the pause.

'No,' said Paul. Laura shook her head. 'Is he a jockey?'

'No,' I said. 'It's not important, I just wondered.'

'Who is he?' Paul asked.

'Just an ex-client of mine,' I said. 'His name has popped up in connection with Barlow a couple of times and I just wondered if you knew him. It doesn't matter.'

There were a few moments of silence as we concentrated on our food.

'Do you know why Barlow and Mitchell hated each other so much?' I asked.

'Wasn't it something to do with Barlow's sister?' Paul said. 'Mitchell had an affair with her or something.'

'Such a shame,' Laura interjected unexpectedly.

'What's a shame?' I asked her.

'About Scot Barlow's sister,' she said.

'What about his sister?' I said.

'Don't you know?' she said. She went on when my blank expression gave her the answer. 'She killed herself in June.'

'How?' I asked, wondering why Steve Mitchell hadn't bothered to mention this to me.

'At a party,' Laura said. 'Apparently she was depressed and injected herself with a huge dose of anaesthetic.'

'How did she get anaesthetic?' I asked.

'She was a vet,' said Paul. 'Specialized in horses.'

'Where?' I asked.

'Lambourn,' Paul replied. 'She worked in the equine hospital there and most of the local trainers used her practice. She was one of a team, of course.'

'You must remember,' said Laura. 'There was a huge fuss on the television and the papers were full of it.'

'I was away for the first half of June,' I said. 'I must have missed it.' I had been away advising a client up on a money-laundering charge in Gibraltar. The long arm of the English law still stretched far to our remaining colonies and dependencies. 'Whose party was it?' I asked.

'Simon Dacey's,' said Paul.

I again looked rather blank.

'He's a trainer,' said Paul. 'Trains on the flat only. Moved to Lambourn about five years ago from Middleham in Wensleydale.' That may account for why I didn't know of him. 'He threw the party after winning the Derby. You know, with Peninsula.'

Now, even I had heard of Peninsula. Hottest horseflesh property in the world. Horse of the Year as a two-year-old and, this season, winner of the Two Thousand Guineas at Newmarket in May, the Derby at Epsom in June, the Breeders Cup the previous month at Santa Anita Park in California, and now on his way to some lucrative earnings at stud.

'That must have gone down well with the guests,' I said rather flippantly.

'It certainly didn't,' said Laura seriously. 'We were there. We've known Simon since our Yorkshire days. Paul worked for him as an assistant when we first started. The party was huge. Massive marquee in the garden with live bands and everything. It was great fun. At least it was until someone found Millie Barlow.'

'Where was she found?' I asked.

'In the house,' said Paul. 'Upstairs, in one of the bedrooms.'

'Who found her?' I said.

'No idea,' said Paul. 'The police arrived and stopped the party about nine at night. It had been going since noon. Started off as Sunday lunch and just went on.'

'What did the police do?' I asked him.

'Took our names and addresses and sent us home,' he said. 'Most of us hadn't even been in the house. They asked for witnesses to tell them when they had last seen Millie Barlow, but we didn't even know what she looked like so we left as soon as we could.'

'And were they sure it was suicide?'

'That's what everyone thought,' he said.

'What was she depressed about?'

'You seem very interested all of a sudden,' said Paul.

'Just my suspicious mind,' I said with a laugh. 'One violent death in a family is unfortunate; two within five months may be more than coincidental.'

'Wow,' said Laura, perking up her interest. 'Are you saying that Millie was murdered?'

'No, of course not,' I said. 'I just wondered if the inquest had found that she had killed herself, and why.'

'I don't know,' she said. 'I don't even know if the inquest has been held.'

I hadn't heard about the case, or read about it, but I knew that the Coroner's Court system, like every other aspect of the law, was slow and tedious at times. It wasn't unusual for an inquest to be opened and adjourned for many months, even years. I made a mental note to look it up on the internet.

'So, how's my horse,' I said, changing the subject.

'Slow and fat,' said Paul, laughing, 'like his owner.'

I toasted our slowness and fatness with good red wine, and added a few more ounces with a second helping of macaroni.

I adored riding out on cold, crisp winter's mornings with my breath showing in the air and the frost white on the ground, glistening in the brightness of the sunlight. Sadly, this Friday was not one of those. Rain fell steadily, the plop, plop of the large drops clearly audible as they struck my helmet from high above.

SILKS

Sandeman and I were number six in Paul's string of ten horses as we walked through Great Milton on the way to the training gallops beyond the village, the horses' metal shoes clicking on the hard roads. Both horses and riders were soaked even before we had left the stable yard with the dawn at seven thirty sharp, and now the water ran in rivulets down my neck inside my semi-waterproof jacket. But I didn't care and neither did Sandeman. I could feel his rippling muscles beneath me. He knew exactly why he had been roused from his stable in the rain, and exactly where we were going. We were both clearly excited in anticipation of the gallop we would soon share.

The wind tore at my jacket and the raindrops stung my face, but nothing could wipe the grin from my mouth as we tore up the gallop at nearly thirty miles an hour with me trying hard to stop Sandeman going any faster. He clearly had recovered fully from the three miles last Saturday and he seemed as eager as I to get back on a racecourse.

Paul sat on horseback at the top of the gallop, watching as we moved smoothly up towards him. I was attempting to comply with the letter of his instructions. A steady three-quarter-speed gallop, he had said, keeping up-sides with one of his other horses. He had implored me not to ride a finish, not to over-tire my horse. I was doing my best to do what he had asked, but Sandeman beneath me seemed determined to race, keen as always to put his nose in front of the other horse. I took another tight hold of the reins and steadied him. In spite of Paul's sometimes casual manner with his owners, he was still a great trainer of racehorses and very rarely did his horses fail on the racecourse due to over- or under-training at home. I had never questioned his judgement in that department.

I pulled Sandeman up into a trot and then a walk, laughing as I did so. What a magnificent way to blow the courtroom cobwebs out of my hair. I walked him round and round in circles while he cooled and the other horses completed their work up the gallop. Then the string wound its way down the hill and back through the village to Paul's stables.

Oxfordshire was coming to life and the road traffic had increased significantly during the time we had been on the gallops. Now, streams of impatient commuters roared past us on their way to join the lines of cars on the nearby M40 making the long drag into London. How lucky I am, I thought, to have this escape from the hurly burly of city life and, as I always did, I resolved to try to do this more often. Life here, deep in rural England, seemed a million miles from baseball bats and smashed computers. Perhaps, I mused, I should stay right here and let it all go away.

My dreams of leaving life's troubles behind lasted only until we arrived back at Paul's yard. Laura came out of the house as I was sliding off Sandeman's back.

'A Mr Lygon called for you about ten minutes ago,' she said as I led Sandeman into his stable. She followed us in. 'He seemed very insistent that you should call him as soon as you got back.'

'Thanks,' I said, wondering how he knew where I was. I looked at my watch. It was ten to nine.

I removed the bridle and saddle from Sandeman and replaced them with his head-collar and a dry rug.

'Sorry, old boy,' I said to him. 'I'll be back to finish you in a while.'

I shut the stable door before the horse bolted and went inside, dripping water all over Laura's clean kitchen floor.

'Bruce,' I said when he answered. 'How did you know where I was?'

'Your clerk told me that you weren't due in court today, and you had told him you wouldn't be in chambers, so he said you were probably riding your nag.' I could almost hear Arthur saying it. 'After that it was easy. I looked up who trained your nag on the *Racing Post* website.'

If Bruce Lygon could find me so easily, then so could young Julian Trent, or, indeed, whoever was behind Julian Trent, the smooth whispering man on the telephone. I must learn to be more careful.

'Do you often frequent the *Racing Post* website?' I asked Bruce sarcastically.

'All the time,' he said eagerly. 'I love my racing.'

'Well, don't tell me if you ever won or lost money on Scot Barlow or Steve Mitchell,' I said. 'I don't want to know.' And neither should anyone else, I thought.

'Blimey,' he said. 'Never thought of that.'

'So how can I help you?' I asked him.

'It's me helping you, actually,' he replied. 'I've managed to get us a visit to the crime scene.'

'Well done,' I said. 'When?'

'Today,' he said. 'The police say we can go there at two this afternoon. But they say it will be an accompanied visit only.'

Fair enough, I thought. I was surprised they would let us in at all this soon.

'That's fine,' I said. 'Where is it?'

'Great Shefford,' he said. 'Small village between Lambourn and Newbury. Place called Honeysuckle Cottage.' It didn't sound like a site of bloody murder. 'Meet you there at two?'

'Is there a pub?' I asked him.

'Yes,' he said. 'I think so. There's one on the main road.'

'Shall we meet there at one o'clock?' I said. 'For some lunch?'

'Ah.' He thought. 'Yes I think that will be fine. But keep your phone on just in case.'

'OK,' I said. 'See you later.'

'How will you know which one is me?' he asked.

'You'll have a rolled up copy of the *Racing Post* under your arm.' I laughed, and so did he.

The *Racing Post* wasn't needed. There were only three other people in the bar when I walked into the Swan Inn at one o'clock sharp and two of them were clearly a couple, heads close together and holding hands as if they were having a secret lovers' tryst far from home.

The third person was a man who looked to be in his mid-to-late forties and who was wearing a light grey suit with white shirt and blue striped tie. He looked at me briefly, then his gaze slid over my shoulder back to the door as if expecting somebody else.

'Bruce?' I asked him, walking up close.

'Yes?' he said as a question, returning his gaze briefly to my face before again looking over my shoulder.

'I'm Geoffrey,' I said. 'Geoffrey Mason.'

'Oh,' he said. He seemed reluctant to take his eyes off the door. 'I was expecting someone . . . you know, a bit older.'

It was a reaction I was used to. I would be thirty-six in January but, it seemed, I appeared somewhat younger. This was not always an asset in court, where some judges often equated age with ability. On this occasion I imagined that Bruce was expecting me to be dressed similarly to him, in suit and tie, while, in fact, I was in jeans and a brown suede bomber jacket over an open-necked check shirt. Maybe it was because I was still trying to tell myself that I couldn't actually represent Steve Mitchell that I had decided against my sober dark suit when I had changed out of my sopping wet riding clothes at Paul's.

'Older and wiser?' I said, adding to Bruce's discomfort.

He laughed. A nervous little laugh. He, too, was not quite what I had expected. Ironically, he was slightly older than I had thought from listening to him on the telephone, and he was less confident than I would have liked.

'What are you drinking?' I asked him.

'I'm fine,' he said pointing at a partially drained pint mug on the bar. 'My round.'

'Diet Coke then, please,' I said.

We also ordered some food and took our drinks over to a table in the corner, where we could talk without the barman listening to every word.

'Did you see Mitchell yesterday?' asked Bruce.

'Yes,' I said without elaborating.

'What did he say?' asked Bruce eagerly.

'Not much,' I replied. 'Says he's being framed.'

'I know that,' said Bruce. 'But do you believe him?'

I didn't answer. 'Did you know Scot Barlow had a sister?' I asked him.

'No,' he said. 'Should I?'

'Seems she killed herself last June,' I said. He didn't look any the wiser. 'During a big party in Lambourn.'

'What? Not that girl vet?' he said.

'One and the same,' I said. 'Millie Barlow.'

'Blimey,' he said. 'That was big news in these parts.'

'Why?' I asked him.

'Speculation, I suppose,' he said. 'And all those celebrities at that party being held by the police.'

'What sort of speculation?'

'Drugs,' he said. 'Lots of cocaine sniffing, apparently. Always the way with celebs. It was initially thought the vet had died of an overdose of it, but it turned out to be horse anaesthetic and it seems she did it on purpose.'

'Do you know or are you guessing?' I asked.

'It's what everyone says,' he replied. 'Seems she left a note or something.'

'Seems a strange place to do it,' I said.

'Suicides do strange things,' he said. 'There was that one near here who drove his car onto the railway line and waited for it to get hit by a train. Stupid sod killed six more with him and injured hundreds of others. Why didn't he just shut himself into his garage and quietly leave the engine running?'

'Yeah, but ruining a party seems a bit . . .' I tailed off.

'Perhaps she had a grudge against the party giver, and she was extracting revenge. I once had a client whose ex-wife killed herself right outside the registry office as he was getting remarried inside.'

'How?' I asked.

'Walked out under a lorry. Just like that. The poor driver had no chance.'

'Bet that went down well with the wedding guests,' I said.

'I actually think my client was delighted,' he said, grinning. 'Saved him a fortune in alimony.' We both laughed.

I was growing to like Bruce, and his confidence was growing too.

'So tell me, what are we looking for at Barlow's place?' he said, changing the subject.

'I'm not sure,' I said. 'I always try to visit scenes of crime if I'm acting in a case. It helps me when it comes to questions in court. Also, it often gives some insight into the victim.'

'So are you now acting in this case?' he asked me.

'Temporarily,' I said, smiling at him. But was I acting for the prosecution or the defence?

We finished our lunch and Bruce drove us the few hundred yards to Church Street, leaving my hired Mondeo in the pub car park. Honeysuckle Cottage was a beautiful old stone building set back from the road amongst a copse of tall horse-chestnut trees, their branches now bare of the leaves that lay deep and uncollected on the driveway. I couldn't actually see or smell any of the honeysuckle after which the cottage had been named, but it was hardly the right season.

The place was surrounded on all sides by grand houses with large gardens, mostly invisible behind tall evergreen hedges or high stone walls. Not much chance here, I thought, of a nosey neighbour witnessing the comings and goings at the Barlow residence.

There were already two cars parked in front of a modern ugly concrete-block garage that had been built alongside the cottage with no respect for its surroundings. The driver's door of one of the cars opened and a young man got out as we pulled up behind him.

'Mr Lygon?' he asked, approaching.

'That's me,' said Bruce, advancing and holding out his hand.

'Detective Constable Hillier,' said the young man, shaking it.

'And this is Geoffrey Mason,' said Bruce, indicating me. 'Barrister in the case.'

DC Hillier looked me up and down and he, too, clearly thought I was under-dressed for the occasion. We shook hands, nevertheless.

'This will have to be a quick visit, I'm afraid. I can give you no more than half an hour,' said the policeman. 'And we are not alone.'

'Who else?' I asked.

'Barlow's parents,' he said. 'Took a coach down from Glasgow. They're inside at the moment.' He nodded towards the house.

Oh bugger, I thought, this could be a more emotional encounter than I had expected.

And so it turned out.

DC Hillier introduced us to Mr and Mrs Barlow in the hallway of the cottage.

'They are lawyers in the case,' he said. Mr Barlow looked at us in disgust, he clearly didn't like lawyers. 'They are acting for Mr Mitchell,' the policeman went on, rather unnecessarily, I thought.

Mr Barlow's demeanour changed from disgust to pure hatred, as if it were we who had killed his son.

'May you all burn in Hell for eternity,' he said with venom. He had a broad Scottish accent and the word 'burn' sounded like it could be spelt as 'berrrrn'. Bruce seemed rather taken aback by this outburst.

'We're only doing our job,' he said, defending himself.

'But why?' Mr Barlow said. 'Why are ye givin' that man any assistance? He is sent from the Devil, that one.'

'Now, now, dear,' said Mrs Barlow laying a hand on her husband's arm. 'Remember what the doctor said. Do not stress yourself.'

Barlow relaxed a fraction. He was a big tall man with heavy jowls and bushy eyebrows and he was wearing an ill-fitting dark suit with no tie. Mrs Barlow, in contrast, had a slight frame, was a good eight inches shorter than her husband and had a head of tightly curled grey hair. She wore an inappropriately cheerful flowery dress that appeared to be at least two sizes too big for her, and which hung on her like a sack.

'Aye, woman,' he said, irritated. He flicked his wife's hand from his sleeve. 'But he is still an evil one, that Mitchell.'

'He hasn't actually been convicted yet,' I said. It was a mistake. His doctor wouldn't have thanked me.

'I tell you,' Mr Barlow almost shouted, jabbing his right index finger towards me. 'That man is guilty and he shall have to answer to our Lord. And it's not just Hamish that he killed, but both of our bairns.'

'Who's Hamish?' I said. Another mistake.

'Hamish, man,' bellowed Barlow in a full rage. 'My son.'

Bruce Lygon grabbed my arm and spoke quickly into

my ear. 'Scot Barlow's real name was Hamish.' I felt a
fool. How could I have not known? On the racecourse,
Barlow was always referred to as Scot, but, I now
realized, that must have been only because he was one.

'But what did you mean about Mitchell killing both
your children?' I asked him, recovering my position a
little.

'He killed our Millie,' said Mrs Barlow quickly in a
quiet, mellow tone that hung in the air

'I thought she killed herself,' I said as gently as
possible.

'Aye, but that man was still responsible,' said Mr
Barlow.

'How so?' I said pressing the point.

'He was fornicating with my daughter,' said Mr Barlow,
his voice rising in both tone and volume. I considered it a
strange turn of phrase. And, surely, I thought, it takes two
to fornicate, like to tango.

'How does that make him responsible for her death?' I
asked.

'Because,' said Mrs Barlow in her gentle tone, 'he
dumped her for someone else on the day she died.'

I wondered again why Steve Mitchell hadn't thought it
was important enough to tell me that. And what was
more, if what the Barlows said was true, then he had lied
to me more than I thought, and I still didn't like being
lied to by my clients. I didn't like it one little bit.

CHAPTER SIX

Mr and Mrs Barlow hovered around us as Bruce and I made an inspection of the rest of their son's house. Everywhere we went they followed and watched. Everything I picked up to look at they took back from me and replaced exactly as it had been.

The police forensic team had previously moved through the house covering every shiny surface with a fine silvery powder, fingerprint powder, hoping, no doubt, to display some of Steve Mitchell's dabs. In due course, at pre-trial disclosure, we would find out how successful they had been.

According to the television reports Scot, or Hamish, had been found lying on his kitchen floor in a pool of blood with the pitchfork stuck in his chest. If there actually had been a pool of blood, someone must have since cleaned it up. However, the floor and the cupboard doors were covered with numerous little yellow labels with numbers written on them, which, I knew from experience, were to show positions where blood spots had been discovered. Unlike on some old American TV murder stories, there was no convenient white outline drawn on the floor to show the position where the body had been found.

Lying face down on the kitchen table was a broken photo frame, its glass badly cracked but still held in place by the silver surround. But there was no photograph in the frame and the back of it was hanging off. As with everything else, it was covered with the slimy fingerprint powder.

'I wonder what was in here,' I said to Bruce, holding up the frame to show him.

'It was a picture of our Millie,' said Mrs Barlow from the doorway.

'Do you have it?' I asked her.

'No,' she said. 'He must have taken it.'

The emphasis she placed on the word 'he' left me in no doubt that she meant Steve Mitchell. But why would he take it? I wondered if the police had found the photograph at Mitchell's house, but, surely, even the most stupid of murderers wouldn't take such a clue home with them from the scene of the crime, although I knew some did, like keeping a souvenir, or a trophy.

'Was it a portrait picture?' I asked her.

'No,' she said. 'It was taken when she was at work in the equine hospital. It showed her with a horse. It used to be hers but Hamish had it when . . .' She couldn't finish. Tears began to well up in her eyes.

'I'm so sorry, Mrs Barlow,' I said. I knew only too well the despair that grief can engender.

'Thank you,' she said, dabbing her face with a white handkerchief that she had deftly removed from the sleeve of her dress. I imagined that she must have shed many a tear over her dead children.

'But it must have been a fairly significant photograph to have been in a silver frame,' I said. 'Do you remember which horse Millie was with?' I looked at Mrs Barlow.

'I'm afraid I don't,' she said. 'We lost touch with them both really, when they moved to England.' She made it sound like England was half-way round the world from Glasgow. 'But I recall seeing the picture in her room after she died. Hamish said he wanted it. To remember her by.'

'Where did she live?' I asked.

'What? When she wasn't living with that man?' she said with unexpected anger. She quickly composed herself. 'She had a flat at the equine hospital. She shared it with another vet.'

'Do you know who?'

'I'm sorry, I can't remember her name,' she replied.

'But you are sure it was a female vet?'

'Oh, I think so,' she said. 'At least I always thought it was a woman. She wouldn't have shared a flat with a man. Not my Millie.' But her Millie had shared a bed with Steve Mitchell.

DC Hillier had listened to most of the exchanges between the Barlows and me but he seemed unconcerned and disinterested. He had been too busy looking at his watch.

'Have you seen all you want?' he asked. 'I've got to go now and I need to lock up.'

Bruce held the Barlows at bay in the hallway while I had a quick peep at the bedrooms and bathrooms upstairs. There was nothing unusual or unexpected. There were no giveaway signs of a permanent female presence, like tampons in the medicine cabinet or a lady's smalls in the airing cupboard. Overall there was not much to see. Hamish Barlow had been a tidy man with a wardrobe of smart designer clothes and two cupboards on his landing full of racing-related memorabilia like piles of race cards, bundled copies of the *Racing Post* and numerous horse-related magazines and books. But there were no skeletons with them for me to find. And no other photo frames, with or without photos. Nothing at all that seemed to me to be in any way abnormal.

The policeman ushered us all out of the house, and then he padlocked the clasp on the front door and invited us all to leave the premises. I would have liked to have had a little longer to look around the garden and the garage. Maybe next time. Oh God, I thought. Next time.

A cold sweat broke out briefly on my forehead and I felt foolish in spinning through 360 degrees just to ensure that Julian Trent was not creeping up behind me. He wasn't. Of course, he wasn't. Calm down, I told myself, and my heartbeat slowly returned to normal.

'Do you have a telephone number where my solicitor could contact you?' I asked the Barlows as they were getting into their car.

Mr Barlow, who had been mostly quiet after his earlier outburst, suddenly turned to me and said, 'Why would he want to contact us?'

'In case he has any more questions for you,' I said.

'I don't want to answer any more of your questions,' he said.

'Look,' I said. 'I know you don't want to help me, but I am as interested as you are in finding out who killed your son.'

'Mitchell killed him,' said Mr Barlow emphatically.

'How can you be so sure?' I asked him.

'Because Hamish used to say that, one day, Mitchell would kill him as sure as he killed his sister. And now he has. I hope he rots in hell.'

There wasn't much answer to that. I stood and watched them drive away. There were other ways of finding their telephone number if I needed it.

'Mr Barlow seems a bit too keen on hell and damnation, if you ask me,' said Bruce as he reversed his car back onto the road.

'He's a good Scottish Presbyterian, I expect,' I said.

'Bit too dour for my liking,' said Bruce. 'And I wouldn't want to cross him in a dark alley.'

'He's all talk,' I said. 'He's far too God fearing to actually break the law. That's God's law, of course. Ten Commandments and all that. All Presbyterians love their Bible.'

'Not really my scene,' said Bruce.

'No,' I said. 'Nor mine either.' Except that English law

owed much to the principles of the Ten Commandments, especially that one about bearing false witness against one's neighbour. Who, I wondered, was bearing false witness against Steve Mitchell?

Bruce dropped me back at the Swan Inn to collect my rental car, before making his apologies and rushing off for a meeting with another client. Meanwhile I decided, as I was almost there, to go and revive some memories by driving around Lambourn, and also to take the opportunity to see Steve Mitchell's place, at least from the outside.

It had been nearly fifteen years since I had lived in Lambourn and I had only been back there a couple of times in the interim, but nothing much had changed, except that there were now many more houses on the outskirts of the village and some of the shops had different names. The place felt the same. Just being here rekindled that feeling of excitement that had gripped me as a twenty-one-year-old starting an adventure, chasing a dream.

I stopped the car on the road opposite the end of the driveway belonging to the trainer for whom I had worked as an unpaid assistant all those years ago. Nicholas Osbourne still trained at the same establishment and I was tempted to drive up to his yard but, in truth, and for reasons I couldn't really understand, our relationship had not been great since my departure. It was why, one day.

I had suddenly transferred my horses from him to Paul Newington, and that hadn't helped Nick's feelings either. So I now moved on and went in search of Steve Mitchell's house.

He lived in a modern red-brick detached monstrosity on the edge of the village set back from the Wantage Road. Behind the house was a small stable yard of half a dozen boxes with a small feed store and tack room. It wasn't yet big enough to be a full commercial racehorse training concern but there was plenty of room for expansion on the grassy field behind. I imagined that Steve had built the place himself with a view to turning to training after retiring from the saddle.

Everywhere was quiet and deserted so I wandered around the empty yard and looked into the six stable boxes. Two of them showed evidence of recent equine habitation with brown peat horse bedding still down on the concrete floor and water in the troughs in the corners. Two of the others had an assortment of contents ranging from some wooden garden furniture put away for the winter and an old push-along mower in one, to an old disconnected central-heating boiler and a stack of large cardboard boxes in the other, the latter obviously still unpacked from some past house move.

The last two stables in the line were empty, as was the tack room, save for a couple of horse rugs bundled in a corner. The feed store contained a small stack of hay and several bags of horse nuts, together with four bales of the brown horse bedding, one of them broken open and half used. Leaning up against the far end wall of the store were two long-handled, double-pronged pitchforks, identical, I imagined, to the one found embedded in Scot Barlow's chest on Monday afternoon.

The house was not so conveniently open as the stable block so I walked round the outside, looking in turn into each of the plentiful ground-floor windows. The daylight was beginning to fade fast before I had made my way completely round the house and I might have missed something, but there was absolutely nothing I could see to help me either way. So dark had it become by the time I had finished that several of the security lights were switched on by their movement sensors as I made my way back to the Hertz Mondeo and drove away.

I looked at the car clock. It told me that it was almost five o'clock. Five o'clock on a Friday afternoon. The start of the weekend. Funny, I thought, I hadn't liked weekends much since Angela had died. Occasionally I went racing and, more occasionally, I actually rode in a race, but overall I found the break from chambers life rather lonely.

I drove back into the centre of Lambourn, to the equine hospital on Upper Lambourn Road, and explained to the receptionist through a sliding glass panel that I was looking for someone who had shared a room with Millie Barlow before last June.

'Sorry,' she said in a high-pitched squeak, 'I'm new here. You'll have to ask one of the vets.'

'OK,' I said looking round the bare vestibule. 'Where are they?'

'We've got a bit of an emergency at the moment,' she went on in her squeak. 'They're all in the operating theatre.'

'How long are they going to be?' I asked.

'Oh, I don't really know,' she squeaked. 'They have been in there for quite some time already. But you're welcome to wait.' I looked about me again, there were no chairs. 'Oh,' she said again with realization. 'You can wait in the waiting room if you like. Through there.' She pointed at a wooden door opposite.

'Thank you,' I said. 'Please will you let the vets know that I am here.'

'Yes, OK,' she said. 'As soon as I can.'

I didn't have much confidence that she would remember.

I went through the door into the waiting room. It reminded me of going to the dentist. A dozen pink upholstered armchairs with pale wooden legs and arms were arranged around the walls with a few occasional tables between some of them. There was another door at the far end with a half-full wire magazine rack standing beside it, and the hard floor was covered with a thin blue carpet. It was functional rather than comfortable.

A man sat on one of the chairs on the right-hand side and he looked up as I entered. We nodded at each other in informal greeting and he went back to reading some of the papers he had spread out around him. I sat down opposite him and glanced through a copy of *Country Life* that someone had left on a chair.

Ten minutes or so passed. I went back out to the receptionist, who assured me that the vets were still operating but shouldn't be much longer. I was sure she actually had no notion how long they would be but, nevertheless, I went back into the waiting room and sat down.

I had looked at all the estate agents' adverts in the *Country Life* and was beginning to read the book reviews when someone came through the far door. It was a woman wearing green scrub tunic and trousers with short green wellington boots. A vet, I surmised, fresh from the operating theatre. But it wasn't me she was after. The other man stood up as she entered.

'How's it going?' he said eagerly.

'Fine,' she replied. 'I think we have managed to save most of the muscle mass in the shoulder. It shouldn't greatly impair him after proper healing.'

The man let out a sigh of relief. 'Mr Radcliffe will be relieved to hear it.' He didn't sound to me like he was the only one.

'I have to get back in there now,' said the vet. 'To finish off. We will keep him here overnight and see how he's doing in the morning.'

'Fine,' said the man. 'Thank you. I'll call you around nine.'

'OK,' she said. The man knelt down and began to collect together some of the papers he had been working on. The vet turned to me and raised her eyebrows as a question. 'Are you being looked after?' she said.

'No, not really,' I said. 'I was hoping to talk to someone who knew one of the vets that used to work here.'

'Which vet?' she asked.

'Millie Barlow,' I said.

The reaction from the man was dramatic. 'Right little bitch,' he said almost under his breath, but quite audibly in the quiet of the waiting room.

'I beg your pardon?' I said to him.

'I said that she was a right little bitch,' he repeated standing up and looking at me. 'And she was.'

'Look, I'm sorry,' the vet said to me. 'I have to go and close up the wound on the horse we have been operating on. If you'd like to wait, I'll talk to you when I'm finished.'

'I'll wait,' I said, and she disappeared through the door.

The man had almost collected his stuff.

'Why was she a right little bitch?' I asked him.

'Who wants to know?' he said.

'Sorry,' I said. 'I'm Geoffrey Mason, I'm a barrister.'

'I know you,' he said. 'You have horses with Paul Newington.'

'I do indeed,' I said. 'But you now have the advantage over me.' I looked at him quizzically.

'Simon Dacey,' he said holding out his hand.

Ah, I thought, no wonder he thinks Millie Barlow was a little bitch, she had ruined his party by killing herself in one of his bedrooms.

'Do you have a problem?' I asked him, nodding towards the door through which the vet had disappeared.

'One of my yearlings got loose,' he said. 'Gashed himself on a parked car. Always happens to one of the good ones.'

'Will he be all right?' I asked.

'I sincerely hope so,' he said. 'He cost almost half a million at the sales last month.'

'But he must be insured,' I said.

'Just for transport home and thirty days,' he said. 'Can you believe it? That ran out last Monday.'

'But surely,' I said, 'aren't all racehorses insured?' I knew mine was.

'Mr Radcliffe, that's the owner, he says that the premiums are too high. He has about a dozen with me and he says he would rather spend the money he saves on another horse. He maintains that's the best insurance.'

I knew that my insurance premium on Sandeman was quite high, more than a tenth of his value. But that was relatively small as he'd been gelded and there were no stud prospects. For a potential stallion with a good bloodline the premium would be enormous. But, even so, it was quite a risk.

'Doesn't he insure any of them?' I asked.

'Not normally, but I know he insured Peninsula against being infertile or being injured so he couldn't perform at stud.'

Oh, I thought, Mr Radcliffe owned Peninsula. He wouldn't be short of a bob or two.

'So tell me why Millie Barlow was a right little bitch,' I said, bringing the subject back to what really interested me.

'She ruined my party,' he said.

'That's a bit ungracious,' I said. 'The poor girl was so troubled that she killed herself. She probably didn't ruin your party on purpose.'

'But she did ruin it, nevertheless,' he said. 'Why didn't she go and do it somewhere else? That party for winning the Derby was the best day of my life until she spoiled it. How would you like it? Some of my guests were royalty. What chance do you think I have of them coming again? I'll tell you. None. The damn police even ended up questioning a Crown Prince about his visa. I ask you.'

I could see his point of view.

'Do you know why she killed herself?' I asked him.

'No idea,' he said. 'I hardly knew her.'

'Did you know she was having an affair with Steve Mitchell?' I asked.

'God, yes,' he said. 'Everybody knew that. Worst kept secret in Lambourn. Look, I really have to go now. Evening stables are already well under way.'

'OK,' I said. 'Thanks. Can I call you again if I need any more answers?'

'Why?' he asked.

'I'm representing Steve Mitchell,' I said, handing him one of my cards.

'Oh, are you?' He smiled, looking at it. 'Seems you may have your work cut out there.'

'Why does everyone think he did it?' I asked him.

'Because everyone in Lambourn would have heard them arguing at one time or another. They have been heard standing in the street shouting at each other. And word is that either of them would have thought nothing of putting the other through the wings.' Putting someone through the wings of a fence by squeezing them for room was one of the worst crimes one jump jockey could do to another. Even though the wings were nowadays made of bendable plastic, it was still one of the most dangerous of falls, and one of the most likely to cause serious injury.

'And no one much cares for either of them,' he went on. 'Barlow was slightly weird, and Steve Mitchell is arrogant.'

'But do you really think he's a murderer?' I asked.

'I don't know,' he said. 'I have to say I was surprised when I heard he'd been arrested. But people do funny things when they're angry. They lose control.'

How right he was. I'd once helped prosecute a psychopath who's family had sworn that he wouldn't normally have even said boo to a goose, but in a rage he had literally torn his wife limb from limb, with nothing more than his bare hands and a potato peeler.

'So can I call you if I need to ask you anything else?' I asked.

'I suppose so,' he said. 'But I can't think I would know anything that everybody else wouldn't know. I didn't have much to do with either of them. I don't have jumpers in my yard.'

'Sometimes even the smallest thing is important in a defence,' I replied.

'Do you really think he's innocent?' he asked me.

'That's not relevant,' I said. 'My job is to cast doubt on the prosecution's case. I don't have to prove his innocence, just create a reasonable doubt in the jury's mind about his guilt.'

'But surely,' he said, 'if you believe he's guilty then you're not doing the public any service by getting him off.'

'It is the prosecution's job to ensure that the jury have no reasonable doubt, not mine.'

He shook his head. 'It's a funny old system,' he said.

'I agree,' I said. 'But it has worked pretty well for hundreds of years.'

The jury system had its origins in Roman times, when huge juries would vote on the guilt or innocence of the accused. The right to be judged by a jury of one's peers was established under law in England as far back as the thirteenth century, although there were semblances of it even before then. Under English law there is a right to trial by jury for all but very minor offences, as there is enshrined in the United States Constitution. But that is not the case around the world, not even across Europe. There is no such thing as a jury trial in modern Germany, for example, where a judge or panel of judges decide alone on guilt or innocence.

'I really must go,' said Simon Dacey, collecting the last of his things.

'Fine,' I said. 'Nice to have met you. Good luck with the yearling.'

'Thanks.'

We didn't shake hands because his were full of papers, so we nodded again as we had done when I had arrived and he departed, me holding the door open for him on his way out.

I sat down again on a red armchair. The clock on the wall read 6.15.

What was I doing? I asked myself. I had now told far too many people that I was the barrister acting for the defence in Steve Mitchell's case, but I knew that I shouldn't act. I couldn't act. I was a potential witness in the case, but only I was aware of that. No one, apart from Scot Barlow and I, knew of our little exchange at Sandown. Or did they? Had Barlow told someone that he had been seen by a 'bloody amateur' in the showers? I doubted it. So what should I do?

All my training told me to go and make the incident known to the police, or at least to the prosecution. All my instincts as a barrister were to walk away from this case and never look back for fear of being turned to a pillar of salt like Lot's wife. Maybe I should just let justice take its course and have nothing to do with it.

But what was justice? I had been emphatically told by someone to take the case and then to lose it. Was that justice? If I walked away would someone else be frightened into ensuring that Steve Mitchell was convicted? Did the very fact that someone was so keen to see him sent down for the murder prove that he didn't do it? Then where would justice be if I walked away? But even if I could successfully defend him, where would that then leave me? *Next time, I'll smash your head*, Trent had said. *Next time, I'll cut your balls right off.* If I walked away and Mitchell was convicted with someone else in the defence chair, would Trent and whoever was behind him still come after me? And that prospect brought a cold sweat to my brow and a tremor to my fingers.

'Angela, my darling,' I said quietly into the empty waiting room. 'Tell me what to do?'

She didn't reply. Once again, I longed for her presence and her wisdom. She had always instinctively known what was right. We had discussed everything, sometimes to the point of exhaustion. She had trained as a psychologist and even the most mundane of family conversations between us could turn readily into a deeper analysis of meaning. I remember one year casually asking her whether we would be going to my father's house or staying with her parents for Christmas. Several hours later we had delved into the inner feelings we each had for our parents, and more particularly our feelings for our parents-in-law. In the end we had remained at home for the festivities, and we had laughed about it. How I now missed laughing with her.

Without warning my eyes began to fill with tears. I couldn't help it.

The lady vet in the green scrubs chose this moment to

reappear. I quickly wiped my eyes on my sleeve and hoped she hadn't noticed.

'Now how can I help you?' she asked wearily.

'Busy day?' It was more of a statement than a question.

'You bet,' she said, smiling. 'But I think we saved Mr Radcliffe his money.'

'Bad?' I said.

'Not life threatening,' she said. 'But it could have stopped him racing if we hadn't been careful. We had to rejoin some tendons and sew back some muscle tissue. He's young. He should heal as good as new. Stupid horse gashed its shoulder on a car wing mirror after breaking free.'

'Yes,' I said. 'Simon Dacey told me.'

She raised her eyebrows in slight surprise.

'And who are you exactly?' she asked.

'Geoffrey Mason,' I said, pulling out another card from my pocket and handing it over.

'Not selling, are you?' she asked, glancing briefly at the card.

'No,' I laughed. 'I'm after some information.'

'Why?' she said. 'What information?'

'I'm a barrister and I'm representing Steve Mitchell.' There I go again, I thought.

'Arrogant little shit,' she said, somewhat surprisingly.

'Is he?' I said. 'Why?'

'Thinks he's God's gift to women,' she said. 'Expects every female round here to drop their knickers on demand.'

'And do they?' I asked.

She looked at me and smiled. 'Remind me never to be in the witness box when you're asking the questions.'

'I'll try.' I smiled back. 'But at least tell me your name so I can be sure.'

'Eleanor Clarke,' she said, reaching out a hand, which I shook. 'I thought you said you wanted to ask about Millie Barlow.'

'I do,' I said. 'Did you know her?'

'Certainly did,' said Eleanor. 'She lived in the house here with three others of us.'

'House?' I asked.

'Yes, there's a house out the back where some of the staff who work here live. I live there and Millie lived there until . . .' she tailed off and looked down.

'Until she killed herself?' I asked, finishing her sentence.

'Yes,' she said, looking back at my face. 'That's right, until she killed herself. But she didn't sleep there every night.'

'Because she was with Steve Mitchell?' I said it as a question.

'Yes,' she replied rather hesitantly.

'Was she sleeping with anyone else?' I asked.

'God, you're sharp,' she said. 'But I'm afraid our Millie would sleep with anyone who asked nicely.'

'Any man, you mean,' I said.

'No,' she replied. 'Millie wasn't really that choosy. But she was a sweet girl. We all missed her after . . .'

'Why do you think she did it?' I asked.

'I don't know,' she said. 'Lots of people said afterwards that she had been depressed but I didn't think so. She was always so happy. She always had a plan to get rich quick.'

'Was she selling sex?' I asked.

'No,' she said with some emphasis. 'I don't think so. I mean, perhaps I exaggerated a bit. She didn't sleep with everyone. She had her favourites. And she would say no occasionally, especially to some of the married ones. She wasn't all bad.'

'But she was living with Steve Mitchell?' I asked.

'Not really,' Eleanor said. 'She lived in the house here but she did spend nights away with Mitchell, yes. Him more than any other, I'd say. But they were hardly living together.' I wondered if Mrs Barlow would be pleased or not. I wondered how strict Millie's upbringing had been. Maybe as soon as she was free of her father's control she went a little mad, sampling life's pleasures in excess.

'How did she get the anaesthetic?' I asked.

'Well, we have it here, of course, but it's funny.' She paused.

'What's funny?' I encouraged.

'The toxicology report on Millie indicated that she had injected herself with thiopental.'

I looked at her quizzically. 'Why is that funny?' I asked.

'We don't use thiopental in the hospital. We use ketamine, usually mixed with either xylazine or detomidine.'

I raised a questioning eyebrow. 'They're sedatives,' she explained, leaving me none the wiser. 'Both types will cause unconsciousness, but thiopental is a barbiturate anaesthetic and ketamine is a hydrochloride salt.'

'Isn't it a bit odd that she used a different drug than you use at the hospital?' I asked.

'Well,' she said, 'a vet can get medicines from any drug supplier just by filling in a form. And anaesthetics are used by vets all the time.'

'But it does mean she didn't kill herself on the spur of the moment,' I said. 'Not if she had to order the stuff especially rather than just take some from here.'

'She may have already had it,' Eleanor said. 'I have a few things in my bag that didn't come from the hospital drug store. And barbiturate anaesthetics are used a lot. Thiopental is what's used every day in most vets' practices to put dogs and cats to sleep.'

'Where does the hospital get its drugs?' I asked her.

'We have a specialist veterinary pharmacist in Reading,' she said. 'We have a delivery almost every day during the week.'

'She must have ordered it separately from them,' I said.

'No,' she replied quickly. 'They had to check their records for the police and there was nothing.'

'How odd,' I said.

'Even if she had wanted to, she would have had trouble using any of the hospital stuff anyway,' said Eleanor. 'We

have a very tight system of control. Anything like anaesthetic has to be signed out of the hospital drug store by
two vets. Look, I've got to go. We aren't normally open
after six and there's someone waiting to lock up.'

'How about the horse you operated on?' I said.

'He's in the stables at the back now for the night. He
has a monitor on him and CCTV to the duty vet's room.
Otherwise we're closed, except, of course, for emergen-
cies.'

'But I would really like to ask you some more questions about Millie,' I said imploringly.

'Let me get changed first,' she said. 'I fancy a drink.
Are you buying?'

'How about supper?' I said.

'Don't push your luck, Mr . . .' She looked again at
my card. 'Geoffrey Mason.'

'No. Sorry,' I mumbled. 'I didn't mean it like that.'

'Oh, thanks,' she said sarcastically. 'Just when I
thought I was being asked out on a date, he says he
didn't mean it.' She laughed. 'Story of my life.'

We went in separate cars to the Queen's Arms in East
Garston, a village a few miles away.

'Let's not go to a pub in Lambourn,' Eleanor had said.
'Too many listening ears and wagging tongues.'

I was there well ahead of her. I ordered myself a Diet
Coke and perched on a bar stool, thinking about what

questions I needed to ask and wondering why I thought that Millie Barlow's death could have anything to do with that of her brother.

I just didn't like coincidences, although they could never be used as evidence on their own. After all, coincidences do happen. Like all the ones involving the assassinated presidents Abraham Lincoln and John F. Kennedy. Lincoln had a secretary called Kennedy, and Kennedy had a secretary called Lincoln, and both were succeeded by a Vice-President Johnson. But I still didn't like them.

I did not immediately recognize Eleanor Clarke when she walked into the dimly lit bar. She had changed out of her functional green scrubs and rubber boots and was now wearing a white rib-pattern roll-neck sweater over blue jeans. However, the main reason I didn't know her at first was because her blonde hair was no longer tied in a ponytail but hung down close to each side of her face. My first instinct was that the change of hairstyle was a mistake as it hid her beautiful arched cheekbones and somewhat reduced the sparkle from her stunning blue eyes.

I was suddenly quite shocked by these thoughts. I had hardly given a woman's face a second glance since the day I had first met and fallen instantly in love with Angela, and I had certainly not thought of beautiful cheekbones or stunning blue eyes on anyone else.

'There you are,' said Eleanor, coming over and sitting on the bar stool next to mine.

'What are you drinking?' I asked her.

'G and T, please.'

I ordered and we sat in silence as the barman poured the tonic over the gin.

'Lovely,' she said, taking a large gulp. 'It's been a long day.'

'I'd better order you another,' I said.

'I'm driving,' she said. 'I'll just have the one.'

'You could stay for dinner,' I said.

'I thought you didn't really mean it.' She looked at me with the sparkly blue eyes. They smiled at me.

'I meant that,' I said. 'I just didn't mean . . .' I was getting lost for words. 'You know, anything else.'

'Like what?' she said all seriously, but now with laughter in her eyes.

'Were you a barrister in a past life?' I said. 'I feel that I'm being questioned in court.'

'Answer the question,' she demanded with a stare.

'I just didn't want you to think I was propositioning you or anything.'

'And were you?' she asked.

'No, of course not,' I said.

'Oh thanks. Am I that unattractive?'

'No. I didn't mean that.'

'We seem to be going round in circles here, Mister Barrister Man,' she said. 'So what did you mean?'

'I thought it was going to be me asking you the questions,' I said. 'Not the other way round.'

'OK,' she said. 'I'm ready. Ask away.'

'Well,' I said. 'Firstly, will you stay to dinner?'

'Yes,' she replied without hesitation.

'Good,' I said.

'Are you married?' she asked suddenly.

'Why?'

'I just wondered,' she said.

I didn't immediately respond.

'Well, are you?' she persisted.

'Why do you want to know?' I asked again.

'Need to know where I stand,' she said.

'But I'm not propositioning you, so why does it matter?' I said.

'You might change your mind,' she said. 'And I can't be bothered to invest any emotion unless I know where I stand. So, are you married?'

'Are you?' I asked her back.

'Only to my job,' she said. She waited a moment in silence. 'Well?'

'I was,' I said slowly.

'Divorced?' she said.

'Widowed.'

'Oh.' She was embarrassed. 'I'm sorry. I shouldn't have asked.'

'It was a long time ago,' I said. But it felt like only yesterday.

She sat silently as if waiting for me to go on. I didn't.

'Still painful?' she asked.

I nodded.

'Sorry,' she said again. Some of the sparkle had gone out of her eyes.

We sat in silence for a while.

'What do you want to know about Millie?' she asked eventually.

'Let's go and eat,' I said.

We opted for a table in the bar rather than in the restaurant. No tablecloth, less formal, but the same menu.

I chose a fillet steak while Eleanor decided on the pan-fried sea bream.

'Would you like a glass of wine?' I asked her.

'I'm still driving,' she said.

'You could leave your car here,' I said. 'I'm sure the pub won't mind if you leave it in their car park. I could drop you back at the hospital and you could collect it in the morning.'

'How about you?' she said. 'What are you drinking?'

'I'm on Diet Coke but I'll have a small glass of red with my dinner,' I said. 'I do have to drive. Back to London tonight.' I had rented the car for only two days.

'Couldn't you stay down here and go in the morning?' she said.

'Are you propositioning me now?' I asked.

She blushed. 'I didn't mean that.'

Pity, I thought, again surprising myself.

I could always have called Hertz to keep the car for another day, but somehow I felt that I was betraying my Angela even to contemplate spending the night away from home, especially in order to have a lengthy dinner with another woman. I told myself not to be such a fool, but I felt it nevertheless.

'How well did you know Millie?' I asked, changing the subject and saving us both some embarrassment.

'Pretty well,' she said. 'We worked together at the hospital for three years and lived in the house together for most of that time.'

'Do you know why she killed herself?' I asked.

'No idea,' she said. 'She seemed pretty happy to me.'

'Did she have money worries?' I asked.

'No,' Eleanor replied emphatically. 'In fact she always seemed rather well off. She bought a brand-new red Mazda sports car the year before she died and she always had lots of nice clothes. I think her father still sent her an allowance, even though we all earn pretty good money at the hospital.'

I thought back to my earlier encounter with the Barlow parents in their ill-fitting clothes. Did they seem the sort of people who could afford to send their high-earning daughter an allowance?

'Was she pregnant?' I said. It was only a wild thought.

'I think it highly unlikely,' said Eleanor. 'She used to boast that she had a good supply of the morning-after pill just in case she forgot to take her other pills. She was medically trained, remember.'

'And medics have a higher suicide rate than almost every other profession,' I said.

'Do they?' She seemed surprised.

'Yes,' I said. 'I had to research the rates last year for a case where a doctor was accused of assisting a suicide.'

'I suppose medics have the knowledge of how to take their own lives,' she said.

'Painlessly, you mean,' I said.

'Absolutely. Just like putting an old dog to sleep,' she said. 'They also have easy access to the necessary drugs.'

'Did Millie get on with her brother?' I asked.

'Well enough, I think,' she said. 'But I don't think he was too happy with her reputation.'

'Reputation?' I asked.

'For being the easiest ride in the village.'

'No,' I said. 'Not really a reputation to cherish.' Especially not in Lambourn, where riding was its life-blood. 'How many casual lovers would you say she had?'

'At least half a dozen on the go at once,' she said. 'I think you could safely say that she wasn't particularly discreet. Suffice to say she liked jockeys.'

'Was Reno Clemens one of them?' I asked.

'Probably,' she said. 'I didn't actually keep a list, but he was often around her. I sometimes saw them together in the pub.'

'But you didn't see him in her room?' I said.

'We have a sort of unwritten rule in the house,' she said. 'Long-term relationships are OK, but no casual partners to stay over. Needless to say, Millie broke it all the time. It was the only thing we argued about. But no, I can't say I ever saw Reno there.'

'How about Steve Mitchell?' I asked. 'Did he stay over?'

'No never,' she said. 'Millie was always too keen to go to his place. She was always telling us about his hot tub.' She lifted her eyebrows in disapproval.

'Why exactly do you dislike Mitchell?' I asked her.

'Is it that obvious?'

'Yes,' I said.

'When I first came to Lambourn about ten years ago he was just starting as a jockey and we went out for a while. I thought he was serious but he wasn't. He was two-timing me with some stable hand and, when the silly bitch got pregnant, he dumped me and married her.' She paused. 'I suppose she did me a favour really.'

'How long did his marriage last?' I asked.

'About six years. They had two children and Steve became very successful. They built the Kremlin together.'

'The Kremlin?' I asked.

'That's what everyone calls that red-brick eyesore he now rattles around in on his own. When Natalie, his ex-wife, finally saw some sense and left him, he came back to my door and wanted to carry on as if nothing had happened. I told him to piss off and Steve didn't like that. He likes to get his own way. I actually think he then made such a fuss over Millie to get back at me.'

So Steve's affair with Millie Barlow hadn't just been a fling as he had claimed, but had continued long after his wife had found out and left him. Mr and Mrs Barlow senior had been right, and Mitchell had indeed lied to me about it.

'Didn't Steve mind that she had other partners as well as him?' I asked.

'Mind? Are you kidding? According to Millie, Steve loved a threesome, or even more.'

'Do you think she was telling the truth?' I said.

'You may have a point there. Millie was a good vet, very good in fact, but she was known to exaggerate things a tad.'

'Do you remember a photo of her and a horse in a silver frame?' I asked.

She nodded. 'Her prized possession.'

'Why?' I asked.

'It was a picture of her with a new-born foal,' she said.

'But why was it so special?'

'It was the first foal she had ever delivered on her own, just after she arrived in Lambourn,' she said. 'Bit of an emergency in the middle of the night. She was the only vet on duty. But she did OK, apparently. I was away.'

I was disappointed. I thought it would be more interesting than that.

'Why are you interested in the photo?' she asked me.

'Because someone took it from Scot Barlow's house,' I said.

'What, when he was murdered?'

'That I don't know,' I said. 'But it is missing now.'

'Perhaps it was for the silver frame,' she said.

'No. Whoever took the photo left the frame. That's how I know the photo's gone.'

'Well, I can tell you that it was of Millie and a foal that was lying in the straw, with the mare and a stud groom behind.'

'Do you know who the stud groom was?' I asked. 'Or who took the photo?'

'No idea,' she said. 'But I know which foal it was. That's why it was Millie's prize possession.'

'Go on,' I encouraged her as she paused.

'Peninsula,' Eleanor said with a flourish.

Was that the reason why Millie Barlow was at Simon Dacey's party? Or was that just a coincidence? But, I didn't like coincidences.

PART TWO

DISCLOSURE

MARCH 2009

CHAPTER SEVEN

By the time of the Steeplechase Festival at Cheltenham in March, Steve Mitchell had been in prison for four months and his name had all but been erased from the racing pages of the newspapers as well as from the consider-ations of the punters. With both Mitchell and Barlow out of the running, Reno Clemens had built up a commanding lead in the battle to be this year's champion jockey and much was expected of him at the festival. Most of his mounts would start as favourite.

Bruce Lygon had done his best at Oxford Crown Court in November to get Steve Mitchell bail but, unsur-prisingly, the judge had listened to him with courtesy and then had promptly declined his application. I had sat beside Bruce in court but I hadn't really helped him much. I don't think it would have made much difference if I had. Letting murder suspects out on bail was never going to endear a judge to the general public and a few recent high-profile cases where the suspects had murdered again while out on bail had put paid to even the slimmest of chances.

I hadn't actually planned to attend the bail hearing but I had received another little reminder from God-knows-who two days before it was due to take place. It had been another slim white envelope delivered as before to my chambers by hand. It had been found on the mat inside the front door and no one had seen who had left it there. Again, in the envelope there had been a single sheet of folded white paper and a photograph. Thankfully the message hadn't been backed up this time by a personal visit from Julian Trent. However, the memory of his previous visit had remained vivid enough in my consciousness for the sweat to break out on my forehead as I had held the envelope tightly in my hands.

As before, there had been four lines of black print across the centre of the paper.

GOOD LITTLE LAWYER
I WILL BE WATCHING YOU IN OXFORD ON WEDNESDAY
DON'T GET MITCHELL BAIL
REMEMBER, LOSE THE CASE OR SOMEONE GETS HURT

The photograph had been of my dead wife Angela. In fact, to be accurate, it had been a photograph of a photograph of Angela in a silver frame. Around the sides I could see a few of the other things on the surface on which the frame had stood. I had known those items. The photograph of Angela was the one of her smiling that I had placed on her dressing table in our bedroom soon after she died. I said 'Good morning, my darling' to that photograph every day. Someone had been into my house

148

to take that shot. It made me very angry, but I was also more than a little afraid. Just who were these people?

I sat at my desk in chambers twiddling my thumbs and thinking. It was Monday morning and I was having a few easy days. In order to prevent a repeat of last year, when I had been stuck in court instead of jumping my way round Cheltenham on Sandeman's back in the Foxhunter Chase, I had instructed Arthur to schedule absolutely nothing for the whole week.

I had recently finished acting for a large high-street supermarket in an out-of-date food case, which my client had won. Such relatively low-key cases were the bread and butter of many junior barristers, and highly sought after. In the big, high-profile criminal cases, the lead for the defence was almost invariably taken by a silk, a Queen's Counsel. However, many companies, especially large well-known firms, often preferred to engage a junior in cases where they were dealing with the 'little people', mostly their staff or their suppliers, or with simple breaks in hygiene regulations. To turn up at a magistrates court with a QC in tow seemed to imply they were guilty, quite apart from the excessive fees of a silk. Many a junior has made a fine reputation and an excellent living from the work. Some juniors, indeed, declined the chance to be promoted to QC for fear of losing their fee-base altogether.

Personally, I enjoyed the criminal Crown Court work

far more, but I earned most of my money either in the magistrates' courts or at the disciplinary hearings of professional institutions.

But not this week. I was determined not to miss out again on a ride in the Foxhunters. Sandeman had qualified partly by virtue of winning the race last year and Paul had assured me at the end of January that the horse was fitter this time, implying that failure to win again this year would not be Sandeman's fault. It had been a direct warning to me not to be the weak link in the partnership, an explicit instruction to get myself fit.

For weeks now I had been running every day, mostly at lunchtime, which had the added advantage of avoiding the temptation to eat with fellow counsel either in the Hall at Gray's Inn, or at one of the many hostelries situated close to our chambers.

In addition, in mid February I had been skiing for a long weekend in Meribel in France and had pushed my aching legs time and again down the mountains. I loved to ski but, on this occasion, it had been ski boot-camp. I had risen early each morning in the chalet I'd shared with four other complete strangers whose sole passion in life was the snow. We had spent the whole day on the slopes, catching the very last lift of the day to the highest point and arriving back at the chalet exhausted, just as the daylight faded. Then I would spend hours in the sauna, sweating off the pounds, before a high-protein dinner and an early bed.

By the second week in March I was toned like I hadn't

been since my time in Lambourn fifteen years before. Bring on Julian Trent, I said to myself. I was at my best fighting weight and relished the chance.

Arthur came into my room. In spite of an excellent internal telephone system, Arthur was of the old school and liked to talk face to face when making arrangements. 'Sir James would like to have a conference about the Mitchell case,' he said. 'I have scheduled it for nine thirty tomorrow. Is that all right with you?'

'I asked you not to schedule anything at all for this week,' I said to him.

'But you're not going to the races until Thursday,' he said. 'You will still be able to watch the Champion Hurdle tomorrow afternoon. The conference won't last all day.'

I looked at him. How did Arthur know I wasn't planning to go to Cheltenham until Thursday? It would be no good asking him. He would reply in the same way as he always did. 'It's my job to know everything about my barristers,' he would say. I wondered for the umpteenth time if he knew more about my little problem than he was letting on.

'Nine thirty tomorrow will be fine,' I said.

He smiled. 'I thought it might,' he said. 'I'll tell Sir James.'

Sir James Horley, QC, was now the lead in Steve Mitchell's defence. When Bruce Lygon had finally called Arthur to engage counsel for the case, Sir James had jumped at it. He could never be accused of not being eager to take on a prominent celebrity client, even if, as in this case, the 'celebrity' status of the client was somewhat dubious and the evidence was stacked up against him. Sir James loved the limelight. He adored the television cameras waiting each day outside court so that they could show him on the six o'clock news replying 'no comment' to each of the journalists' questions.

My heart had dropped when Arthur told me that Sir James would lead and I would be acting as his junior. Sir James has a reputation of doing very little, or nothing, in preparation for a trial while still expecting everything to be in order and complete on day one. He also had a reputation, richly deserved, for publicly blaming his junior whenever anything went wrong, whether or not they had anything to do with it. He seemed to expect his juniors to have powers of clairvoyance over the facts, yet be unable to stand up in court to question a witness, something he reserved solely for himself.

Needless to say, I still had not yet told anyone of my encounter with the murder victim in the showers at Sandown, even though I had been sorely tempted to do so in order to disqualify myself from acting alongside Sir James. But it had been so long since I should have said something that I couldn't really do so now without placing myself in a very compromising position. I would be damned if I did, and damned if I didn't, but, in the latter case, only if anyone else knew about it from Barlow. Was I prepared to take that risk? Perhaps I should simply plead insanity, excuse myself from the case altogether and commit myself to a mental hospital until it was all over.

'Didn't Steve mind that she had other partners as well as him?' I asked.

'Mind? Are you kidding? According to Millie, Steve loved a threesome, or even more.'

'Do you think she was telling the truth?' I said.

'You may have a point there. Millie was a good vet, very good in fact, but she was known to exaggerate things a tad.'

'Do you remember a photo of her and a horse in a silver frame?' I asked.

She nodded. 'Her prized possession.'

'Why?' I asked

'It was a picture of her with a new-born foal,' she said.

'But why was it so special?'

'It was the first foal she had ever delivered on her own, just after she arrived in Lambourn,' she said. 'Bit of an emergency in the middle of the night. She was the only vet on duty. But she did OK, apparently. I was away.'

I was disappointed. I thought it would be more interesting than that.

'Why are you interested in the photo?' she asked me.

'Because someone took it from Scot Barlow's house,' I said.

'What, when he was murdered?'

'That I don't know,' I said. 'But it is missing now.'

'Perhaps it was for the silver frame,' she said.

'No. Whoever took the photo left the frame. That's how I know the photo's gone.'

'Well, I can tell you that it was of Millie and a foal that was lying in the straw, with the mare and a stud groom behind.'

'Do you know who the stud groom was?' I asked. 'Or who took the photo?'

'No idea,' she said. 'But I know which foal it was. That's why it was Millie's prize possession.'

'Go on,' I encouraged her as she paused.

'Peninsula,' Eleanor said with a flourish.

Was that the reason why Millie Barlow was at Simon Dacey's party? Or was that just a coincidence? But, I didn't like coincidences.

By then Steve Mitchell would have been tried, convicted and sentenced to life imprisonment for a crime for which I didn't believe he was responsible. I would then be safe from Julian Trent and life could go back to normal. That is, until the next time someone wanted to manipulate the outcome of a trial, and young Mr Trent and his baseball bat were sent to pass the message.

The news that I was no longer acting as the sole barrister in the case had spread far and wide to ears I didn't know, but ears of those who most definitely had an interest in the outcome.

Within only a few hours of the appointment of Sir James Horley as defence QC being posted on the courts' website, I had received a call on my mobile.

'I told you to take the Mitchell case,' the quiet well-spoken whisperer had said. 'Why are you not listed as the defence barrister?'

I had tried to explain that a QC would always have to lead in such a high-profile case and I wasn't one. I had told him that I would be assisting.

'You are to ensure Mitchell loses,' he had said.

'Why?' I had asked him.

'Just do it,' he had said, and then he'd hung up.

As before, and as expected, he had withheld his number.

Why, indeed, did they, whoever 'they' were, want Mitchell to lose? Was it solely to have someone else convicted of their crime or was there something else? Was it anything to do with Mitchell himself? Had Mitchell in fact done the crime and they were just making sure he got his just deserts? But how would they know he was definitely guilty unless they were there with him at the time?

No, I still believed that Steve was being set up. All the disclosed prosecution evidence put together would be very convincing to a jury, although any single part of it on its own could be described as circumstantial. No one questioned that the pitchfork, the murder weapon, had belonged to Steve Mitchell, but, as I had seen myself, his pitchforks had not been kept locked away and anyone could have taken one of them from the open feed store to stick into Barlow's chest. Blood and hairs from the victim had been found on a pair of Mitchell's wellington boots as well as in his car, but the boots had been kept in the same feed store as the pitchfork, and Mitchell swore that he had left his car unlocked on his driveway, as he always did, on the day of the murder. The Defence Case Statement stated that Mr Mitchell was being framed for the crime that someone else, unknown, had committed. And that the crime in question had been premeditated and planned meticulously so as to appear to have been perpetrated by our client.

The prosecution had been unable to establish definitively that Mitchell had indeed sent the text message to Barlow threatening to 'come round and sort you out

properly you sneaking little bastard'. In spite of the
message being signed with Mitchell's name, it could only
be determined by the police that it had been sent by a free
texting service accessible from any computer, by anyone,
anywhere in the world.

The betting receipts, however, did indeed belong to
Steve Mitchell and he had been stupid enough to have his
own name on them. They were, in fact, debit-card receipts
from a bookmaker rather than actual betting slips. Steve
denied that they were his but even I knew he wasn't
telling the truth. I had explained to him that the time for
lying about betting was now over, he had more serious
allegations to deal with, but he was so used to denying
that he gambled that it came naturally to him to continue
to do so.

Add the mass of physical evidence, the well-known
and well-documented antagonism between the victim and
the accused, the lack of any semblance of an alibi and the
defence's seeming inability to demonstrate who or why
anyone would want to frame him, and I could imagine a
jury returning a unanimous guilty verdict so quickly that
they would hardly have to retire from the courtroom.

I had explained to Steve, during another trip to talk
with him in prison, that if he had an alibi he must declare
it prior to the trial. To suddenly produce one in court
would not assist his case. The jury would be invited by
the prosecution to draw whatever inferences they wished
from the fact that no previous mention had been made of

an alibi. However, he had remained adamant that he had been on his own at home reading all afternoon on that Monday.

'Steve,' I had implored. 'I am afraid I don't believe you. If you were with someone, perhaps someone you shouldn't have been with, you must tell me now. At the trial or afterwards will be too late.'

'I tell you I was on my own,' he had said. 'That's the truth. What do you want me to do? Lie?'

I had thought that it would be counter-productive to say that I knew he had lied to me before, about the ending of his affair with Millie Barlow.

'Don't you realize the mess you are in?' I'd shouted at him while banging on the grey metal table with my fist. 'You're facing a long stretch in prison for this. It's not some game in the park, you know.'

'I can't,' he had said finally.

'Yes, you can,' I'd screamed at him. 'No one would expect you to keep quiet if it meant you would be convicted of a murder you didn't do.'

'It's not that simple,' he had said, looking down at the table.

'Is she married?' I had asked, guessing the reason.

'Yes,' he'd said emphatically. 'And I don't even think I was with her when that bastard Barlow got himself killed. It was only a last-minute lunchtime bonk, arranged when the racing at Ludlow was called off. I'm certainly not embroiling her in this mess when it wouldn't even give me an alibi for the right time.'

The prosecution case was that Barlow had died some-time between two and four in the afternoon. His body had been discovered around six by a policeman responding to an anonymous call to Newbury police station's front desk about an intruder at Honeysuckle Cottage. As the caller had used the local landline and not the emergency 999 service there had been no record of the telephone number or any recording of the conversation.

This fact was one of the few plus points for our side because, as I had pointed out in our Defence Case Statement, Mitchell was hardly likely to call the police if he had, in fact, murdered Barlow, and the prosecution case was that he had acted alone in the killing. It was a minor point in the face of the wealth of prosecution evidence, but one I planned to exploit to the full at the trial.

'The fact that you were not alone all of the time from one o'clock until six might help to plant some doubt in the minds of the jury,' I had told him 'And, at the moment, we need all the help we can get.'

'She was gone by two thirty at the latest,' he'd said. 'So what difference would it make? Barlow's bloody house is only ten minutes' drive from mine. I could easily have been there well before three anyway so it's not a bloody alibi.' He'd paused. 'No. I won't get her involved.'

'Tell me who it was,' I had said to him. 'Then I can ask her if she would be prepared to give a statement to the police.'

'No,' he had said. And he had been silent on the matter ever since.

I had also asked him about Millie Barlow and why he hadn't told me about her death at our first meeting.

'I didn't think that it was that important,' he'd said.

'Of course it was important,' I had shouted at him. 'You tell me absolutely everything and I'll decide whether it's important or not.'

He had looked at me with big eyes, like a scolded puppy. 'I'm in a bit of the shit here, aren't I?'

'Yes,' I'd said. 'Big shit.'

'I didn't do it, you know,' he'd said mournfully.

'Were you drunk that afternoon?' I'd asked him. 'Or high?'

'Nothing like that,' he'd replied quite sharply. 'We'd had a bit of red wine, I suppose, but not more than a bottle. That's why I stayed in after. Because I didn't want to get done for drunken driving.'

Shame, I'd thought, being banged up for a bit of driving under the influence would have provided a cast-iron alibi for Barlow's murder.

'So did Barlow blame you for his sister's suicide?' I had asked him.

'All the bloody time,' he'd replied. 'Kept going on and on about it. Called me a bloody murderer. I told him to shut up or I'd bloody murder him.' Steve had suddenly stopped and he had looked up at my face. 'But I didn't, I promise you I didn't.' He had then buried his head in his hands and begun to sob.

158

'It's all right, Steve,' I'd said, trying to reassure him. 'I know you didn't do it.'

He had looked back at my face. 'How do you know? How can you be sure?'

'I just am,' I'd said.

'Convince the bloody jury then.'

Maybe that is what I should do, I thought, sitting here at my desk. Perhaps I should tell the jury that I had been threatened to make sure I lost in court. That was it. I must tell Sir James that I had been approached and intimidated. Then I could become a witness instead of a barrister in the case and I could tell the jury all about baseball bats and Julian Trent. But would that be enough to help Steve? Probably not. The judge might not even allow testimony concerning intimidation of one of the lawyers to be admitted. It was hardly significant evidence in the case, irrespective of what I might think. It might just be relevant if the defence could use it as support for our belief that Steve was being framed. But in the face of the prosecution case, would the jury believe it?

And where would that leave me, I wondered. Did I just sit and wait to have my head smashed in and my balls cut off? And how about my elderly father in his holey green jumper? What danger would I be putting him in?

It seemed to me that the only solution to my multiple dilemmas was to discover who was intimidating me and then show that they were the true murderers of Scot Barlow, and to do it quickly, before any 'next time'.

Simple, I thought. But where do I start?

Julian Trent. He must be the key.

The following morning, I didn't tell Sir James Horley QC anything about intimidation, or anything about an encounter in the Sandown showers. He and I sat on one side of the table in the small conference room in the lower ground floor of chambers. Bruce Lygon sat opposite us. For two hours we had been once again going through every aspect of the prosecution case. We had received their secondary disclosure, but there was nothing new to help us.

The prosecution was required to disclose to the defence anything that they, or the police, had discovered which would assist us based on our Defence Case Statement. The response had been short but to the point. Their letter simply stated that they had no information other than that already disclosed in their primary disclosure and Statement of Case. We hadn't really expected anything.

'Are you sure that Mitchell shouldn't plead guilty?' said Sir James. 'The case against him is very strong.' I wondered, ungraciously, if Sir James liked the idea of a guilty plea to save him a courtroom loss. Maybe he was having second thoughts about taking this case.

'He says he didn't do it,' I said. 'He's adamant that he will not plead guilty to something he didn't do.'

'How about a plea based on a lesser charge?' said Bruce. 'Or on diminished responsibility, or temporary insanity.'

Insanity was right, I thought. They were clutching at straws.

'Our defence is that our client didn't do it and is being framed, so we shall have no guilty pleas to anything, OK?' I said firmly.

'Then we had better find out who's framing him,' said Sir James. 'Otherwise we shall have egg on our faces. Trial date is set for the second week in May at Oxford. That's eight weeks from now. I suggest we meet again in two weeks to see if we are any further on.' He stood up and tied the papers together with ribbon and bows, as if they were Christmas presents. The ribbon was pink. Pink for defence. Prosecution briefs were tied up in white ribbon.

Papers so tied could not be looked at by any member of chambers except those acting for the appropriate side in that case. It was not unusual for different counsel within chambers to be acting for both sides in the same trial. I had once been prosecuting an armed robbery case while a colleague who normally shared the same room as me was acting for the defendant. We had temporarily been separated to opposite ends of the building, but we still needed to be very careful not to discuss aspects of the trial in the other's hearing. Arthur had even installed segregated photocopiers so that a document carelessly left in one machine would not fall into the other camp's hands.

I went back to my room and looked at the desk of that colleague. As always, it was almost impossible to see the wood from which it had been constructed. The tough old

English oak was doing its duty supporting stack upon stack of papers and box files. I was the tidiest of the three of us who shared this space, and even my area could look like a war zone at times. Stuff that couldn't fit on our desks was stacked in boxes on the floor or in the full-length bookshelves down the side of the room, opposite the windows. But nothing was ever lost. At least that's what we told everyone and it was almost the truth, although maybe not the whole truth.

There had been a large white envelope in my box in the clerks' room and I sat at my desk and looked at it. This envelope, however, had been expected and contained no sinister threatening note, and no photograph. I had ordered a full transcript of the Julian Trent appeal hearing from last November and now I eagerly scanned its close-typed pages looking for a certain name.

Josef Hughes of 845 Finchley Road, Golders Green, north London, was the rogue solicitor who had forced the appeal in the first place. It was his supposed intervention with the jury that had got Trent off. If, as I suspected, he had been coerced into giving his evidence to the Court of Appeal, then he might be prepared to help me find out how and why Julian Trent was connected to Scot Barlow's murder. I went to Golders Green first thing on Wednesday morning.

Josef Hughes went white and his knees buckled as soon as I mentioned Julian Trent. I thought he was going to pass out completely in the doorway of his bed-sit, one of half a dozen or so bed-sits crammed into the large 1930s-built semi-detached house at 845 Finchley Road.

He might have collapsed right down to the floor if I hadn't held him by his left elbow and helped him through the door and into the room. He sat down heavily on the side of the double bed that took up most of the available floor space. We were not alone. A young woman, not much more than a child, sat on an upright wooden chair nursing a young baby. She didn't move as I helped Josef over to the bed but sat silently staring at me with big brown, frightened eyes.

I looked around. Apart from the green blanket-covered bed and the chair there was a small square table under the window, another upright chair that matched the first, and a tiny kitchenette in the corner, half hidden by a thin curtain that was badly in need of a wash.

I went over to the kitchen sink to fetch Josef a glass of water. There were no glasses visible but there was a moderately clean though badly chipped coffee mug upturned on the drainer. I splashed some water into it and held it out to him.

He looked up at me in real horror, but he took the mug and drank some of the water. The colour in his face improved fractionally.

'It's all right,' I said in as comforting manner as I could muster. 'I haven't been sent here by Julian Trent.'

At the sound of the name, the young woman gave out a slight moan and I was suddenly afraid that she too was

163

about to pass out. I stepped towards her as if to catch her baby but she pulled the child away from me and curled her body round it as protection.

What on earth had Julian Trent done to these people to make them so afraid?

I looked around the room again. Everything was very basic, with threadbare carpets, paper-thin curtains and bare cream-painted walls that were overdue a redecoration. A plastic tubular travel cot was folded and leaned up against the wall behind the door with three blue baby romper suits hanging on it to dry.

'We used to have the big flat on the top floor,' said the girl, watching me look. 'With our own bathroom. Then Joe lost his job and we had to move down here. Now, we share a bathroom on the landing with three other rooms.'

'How old is the baby?' I asked her.

'Eight months on Friday,' she said. I thought she was close to tears.

'What's his name?' I asked her, smiling.

'Rory,' she said.

'That's nice,' I said, smiling at her again. 'And what's your name?'

'Bridget,' she said.

We sat there in silence for a while, Josef and me on the bed, with Bridget holding Rory on the upright chair.

'What do you want?' Josef said eventually.

'Tell me what happened,' I said quietly.

Josef shivered next to me.

'It was a man,' said Bridget. 'He came here, to our flat upstairs.'

'No,' said Josef suddenly and forcefully.

'Yes,' said Bridget back to him. 'We need to tell someone.'

'No, Bee,' he said again firmly. 'We mustn't.'

'We must,' she pleaded. 'We must. I can't go on living like this.' She started to cry.

'I promise you,' I said, 'I'm here to try and help you.' And to help myself.

'He broke my arm,' said Bridget quietly. 'I was six months pregnant with Rory and he came into our flat, hit me in the face and punched me in my stomach. Then he broke my arm by slamming it in the door.'

'Who did?' I asked her. Surely, I thought, Julian Trent had been in prison.

'Julian Trent's father.'

CHAPTER EIGHT

In the end, between them, they told me everything. It was a horror show.

The man who had said he was Julian Trent's father had arrived wearing a smart suit and tie one evening soon after Josef had arrived home from his work at the Crown Prosecution Service. Josef had qualified as a solicitor only the year before and the CPS was his first job and he had loved it. He and Bridget had married while he was at the College of Law and they had moved into their first family home together in preparation for the birth of their first child. Everything was fine and they had been blissfully happy together. That is, until the shadow of Julian Trent had been cast over their lives.

At first the man had been nice and had even offered Josef some money to get some information for him.

'What information?' I asked him.

'Stuff that was already in the public domain,' he said.

'What sort of stuff?' I asked again.

'Names and addresses of jurors,' he said.

'In the Julian Trent trial?' I asked, but I already knew what the answer would be.

He nodded. 'It was the first trial I had worked on at the Old Bailey. And the jurors' names are in the transcript,' he said in his defence. 'Their names had been read out in open court.' He was trying to justify his actions. The jurors' names may have been in the public domain, but their addresses wouldn't have been.

'And we really needed the money,' said Bridget. 'What with the baby coming, there were things we had to buy.'

'And it wasn't against the law,' said Josef, almost in despair.

'But you knew it was wrong,' I said to him. It may or may not have been against the letter of the law, I wasn't sure, but it was definitely against the Law Society rules, and would quite likely have been in contempt of court.

He nodded again.

'So when did he come back?' I asked them.

'The following day,' Josef said. 'He was meant to be bringing the money for the information I had ready for him.'

'But he hit Bridget instead?' I said.

He nodded again, and now tears welled up in his eyes. 'I couldn't believe it. He just walked straight into the flat and hit her. He knocked her down, then he dragged her over to the door and broke her arm while she was lying on the floor. It was horrible.' The tears began to flow and he swallowed hard. 'I felt so helpless to stop it.'

Bridget placed a hand on his arm. His tears flowed

faster. 'It all happened so fast,' he wailed. It was obviously his inability to protect his wife that hurt him most.

'Then what happened?' I said.

'He demanded the information,' Josef said.

'Did you give it to him?' I asked.

'I asked him for the money,' he said. 'But he said to give him the stuff immediately or he'd break Bridget's other arm.' He sobbed again.

'What happened next?' I asked when his sobs had diminished a little.

'I had to get an ambulance,' he said. 'We were so afraid we would lose the baby. Bridget was in hospital for nearly a week.'

I had really meant what happened next with the man.

'Did you call the police?' I asked him.

'The hospital did. They seemed to think that I had done it,' he said. 'The police didn't believe me when I said it was another man.'

'Did you tell them who he was?' I asked. 'Or what he wanted?'

'No.' He cried again. 'He said he would come back and make Bridget lose the baby if we told anyone.' He looked at me and I wondered if he was now thinking that telling me had been a mistake. 'The man said that if we told anyone, he would make sure we would never be able to have any children ever.'

I was certain that Josef had believed it. *Next time I'll smash your head, next time I'll cut your balls right off.* I believed it, too.

'But the man came back?' I asked him.

'Not in person,' he said. 'He sent me a letter at work the month after the trial was over.'

'Saying what?' I asked, but I suspected I already knew that, too.

'He told me to go to Julian Trent's lawyer and tell him that I had talked to some of the jury to try and ensure that Julian Trent was convicted,' he said in a rush. 'But I hadn't, I swear it.' But he had sworn at the appeal hearing that he had. I had read the transcript.

'Did the letter say which jurors you had to say you had approached?' I asked him.

'Yes,' he said. 'Three of them.'

I knew their names too. They were also in the transcript.

'What was the name of the lawyer?' I asked. I had been Julian Trent's defence lawyer at the trial.

'Some solicitor in Weybridge,' he said. 'I can't remember the name of the firm. Funny, though, I felt sure he was somehow expecting me when I arrived. He knew exactly what I was going to say.'

'Please try and remember who it was,' I said to him. The solicitor who had engaged me to act for Trent at his first trial had been from a central London firm, not one in Weybridge.

'I can't,' he said. 'I had it on the letter, but the lawyer took that. I know it was in Weybridge High Street, above some shops. I could probably find it again. I was all in a bit of a daze.'

'Was there anything else with the letter?' I asked.

'There was a photograph.' He gulped. 'It showed Bridget and me coming out of her ante-natal class at the local hospital. Someone had drawn an arrow on it with a red marker pen. The arrow was sticking into her stomach.'

Altogether I spent more than an hour with Josef and Bridget Hughes. Their lives had been totally destroyed by the visit of the friendly, well-dressed man offering money for information. He must have known they were young and vulnerable. He had drawn them into his scheme and tossed their futures away without a second thought. Josef had been stripped of the professional qualifications that he had worked so hard to obtain and had avoided a criminal prosecution only by a whisker.

But it was what he had done to their confidence that was worse. Bridget was now almost too timid to step out of her door. They were prisoners in a bed-sit, a bed-sit they could now hardly afford to live in with Josef having to do casual work stacking supermarket shelves at night. He would come home in the mornings with out-of-date food as part of his wages.

'Please help us,' Josef had pleaded as he came downstairs to the main door of the property. 'I only keep going for Bee and Rory.'

'How can I contact you?' I asked him.

'There's a pay phone here.' He pointed at it just inside

the front door and I took down the number. I also gave him one of my cards.

'Call me if you need anything,' I said.

He nodded slightly, but I doubted that he would. His life may have been in tatters but he had kept his pride.

We shook hands inside the hallway and Josef peered cautiously round the door as he opened it to the street. I pressed some banknotes into his hand. He looked at the money and started as if to refuse it.

'Buy some food for the baby,' I said.

He looked up at my face. 'Thank you,' he mumbled, fighting back the tears. Things were so bad that he couldn't refuse the cash, even though he clearly hated not doing so.

Next I went to see one of the three jurors from the original trial who had testified at the appeal and who lived in Hendon, close to Golders Green in north London.

George Barnett tried to slam the door in my face as soon as he saw who it was. He obviously recognized me from the trial, as I did him. He was the schoolmasterly white-haired gentleman who had been the jury foreman, but he seemed a shadow of his former self. Gone were the upright posture and the air of self-assurance. In their place there was an old-age stoop, and fear. Lots of fear.

'Go away,' he shouted through the crack in the door that my foot was preventing from closing. 'I did what you asked. Now leave me alone.'

'Mr Barnett,' I called to him round the door. 'I've come here to try and help you.'

'That's what he told me,' he said.

'I have not been sent by Mr Trent,' I said back to him. There was a muffled 'Oh God' from inside and he pushed harder on the door so that the wood bent. 'Go away,' he shouted again.

'Mr Barnett,' I called again, not moving my foot out of the door. 'I was also beaten up by Julian Trent. I want to find out why. I need your help.'

'Please go away,' he said again, but this time he sounded tired.

'All right,' I said. 'I am going to move my foot now.' I lifted it and he slammed the door shut.

'Mr Barnett,' I called through the door. 'Do you want to spend the rest of your life in fear, or do you want to help me stop these people?'

'Go away,' he said again, pleading.

I pushed one of my business cards through his letter box. 'Call me if you change your mind,' I said. 'I promise I'm on your side.'

He hadn't actually told me anything useful but he had at least confirmed what I had suspected. Julian Trent, together with his friends and relations, had left a trail of broken lives wherever they went, attacking and then intimidating good people into doing what they wouldn't normally contemplate, perverting the course of justice for their own ends and to hell with the consequences for everyone else, including me.

But I had no intention of living in fear for the rest of my life.

It was time to take a stand.

On Thursday, I left my troubles behind and went to Cheltenham for the races.

The Foxhunter Chase, my ambition, was the following afternoon, directly after the Gold Cup. Thursday was World Hurdle day, the long-distance hurdle race for the best 'stayers' in the country.

Today I was having a day off as a guest of a Lambourn horse-transport company that had hired a private box. I had acted for them the previous year when I had successfully defended a charge of careless driving against one of their drivers, and they were honouring their promise to give me a day at Cheltenham as a bonus.

The private box was on the top level of the huge grandstand that would later hold tens of thousands of cheering race fans, shouting home the winners at the greatest jump-race festival in the world. This was the meeting that all owners, trainers and jockeys worked towards for the preceding twelve months. The Grand National may be the most famous English steeplechase, known around the world, but the Cheltenham Festival is where most would love to win, especially one of the two major Blue Riband events, the Gold Cup and the Champion Hurdle.

The festival excitement can be almost cut with a knife

as the crowds stream through the turnstiles, eager to find themselves a pie and a pint before the serious business of choosing their fancies and placing their bets in good time to bag a vantage point on the grandstand steps.

Fortunately, for me, my vantage point was assured on the viewing balcony of the private box, so I had time to absorb the atmosphere, to walk amongst the tented village of shops and galleries, and to stroll through the Racing Hall of Fame on my way to level 5.

'Ah, Geoffrey.' Edward Cartwright, the transport-company owner extended a large plump hand as he came to meet me at the door. I shook it warmly. 'Welcome to Cheltenham,' he said. 'Let's hope for a great day.' His gaze slid past me as another guest appeared behind me, his attention moving in turn to the new arrival.

The box was about four metres square and the centre was taken up with a large rectangular cloth-covered table set for lunch. I quickly scanned the places. There would be twelve of us in all, about half of whom had so far arrived. I gratefully accepted a glass of champagne that was offered by a small dark-haired waitress and then went out to join some of the other guests that I could see on the balcony outside.

'Hello,' said one of them. 'Remember me?'

'Of course,' I said, shaking his hand. I had last seen him at the equine hospital in November. 'How's the yearling?'

'Two-year-old now,' Simon Dacey said. 'Almost ready for the racecourse. No apparent ill effects, but you never know. He may have been faster still without the muscle damage.'

I looked at the other three people on the balcony.

'Oh, sorry,' said Simon. 'Can I introduce you to my wife, Francesca?' I shook the offered petite hand. Francesca Dacey was blonde, tall, slim and wearing a yellow suit that touched her in all the right places. We smiled at each other. Simon waved towards the other two, a middle-aged couple, he in a pinstripe suit and she in an elegant long brown open jacket over a cream top and brown slacks. 'And Roger and Deborah Radcliffe.' Ah, I realized, they were the Peninsula connections.

'Congratulations last June,' I said. 'With the Derby.'

'Thank you,' said Deborah Radcliffe. 'Greatest day of our lives.'

I could imagine. I was hoping that the following day would prove to be mine. To win at Cheltenham was a dream, to have done so at Epsom in the Derby must be anyone's lifetime ambition. But I could remember Simon Dacey saying when we met in the _____ that his _____ herself in the middle

_____ _____, said Simon Dacey. 'I remember you party ____ with Paul Newington, but I'm afraid I have forgotten your name.'

'Geoffrey Mason,' I said.

'Ah yes, Geoffrey Mason.' The introductions were completed and hands shaken. 'Lawyer, I think you said?'

'Yes, that's right,' I replied. 'But I'm here as an amateur jockey.' I smiled. 'I have a ride in the Foxhunters tomorrow.'

'Best of luck,' said Deborah Radcliffe, rather dismissively. 'We don't have any jumpers.' She said it in a way that gave the impression that she believed jumpers weren't real racehorses and were more of a hobby than proper racing, not like the flat. More fool her, I thought. I had always believed the reverse.

Roger Radcliffe, who obviously agreed with her, took the opportunity to move back inside the box to replenish his champagne. Why, I wondered, did they bother to come if they weren't excited by the racing? But it was not my problem. I was in seventh heaven and my only concern was having too much to eat and drink today and having to put up overweight in the race tomorrow.

Francesca Dacey and Deborah Radcliffe moved to the far end of the balcony for, I imagined, some girly talk. It left silence for a 1 ___ champagne glasses.

'Didn't you say you were acting for Stev___

Simon Dacey finally asked, almost with relief.

'That's right,' I said, relaxing. 'I'm one of his barristers.'

'When's the trial?' he asked.

'Second week in May.'

'Has Mitchell been inside all this time?' he said.

'Certainly has,' I said. The defence had applied twice for bail without success. Two chances were all you had.

'Can you get him off?' he asked.

'One doesn't get people off,' I said sarcastically. 'It is my job to help the jury determine if he is guilty or not. I hope to provide them with sufficient doubt.'

'Beyond a reasonable doubt,' he said as if quoting.

'Exactly.'

'But there is always some doubt, isn't there?' he said. 'Unless you have it on film.'

'There's some doubt even then,' I said. 'Gone are the days of a hard negative to work from. Don't let anyone ever tell you that a digital camera never lies. They do, and often. No, my job is to persuade the jury that any doubt they may have is at least reasonable.'

'How genteel.' He laughed.

Genteel is not how I would describe the Julian Trent baseball-bat approach to persuasion.

'Have you ever heard of anyone called Julian Trent?' I asked him.

'No,' he said. 'Should I?'

'I just wondered,' I said. He hadn't appeared to be lying. If he was, he was good at it.

'Is he in racing?' he asked.

'No, I don't think so,' I said. 'I asked just on the off chance.'

'It's funny,' he said. 'Our industry, racing that is, it's very insular. Everyone in it knows everyone else but we really don't know anyone not connected, anyone from outside.'

I knew what he meant. The law could be like that too. It was one of the reasons I had chosen to continue taking my pleasure from a sport so far removed from the formality and deathly slow pace of the courts.

The small dark-haired waitress popped her head out of the door and informed us that lunch was about to be served, so would we please take our seats.

The remaining guests had arrived while I had been out on the balcony and I found myself sitting on the long side of the table between Francesca Dacey and Joanna, wife of Nicholas Osbourne, the trainer I had gone to in Lambourn all those years ago. Nicholas and I had nodded cordially to each other as we had sat down. Sadly, there had been no warmth in our greeting. Too many years of animosity, I thought, and I couldn't even remember why.

Joanna, meanwhile, couldn't have been friendlier and even squeezed my knee beneath the table cloth as I sat down. She had always flirted with me. I suddenly wondered if that was why Nick had become so antagonistic towards me. I looked across the table at him. He was fuming, so I winked at him and laughed. He didn't seem at all certain how to react.

'Nick,' I said loudly. 'Will you please tell your wife to stop flirting with me, I'm a married man.'

He seemed unsure how to reply.

'But . .,' he tailed off.

'My wife might be dead,' I said, with a smile that I didn't feel. 'But I'm still in love with her.'

He seemed to relax a little. 'Joanna, my darling,' he said. 'Leave the poor boy alone.' And he smiled back at me with the first genuine sign of friendship for fifteen years.

'Silly old fool,' Joanna said quietly to me. 'He gets so jealous. I'd have left him years ago if I was ever going to.'

I squeezed her knee back. Nicholas would have had a fit.

'So tell me what you're up to,' she said as we ate the starter of steamed asparagus with Hollandaise sauce.

'I'm representing Steve Mitchell,' I said.

Francesca Dacey, on my other side, jumped a little in her seat. The chairs were so close together round the table that I felt it clearly.

'How exciting,' said Joanna with relish. 'Is he guilty?'

'That's for the jury to decide,' I said.

'Don't be so boring,' Joanna said, grabbing my knee again beneath the table. 'Tell me. Did he do it?'

'What do you think?' I asked her. Francesca was trying not to show that she was listening.

'He must have,' she said. 'Otherwise why have they kept him in prison for so long?'

'But he hasn't been tried yet,' I said.

'Yeah, but it stands to reason,' she said. 'They wouldn't have arrested him if he didn't do it. And everyone knows that Barlow and Mitchell hated each other's guts.'

'That doesn't make him a murderer,' I said. 'In fact, if everyone knew that he hated Barlow so much then he was the obvious person to frame for his murder.'

'That's a bit far-fetched though, isn't it?' she said. 'Doesn't everyone who's guilty say they were framed?'

'A few must be telling the truth,' I said.

Our empty starter plates were removed and were replaced with the main course of chicken breast in a mustard sauce. Francesca Dacey had the vegetarian option of penne pasta with pesto.

Joanna Osbourne turned to talk to the man on her left, another Lambourn trainer whose reputation I knew rather better than the man himself. I, meanwhile, turned to Francesca on my right. She was giving a good impression of a health inspector, so keen was she to keep her eyes firmly fixed on her food.

'So how long have you known Steve Mitchell?' I asked her quietly.

'I don't,' she said. But both of us knew she was lying.

'Were you with him the day Scot Barlow died?' I asked her, so quietly that no one else would have been able to hear.

'No,' she replied in the same manner. 'I don't know what you mean.' But we both did.

'Were you really gone from Steve's house by two thirty?' I said, keeping my eyes firmly on my chicken.

'Oh God,' she said under her breath. I thought for a

moment that she was going to get up and leave, but she took a couple of deep breaths and went on studying her pasta. 'Yes,' she said. 'Absolutely I had to be home by two thirty to meet the plumber. He came to fix the dishwasher.'

So, just as Steve had told me, getting her involved wouldn't actually give him an alibi for Barlow's murder.

'Steve didn't tell me,' I said to her, turning towards her ear so that others wouldn't hear. 'He refused to say who it was he was with.'

I wasn't sure whether she was pleased or not.

'Please.' She gulped. 'Please don't tell my husband,' she pleaded in a whisper.

'No,' I said. 'No need to.'

She half coughed, half sobbed and then suddenly stood up.

'Sorry,' she croaked to our host, 'Something went down the wrong way.' She rushed out, holding a white linen napkin to her face. One of the other ladies followed her out. Simon Dacey watched in obvious embarrassment.

Cheltenham during the Festival is like no other day at the races anywhere in the world. After lunch I wandered around absorbing the atmosphere. I walked down to the Guinness Village, now an institution at the track and the transient home to thousands of Irish whose annual pilgrimage to Gloucestershire does much to make this event so unique. Irish folk bands and English rock bands vied for favour in the huge marquee behind a scaffold-built temporary grandstand, entertaining the crowd prior to the main attraction of the afternoon, the racing itself.

I leaned on the white plastic rail next to the horse walk to watch a quartet of happy punters from across the Irish Sea. They all wore outrageous green and black huge leprechaun hats and they had linked arms in a line like a scene from *Zorba the Greek*. They were trying to perform an Irish jig and I laughed out loud as they came a cropper and sat down heavily on a grassy bank. All were in good humour, aided and abetted by a continuous flow of the black stuff, the Guinness.

'Hello, stranger,' said a familiar voice behind me. I smiled broadly and turned round.

'Hello, Eleanor,' I said, and I gave her a kiss on the cheek. 'How lovely to see you. Are you here for work or pleasure?

'Both really,' she said. 'Busman's holiday for me today. I am technically on call but that means I can do pretty much what I want. I just have to carry this bleep.' She produced a small rectangular black item from her cavernous handbag.

'Fancy a drink?' I asked.

'Yes, but not here,' she said indicating the Guinness bar.

'No,' I agreed.

We went in search of one of the bars under the grandstand but they were all packed with a scrum ten deep to get served.

'Come on,' I said. 'Let's go up to the boxes.'

I was sure that Edward Cartwright, my host, wouldn't mind me bringing Eleanor into his box and so it turned out. In fact, he rather monopolized her and left me wishing we had stayed in the crush downstairs.

I had seen Eleanor twice since the previous November. The first time had been in London just a week later, when I had asked her to a black-tie dinner in the Hall at Gray's Inn. It hadn't been a particularly successful evening. I should have opted for a table for two in a candle-lit Italian restaurant rather than the long refectory tables and benches in Hall.

The seating plan had us sitting opposite each other rather than side by side as I had hoped and conversation between us had been difficult, not only due to the noise of three hundred people eating and talking at once, but also because the centre of the table was full of flowers, silver candelabras, and a detritus of wine glasses, condiments and place-cards.

We had hardly spoken a word to each other the whole evening and I think she had been bored by the speeches, which had contained too many 'in' jokes for the lawyers. At the end of the dinner she had jumped straight back into a cab and rushed off to Paddington for the last train home.

Why I had asked her to that dinner, I could not imagine. If I had wanted a romantic evening à deux, I couldn't have chosen anything less appropriate. Maybe that was the trouble. Maybe I hadn't actually wanted a romantic evening à deux in the first place. It was silly to admit, but perhaps I was scared to embark on a new amorous adventure. It also made me feel guilty. Guilty that I was somehow deserting Angela.

The second time we had met had been even more of a disaster. We had both been guests at a Christmas ball thrown by a big racing sponsor in the grandstand at Newbury racecourse. I had been there in a party put together by Paul and Laura Newington, and Eleanor had been in another group, one of the many from Lambourn. I had been so delighted to see her again and had immediately asked her to dance. But she had been with someone else and he'd been determined that I wouldn't get a look-in with 'his' girl. I had felt wretched all evening. It was not just that I had lost out to another, it was that, maybe, I had suddenly realized that the time was now right and I had missed my chance. The bus had come along willingly and had opened its doors to pick me up, but I had declined the offer and now it had driven off, leaving me standing alone at the bus-stop. I now worried that it might have been the last bus, and that I would remain waiting at the stop for ever.

'Penny for your thoughts,' Eleanor said, coming up behind me again. I had been leaning on the balcony rail aimlessly watching the massed crowds below and I hadn't noticed her escape the clutches of Edward and come outside to join me.

'You,' I said, turning and looking into her blue eyes.

She blushed, the crimson colouring spreading up from her neck and over her face.

'Did you know,' I said, 'that if you are naked you blush all over your body.'

'Bastard,' she said. She turned away and laughed.

'What are you doing tonight?' I asked her.

'I'm not coming to another of your awful dining-in nights, that's for sure.'

We laughed together.

'I have to admit that it was a bit of a disaster,' I agreed, 'But I'm sure the next one will be better.'

'Forget it,' she said. 'I had always thought lawyers were boring, and now I know they are.'

'You just haven't met the right lawyers,' I said.

She paused and smiled at me. 'Oh yes I have,' she said.

Wow, I thought. The bus had made a round trip. Now do I get on?

CHAPTER NINE

Sadly, I didn't spend the evening with Eleanor, nor the night.

In fact, I spent very little time with her at all. Her bleep went off as we were still on the balcony and she rushed off to find a quiet spot to make a call, returning only briefly to tell me that she had to go back to Lambourn. There was an emergency at the hospital, something about a prize stallion and a twisted gut.

'Will you be here tomorrow?' I shouted after her rather forlornly as she rushed away.

'Hope so,' she called back. 'Call me on the mobile in the morning.'

Suddenly she was gone. I was surprised at how disappointed I felt. Was I really ready after seven and a half years? Don't rush things, I told myself.

I spent much of the rest of the afternoon drifting between the box upstairs and the parade ring. I had intended to use the time to familiarize myself with the surroundings, the sounds and the smells of the Festival in mental preparation for the race the following day. Instead,

I spent most of the time thinking about Eleanor, and about Angela. They were quite different but in many ways they were the same. Eleanor was blonde with blue eyes whereas Angela had been dark with brown, but they both had a similar sense of humour, and a love for life and fun.

'Which one do you fancy?'

I looked at the man standing next to me who had spoken. I didn't know him.

'I beg your pardon?' I said.

'Which one do you fancy?' he said again, nodding at the horses. We were leaning up against the rail of the parade ring where the horses for the next race were walking round and round.

'Oh,' I said in sudden understanding. 'Sorry, I don't even know what's running.'

He lost interest in me instantly, and went on studying the horseflesh on parade in front of him prior, no doubt, to making an investment with the bookies.

I went back upstairs to the box, telling myself to snap out of this daydreaming and pay attention to the racing.

'How's he doing?' Francesca Dacey whispered in my ear as she stood behind me to watch the race on the balcony.

'Fed up,' I said, turning slightly. 'But otherwise OK.'

'Say hi to him for me if you get the chance,' she whispered again before moving away to her left and talking to another of the guests.

The World Hurdle, the big race of the day, was a

three-mile hurdle race for horses with stamina for the long distance, especially the uphill finish in the March mud. And stamina they had. Four horses crossed the last obstacle in line abreast and each was driven hard for the line, the crowd cheering them on with fervour, the result to be determined only by the race judge and his photographs.

There was a buzz in the crowd after the horses swept past the winning post, such had been the exhilarating effect of the closest of finishes; the adrenalin still rushed round our veins, our breathing was still just a tad faster than normal. Such moments were what brought the crowds back time and again to Cheltenham. The best horses, ridden by the best jockeys, stretching to reach the line first. Winning was everything.

'First, number seven,' said the announcer to a huge cheer from some and a groan of misery from others. Reno Clemens on horse number seven stood bolt upright in his stirrups and punched the air, saluting the crowd, who roared back their appreciation. How I longed for it to be me doing just that the following afternoon.

Most of the guests rushed off to watch the winner come back to the unsaddling enclosure, where he would receive a fresh wave of cheering and applause. I, however, decided to stay put. I had done my share of aimlessly wandering the racecourse wishing that Eleanor had been with me to share it.

The lunch table had been pushed up against one wall and was now heaving under large trays of sandwiches and cakes ready for tea. I looked longingly at a cream-filled chocolate éclair and opted instead for the smallest cucumber sandwich I could find.

'I hear you are a lawyer,' said a female voice on my right.

I turned to find Deborah Radcliffe standing next to me. Why did I think she didn't like lawyers? Maybe it was the way she looked down her nose at me. Lots of people didn't like lawyers, that is until they got themselves into trouble. Then their lawyer became their best friend, maybe their only friend.

'That's right,' I said, smiling at her. 'I'm a barrister.'

'Do you wear a wig?' she asked.

'Only in court,' I said. 'Lots of my work is not done in courts. I represent people at professional disciplinary hearings and the like.'

'Oh,' she said, as if bored. 'And do you represent jockeys at enquiries?'

'I have done,' I said. 'But not very often.'

She seemed to lose interest completely.

'How is Peninsula?' I asked her.

'Fine, as far as I know,' she said. 'He's now at Rushmore Stud in Ireland. In his first season.'

Retired at age three to spend the rest of his life treated like royalty, passing his days eating, sleeping and covering mares. Horse paradise.

'But he wasn't born himself at Rushmore?' I said.

'Oh no,' she replied. 'We bred him at home.'

'Where's home?' I asked her.

'Near Uffington,' she said. 'In south Oxfordshire.'

'Where the White Horse is,' I said. The Uffington White Horse was a highly stylized Bronze Age horse figure carved into the chalk of the Downs a few miles north of Lambourn.

'Exactly,' she replied, suddenly showing more interest in me. 'I can almost see White Horse Hill from my kitchen window.'

'I've never actually seen the horse,' I said. 'Except in photos.'

'It's not that easy to see unless you get up in the air,' she said. 'We are forever getting tourists who ask us where it is. They seem disappointed when you show them the hill. The horse is almost on the top of it and you can't even see it properly if you walk up to it. Goodness knows how they made it in the first place.'

'Perhaps it was the fact that they couldn't see it properly that made it such a weird-looking horse,' I said.

'Good point,' she said.

'Do you remember Millie Barlow being there when Peninsula was born?' I asked.

'Who?' she said.

'Millie Barlow,' I repeated. 'She was the vet who was present.'

'Not really,' she said. 'We have foals being born all the time. We have a sort of maternity hospital for horses. They come to us to deliver, especially if they are to then be covered by a local stallion.'

'But I would have thought you would remember Peninsula,' I said.

'Why?' she said, 'We didn't know at the time that he would turn out so good. He had good breeding but it was not exceptional. We were just lucky.'

It made sense. After all, the world knows that William Shakespeare died on 23 April 1616, but it is not known for sure exactly where and on which day he was born, although it is often assumed, for neatness, to be the same day of the year as his death. All that is actually recorded is that he was baptized on 26 April 1564.

'Why do you ask about this vet?' Deborah asked me.

'It's just that she killed herself last June and I wondered if you remembered her at Peninsula's birth,' I said.

'Not that vet who killed herself during the party?' she said.

I nodded.

'I remember her doing that, of course,' she said. 'But I didn't know it was the same vet who had been there to foal Peninsula.'

'So you didn't see a photo of her with Peninsula after the birth?' I asked.

'No,' she said emphatically. 'Why? Should I have done?'

'It seems to have gone missing,' I said.

'Sorry,' she said, losing interest again. 'I can't help you.'

A large group of the other guests suddenly returned to

the box for their tea and I decided to go back outside onto the balcony rather than be continuously beguiled by the chocolate cream éclairs.

I woke early the following morning with butterflies rather than éclairs hovering in my stomach. I was used to that feeling. It happened almost every time I had a ride in a race but this time it was something special. The Foxhunter Chase at Cheltenham is known as the amateur riders' Gold Cup. It is run over the same course and distance as its big brother, although, while the Gold Cup had the highest prize money at the Festival, the Foxhunter Chase had the lowest. But it wasn't the prize money that mattered. For me as a jockey, winning the Foxhunters would be like winning the Gold Cup, the Grand National and the Derby all rolled into one.

I spent some of the morning on the phone, chasing some information for the Mitchell case that we had requested several weeks before. As a matter of course we had received copies of Scot Barlow's bank statements with the rest of the prosecution disclosure, but I had also asked for those of his sister, Millie. The bank had kicked up a bit of a fuss about confidentiality and I had needed to go back to court and argue in front of a judge as to why they were needed.

It had now been two weeks since the hearing. I had referred to our Defence Case Statement in so far as we believed that Mitchell had been framed and that therefore, in our opinion, some unknown third party had been involved in the crime. Thus Barlow's bank statements had been needed to determine if any unusual or relevant transactions had occurred between him and an unknown third party. I further pointed out that Millie Barlow, sister of the victim and lover of the accused, had, according to her friends, seemed quite well off prior to her suicide the previous June. More well off than might have been expected from her salary alone. I had argued that she might have been receiving an allowance from her brother, a successful sportsman who, at the time, had been earning near the top of his profession. Millie Barlow's bank statements were needed therefore to cross reference with his, so as to be able to eliminate transactions on his statements made by him to her during her lifetime.

I was not altogether sure if the judge had believed me, or even if he had understood my argument, but he could see no reason why the bank statements of a suicide, whether or not she was the sister of a murder victim, should still have been covered by the bank's confidentiality policy, and he made an order for the bank to produce them. He clearly rated suicides lower than criminals.

However, the bank was being very slow in complying with the order. Arthur had finally found me a telephone number that didn't connect to an overseas call centre, so I rang Bruce Lygon and asked him to telephone the bank and tell them that, unless the statements were on my desk by Monday morning, we would have no option but to go back to the judge and argue that the bank was in contempt. I also told Bruce to ensure that he dropped into his conversation that the punishment for criminal contempt of court was a two-year term of imprisonment and/or an unlimited fine.

Bruce called me back within five minutes. He was laughing. He had clearly laid on thick the bit about a prison sentence and the bank's commercial director had promised him absolutely that the statements would be couriered to our chambers this very day. I congratulated him.

Next I called Eleanor.

'Hello,' she said, sounding sleepy.

'Late night?' I asked.

'More like early morning,' she said. 'I was in theatre until nearly four.'

My heart sank. I had so hoped she would be there to see me ride.

'Are you coming today?' I asked without any real hope.

'Probably not,' she said. 'Believe it or not, but I'm still technically on call if there's another emergency. I must get some sleep sometime.'

'Yes,' I said. 'I suppose so.'

'I'll try and be there if I can,' she said. 'What time is the race?'

'Four,' I said.

'If I don't make it, I'll make sure I watch it on the telly,' she said. 'Call me after. OK?'

'Yes,' I said. 'OK.'

'From the winner's circle,' she said.

'I hope so,' I replied with more of a smile in my voice.

'I must dash,' she said. 'Good luck.'

'Thanks,' I said, but the line was already dead.

I surprised myself by the degree of my disappointment. Angela had always hated watching me ride. She used to say that she couldn't eat beforehand and that her stomach was twisted into knots by the fear that I would be injured. I had almost stopped riding altogether towards the end of her life as I could see how much she hated it. After she died I had slowly returned to the saddle, using early mornings on Paul Newington's gallops as a sort of therapy for the agony and the loneliness. It had been a natural progression to return to riding in races as well.

Now I wished so much that Eleanor would be there this afternoon. But perhaps she would hate it too, and maybe, I thought with hope, for the same reason.

I arrived at the racecourse early to miss the traffic. I had stayed the night in a small hotel on Cleeve Hill overlooking the track. It was where I should have been a year ago and the couple who owned and ran the place had been very happy to have pocketed my non-refundable 100 per cent deposit and then re-let the room when I couldn't make it. To their credit, they had eagerly accepted my booking for this year, perhaps in the hope of again making a sizable profit. There was not a hotel room within fifty miles of Cheltenham that wasn't filled and pre-purchased at least twelve months in advance for these four days.

I parked my rented car in the jockeys' car park, made my way into the racecourse enclosures, through to the weighing room and then on into the inner sanctum, the jockeys' changing room. I slung my bag of kit on a peg and walked out onto the weighing-room terrace, feeling completely at home amongst the crowd of trainers, journalists and other jockeys. This was where I loved to be, not in some musty courtroom where the pace of the action was so slow as to be painful.

A racing correspondent from one of the national dailies came up to me.

'Hi, Perry,' he said. 'How's that client of yours?'

'Which client?' I asked. 'And the name's Geoffrey.'

He laughed. I knew that he knew my real name as well as I did.

'OK, Geoffrey,' he said with sarcasm. 'How's your client, Steve Mitchell?'

'Fine,' I said. 'As far as I'm aware. But you probably know better than me.'

'Is he guilty?' he asked.

'I couldn't possibly comment on a case that's still before the courts,' I said. 'I would be in contempt.'

'I know that,' he said. 'But, off the record?'

'Wait for the trial,' I said. 'Then the jury will decide.'

'Won't take 'em long if what I hear is true?' he said with a laugh.

'And what have you heard?' I asked him.

'That Mitchell stuck him one because Barlow accused him of killing his sister.'

'And who exactly told you that?' I asked him.

'That's the word in the press room,' he said. 'Everyone's saying it.'

'And is that what you think?' I asked him.

'Yeah,' he said uncertainly. 'Suppose so.'

We stood together in awkward silence for a moment before he turned away with a slight wave of a hand and went off in search of someone else.

I stood and drank in the atmosphere. Even the weather was joining in the enthusiasm. The sun peeped out from behind a fluffy white cumulus cloud to warm the hearts and souls of seventy thousand racegoers. This was Cheltenham on Gold Cup day and there was nothing quite like it.

'Hi, Geoff.' It was Nick Osbourne, with a smile.

'Hello, Nick.' We shook hands warmly. The truce from the previous day was still holding. 'Any runners today?' I knew he didn't have one in the Gold Cup or the Foxhunters but, apart from those races, I had no idea what was running.

'One in the novice hurdle,' he said. 'Not much chance really.'

'Good luck anyway,' I said.

'Good luck to you too,' he replied. 'On Sandeman.'

'Thanks.'

We stood in easy companionship for a while discussing

our chances and, as always on this day, coming back to who we thought would win the big one.

By the time of the first race at two o'clock my guts were twisted tighter than those of Eleanor's equine patient, and the nerves were beginning to get to me. I sat on the bench around the changing room and made myself calm down. I even managed to force down a cheese and pickle sandwich and a cup of tea that had thoughtfully been provided for the jockeys in the weighing room.

I was not alone in feeling nervous. Even for the top professionals, chances on good horses at Cheltenham were few and far between. For the jockeys of the three or four top-rated horses in the Gold Cup this was a day that could define their careers. Gold Cup winners, both horses and jockeys, were remembered and revered.

I spent much of the afternoon sitting in the changing room alone with my thoughts, mentally running the race over and over in my head, deciding where I wanted to be and when, whether to be on the inside to take the shortest route or to run further wide and give myself more room. Sandeman was fit and so was I. There would be no repeat of Sandown the previous November when it had been my fault we hadn't won. On this day the horse and jockey would both have the stamina to come up the Cheltenham hill after three and a quarter miles.

I stood on the scales in my riding clothes holding my saddle, together with the felt pad that goes under it, the number cloth and the weightcloth, a devious contraption that sits beneath the saddle with lead sheets in pockets to add weight. The digital read-out settled on twelve stone, the required mark, and the clerk of the scales ticked me off on his list. As a rule jockeys don't like carrying extra lead as it sits as dead weight on the horse's back, but I was secretly quite pleased that I had eight pounds of it in my weightcloth, especially as I was using a heavier saddle than many of the other amateurs waiting for their turn on the scales. All that running and skiing had done the trick and I was lighter than I had been for quite a while. I was now well under eleven stone in my birthday suit, so carrying twelve was easy.

I had never really had much trouble doing the weight on Sandeman as he had always been fairly highly rated and, even in handicaps, he had always been near to top weight. Some jockeys, however, had an ongoing struggle every day to keep their weight down, a problem that to me seemed to be getting worse as the average size of the population grew while the racing weights stayed the same.

You could always tell when someone was in trouble doing the weight. There were little games they would play with the clerk of the scales, who was probably wise to every one. They would leave their cap on their helmet and place it on the table. The rule stated that the cap should be weighed even if the helmet wasn't. Others would weigh-out using paper-thin boots, known by jockeys as cheating boots, which they would then change for their regular riding boots when safely back in the changing room. It had also been known for jockeys to weigh-out with a much lighter saddle than they actually intended using, or indeed, if things were desperate, with no saddle at all. Overweight was frowned upon by the stewards, and by owners and trainers alike, and could make the difference between keeping or losing the ride on that horse in the future.

Having successfully cleared the scales, I handed my saddle and the rest of the tack to Paul Newington, who was standing by waiting to receive it.

'See you in the parade ring,' he said, and turned on his heel.

I could tell that he was nervous as well and I watched his back as he hurried away to get Sandeman ready in the saddling boxes.

I went into the changing room to get a jacket to put over my silks and then back out onto the weighing-room terrace to watch the Gold Cup on the big screen set up near the paddock. The favourite won easily with Reno Clemens in the saddle. They had jumped clear of the chasing pack over the last two fences in the straight and stormed up the hill to win by eight lengths. They received a hero's welcome from the huge crowd. But Steve Mitchell in his prison cell wouldn't like it, I thought. He should have been riding that winner. He had ridden the horse all the way through its career only to miss out on its crowning glory.

With the Gold Cup over, now it was my turn. The Foxhunter Chase was less than half an hour away and the butterflies in my stomach had turned into full size eagles. I went back into the changing room and made all my last-minute adjustments once again, making sure I was wearing my back protector and that it was correctly fitted, checking that my silks were on properly with rubber bands around the wrists to stop the wind rushing up the sleeves, tying and retying the cords on my cap to get them right, to ensure it didn't fly off my helmet during the race.

I went once again to the loo and nervously paced around. It was like waiting outside the exam room before my law finals at university, or being in a dentist's waiting room before an extraction.

Finally, the call was made for the jockeys to go out to the parade ring. As always, I felt the burst of adrenalin course through my body but, this time, I wasn't so sure I was enjoying it. The expectation was too great. Riding last year's winner and this year's favourite, as well as carrying so many punters' hopes, was taking much of the fun out of it.

Paul and Laura stood on the grass in the paddock and both seemed to hop from foot to foot with nervousness.

'Good luck,' said Laura breathlessly, giving me a kiss on the cheek.

'Look,' I said. 'Let's just enjoy it. Eh?' They both looked at me as if I were mad. 'Win or lose, it's been a great day out.'

I smiled at them. They didn't smile back. Oh no, I thought, they've had a big bet on us to win. I could read it in their faces. Oh, woe is me. Just another load of pressure I could have done without.

Paul gave me a leg-up onto Sandeman's back and he slapped a hand on his neck. 'Go get 'em, cowboy,' he said nervously in a mock American accent, looking up at me.

'Do my best, pardner,' I said back to him in the same manner.

We circled around the ring a couple of times as the horses sorted themselves out and then we were led out towards the course by two huntsmen in scarlet jackets.

Sandeman beneath me was eager to get going and he didn't like being crammed in on all sides by the massive crowd five deep against the horse-walk rail.

'Good luck, Geoffrey,' called a voice to my left.

I looked down from my vantage point atop a seventeen-hand horse and there was Eleanor, waving madly. She had made it after all. How wonderful.

'Thanks,' I shouted at her inadequately above the bustle of the crowd.

I turned to take one last look at her before Sandeman and I went out onto the course. She was smiling broadly, still waving, but something else caught my eye. Standing just behind her and a little to her right was someone else I recognized.

It was Julian Trent, and he was smiling at me too.

Oh shit. I tried to stop and turn round, to go back and warn her, but the stable lad just thought that Sandeman was playing up a little so he took a tighter hold of the reins and pulled us forward.

I turned right round in the saddle and tried to shout

to Eleanor but she didn't hear me. What should I do? I wanted to jump off, to run back, to protect her. But Sandeman and I were now out of the horse walk and on the course, walking up in front of the expectant crowd. Surely, I told myself, Eleanor would be safe amongst all those people. Perhaps Trent had not seen the exchange between us and he would think of her as just another eager spectator.

The horses were to be led up in front of the grandstand and then we would turn and canter back past the horse walk and on to the start of the race at the far end of the finishing straight.

So distracted was I that I almost fell off when the stable lad turned Sandeman and let him go with a reminding slap on his rump. Instinct made me gather the reins tight in my hands and set off in a gentle canter to the start while I searched the thousands of faces in the crowd, desperate for a glimpse of Eleanor, or of Trent, but unable to spot either.

I felt sick.

All my pre-race planning of where I wanted to be at the start went out the window as my mind was elsewhere. When the tapes flew up Sandeman was caught flat-footed owing to my negligence and I instantly gave the rest of the field ten lengths' start. I could imagine Paul swearing on the trainers' stand and wishing that he had convinced me to let last year's jockey ride again. And he wouldn't be the only one, I thought. This was a televised race and I had been napping at the start. In any other circumstances it would have been unforgivable, but somehow I didn't care. I was more concerned about Eleanor's safety.

Sandeman set off in pursuit of the others and made a magnificent leap at the first with me hardly participating at all. Come on, I said to myself, Eleanor will be fine, concentrate on the matter in hand.

I eased Sandeman back from his headlong gallop to a steadier pace. There was plenty of time to get back to the pack. This was a three-and-a-quarter-mile chase with twenty-two jumps, twice round the Cheltenham course. I settled him down and we steadily closed the gap until, although still last, there was no air between us and the rest. Fortunately the first circuit was not being run too fast as everyone realized there was a long way to go in fairly heavy ground.

At the top of the hill for the first time, I pulled Sandeman slightly wider and we overtook eight other horses easily in the run down to the point where we had started. As we began the second circuit we were in the middle of the pack, lying about tenth, but with those ahead tightly bunched.

By the time we reached the water jump half-way down the back straight the race was really on in earnest. Sandeman flattened his back and sailed over the water like a hurdler. We passed three horses in mid-air and landed running fast. But two other horses had got away at the front of the pack and a three-length gap had opened up behind them.

I kicked Sandeman hard in the ribs.

'Come on boy,' I shouted in his ear. 'Now is the time.'

It was as if he changed gear. We were eating up the ground and two great leaps at the open ditches found us lying third, turning sharp left and starting down the hill for the last time.

I was exhilarated. I wasn't tired and Sandeman didn't feel a bit tired beneath me. I looked ahead. The two horses in front seemed also to be going well and they were about four lengths away, running side by side.

I gave Sandeman a little bit of a breather for a few paces, sitting easily on his back rather than pushing hard at his neck. There were two fences down the hill and I took a measured look at the first one. I adjusted Sandeman's stride and asked him for a big leap. He responded immediately and flew through the top of the fence, gaining half the distance on his rivals ahead. So full of energy had he been that for the first time I thought I might win.

I now kicked him and asked for his final effort. Sandeman had always been a horse with great stamina but without an amazing sprint finish. We needed to be ahead at the last with the momentum to carry us up the hill to the finish in front.

'Come on boy,' I shouted again in his ear. 'Now, now, now.'

Both the horses in front wavered slightly as they approached the fence and I knew, I suddenly knew, that we were going to win.

I gave a slight pull on the reins, setting Sandeman right for another great leap. I was watching the ground, looking at our take-off point, and only peripherally did I see one of the horses ahead hit the top of the fence hard. I pulled Sandeman slightly wider, but it was the wrong way. The horse in front overbalanced badly on landing, rolled sharply to its right and onto the ground, straight into our path. Sandeman and I were in mid-air before I realized that we had nowhere to land. My horse did his best to avoid the carnage but without any real hope of success.

Sandeman tripped over the bulk of prostrate horseflesh in front of him and somersaulted through the air. My last memory of the day was of the green grass rushing up to meet me, just before the blackness came.

PART THREE

TRIAL AND PUNISHMENT

MAY 2009

CHAPTER TEN

I sat at my desk in chambers reading through the paperwork for an upcoming disciplinary hearing at which I would be representing one of a group of senior doctors who had been accused of professional misconduct over the untimely death of a patient in their hospital.

The phone on my desk rang. It was Arthur.

'Mr Mason,' he said 'There's someone here to see you. He's in the clerks' room.'

'Who is it?' I asked.

'He won't say,' said Arthur, clearly disapproving. 'He just insists on talking to you, and only you.'

How odd, I thought.

'Shall I bring him along?' Arthur asked.

'Yes please,' I said. 'But will you stay here until I ask you to leave?'

'All right,' he said. 'But why?'

'Just in case I need a witness,' I said. But I hoped I wouldn't. Surely Julian Trent wouldn't show up and demand to see me in my room.

I put the phone down. It was a general rule hereabouts

that members of chambers met with clients and visitors only in one of the conference rooms on the lower ground floor but, since I had returned to work after Cheltenham, Arthur had been kind enough to grant me special dispensation to meet people in my room. Climbing up and down even just a few stairs on crutches wasn't easy, particularly as the stairs in question were narrow and turning.

There was a brief knock on the door and Arthur entered, followed by a nervous looking man with white hair wearing the same light coloured tweed jacket and blue and white striped shirt that I had seen before in court number 3 at the Old Bailey. However, his shirt had then been open at the collar whereas now a neat red and gold tie completed his ensemble. It was the schoolmasterly foreman of the jury whom I had last glimpsed when I'd had my foot in his front door in Hendon.

'Hello, Mr Barnett,' I said to him. 'Come on in. Thank you, Arthur, that will be all.'

Arthur looked at me with a questioning expression and I smiled back at him. Eventually, he turned on his heel and left me alone with my visitor. I stood up clumsily and held out my hand. George Barnett approached cautiously and briefly shook it.

'Please sit down,' I said to him, indicating the chair in front of my desk.

'Did Trent do that?' he asked, pointing at the cast that stretched from my left foot to my upper thigh.

'No,' I replied. 'I had a fall.'

'I had one of those last June,' he said. 'In my bathroom. Cracked my pelvis.'

'Mine was from a horse,' I said. 'In a race.'

'Oh,' he said.

'Smashed my knee,' I said.

'Oh,' he said again.

I didn't bother telling him about the cracked vertebrae, the broken ribs and the collapsed lung. Or the concussion that, seven weeks later, still plagued me with headaches.

We sat for a moment in silence while he looked around at the mass of papers and boxes that filled almost every available inch of space in my room.

'Mr Barnett,' I said, bringing his attention back to my face. 'How can I help you?'

'I thought it was me who needed to help you,' he said.

'Yes, indeed,' I said, slightly surprised. 'Yes, please. Would you like some coffee or tea?'

'Tea would be lovely,' he said. 'Milk and one sugar.'

I lifted the phone on my desk and asked one of the junior clerks if he would be kind enough to fix it.

'Now, Mr Barnett,' I said. 'Tell me everything.'

He was reluctant at first but he relaxed when the tea arrived, and the whole sorry story was spilled out.

'I was initially pleased when I received the summons for jury service,' he said. 'I had been retired for about four years and I thought it would be interesting, you know, stimulating for the mind.'

'What had you retired from?' I asked him.

'I was in the Civil Service,' he said. I had been wrong about him having been a schoolmaster. 'I was a permanent undersecretary in the Lord Chancellor's Department, but it's called something else now, Constitutional Affairs or something. They change everything, this government.' It didn't sound like he approved.

'Had you done jury service before?' I asked.

'No,' he said. 'I was called once, years ago, but I was exempt through my work in the administration of justice. But they've changed the law on that now too. Even judges and the police now have to serve on juries if they are summoned.'

I knew. Lawyers used to be excluded too, but not any more.

'So tell me what happened,' I encouraged.

He looked around him as if about to tell a big secret that he didn't want anyone else to overhear. 'I turned up at the Old Bailey as I had been asked to and there were a whole load of us. We sat around for ages in the jury area. Then we were given a talk about being a juror and it was all rather exciting. We were made to feel important, if you know what I mean.'

I nodded. I suspected that, as a permanent under-secretary, he had indeed been quite important in the Civil Service but retirement had brought a return to anonymity. Like the headmasters of the great British public schools who may have princes and lords hanging on their every word while they are in post, only to be turned out to fairly low-paid pasture and obscurity on the day they depart.

George Barnett would have enjoyed once again being made to feel important, as we all would.

'In the end,' he said. 'I spent the whole of the first day sitting in the jury collection area reading the newspapers. When I was told I could go home, I was rather disappointed. But the following day I was selected for a trial. I remember being so excited by the prospect.' He paused. 'That was a mistake.' He smiled ruefully at me.

'The Trent trial?' I said.

He nodded. 'It was all right for a while,' he said. 'Then during the first weekend a man came to see me at home.' He paused again. 'He said he was from the jury service so I let him in.'

'Did he give a name?' I asked him.

'Not at first,' he said. 'But then he said he was Julian Trent's father, but I don't think he actually was.'

'Why not?' I said.

'I called him Mr Trent a couple of times and I didn't think he realized I was talking to him.'

'What did he say?'

'Well, when he gave me that name I immediately told him to leave,' he said. 'I knew that we shouldn't talk to anyone about the case, especially not to the defendant's family. But he wouldn't go away. Instead, he offered me money to vote not guilty.'

I sat quietly, waiting for him to continue.

'I told him to go to hell,' he said. 'But . . .' He tailed off, clearly distressed by the memory. I waited some more.

'But he just sat there on a chair in my living room and looked around him. He said that I had a nice place and it would be a shame if I lost it all, or if my wife was injured in an accident.' He stopped again. 'I asked him what he meant. He just smiled and said to work it out.'

'So did you vote not guilty?' I asked.

'My wife has Parkinson's disease,' he said. 'And a bad heart.' I assumed that meant yes, he had. 'I knew that you only need ten of the twelve people on the jury to vote guilty in England to convict, so my vote wouldn't really matter.' I suppose he was trying to justify himself, and to excuse his behaviour. But he must surely have realized that the man would approach other jurors too.

'So what happened in the jury room?' I asked him. It was against the law for him to tell me and I could quite likely get disbarred for even just asking him, but what difference did one more misdemeanour matter, I thought. I could have been disbarred for lots of things I had done, or not done, recently.

'There was a terrific row,' he said. 'Nine of them said straight away that they thought he was guilty as hell. There were three of us who didn't.' He stopped and looked up at the ceiling. 'I think now that the man must have been to see all three of us. None of us could give any reason for saying he was not guilty. We just did. The others thought we were mad. One or two of them got really angry as the time dragged on and on.'

I remembered. I'd been really angry as well.

'But you did return a guilty verdict in the end,' I said.

'I know,' he said. 'And it was me who had to say it in court as they had made me foreman right at the start. It was terrible.'

I remembered back a year, to the nervousness with which he had delivered the verdicts.

'Who cracked?' I said, trying to make light of the situation.

'One of the other two,' he said. 'A woman. She did nothing for days and days but cry. It was enough to send anyone mad.'

I could imagine the emotions in that room. It had taken more than six days for one of the three to change their vote to guilty.

'I was so relieved,' he said. 'I had often so nearly changed my vote, but every morning the man had called me and reminded me that my wife would have an accident if I didn't stay firm. I just couldn't believe that it went on for so long.'

Neither could I. I had fully expected the judge to declare a mistrial because the jury couldn't make a decision. But he hadn't. He had kept calling the jury back into court to ask them to try again to reach a verdict on which at least ten of them agreed. We would never know for how much longer he would have persevered.

'So what happened afterwards?' I asked him.

'Nothing for ages, at least a month,' he said. 'Then the man turned up at my door and pushed me over when I tried to shut him out. He simply walked into the house and kicked me.' It was clearly painful for him simply to describe it. 'It was awful,' he went on. 'He kicked me twice in the stomach. I could hardly breathe. Then he went over to Molly, that's my wife, and just tipped her out of her wheelchair onto the floor. I ask you, who could do such a thing.' His eyes filled with tears but he choked them back. 'Then he put his foot on her oxygen tube. It was absolutely horrid.'

I could see that it was.

'And he told you,' I said, 'to go to the police and say that you had been approached by a solicitor who had asked you to make sure you found Trent guilty?' It was a question but, as all barristers know, one should never ask a question to which you don't already know the answer.

He nodded and looked down into his lap.

'It was dreadful, lying like that in the court,' he said. 'The appeal judges kept asking me if I was telling the truth or was I saying it because I had been told to do so by someone else. I was sure they knew I was lying. I felt so ashamed.' He said the last part in little more than a whisper. 'That's why I'm here,' he said more strongly. 'When you came to my house I was afraid of you. I've been afraid of nearly everyone for the past year. I've hardly been out of the house since the trial. I've been looking at your business card for weeks and been trying to pluck up the courage to come here.'

'I'm so glad you did,' I said. He smiled a little. 'And how is your wife?'

'They took her into a nursing home yesterday, poor

thing. The Parkinson's is beginning to affect her mind and it's becoming too much for me to manage on my own. She's so confused. That's another reason I'm here today,' he said. 'She's safe now. The security at the nursing home is pretty good, mostly to stop the patients wandering off. Now I only have to worry about myself.'

'And what would you like me to do about what you have told me?' I asked.

'What do you mean?' he said, looking nervous again.

'Do you want to go to the police?' I asked him.

'No,' he said quite firmly. He paused. 'I don't think so.'

'Are you still frightened of this man?' I asked.

'Damn right I am,' he said. 'But you can't live your life being too frightened to step out of your own house.'

Bridget Hughes was, I thought.

'So what do we do?' I said.

'I don't know,' he said. 'Perhaps I shouldn't have come here. I'm sorry I think I should go now.' He stood up.

'Mr Barnett,' I said to him. 'I won't tell anyone what you have told me, I promise. But if I try to stop this man and put him behind bars where he belongs, will you help me?'

'How?' he asked.

'I don't know yet,' I said. I didn't even know who the enemy was. 'Would you recognize the man again?'

'I certainly would,' he said. 'I'll never forget him.'

'Tell me what he looked like,' I said.

Mr Barnett did his best but he often contradicted himself. He said he was big but then he also said he was shorter than me. He described him as muscular but also as fat. He was a little confused himself, I thought. In the end I had very little idea about the man who said he was Julian Trent's father other than he was white, middle aged and fairly average in every way. Much the same as Josef Hughes had said and not very helpful. Short of getting a police artist or a photofit expert, it was the best he could do.

He departed back to his home in north London, again looking nervously from side to side. I was left to ponder whether I was any further on in finding out how, and why, Julian Trent had his fingers into the Scot Barlow murder.

Steve Mitchell's trial was now less than a week away and we still had almost nothing to use in his defence except to claim that he definitely didn't murder Scot Barlow, that someone else did – someone who was making it appear that our client was responsible. A classic frame-up, in fact, that no one else could see, not least because Steve Mitchell was not the most likable of characters and people didn't seem to care enough whether he was convicted or not. But I cared. I cared for the sake of justice, and I also cared for the sake of my personal survival. But were the two compatible?

I could foresee that the trial was unlikely to fill the two weeks that had been allocated for it on the Oxford Crown

Court calendar unless we came up with something a bit more substantial, and quickly.

After a sandwich lunch at my desk, I took a taxi to University College Hospital to see an orthopaedic surgeon, with my left leg resting straight across the back seat. Seven whole weeks had now passed since I had woken up in Cheltenham General Hospital with a pile-driver of a headache that had made my skull feel as if it were bursting. With a return to consciousness had also come the discovery that I had to remain flat on my back, my left leg in traction, with a myriad of tubes running from an impressive collection of clear plastic bags above my left shoulder to an intravenous needle contraption in my forearm.

'You are lucky to be alive,' a smiling nurse had cheerfully informed me. 'You've been in a coma for three days.'

My head had hurt so much that I had rather wished that I had remained so for another three.

'What happened?' I had croaked at her from inside a clear plastic mask that had sat over my nose and mouth and which, I'd assumed, was to deliver oxygen to the patient.

'You fell off your horse.'

I had suddenly remembered everything – everything, that is, up to the point of the fall.

'I didn't fall off,' I had croaked back at her. 'The horse fell.' An important distinction for every jockey, although the nurse hadn't seemed to appreciate the difference.

'How is my horse?' I had asked her.

She had looked at me in amazement. 'I have no idea,' she had said. 'I'm only concerned with you.'

Over the next few hours my headache had finally succumbed to increasing doses of intravenous morphine and the roaring fire in my throat had been extinguished by countless sips of iced water via a green sponge on a stick.

Sometime after it was dark, a doctor had arrived to check on my now-conscious form and he had informed me of the full catalogue of injuries that I had sustained, first by hitting the ground at thirty miles and hour and then having more than half a ton of horse land on top of me.

My back was broken, he had said, with three vertebrae cracked right through but, fortunately for me, my spinal cord was intact, thanks probably to the back protector that I had been wearing under my silks. Four of my ribs had been cracked and one of those had punctured a lung that had subsequently partially collapsed. My head had made hard contact with something or other and my brain had been badly bruised, so much so that a neuro-surgeon had been called to operate to reduce the pressure inside my skull by fitting a valve above my right ear that would drain away the excess fluid. My left knee had been broken, the doctor had explained, and he himself had operated to fix it as best he could, but only time would tell how successful he had been.

'So will I live?' I had asked him flippantly.

'It was a bit touch and go for a while,' he had replied seriously. 'But I think you will. There was no real damage to your main internal organs other than a little bruising to the left kidney, and a small tear in your left lung that will heal itself. Yes, I think you'll be fine in time, especially now you are conscious and there doesn't appear to be any major damage to your brain either.'

'And will I ride again?' I'd asked him more seriously.

'More difficult to say,' he'd replied. 'Again, time will tell. I suspect it will depend on how mad you are. I personally think that all you jump jockeys have a screw loose. The same ones come in here year after year to be patched up and plastered.' He shook his head. 'They're completely bonkers.'

'How about my horse?' I had asked him.

'I don't know,' he'd said. 'But surely it wasn't your own horse you were riding?'

'Yes it was,' I'd said. I had tried explaining about being an amateur jockey and the Foxhunter Chase but he hadn't really been interested, and he had no idea whether Sandeman had been injured or not, or even if he was alive. It had only been when Paul and Laura Newington had come to see me later that evening that I had heard the full story of the disaster.

They had been watching the race from the stands and

they were just getting excited about the prospect of another famous win when Sandeman and I had so spectacularly disappeared in a flurry of legs, and then we had both lain prostrate and unmoving on the turf.

Paul, it seemed, had run the half-mile from the grandstands, down the course, to where we had both been hidden from the sight of the thousands of spectators behind hastily erected green canvas screens. Sandeman, it appeared, had been badly winded and had also damaged his back. He had taken a full fifteen minutes to get gingerly to his feet and only Paul's personal intervention had prevented the racecourse vet from putting him down there and then. Fortunately for me, no questions had been asked about whether or not to shoot the jockey. Paul told me that I had been lying on the turf being attended to by the paramedics and the racecourse doctor for nearly an hour before being lifted ever so carefully into an ambulance and driven away at a snail's pace. The following race had been required to bypass the fence and was nearly abandoned altogether.

'There was someone else down there as well,' he had said. I had thought he must have meant Julian Trent but I'd been wrong. 'A girl. Ran all the way down the course in high-heeled shoes. Nice looker. Called herself Eleanor. Do you know her?'

I'd nodded to him.

'She seemed a bit cut up about you,' he'd said, almost surprised. 'I thought she must have the wrong guy but she was certain it was you. She said she had met me before at that do at Newbury in December but I don't remember.'

'What happened to her?' I'd asked him.

'I think she went in the ambulance with you but I don't know. I was so busy trying to get Sandeman sorted out.'

'How is he?' I'd asked him.

'Not great,' he'd said. 'He was taken straight to the equine hospital in Lambourn. They are treating him for a badly strained back and severe bruising.'

I'd laughed at him. 'Eleanor is a vet at that hospital.'

'What a coincidence,' he'd said laughing back.

But I didn't like coincidences.

'I think that cast can come off your leg,' said the ortho-paedic surgeon. 'The X-rays show the knee mending well and there's no reason why it needs to be immobilized any longer. How long is it now?'

'Seven and a half weeks,' I said.

'Mmm,' he pondered. 'Should be fine, but you will need to keep using the crutches and just put a little weight on it for a while. Build up the weight over the next few weeks.'

'What about my back?' I asked him.

'The scans show that the bones are mending slowly but you still need to keep that straightjacket on for another six weeks at least.'

He was referring to the hard white plastic shell that I

wore to prevent me bending my back. The damned thing reached from just below my neck almost to my groin in the front and from my shoulder blades to the top of my buttocks behind. It was very uncomfortable and made sitting at a desk near impossible, but wearing it had at least allowed me to walk around. Without it I would probably still be lying flat on my back.

'Six weeks?' I said in exasperation.

'You broke the T10, T11 and T12 vertebrae right through and you don't want to finish now what your fall started,' he said. 'You are a very lucky man. With that injury you could have so easily been paralysed, or dead.'

I would just have to put up with the discomfort, and the ignominy of having to ask my downstairs neighbour to come and help me get out of the wretched thing at night and back into it in the morning. The shell was actually made in two halves that had been heat moulded to fit my torso exactly, the two parts being held together round my upper body by half a dozen Velcro-covered nylon straps that needed to be fed through metal loops and pulled tight. I even had to shower in the damn thing.

The surgeon inspected the device before I gratefully hid it again from sight beneath my shirt.

'It's damned uncomfortable, you know,' I said to him. 'It makes me itch all the time.'

'Better than being paralysed,' he replied.

And there was no answer to that.

'How's the head?' he asked. It wasn't technically his department.

'Getting better slowly,' I said. 'I saw the neurologist last week and he is happy with my progress, but I still have some headaches.'

'Do you still have the valve implant?' he asked.

'No,' I said putting my hand up to my right ear. 'He took it out four weeks ago now.'

'No problems?' he asked.

'A little dizziness at first,' I said. 'But that went after a couple of days. No, I feel fine, just a few headaches and they are getting more infrequent and less troublesome.'

'Good,' he said looking down and making some notes.

'When can I start riding again?' I asked him.

He stopped writing and looked up. 'Are you serious?'

'Absolutely,' I said.

He put his pen down and looked at me with his head inclined to the side. 'Well, I suppose from my point of view, all your bones will heal and they'll be as good as new in a few months, but I would be worried about your head. The brain can only take so many knocks like that.'

I had to admit that it had been quite a bang. I had seen what was left of my racing helmet and it was cracked right through from front to back. Without it, I would have certainly died.

'But I don't intend to ever land on my head again,' I said.

'No one intended there to be a second world war after the first one. But there was.'

'That's a bit different,' I said.

'OK,' he conceded. 'But you should never try to predict the future.'

I knew that well enough. Especially in the law.

When I returned to chambers later that afternoon I felt I was walking on air, albeit with only one leg. In spite of the fibreglass and polyurethane material being much lighter than the old-fashioned white plaster of Paris, the full-length cast had still been very heavy and annoyingly restrictive. Without it, I felt at least partially released from the cage in which I had been existing.

The surgeon had told me that I would need lots of physiotherapy to get the knee back to full movement, and I still had to walk using the crutches, but it was such a joy to once again scratch an itch in my thigh, or to rub away an ache in my kneecap.

Arthur looked up at me from his desk as I hopped my way through the clerks' room. 'On the mend, I see,' he said.

'Slowly,' I agreed. 'I still have to wear this body armour for another six weeks.' I tapped the hard shell beneath my shirt.

'Still need the recliner then?' he said, smiling.

He referred to the new chair I had acquired from a friend that sat behind my desk. It allowed me to lean right back and reduce the pressure that the shell made on my groin.

'I might just keep it anyway,' I said to him with a laugh. He had found me asleep in the chair two or three times when I had first returned to chambers about three weeks previously.

'There's another one of those hand-delivered envelopes in your box,' Arthur said, immediately wiping the smile from my face. 'It came while you were out.'

'Right,' I said. 'Thanks.'

Arthur looked me in the eye and I thought for a moment that he was going to ask me straight out what was in the envelope, but he didn't, instead returning his attention to something on his desk.

I went over to the boxes and looked into mine. I had been temporarily promoted to the top row as I was unable to bend down to my usual level, and there, on its own, was a slim A5-sized white envelope, just as before.

I was sure that Arthur was watching me so I picked it up casually and stuffed it into my trouser pocket before negotiating the corridor on my crutches to the safety and privacy of my room. Thankfully, the two others junior barristers who also shared this space with me were both away in Manchester acting for a big local football club that was up to its neck in a tax evasion scandal involving half a dozen of their most highly paid players.

I sat in my recliner chair and carefully opened the envelope. As before there was a single sheet of folded paper, and a photograph. On the sheet of paper there were just two short lines, again in black capital letters.

JUST REMEMBER, LOSE THE CASE
MITCHELL GETS CONVICTED

The photograph showed Eleanor in her blue scrub tunic and trousers walking along the gravel path between the house she lived in and the equine hospital in Lambourn.

CHAPTER ELEVEN

Why was it, I wondered, that I felt like I was being dangled on a string by an unknown hand, being made to dance a jig by some puppet-master hidden from the light. My house, my job, my father and even my friends were somehow under his spell. Sometimes I even began to wonder if my fall at Cheltenham had been his doing, but I knew that was ridiculous.

I sat at my desk and turned the photo of Eleanor over and over in my hands. Even if Julian Trent had seen her call and wave to me at Cheltenham, how did he know where she worked or how to get her photograph?

Photograph, photograph. Why did I keep thinking about the photograph taken from Scot Barlow's house the day he was murdered? Why not steal the frame as well? If someone had wanted to keep that picture then, surely, wouldn't they have taken the frame with it? Not, I supposed, if it had been highly individual and easily recognizable. But it hadn't. It had been a simple silver frame available in any high-street jeweller or department store.

So had the photograph been taken simply to destroy it? Was the image in fact a clue to whoever had been the murderer?

I was pondering these questions when my phone rang.

I picked it up with some trepidation but there was a familiar voice at the other end, one I was beginning to hope might become more familiar still.

'What did the doctor say?' Eleanor asked immediately.

'He told me I can go on living,' I replied with a smile.

'Good,' she said. 'So he must have told you that you were quite well enough to take me out to dinner tonight?'

'He said that it was completely out of the question,' I replied. 'He insisted that I should eat in at my place, alone. Matter of life or death.'

'Well, you'll just have to die then,' she said laughing. 'Because you, sunshine, are taking me out to Maximillian's tonight whether you like it or not.'

I liked it.

'How's the conference?' I asked her. She was attending a two-day international equine-medicine symposium at the London Veterinary School.

'Boring,' she said. 'Look, I must dash. They're about to start a lecture about the caecum and its role in colic.'

'Sounds like fun,' I said.

'Anything but,' she said. 'See you at the restaurant at seven thirty.' She disconnected before I had time to say goodbye.

I think she had applied to attend the symposium only so that she could spend a night in a London hotel, and spend the evening with me.

I had seen her four or five times since my fall at Cheltenham.

'Typical,' she had said when she first came to see me in hospital after I had woken up.

'What's typical?' I'd replied.

'I sit here beside him trying to wake him up for nearly three whole days and nights and then, when I have to go to work, hey presto, he opens his eyes.'

I had smiled at her. 'You didn't have to do that,' I'd said.

'I didn't have to,' she'd said. 'But I wanted to.'

That was nice, I'd thought.

She had been back to see me a couple more times during the week that they had insisted on keeping me in Cheltenham hospital, and then she had helped me on the day I went back home to Ranelagh Avenue, SW13.

Strangely, for the first two weeks after hospital I had been permitted only to lie flat on my back or to stand upright. Sitting, other than for a few minutes at a time, had been banned by the doctors. It had made life very complicated as it was impossible to travel anywhere by car. An ambulance had been needed to take me home on a stretcher, yet I was able to climb the stairs to my house, albeit on one leg and a pair of crutches, with Eleanor standing behind me so I didn't topple over backwards and do myself more mischief.

She had stayed that first night I was home, sleeping in the room that, seven and a half years before, Angela and I had so gleefully decorated with teddy bears' picnic wallpaper as a nursery for our unborn son, and which I hadn't yet bothered to change. I realized that, since my father had gone home soon after Angela's funeral, Eleanor was the first person other than me to have slept in my home. It wasn't that I was particularly averse to having guests, it was just that I hadn't yet got round to actually asking anyone to stay. I kept thinking that there was plenty of time, and the last seven years had seemingly passed in a flash.

But I think Eleanor had felt uneasy sleeping at my place, as uneasy as I had at her being there. She had stayed only one night in Barnes before returning to Lambourn, and she hadn't been back, although we had twice met elsewhere, on neutral territory, as it were, and we had spoken often on the telephone.

I liked her. I liked her a lot. But I still wasn't sure if I was yet ready for a serious relationship. I had become used to my solitary existence. I had grown accustomed to looking after myself and not having to worry about getting home from work at a reasonable time. Maybe I was set in my ways, and not very sure that I was prepared to change them.

However, I was greatly looking forward to seeing her again for dinner, and I had a spring in my one-footed step as I finally left chambers at seven o'clock and went in search of a taxi.

Julian Trent was standing next to the gate onto Theobald's Road, leaning on the brick-built gatepost, and I saw him immediately when I walked out of chambers. He was making no attempt at concealment as he had done before, the previous November, when he had hidden between the parked cars before stepping out to hit me with his baseball bat.

I realized there was no point in me trying to run away. The best speed I could manage on one leg and two crutches would have hardly outrun a two-year-old toddler let alone a fit and healthy young man of twenty-four. I turned towards him and he watched me as I carefully and slowly covered the sixty or so yards between us. He stood up straight and stopped leaning on the brickwork as I approached. I hoped he couldn't actually see my heart beating fast inside my chest.

He took a few steps forward and I was beginning to regret that I hadn't simply gone back inside my chambers as soon as I had seen him. However, I did gratefully note that he wasn't accompanied today by his sidekick, the baseball bat, but it might, I thought, have been lurking somewhere nearby.

He seemed about to say something to me but I beat him to it. 'What the hell do you want?' I shouted at him.

He seemed a little taken aback and looked around to see if anyone else had heard me. Theobald's Road was a busy place at seven o'clock on a sunny May evening and a continuous stream of pedestrians flowed past the gated entrance. A few heads had turned as I'd shouted but no one had actually stopped.

'Didn't you hear me?' I shouted again. 'I asked you what the hell do you want.'

He was definitely unnerved by a reaction he hadn't been expecting.

'Did you get the message?' he said.

'Do you mean this?' I shouted at him pulling the envelope and the paper out of my trouser pocket and ripping them both into several pieces. By this time he was standing less than ten feet from me. I threw the bits of paper into the air and they fluttered to the ground at his feet. 'Now sod off,' I shouted at him.

'Stop shouting,' he said.

'Why should I?' I shouted even louder, the sound of my voice echoing back to me from the buildings all around us. 'What are you afraid of?'

'Shut up,' he said, hissing at me.

I stood my ground and raised one of the crutches as a potential weapon. 'I'll shut up,' I shouted at the top of my voice, 'when you go away and leave me in peace.'

He clenched and unclenched his right fist. Perhaps he was regretting not bringing his baseball bat with him after all.

'Do as you're told,' he said menacingly, again almost under his breath, as if being extra quiet might compensate for my extra noisiness.

'Why?' I shouted again at full volume. 'Who wants me to? Who are you working for, you little creep? Get out of my life, do you hear? And stay out.'

One or two heads out on Theobald's Road were turned

our way and one man stopped and stared at us. Julian Trent seemed to be losing his nerve.

'You'll regret this,' he said quietly through gritted teeth. 'You'll bloody regret this.'

And with that, he was gone, dodging out through the gateway, past the staring pedestrian, and off down Theobald's Road towards Clerkenwell. I stood there for a moment breathing deeply and wondered if I had made a big mistake. Perhaps, as Trent had said, I would regret it. But simply rolling over was not an option. I would not be dictated to, and my father and Eleanor would, like me, have to take their chances. To succumb to these threats in this case would simply invite more threats in the future. Both Josef Hughes and George Barnett had complied with the first demands and, in each case, the menace had returned for more.

I was aware that over the past few months I had become fairly ambivalent about the outcome of the Steve Mitchell trial. If he was convicted, then I would have nothing to fear from Julian Trent, or whoever was behind him. If he was acquitted then I could hold my head up for justice.

Now, suddenly, the result became incredibly important to me. If Mitchell was innocent, and I was sure that he must be, then I had to find a way to show it. And to do that, I had to find out who actually had committed the murder, and soon.

As things stood, I was pretty sure that he would be convicted simply because there was no credible indication to show that he didn't do it and the circumstantial evidence would be enough to sway the jury. True, there was none of Mitchell's DNA at the scene, but Barlow's blood and DNA had been found on Mitchell's boots and in his car, and that alone was very damning. If I were the prosecutor in the case, I would be highly confident of a guilty verdict. Even Sir James Horley QC, who was meant to be leading for the defence, seemed sure of the defendant's guilt and had even suggested to me that I go and see Mitchell in prison and encourage him to plead guilty. I had the distinct impression that, just this time, Sir James was going to be happy to let me conduct the case throughout. I suspected that he would find a good reason not to go to Oxford on the first day, and then he would use that as the excuse for not going at all. And that would suit me just fine.

But, short of resorting to the Trent method of intimidating the jury into returning a 'not guilty' verdict, I still couldn't see what I could do to get Mitchell off the charge.

What exactly was Julian Trent's connection with racing, and with a murdered jockey? Was the man who had been to see both Josef Hughes and George Barnett actually Julian Trent's father or was it somebody else? It was time to find out.

Eleanor was at the restaurant in Berkeley Square before me. She was seated on a stool at the bar facing away from me. I could see her back. I had been looking forward to this evening all day, so why did I now have cold feet? Why, all of a sudden, did I experience the urge to run away? Why did I feel so afraid? I had just faced up to Julian Trent, so why should I have any fears of Eleanor?

She turned round on the stool, saw me at the door, smiled and waved. I waved back. What, I asked myself, was I really afraid of here? It was a question I couldn't even begin to answer.

Over dinner, Eleanor and I discussed everything except ourselves, and specifically our relationship. I asked her about the equine symposium and she seemed to be surprised at how useful it was being.

'I've learned a lot,' she said over our starters. 'Some of the new treatments have potential for us in Lambourn, especially in the treatment of ligaments and tendons. There are some wonderful things being done with artificial replacements. Some horses that in the past would have been retired due to tendon trouble will soon be able to continue racing.'

'Bionic horses,' I said flippantly. 'The six-million-dollar horse.'

'No. Much much more than that,' she said, laughing. 'Peninsula was syndicated to stud for ten times that.'

'Wow,' I said. 'And to think he was foaled by a first-time vet.'

'Quite a responsibility,' she agreed. 'But, of course, they didn't know then how good he'd turn out to be.'

'I wish I had a copy of that photograph,' I said.

'The one of Millie with Peninsula as a foal?' Eleanor said.

'Yes,' I said. 'It was taken from Scot Barlow's house the day he was murdered.'

'You really think it's important?' she asked.

'I don't know,' I said. 'But the murderer must have thought it was important enough to remove from its frame and take away with him.'

'How do you know it was the murderer who took it?' she asked.

'I don't for sure,' I said. 'But whoever did take it also took care to wipe the frame clean. There were no finger-prints on it.'

'I remember that photograph so well,' Eleanor said. 'Millie showed it to everyone. She kept it on the mantel-piece in her room and she was always polishing the frame.'

'Describe it,' I said.

'It was just a photo,' she said. 'Millie was kneeling on the straw with the foal's head in her lap. The mare was standing behind them but you couldn't really see her properly. You could only see her hind quarters.'

'Wasn't there someone else in it as well?' I asked.

'There was the stud groom standing behind Millie. I think he was cleaning the mare after foaling, you know.'

I couldn't see how it was so important.

'And you don't know who took the picture?' I asked her.

'No idea,' she said.

'Wasn't Peninsula foaled at the Radcliffe place?' I said.

'They have lots of foals born there,' Eleanor said. 'They've made quite a business out of it. But we have less to do with them than we used to.'

'Why?' I asked.

'They've got so big that they now have a resident vet. They don't use the hospital practice any more unless one of their horses needs surgery.'

Our main courses arrived and we ate in silence for a few minutes.

'Tell me what the doctor told you,' Eleanor said between mouthfuls of sea bass.

'I've got to wear this damned body shell for another six weeks at least,' I said, 'and it's very uncomfortable.'

The restaurant had kindly given us a booth table and I was able to sit half sideways and lean back against the wall whenever it began to hurt too much.

'But at least that cast is off your leg,' she said.

'Thank goodness,' I said. I had been trying to bend my knee ever since the hospital circular saw had sliced through the last inch of the cast and set my leg free. So far I had only managed about twenty to thirty degrees, but that was a huge improvement over dead straight.

Main course finally gave way to coffee, with a Baileys on the rocks for her and a glass of port for me.

'I asked the surgeon when I could ride again,' I said, watching her face carefully to spot any reaction.

'And?'

'He said that my bones would be fully healed and as good as new in about three months, but he wasn't so sure about my brain.'

'What about your brain?' she asked.

'He said it couldn't take too many bangs like that.'

'Seems all right to me,' she said, smiling at me broadly with her mouth slightly open and all her perfect top teeth showing. The sparkle in her lovely blue eyes was there again, the same sparkle I had noticed at the equine hospital at our first meeting.

I sat opposite her and smiled back. But then suddenly I looked away, almost in embarrassment.

'Tell me about her,' she said.

'About who?' I asked. But I knew who she meant before she replied.

'Angela.'

'There's not much to tell really,' I said, trying to deflect her direct approach. 'Why do you want to know?'

She sat silently for a while, looking up at the ceiling as if making a decision. The jury was out deliberating.

Finally, she looked down again at my face and answered softly, 'I need to know what I'm up against.'

I looked down at the table and cupped my mouth and nose in my hands. I breathed out heavily once or twice, feeling the hot air on my skin. Eleanor just sat quietly, leaning forward slightly, with an expectant expression on her face.

'We met while I was doing the Bar Vocational Course, that's the course you study to become a barrister,' I said.

'Angela was a second-year student at King's reading clinical psychology. We were both guests at the same party and we just clicked. Right there and then.

'We got married six months after that first meeting, in spite of her parents' disapproval. They wanted her to wait until after she had finished her degree but we were so keen to marry straight away. There was a huge row and they never really forgave us. Silly really, but it seemed to matter so much to us back then. Now her mother blames me for her death.'

Eleanor reached forward across the table and took my hand.

'We were so blissfully happy together for five years. She wanted to have a baby as soon as we were married but I talked her into waiting until she had qualified, but then we discovered that having a child was not as straight-forward as we thought. We tried for ages without success, but a scan then showed that her tubes were blocked so we had to try for *in vitro*, you know, test-tube baby and all that. And that worked absolutely straight away. It was brilliant. And we were both so pleased that she was carrying a boy.'

I stopped. Tears welled in my eyes for Angela and our unborn son.

'She was eight months pregnant when she died.' I had to stop again and take a few deep breaths. Eleanor went on holding my hand and saying nothing.

'It was a pulmonary embolism,' I said. 'I found her lying on the floor. The doctors said it would have been very sudden.' I sighed loudly. 'That was more than seven years ago now. Sometimes it seems like yesterday.' I let go of Eleanor's hand and held the cotton table napkin up to my face. It was as much as I could do not to sob.

We sat there together in silence for what felt like ages until a waiter came over and asked us if we wanted some more coffee.

'Thanks,' I said, back in control. He poured the hot black liquid into our cups and then left us alone again.

'So,' said Eleanor with a sigh. 'Not much chance for me then.'

We laughed, a short embarrassed laugh.

'Give me some more time,' I said. But I'd had seven years. How much longer did I need?

'How much more time?' she said.

'I don't know,' I said in exasperation.

'But I need to,' she said in all seriousness. She stared at my face. 'I like you, Mister Barrister. I like you a lot. But I do need some response if I'm going to invest my time and my emotions. I'm thirty-three years old and, as they say, my body clock is ticking. I want . . .' She tailed off and dropped her eyes.

'What?' I said.

'You . . . I think,' she said, suddenly looking back up at my face. 'And a house and kids and . . . family life.' She paused and I waited patiently. 'When I started out as a vet, with all the years of training, I only cared about my job and my career. I loved it, and I still do. But now I find I need more than just that. I realize that I want what my parents had,' she said. 'Love, home and family.' She paused again for a moment and took my hand again in hers. 'And I think I want it with you.'

CHAPTER TWELVE

Eleanor went back to her hotel near Tower Bridge for the night and I took a taxi home to Barnes. It wasn't that we took a conscious decision to go in diametrically opposite directions, it was just sensible logistically. The equine symposium would start again for her at nine in the morning while, at the same time, I was due to be collected from my home by a car from a private hire company and taken to Bullingdon Prison to see my client. However, I now spent the whole journey home from the restaurant, along the Cromwell Road, past the V&A and Natural History museums, under the dark sloping walls of the London Ark and across Hammersmith Bridge, wondering whether I should ask the taxi driver to turn round and take me back to Eleanor at the Tower.

Then, quite suddenly and before I had made up my mind, we were outside my home at Ranelagh Avenue in Barnes. I clambered unsteadily out of the cab and paid off the driver, who gunned his engine and noisily departed, no doubt back to the West End to find another late-night passenger in need of a ride home.

I stood for a moment on my crutches and looked at the old Edwardian property with its two side-by-side front doors and I speculated about what it was that had kept me here these past seven years. Perhaps I really had been foolish enough to think that life would have somehow returned to the blissful time with Angela. Maybe I had been living too long with my head in the sand and now was the time to make a fresh start with someone different. But how could I dispel the feeling that doing so would somehow be disloyal to Angela's memory?

A car turned slowly into the far end of the avenue and all of a sudden I felt very vulnerable, standing alone on the poorly lit pavement at nearly midnight with no one else about, no one this time to come running to my rescue if I shouted. Even my downstairs neighbour's lights were out. And Julian Trent, or whoever had been into my house to take that photograph, knew exactly where I lived.

I hurried as best I could up the half a dozen outside steps to the front doors and fumbled with my keys and the crutches. The car's headlights moved little by little down the road towards me and then swept on past, round the bend and out of sight.

I breathed a huge sigh of relief, found the right key, and let myself in. I leaned up against the closed front door and found that I was trembling. I slid the bolt across behind me and carefully negotiated the stairs.

Why did I exist like this? I had asked myself that question umpteen times over the past weeks as I had struggled with the six steps up from the street to my front door and then the thirteen steps up from there to my sitting room. I had often not bothered with the twelve more to my bedroom, sleeping, instead, stretched out on the sofa. I had no garden, no terrace, no deck, not even a balcony. Just a view of Barnes Common, and even that was obscured in the summer months from all but the topmost bedroom windows by the leaves on the trees.

I had stayed here for the memories but maybe it was time now to make more memories elsewhere. Time to shake off this half-life existence. Time to live my life again to the full.

Steve Mitchell was a shell of his former self. As a jockey, he was well used to existing on meagre rations, and prison food was not exactly appealing to the discerning palate. But it was not the lack of food that had made the greatest difference to Steve, it was the lack of his daily diet of riding up to six races with the muscle toning and stamina which comes from regular exercise as a professional sportsman. He looked pale, thin and unfit, because he was, but he seemed to be coping fairly well mentally, considering the circumstances. Steeplechase jockeys had to be strong in mind as well as in body, to cope with the inevitable injuries that came with the job.

'What news?' he said, sitting down opposite me at the grey table in the grey interview room.

'Not much, I'm afraid,' I said.

He looked at the crutches lying on the floor beside me. This was the first visit I had been able to make to see him since my fall at Cheltenham.

'Sandeman?' he asked.

'Yes,' I said.

'Read about it in the paper,' he said. 'Knees are a bugger.'

'Yes,' I agreed.

'Also read about that bastard Clemens winning the Gold Cup on my bloody horse,' he said. The 'bastard' tag, I noticed, had now been moved from Scot Barlow to Reno Clemens. 'It's bloody unfair.'

Yes, it was, but, as my mother had told me as a child, life is unfair.

'But you did meet with Sir James Horley?' I said it as a question. 'When I couldn't make it last time.'

'Bit of a cold fish, if you ask me,' said Steve. 'Didn't like him much. He kept talking to me as if I'd done it. Even asked me to examine my conscience. I told him to bloody sod off, I can tell you.'

I knew. I had heard about it at length from Sir James on his return from Bullingdon to Gray's Inn. As a rule Sir James didn't much care for visiting his clients on remand, and this time had been no exception. He preferred that to be a job for his junior, but I had been rather incapacitated and he'd had no alternative but to go himself. The interview had clearly not gone well. Mitchell may not have liked his lead counsel very much but that was nothing compared to the utter disdain in which Sir James now held his client. Not for the first time I thought that Sir James would be rather pleased to lose this case.

'Can't you act without that silly old buffer?' he said.

'He is a very experienced Queen's Counsel,' I replied.

'I don't care if he's the Queen herself in drag,' he said, 'I would much rather have you defending me in court.'

'Steve,' I said seriously. 'I'm not altogether sure it would make much difference who defended you in court at the moment.' I paused while my underlying meaning sank in.

'I didn't do it,' he said finally. 'I tell you. I didn't bloody do it. Why will no one believe me?'

'I believe you,' I said. 'But we need something to make the jury believe you, and there's nothing. The evidence is quite compelling. There's the blood in your car and on your boots, and the fact that the pitchfork was also yours doesn't help. And everyone knows you hated Barlow. Those betting receipts and your lack of any sort of alibi are going to hold considerable sway with the jury.'

'There must be something you can do,' he said rather forlornly.

'I haven't given up hope yet,' I said, trying to sound more optimistic than I felt. 'The evidence is either circumstantial or can be explained away. When the prosecution finish presenting their case, I will make a submission to the judge that you have no case to answer. But I think it's unlikely that he or she will agree and, with nothing new turning up, I fear that things may not go well.'

'So what's the down side?' he said.

'In what way?' I said.

'How long if I get convicted?'

'How long a sentence?' I asked.

'No,' he said, irritated. 'How long until I get an appeal? Until something comes up to show I didn't do it.'

'There's no guarantee you would get an appeal,' I said. 'It would have to be either because there is a question of law, say a ruling or the summing up by the trial judge was considered questionable or biased, or if new evidence has appeared in the case. Either way it would be quite some time. Appeals against short sentences are heard more quickly than those for longer ones. It's not much good waiting two years for an appeal against a three-year sentence, you'd already be out. But life . . .'

'Life?' Steve said loudly, interrupting me.

'Murder carries a life sentence,' I said. 'Mandatory. But life doesn't actually mean life in most cases.'

'Oh God,' he said resting his forehead on his hand. 'I'll go bloody mad if I have to stay in here much longer.'

The private hire silver Mercedes was waiting for me outside the prison and it pulled up to the main gate when I appeared. Bob, the driver, stepped out to hold the door for me as I clambered awkwardly into the back seat. Then he carefully placed the crutches in the boot. I could get quite used to this, I thought.

'Back to London, sir?' Bob asked.

'Not yet,' I said, and I gave him directions to our next stop.

Sandeman was eating from his manger when I went in to see him. He looked casually in my direction, blew hard down his nostrils and then went back to concentrating on his oats. I hobbled over to him and slapped him down his neck with the palm of my hand while feeding him an apple from my pocket.

'Hello, old boy,' I said to him as I fondled his ears and rubbed his neck. He put his head down against me and pushed me playfully.

'Whoa,' I said amused. 'Careful, my old boy, I'm not yet able to play.' I slapped him again a couple of times and left him in peace.

'He's doing well,' said Paul Newington at the door, from where he'd watched the exchange. 'We've started walking him around the village every morning, and he has even trotted a bit round the paddock on a lunge. Still too early to put any weight on that back, of course, but he doesn't seem to be in any pain.'

'Good,' I said. 'He looks well.'

'Plenty of time for Kit to brush his coat.' Kit was the stable lad that 'did' for Sandeman.

'Will he ever be able to race again?' I asked Paul. I had asked him that several times before on the telephone and he'd always been rather noncommittal in his answer.

'I suspect he could,' he said. 'But he's thirteen now and he would quite likely not be fit enough to run before he becomes fourteen.' All horses in the northern hemisphere became a year older on 1 January, irrespective of the actual day on which they were born. In the south the date was, for some reason I had never worked out, not 1 July as one would expect, but a month later on 1 August.

'Are you saying he'd be too old?' I asked.

'Racehorses can race at that age,' he said. 'I looked it up on the internet. The oldest ever winner was eighteen, but that was over two hundred years ago.'

We stood there leaning on the lower half of the stable door, looking at my dear old horse.

'I'm not saying he couldn't get back to fitness,' Paul went on. 'I'm just not sure it would be cost effective, or even if it's fair on the old boy.'

'You think it's time to retire him?' I was miserable. Retiring Sandeman from the racecourse would be tantamount to retiring myself from race riding. I knew that I was too old to start again with a new horse.

'I do,' he said bluntly. 'And I do realize that it would quite likely mean that you wouldn't have a horse with me again.'

'But what would we do with him?' I asked forlornly.

'Now don't take this the wrong way,' he said, 'but I am in need of a new hack. And that's not, I promise, the reason I think you should retire Sandeman.'

'I know that,' I said. 'But what about old Debenture?'

Debenture had been Paul's hack for almost as long as

I could remember and Paul rode him up to the gallops every morning to watch his horses work.

'He's too old now,' said Paul. 'It's time to put him out to grass. Every time I've got on him recently I've feared he's about to collapse under me.'

'So you'd replace him with Sandeman?' I asked.

'I would like to, if Sandeman recovers sufficiently,' he said. 'And I think he probably will, if his progress so far is anything to go by.'

'Well, I suppose that would be fine by me,' I said. 'But can he go on living in this stable?'

'Geoffrey, you are far too sentimental,' he said, laughing. 'No way. He'll have to live in the dog kennel.' He laughed loudly, mostly at my expense. 'Of course he can stay here and Kit will continue to look after him.'

'Can I still ride him?' I asked.

'Geoffrey,' he said laying a hand on my shoulder. 'You don't want to ride him as a hack. I would simply walk him through the village at the head of the string and then I'd sit on him as I watched the other horses, before he walked back here. If you really want to ride out, you can ride one of the others.'

'Do you mean that?' I asked, surprised.

'Of course I do,' he said. 'And I won't even make you pay training fees for the privilege. Come any time you like, as long as you stay reasonably fit, and light. I won't let you if you go over twelve stone.'

'I have absolutely no intention of doing that,' I said.

'That's what all those fat ex-jockeys said.' He laughed.

Sandeman finished his lunch and came over to the stable door for another apple from my pocket. I rubbed his ears and massaged his neck. If only he could talk, I thought yet again, he could tell me what he wanted.

'Well, old boy,' I said to him. 'Seems like you and I have run our last race. Welcome to old age.'

'We'll look after him,' said Paul, stroking Sandeman's nose.

I didn't doubt it, but somehow this felt like a defining moment in my life. Gone, abruptly and unexpectedly, were the days of excitement and adrenalin that I had coveted for so long. My racing days had been what I had lived for. When one was past, I spent my time working but with half an eye on the calendar to show me when I was next due to weigh out and hear the familiar call for 'jockeys'. But suddenly, this minute, I was no longer an injured jockey on the road to recovery and my next ride. I had become, here and now, an ex-jockey, and I was very aware of having lost something. There was an emptiness in me as if a part of my soul had been surgically excised.

'Are you OK?' said Paul, as if he, too, was aware of the significance of the moment.

'Fine,' I said to him with a smile. But I wasn't really fine. Inside I was hurting.

'You'll just have to get a new hobby,' Paul said.

But riding races had never felt like a hobby to me. It

had been what I had lived for, especially these past seven years. It really was time to get a new life, and now I didn't have any choice in the matter.

I stayed for a leisurely lunch with Paul and Laura and then Bob drove me further west to Uffington and the Radcliffe Foaling Centre. I had called ahead and spoken to the manager, Larry Clayton, who seemed bored with his job and quite keen to show a visitor around the place.

The tyres of the Mercedes crunched over the gravel as we drove slowly up the driveway and pulled up in front of a new looking red-brick single-storey building to the side of the main house. 'Visitors Report Here' ordered a smartly painted notice stuck into the grass verge. So I did.

'It's very quiet at this time of the year,' said Larry Clayton as we sat in his office. 'Most of the mares and foals are gone by now.'

'Where to?' I asked.

'Back to their owners for the summer, most of them,' he said. 'Some have gone to Ireland. A few of the mares have gone back into training. I don't really know.' And it sounded like he didn't really care.

'So when's your busy time?' I asked.

'January to April,' he said. 'That's when most of them are born. Absolutely crazy here in February and March. Foals dropping every five minutes.'

'How many?' I asked.

'Too many,' he said with a wry smile. 'About a hundred, and they want to double that next year.'

'Is that more than in the past?' I said.

'Dunno,' he said putting his feet up on his desk. 'My first year here. But I think it must be. The Radcliffes built more foaling boxes last summer, and these offices. I think it was pretty small fry before then.'

I looked at his feet on the desk. He was wearing badly scuffed cowboy boots under tight blue jeans with a check-pattern open-necked shirt. I wondered if the Radcliffes knew that their manager was so casual with their guests. I had picked up some of their marketing material stacked upright in a rack in the reception area on my way in. It was a well produced large glossy brochure with plenty of impressive facts and figures about the equine care provided for the expectant mothers, and a smiling picture on the front of Roger and Deborah Radcliffe standing together next to some mares and foals in a paddock.

'Are they at home?' I asked Larry, indicating the picture. 'I didn't get an answer on their home phone when I called them yesterday.'

'Nope,' he said. 'They are in Kentucky for the sales and the Derby. Not back until next week.'

'Can I have a look round?' I asked.

'Sure,' he said, lifting both his feet together off the desk. 'Not much to see.'

We walked around the new complex of foaling boxes and other stalls, each angle covered by a closed-circuit television camera.

'How many staff do you have?' I asked.

'About a dozen in the high season but only a couple now,' he said. 'We have an onsite delivery team who are on constant standby when we're foaling. But they've gone now. We only have a few horses here at the moment and they mostly belong to the Radcliffes. Two of them are mares that dropped in early March and their foals will be fully weaned by the end of July, ready for the sales.'

We walked past the rows of deserted stables and looked into the new foaling boxes. They had hard concrete floors devoid of the soft cushion of straw that would be laid down for the arrival of a new foal, possibly a new superstar like Peninsula.

'Where was Peninsula foaled?' I asked.

'No idea,' he said. 'Here somewhere. But lots has changed.'

'Do you know if the stud groom still works here?' I asked. 'The one who helped with Peninsula.'

'No idea,' he said again. 'Do you know who it was? Stud grooms come and go round here like wet Sundays.'

'Have you ever heard of anyone called Julian Trent?' I asked him.

'Nope,' he said. 'Should I?'

I decided that it really hadn't been a very helpful excursion. In fact, the whole day had been rather disappointing so far from start to finish. I could only hope that it would get better.

*

Bob dropped me back at Ranelagh Avenue around quarter to eight and, in spite of the bright spring evening light, I asked him to wait while I made it up the steps to the front door and then safely inside it.

But he had driven away before I realized that there was something very wrong. I was about half-way up the stairs when I first heard the sound of running water where there shouldn't have been.

It was running through the light fitting in the ceiling of my sitting room onto the floor below. It wasn't just a trickle, more of a torrent. And that wasn't the only problem. My home had been well and truly trashed.

I made my way as quickly as possible up to the top floor to turn off the water only to discover that doing so was not going to be that easy. The washbasin in the second bathroom had been torn completely away from its fittings and the water was jetting out of a hole in the wall left by a broken pipe. The stream was adding to the inch depth that already existed on the bathroom floor and which was spreading across the landing and down the top few steps like a waterfall.

Where, I wondered, was the stop cock?

I carefully descended the wet stairs again and used the telephone to call my downstairs neighbours to ask for help. There was no answer. There wouldn't be. It was Wednesday and they were always out late on Wednesdays, organizing a badminton evening class at the school where they both taught. I had become quite acquainted with their routine since I had needed to call on their assistance over the past six weeks. They would have stayed on at the school after lessons and would usually be back by nine, unless they stopped for some dinner on the way home, in which case it would be ten or even half past. By then, I thought, their lower floor, set as it was below ground level, might be more akin to an indoor swimming pool than a kitchen.

I sat on the torn arm of my sofa and looked about me. Everything that could have been broken had been. My brand-new expensive large flat-screen plasma television would show no pictures ever again. Angela's collection of Royal Worcester figurines was no more, and the kitchen floor was littered deep with broken crockery and glass.

I looked at the phone in my hand. At least that was working, so I used it to dial 999 and I asked the emergency operator for the police.

They promised to try and send someone as soon as possible but it didn't sound to me like it was an urgent case in their eyes. No one was hurt or imminently dying, they said, so I would have to wait. So I thumbed through a sopping copy of Yellow Pages to find an emergency plumbing service and promised them a big bonus to get here as soon as humanly possible. I was still speaking to them when the ceiling around the light fitting, which had been bulging alarmingly, decided to give up the struggle and collapsed with a crash. A huge mass of water suddenly fell into the centre of my sitting room and spread out towards my open-plan kitchen area like a mini tidal wave.

I lifted my feet as it passed me by. The plumbing company promised that someone was already on the way.

I hobbled around my house inspecting the damage. There was almost nothing left that was usable. Everything had been broken or sliced through with what must have been a box cutter or a Stanley knife. My leather sofa would surely be unrepairable with so many cuts through the hide, all of which showed white from the stuffing beneath. A mirror that had hung this morning on my sitting-room wall now lay smashed amongst the remains of a glass-and-brass coffee table, and an original oil painting of a coastal landscape by a successful artist friend was impaled over the back of a dining chair.

Upstairs in my bedroom the mattress had also received the box-cutter treatment and so had most of the clothes hanging in my wardrobe. This had been a prolonged and determined assault on my belongings of which almost nothing had survived. Worst of all was that the perpetrator, and I had little doubt as to who was responsible, had smashed the glass and twisted to destruction the silver frame that had stood on the dressing table, and had then torn the photograph of Angela into dozens of tiny pieces.

I stood there looking at these confetti remains and felt not grief for my dead wife, but raging anger that her image had been so violated.

The telephone rang. How was it, I wondered, that he hadn't broken that too?

I found out. 'I told you that you'd regret it,' Julian Trent said down the wire, his voice full of menace.

'Fuck off, you little creep,' I said and I slammed down the receiver.

The phone rang again almost immediately and I snatched it up.

'I said to fuck off,' I shouted into the mouthpiece.

There was a pause. 'Geoffrey, is that you?' Eleanor sounded hesitant.

'Oh God. I'm so sorry,' I said. 'I thought you were someone else.'

'I should hope so,' she said with slight admonishment. 'I called because I have some good news for you.'

I could do with some.

'I've found a copy of the photo of Millie with the foal.'

CHAPTER THIRTEEN

It took the emergency plumbers forty-five minutes to arrive at Ranelagh Avenue, by which time not only had the ceiling in my sitting room collapsed but also two ceilings below. I know because I heard about it at full volume from my neighbours when they arrived home at five past nine. It was a shame, I thought, that they had decided not to eat out. They wouldn't be able to produce much of a dinner in the flood. Only when they came upstairs and saw the state of my place did they understand that it hadn't been a simple thing like leaving a tap running or overflowing a bath.

The police showed up at least an hour after the plumbers had successfully capped off the broken pipe and departed. Two uniformed officers arrived in a patrol car and wandered through the mess, shaking their heads and denigrating the youth of today under their breath.

'Do you have any idea who may have done this?' they asked me.

I shook my head. Somehow not actually speaking seemed to reduce the lie. Why didn't I just tell them that

I knew exactly who had done it. It had been Julian Trent and I could probably find his address, or, at least, that of his parents.

But I also knew that Julian Trent was far from stupid, and that he would not have been careless enough to have left any fingerprints or other incriminating evidence in my house, and that he would have half of London lined up to swear that he was nowhere near Barnes at any time during this day. If he could get himself off an attempted murder rap, I had no doubts that he would easily escape a charge of malicious damage to property. To have told the police the truth would simply have given him an additional reason to come back for another dose of destruction – of me, of my father, or, as I feared most, of Eleanor.

The police spent some time going all round my house both outside and in.

'Whoever did this probably got in through that window,' one of the policemen said, pointing at the now-broken glass in my utility room. 'He must have climbed the drainpipe.'

I had changed the locks and bolstered my security on the front door after the time I'd had an unwanted guest with his camera. I now wished I had put in an alarm as well.

'Is there anything missing?' asked one of the policemen finally.

'I have no idea,' I said. 'It doesn't seem so. It's just all broken or slashed.'

'Mmm,' said the policeman. 'Mindless vandalism.

Happens all the time, sadly. You should be grateful that the whole place isn't also smeared with shit.'

'Oh thanks,' I said rather sarcastically. But Julian Trent wouldn't have done that for fear of leaving some speck of his own DNA along with it. 'So what happens now?' I asked them.

'If nothing's been stolen then CID won't really be interested,' he sounded bored himself. 'If you call Richmond police station in the morning they will give you a crime number. You'll need that for your insurers.'

That's why I had called them in the first place.

And with that, they left. No photos, no tests, no search for fingerprints, nothing. As they said, no one was hurt and nothing had been stolen, and the insurance would deal with the rest. End of their problem. They had no hope or expectation of ever catching the person responsible, and, to be fair, I hadn't exactly been very helpful with their inquiries.

I sat on a chrome kitchen stool and surveyed my ruined castle.

Surprisingly the electrical system seemed to have suffered no ill effects from the cascade of water through the sitting-room light fitting. I had quite expected there to be a blue flash followed by darkness when I chanced turning on the switch, but instead I was rewarded with two bulbs coming on brightly. The remaining bulbs, those in the wall brackets, had received the baseball bat treatment. At least, I assumed that Trent had been accompanied by his weapon of choice. The damage to some of the fittings was too much to have been the result of only a kick or a punch. Even the marble worktops in the kitchen were now cracked right through. Young Julian clearly had considerable prowess in the swing of his bat.

Eleanor arrived at just before ten. She had been so distressed to hear me on the telephone describing the shambles that was now my home that she had driven up from Lambourn as soon as she could. She had only been back there an hour, having caught the train from London to Newbury at the end of the veterinary symposium.

I hobbled down the stairs to the front door to let her in and we stood in the hallway and hugged. I kissed her briefly with closed lips. It was a start.

She was absolutely horrified at the damage and I was pleased that she cared. For me, over the past couple of hours since I had first discovered it, I had grown somehow accustomed to the mess, anaesthetized by its familiarity. Seen through a fresh pair of eyes, the true scale of the devastation was indeed shocking.

It wasn't that I didn't care about my stuff – I cared a lot. It was just that the loss of everything fitted in quite well with the feeling I had of moving on, of starting again. Perhaps it might even make things easier.

'Have you called the police?' she asked.

'They've just left,' I said. 'They didn't hold out much hope of catching whoever did this.'

'But Geoffrey,' she said seriously. 'This isn't some random attack by an opportunistic vandal. This was targeted directly at you personally.' She paused and fingered a tear in my sofa. 'You must have some idea who did this.'

I said nothing. It was answer enough.

'Tell me,' she said.

We sat amid the wreckage of my home for two hours while I told her what I knew about Julian Trent and his apparent connection with the murder of Scot Barlow. I told her how I shouldn't be acting in this case and how I had withheld information from the police and from my colleagues. I told her about Josef Hughes and George Barnett. And I told her about seeing Trent standing behind her at Cheltenham races before the Fox-hunter Chase. I showed her the photograph I had received in the white envelope showing her walking down the path near the hospital in Lambourn. I had kept it in the pocket of the jacket I'd been wearing, and it had consequently survived the demolition.

She held the photograph in slightly shaking hands and went quite pale.

I dug around in the kitchen and finally found a pair of unbroken plastic mugs and a bottle of mineral water from the fridge.

'I'd rather have some wine,' Eleanor said.

My designer chrome wine rack, along with its dozen bottles of expensive claret that a client had given me as a gift for getting him off a drink-driving charge of which he had really been guilty, lay smashed and mangled, a red stain spreading inexorably across the mushroom-coloured rug that lay in my hallway.

I went back to the fridge and discovered an unbroken bottle of champagne nestling in a door rack. So we sat on my ruined sofa next to the damp ceiling plaster and amongst the other carnage, and drank vintage Veuve Clicquot out of plastic mugs. How romantic was that?

'But why didn't you tell me about this photo sooner?' she asked accusingly. 'I might have been in danger.'

'I don't believe you are in real danger as long as Trent, or whoever is behind him, still thinks I will do as they say. It's the threat of danger that's their hold.'

'So what are you going to do about it?' Eleanor asked. 'How can you defeat this Trent man? Surely you have to go to the police and tell them.'

'I don't know,' I said inadequately.

'Darling,' she said, using the term for the first time, and raising my eyebrows. 'You absolutely have to go to the authorities and explain everything to them. Let them deal with the little horror.'

'It really isn't that simple,' I said to her. 'In an ideal world, then yes, that would be the best route, but we don't live in an ideal world. For a start, doing that might cost me my career.'

'Surely not,' she said.

'Oh yes,' I said. 'I have been very economical with the truth in a business where it is the truth, the whole truth and nothing but. In fact I have told outright lies to the police, and the law is pretty unforgiving of lies. I may have even been guilty of holding the court in contempt. I have certainly misled the court and that is the most heinous of crimes for a barrister. That alone is enough to get disbarred.'

'But you have a good reason,' she said.

'Yes, indeed I have,' I said. 'I was scared. And I still am. When I saw Trent outside my chambers yesterday I was so scared I nearly wet myself. But all that will have little bearing for the court. I know. I have dealt with intimidation in some form or other almost every week of my working life and, until recently, I was like every other lawyer who would tell their client not to be such a wimp and to tell the truth no matter what the consequences. The courts are not very forgiving of those who fail to tell the truth, even if they are frightened out of their wits. I've seen witnesses sent to prison for the night because they refuse to tell the judge something they know but are too afraid to say. People don't understand until it happens to them. And it's happening to me now. Look around you. Do you think I wanted this to happen?'

I was almost in tears. And they were tears of frustration.

'So what are you going to do?' she asked finally.

'I am going to defeat him by getting Steve Mitchell acquitted,' I said. 'The only problem is that I'm not quite sure how I'm going to manage it.'

'But then what?' she said. 'He won't just go away.'

'I'll cross that bridge when I get to it,' I said with a laugh. But it wasn't really a laughing matter.

'But won't that get you even deeper into trouble?' she said.

'Maybe,' I said. 'But at least if Mitchell gets convicted he would then have grounds for an appeal. And I'm sure he didn't murder anyone.'

'Does the picture of Millie help?' she asked.

'It might,' I said. 'Where is it?'

'Here,' she said, pulling out a digital camera from her handbag. 'It's not that good. That photo frame was in the background of some pictures I took in Millie's room when we had a drinks party there for her birthday. I thought about it during a boring lecture this morning after what you said last night. I checked when I got home and there it was.' She smiled in triumph.

She turned on the camera and scrolled through the pictures until she arrived at one of three girls standing with glasses in their hands in front of a mantelpiece. And there between the heads of two of them could be clearly seen the frame and the missing photo. Eleanor zoomed in on the image.

'Amazing things, these cameras,' she said. 'Over eight million pixels, whatever that means.'

It meant that she could zoom right in and fill the whole screen with the picture of Millie Barlow with Peninsula's head in her lap with the mare standing behind with the stud groom. At such a magnification it was a little blurred but it was just as Eleanor had described it.

'Well?' she said as I studied the image.

'I don't know,' I said. 'It surely has to be important, otherwise why was it stolen from Barlow's house? But I just can't see why. It must be something to do with the stud groom, but I don't recognize him. You can see his face quite clearly in spite of the blurring, but I'm certain I've never seen him before. It's not Julian Trent, that's for sure.' Somehow I had suspected that it might have been.

Eleanor spent her second night in my house and, this time, she didn't sleep in the room with the teddy bears' picnic wallpaper. She slept alone in my bed, or what was left of it, while I dozed fully clothed on the torn-up sofa downstairs with my crutches close to hand. Neither of us felt that it had been the right circumstance to make any further moves towards each other and I was still worried that, with a broken window in the utility room, my castle was far from secure.

I woke early with the daylight, and what it revealed was no better than it had been the night before.

Julian Trent had been vindictive in his approach to the destruction and had even cut up my passport. It wasn't that I couldn't replace what he had destroyed, but he had made my life so much more complicated and annoying. Where did one start to get rid of all this mess?

I looked in the drawers of my desk for my insurance policy. Clearly not all the wine was soaking into the rug.

Trent had saved a couple of bottles to pour into my paperwork, which was now red and still dripping.

Eleanor padded down the stairs wearing my dressing gown.

'Careful,' I said, looking at her bare feet. 'There's broken glass all over the floor.'

She stopped on the bottom stair and looked around. 'Must have been quite a party,' she said with a smile.

'The best,' I said, smiling back.

She retreated back to my bedroom and soon re-appeared, dressed and with her shoes on. I was a little disappointed at the transformation from my dressing gown.

'I'd better be going,' she said, more serious now. 'It's well gone six and I need to be at work at eight. Will you be all right?'

'I'll be fine,' I said. 'I have a car picking me up at eight.'

'You'd better have this,' she said, handing me her camera.

'Right,' I said. 'Thanks. I may use it to take some shots of this lot for the insurance company.'

'Good idea,' she said, standing still in the middle of the hallway.

It was as if she didn't really want to go.

'What are you doing tonight?' I asked.

'I'm on call,' she said miserably. 'I have to stay in Lambourn.'

'Then can I come down there and return your camera to you this evening?' I asked.

'Oh, yes please,' she said with a wide grin.

'Right, I will. Now get going or you'll be late for your patients.'

She skipped down the stairs, and I waved at her from the kitchen window as she drove away, her right arm gesticulating wildly out of the driver's window until she disappeared round the corner at the top of the road.

I used the rest of the free memory in Eleanor's camera to take shots of every aspect of Julian Trent's handiwork, right down to the way he had poured all the contents from the packets in my kitchen cupboards into the sink, which was now blocked. I didn't know what good the photos would be but it took up the time while I waited for the car.

I found a clean shirt lurking in the tumble drier that young Mr Trent had missed with his knife and, even though there was no water in the bathrooms with which to shower or wash, I had managed to shave with an unbroken electric razor and I felt quite respectable as I hobbled down the steps and into Bob's waiting Mercedes at eight o'clock sharp.

I had brought my mobile phone and the Yellow Pages into the car and, while Bob drove, I set to work finding someone to fix the utility-room window.

'Don't worry about the mess,' I said to the first glazier I called, who finally agreed to do the job for a fat fee.

'Just go through the kitchen to the utility room and fix the window.'

'How shall I get in?' he asked. 'Is there someone there?'

'I left the front door open,' I said. After all, there wasn't much left to steal. 'The keys are on the stairs. Lock the door when you are finished and put the keys back through the letter box. I've got another set.'

'Fine,' he said. 'Will do.'

Next I called my insurance company and asked them to send me a claim form. They might want to come and have a look, they said. Be my guest, I replied, and I fixed for them to come on the following afternoon at five o'clock. They could get a key from my downstairs neighbours, who would be back from their school by then.

Bob took me first to chambers, where he went in to collect my mail while I half sat and half lay on the back seat of the car. Bob reappeared with a bundle of papers which he passed in to me through the window. And he also had Arthur in tow.

'Mr Mason,' said Arthur through the window, formal as always.

'Morning, Arthur,' I said. 'What's the problem?'

'Sir James is very keen to see you,' he said. I bet I knew why. 'He needs to speak to you about Monday.' Monday was the first day of Steve Mitchell's trial in Oxford.

'What about Monday?' I said. I, too, could play this little game.

'He thinks it may be impossible for him to attend on Monday as the case he is on at the moment is over-running.'

What a surprise, I thought. I bet it's overrunning because Sir James keeps asking for delays.

'Tell Sir James that I will be fine on my own on Monday,' I said. 'Ask him to call me over the weekend on my mobile if he wants me to request an adjournment for a day.' I wouldn't hold my breath for the call, I thought.

'Right,' said Arthur. 'I will.'

Both he and I were plainly aware of what was going on, but protocol and good manners had won the day. So I refrained from asking Arthur to also inform Sir James that he was a stupid old codger and a fraud, and it was well past the time he should have hung up his silk gown and wig for good.

Next, Bob drove me just round the corner to Euston Road, to the offices of the General Medical Council, where I spent most of the day sitting around waiting and very little time standing on my right foot, leaning on my crutches, arguing my client's case against a charge of professional misconduct in front of the GMC Fitness to Practise Panel. Each of the three accused doctors had a different barrister and the GMC had a whole team of them. It made for a very crowded hearing and also a very slow one. By the time we had all finished our representations and each of the witnesses had been examined and cross-examined, there was no time left in the day for any judgments and the proceedings were adjourned until the following morning, which was a real pain for me as I wanted to be in Lambourn.

I tut-tutted to my client and told him, most unprofessionally, that it would mean much greater expense, another day's fees. He almost fell over himself to ask the chairman of the panel if I would be required on the following day. He seemed greatly relieved when the chairman informed him that it was up to the accused to decide if and when they had professional representation, and not the members of the GMC. I was consequently rapidly released by my client. My fellow barristers looked at me with incredulity and annoyance. Two days' fees may have been better for them than just one but, there again, they hadn't planned to go and see Eleanor tonight.

I called Arthur on my mobile and asked him to arrange for all my boxes, papers, files, gown, wig, and so on for the Mitchell trial, to be sent direct to my hotel in Oxford, where I would be spending the weekend in preparation for Monday. No problem, he said. Sending boxes of papers by courier all over the country for court hearings was normal practice.

Bob was waiting for me in the Mercedes outside the GMC offices.

'Back to Barnes?' he asked.

'No, Bob,' I said. 'Could you take me to Lambourn?'

'Be delighted to,' he said with a big smile. Bob was being paid by the mile. 'Round trip or one way?' he asked.

'One way for tonight, I think,' I said. 'I need to make

a call or two. And, Bob, can we find a photo shop that's still open, one where you can stop outside to drop me off?'

He found one in Victoria Street and I spent about half an hour at a self-service digital photo machine printing out the pictures I had taken that morning with Eleanor's camera. I also printed out ten six-by-four-inch copies of the blown-up image of the Millie and foal picture. They weren't perfect, and looked a little more blurred than on the camera, but they would have to do.

Eleanor was delighted when I called her to say I was still coming to Lambourn, but she seemed a little hesitant when I told her that I had nowhere yet to stay.

'Oh,' she said. 'I suppose . . .'

'I'll find a pub or a hotel,' I said, interrupting her.

'Oh, right,' she said, sounding relieved. 'It's just we have the house rule . . .' she tailed off.

'It's all right,' I said. 'I hadn't expected to stay with you anyway.'

From the house-rule point of view, I was clearly still seen as a casual rather than a long-term relationship. And I suppose that was fair, I thought. Eleanor and I had hardly kissed, so staying the night with her would have been a huge step.

I phoned ahead to the Queen's Arms Hotel in East Garston, the pub where Eleanor and I had met for our first drink and meal back in the previous November.

'Yes,' they said. 'We have rooms available for tonight. For how many people?'

'For one,' I said. 'But I would like a double-bedded room please.' Well, you never knew.

Bob took me straight to the hotel, where the receptionist was surprised that I had no luggage, not even a wash bag. It was too complicated to explain, so I didn't. She kindly allocated me a room on the ground floor in a modern extension alongside the eighteenth-century inn, and I went and lay down on the bed to rest my aching back and to wait for Eleanor to arrive to look after me.

We had dinner at the same table as before but, on this occasion, our evening was interrupted by an emergency call on her pager.

'I just don't believe it,' said Eleanor, disconnecting from her mobile phone. 'No one who's been on call this week has been needed and now this.' She took another mouthful of her fish. 'I'll try and come back.' She stood up.

'Do you want me to save your dinner?' I said.

'No, I'll be longer than that,' she said. 'I'll call you.'

She rushed off to her car and left me sitting alone. I was disappointed. And, for the first time, I realized that I didn't feel guilty about being out with someone other than Angela.

I finished my dinner alone, drank my wine alone and, in time, went along the corridor to my bed, alone.

Eleanor did call eventually, at five to midnight.

'I'm so sorry,' she said. 'A two-year-old with a bad haemorrhage in its lung. Still a bit touch and go. I'll have to stay here. Also it's a bit late for dessert and coffee.' She laughed nervously at her own little joke.

'I'm in bed anyway,' I said. 'It's fine. I'll call you in the morning.'

'Right.' Did she sound relieved? Or was it my imagination? 'Goodnight.'

'Night,' I replied, and disconnected.

Life and love were very complicated, I reflected, as I drifted off to sleep.

CHAPTER FOURTEEN

On Friday morning I went shopping in Newbury. A taxi picked me up from the hotel and I spent a couple of hours buying myself, maybe not a complete new wardrobe, but enough to see me through the next few weeks at Oxford Crown Court.

The hotel receptionist raised a questioning eyebrow when I arrived back at the Queen's Arms with two suitcases of luggage that I hadn't had the previous night.

'Lost by the airline,' I said to her, and she nodded knowingly.

She carried the cases to my room as I struggled along behind her with the damn crutches.

'Are you staying tonight, then?' she asked.

'I'm not sure yet,' I said. 'Someone told me at breakfast that late check-out would be OK.' For a fee, of course.

'Oh yes, that's fine,' she said. 'The room is free tonight if you want it.' I presumed she didn't mean free as in money, but free as in unoccupied.

'Thank you,' I said. 'I'll let you know.' And I closed the door.

I eased myself out of the white plastic shell and chanced standing in the shower without it, letting a stream of cool water wash away the grime and bring relief to my itching body. I washed my hair with new shampoo, brushed my teeth with a new toothbrush, and shaved my chin with a new razor. I then reluctantly put myself back in the plastic straightjacket before dressing in crisp clean new shirt and trousers. I suddenly felt so much better. Almost a new man, in fact.

The taxi returned after lunch and took me to Uffington, back to the Radcliffes' place. I had called Larry Clayton to say I was coming and he was sitting in his office when I arrived about two thirty, the same scuffed cowboy boots resting on his desk. It had been only two days since I had been here, but somehow it seemed longer.

'How can I help?' he said, not getting up.

I handed him a copy of the Millie and foal photo.

'Do you recognize anyone in this picture?' I asked him.

He studied it quite closely. 'Nope,' he said finally.

'The foal is Peninsula,' I said.

He looked again at the picture.

'Sorry,' he said. 'Still can't help you.'

'When did you say you arrived here?' I asked him.

'Last September,' he said.

'Where were you before?' I said.

'Up in Cheshire,' he said. 'I managed a meat-packing plant in Runcorn.'

'Bit different from this,' I said. 'How did you get this job?'

'I applied,' he said. 'Why, what's your problem?' He lifted his feet off the desk and sat upright in his chair.

'Sorry,' I said. 'No problem. Just seems funny to move from meat packing to foals.'

'Perhaps they wanted me for my man-management skills,' he said, clearly annoyed with my questions.

'Is there anyone working here now who was here when Peninsula was born?' I asked, trying to change direction.

'Doubt it,' he said unhelpfully, leaning back and replacing his feet on the desk. It was his way of telling me that my time was up.

'Well, keep the photo anyway,' I said. 'If anyone recognizes the man will you ask them to give me a call.' I handed him one of my business cards but I suspected that he would put it in the waste bin beside his desk as soon as I was through the door, together with the photo.

'When did you say the Radcliffes will be back?' I asked him from the doorway.

'The Kentucky Derby is at Louisville tomorrow,' he said, leaning further back in his chair. 'They'll be back sometime after that.' He seemed determined not to be too helpful.

'Right,' I said. 'Would you ask them to look at the picture as well, please?'

'Maybe,' he said.

The taxi had waited for me and I asked the driver to take me back to the Queen's Arms. That had all been a waste of time, I thought.

I called Eleanor and asked her if I should stay for a

second night or go on to Oxford. Arthur had booked my hotel from the Friday, and I had already called to check that all my boxes had arrived there safely.

'I'm on call again,' she said.

'Is everything all right?' I asked her. She seemed strangely reticent for someone who had previously been so forthcoming, almost eager.

'Fine,' she said. 'I'm just very busy at the moment.'

Was it something I had said, I wondered.

'But would you like to have dinner together?' I asked. 'You may not be paged tonight.' There was a pause from the other end of the line. 'But we can leave it if you like,' I went on quickly. Was I being too pushy?

'Geoffrey,' she said seriously. 'I'd love to have dinner with you, but . . .'

'Yes?' I said.

'I'll have to come back here afterwards.'

'That's fine,' I said, upbeat. 'Why don't we have dinner at the Fox and Hounds in Uffington, and then I'll get a taxi to take me on to Oxford while you go back to Lambourn.'

'Great,' she said, sounding a little relieved.

'Are you sure everything's all right?' I asked her again.

'Yes,' she said. 'I promise. Everything is fine.'

We disconnected and I was left wondering whether men could ever fully understand women.

*

We had arranged to meet at the Fox and Hounds at eight. I had noticed the pub on both my trips to the Radcliffe place. It was a yellow plastered building set close to the road in Uffington High Street and I arrived early at ten past seven in a taxi with my two suitcases.

'I'm sorry,' said the publican as I struggled in through the door with both cases and my crutches. 'We don't have any accommodation, we're only a pub.'

I explained to him that another taxi was picking me up later and he kindly allowed me to store my bags in his office in the interim.

'Now,' he said as I half sat myself on one of the Windsor-style bar stools. 'What can I get you?'

'Glass of red, please,' I said. 'Merlot, if you have it.'

He poured a generous measure and set the glass down on the wooden bar top.

'I called and booked for dinner,' I said.

'Mr Mason?' he said. I nodded. 'For two? At eight?'

'Yes,' I said. 'I'm early.' I looked around the bar. I was so early that, even on a Friday evening, I was his only customer. 'Quiet tonight,' I said to him.

'It'll be much busier later,' he said. 'All my regulars will be in soon.'

I rather hoped that Larry Clayton would not be amongst them.

I pulled a copy of the Millie and foal photograph from my jacket and placed it on the bar. 'Do you recognize either of the people in this picture?' I said, pushing it towards him.

He had a good look. 'I don't know the woman,' he said. 'But I think the man is Jack Rensburg.'

'Does he live round here?' I said. I could hardly control my excitement. I had thought the pub might be a long shot and hadn't expected to get an answer so quickly.

'He used to,' the publican replied. 'He worked at the stables on the Woolstone road. He's been gone for two or three years, at least.'

'How well did you know him?' I asked.

'Is he in trouble?' he said.

'No, nothing like that,' I assured him with a laugh.

'He used to talk a lot about cricket,' he said. 'He's South African. He played for the village team here and they come into the pub after matches in the summer. He was always going on about how much better the South Africans were than the English team. But it was just banter. He's a nice enough chap.'

'Do you know why he left?' I asked.

'No idea,' he said. 'I think he went away on holiday and never came back.'

'And you don't know when exactly?' I asked him.

He thought for a moment but shook his head. 'Sorry.'

Some more customers arrived and he went off to serve them.

So, I thought, the stud groom was called Jack Rensburg and he was a South African who liked cricket and he had left Uffington at least two or three years ago, possibly to go on a holiday from which he had not returned. Young men the world over, especially those living away from their homeland, went on holidays all the time from which they didn't return. The nomadic life of the young expatriate male should not be a surprise to anyone. Perhaps he met a girl, or simply went home and stayed there.

Eleanor arrived promptly at eight and I was still half standing, half sitting on the bar stool enjoying a second glass of Merlot.

She came over, gave me a peck on the cheek and sat on the stool next to me and ordered a glass of white. Where, I thought, had the kiss on the lips gone?

'Had a good day?' she asked rather gloomily, tasting her wine.

'Yes, actually, I have. I've bought up most of the menswear in Newbury, washed, shaved and preened my body, and,' I said with a flourish, 'I've discovered the name of the man in the picture.'

'Wow,' she said, mocking. 'You have been a busy boy.' She smiled and it felt like the sun had come out.

'That's better,' I said, smiling back. 'And what have you been up to?'

'I've spent most of the day monitoring the two-year-old from last night. And discussing his future with the owner.' She raised her eyes to the heavens. 'He would have much rather I put the animal down than save its life.'

'How come?' I said.

'Seems it's insured against being dead, but not against being a hopeless racehorse.'

'And is it a hopeless racehorse?' I asked.

'It might be after yesterday,' she said. 'Might not be able to race at all. Much more profitable to him dead.'

'Is bleeding in the lungs common in horses?' I asked.

'Fairly,' she said. 'But mostly EIPH. This one was a static bleed.'

'EIPH?' I said.

'Sorry,' she replied, smiling. 'Exercise-induced pulmonary haemorrhage.'

I began to wish I'd never asked.

'Lots of horses bleed slightly into their lungs during stressful exercise but that usually clears up quickly and spontaneously without too much damage and without any blood showing externally. Horses' lungs are big and efficient but they need to be. A racehorse needs masses of oxygen delivered to its muscles to run fast. You just have to see how hard they blow after the finish.' She paused, but only for breath herself. 'During the race their action helps their breathing. As they stretch out their hind quarters, they draw air in, and then that's blown out again by their legs coming forward in the stride. It makes Thoroughbreds very efficient gallopers when both their hind legs move together, pumping air in and out of their lungs like pistons. But it also means that the air fairly rushes in and out at hurricane speeds and that sometimes damages the lining, which, by definition, has to be flimsy and fragile to let the oxygen pass into the bloodstream in the first place.'

I sat there listening to her, understanding every word and loving it. Not since Angela had died had I enjoyed the experience of a bright, educated and enthusiastic female companion describing to me something complicated because it interested her, and not just because I had asked her to do so as part of my job.

'So, is a static bleed worse?' I asked her.

'Not necessarily,' she said. 'But it might make EIPH more likely. And horses that regularly show blood on their nostrils after racing are discouraged from running again and, in some countries, they're not allowed to. The horses are usually referred to as having burst a blood vessel, or having had a nosebleed.'

I had heard both the terms used often on the racecourse.

'It's not really a blood vessel as such,' she said. 'And the blood comes not from the nose but from the alveoli in the lungs. In America they all use a drug called Lasix to help prevent it, but that's against the Rules of Racing here.'

I didn't really want to stop her but the publican came over and asked us if we were ready to eat, so we moved to a table in the corner of the bar.

'Tell me about the man in the picture,' Eleanor said as we sat down.

'Not really much to tell,' I said. 'His name is Jack Rensburg, and he's a South African who used to work for the Radcliffes but has now gone away.'

'Where to?' she said.

'I haven't found that out yet,' I said.

'Is he coming back?' she said.

'I don't know that either, but I doubt it. He's been gone for two years or more.'

'Bit of a dead end, then?' she said.

'Yeah,' I agreed. 'But I'll set Arthur onto it on Monday. He loves a challenge.'

'Arthur?' she asked.

'Chief Clerk at my chambers,' I said. 'Knows everything, walks on water, that sort of thing.'

'Useful,' she said, smiling broadly, but the smile faded.

'Horse walks into a bar – ' I said.

'What?' said Eleanor, interrupting.

'Horse walks into a bar,' I repeated. 'Barman says, "Why the long face?"'

She laughed. 'The old ones are always the best.'

'So, why the long face?' I said to her again.

She stopped laughing. 'It's nothing,' she said. 'I'm just being silly.'

'If it's nothing,' I said. 'Tell me.'

'No,' she said in mock seriousness. 'It's private.'

'Have I done something wrong?' I said.

'No, of course not,' she said. 'It's nothing. Forget it.'

'I can't,' I said. 'For the first time in more than seven years I don't feel guilty at being out with another woman and, suddenly, there's something wrong. And I'm worried it's because of what I've said or done.'

'Geoffrey,' she said laying a hand on my arm. 'It's nothing like that.' She laughed, throwing her head back.

'Well what is it, then?' I asked determinedly.

She leaned forward close to me. 'Wrong time of the

month,' she said. 'I was so afraid you would ask me to sleep with you, and I don't want to, not like this.'

'Oh,' I said, embarrassed. 'I'm so sorry.'

'It's not a disease you know,' she said with a laugh, the sparkle back in her eyes. 'It'll be gone by Monday, or Tuesday.'

'Oh,' I said again. 'Monday or Tuesday,' I repeated rather vaguely.

'And I'm not on call on either night,' she giggled.

I didn't know whether to feel embarrassed, excited or just plain foolish.

The publican came over to our table to save me from further blushes. There was another man behind him. 'There's a chap here who used to play cricket with Jack,' he said. 'He may be able to help you.'

'Thank you very much,' I said.

The man pulled up a chair and sat down at the table.

'Pete Ritch,' the man said by way of introduction. 'Hear you're looking for Jack Rensburg.'

'Yes,' I said. 'I'm Geoffrey Mason and this is Eleanor.' He nodded at her.

'What do you want him for?' he asked.

'I'm a lawyer and I'd like to talk to him,' I said.

'Is he in trouble?' he said.

He was the second person who thought he might have been in trouble.

'No. No trouble,' I said. 'I just need to talk to him.'

'Is it some inheritance thing?' he asked. 'Has some aunt left him a pile?'

'Something like that,' I said.

'Well, I'm sorry, then, 'cause I don't rightly know where he is no more.'

'When did you last see him?' I asked.

'Years ago now,' he said. 'He went on holiday and just never came back.'

'Do you know where he went?'

'Somewhere exotic it was,' said Pete. I thought that anywhere out of Oxfordshire might seem exotic to him. 'Far East or something.'

'Can you think exactly when that was?'

'It was during the last England tour to South Africa,' he said with some certainty. 'Him and me had a wager on the result and he never came back to pay me when England won. I remember that.'

'Cricket tour?' I asked.

'Yeah,' he said. 'Dead keen on his cricket was Jack. His name was actually spelt with a "ques" at the end, like that famous South African cricketer Jacques Kallis. He was proud of that. But we all just called him Jack.'

'Do you know anything else about him?' I asked. 'Does he have any family here, or did he own a house or a car?'

'No idea,' he said. 'I only knew him from in here, and at the cricket club. He could bowl a bit. Spinners, mostly.'

'Thank you so much, Pete,' I said to him. 'You've been most helpful.'

He made no move to stand up or to leave our table.

'Sorry,' I said, understanding. 'Can I buy you a drink?'

'That would be handsome,' he said.

I waved at the publican, who came over.

'Would you please give Pete here a drink on me,' I said. 'And one for yourself as well.'

They went off together to the bar and, subsequently, Pete waved a full pint in my direction. I nodded at him and smiled. Eleanor was trying very hard not to completely collapse in a fit of giggles.

'Stop it,' I said to her under my breath while trying hard not to join in. 'For goodness' sake, stop it.' But she didn't, or she couldn't.

My taxi arrived at ten fifteen sharp, as I had ordered, and it whisked me off to Oxford, leaving Eleanor waving to me from the pub car park. The evening had flown by and I wasn't at all ready to go when the driver arrived. But he couldn't wait. He had other trips booked after mine.

'Now or never,' he'd said.

I was tempted to say never, but I would just have to wait until Monday, or Tuesday.

Eleanor and I kissed each other goodnight firmly, with open mouths. It was a revelation to me after such a long time. Something stirred inside me and I so reluctantly struggled into the back seat of the taxi to be borne away from her to the City of Dreaming Spires. I, meanwhile, was dreaming of the future, and especially of Monday, or Tuesday.

CHAPTER FIFTEEN

I spent an hour early on Saturday connected to the internet, dealing with my e-mails, paying bills and generally managing my bank account. I also looked up when England had last played cricket on tour in South Africa. The rest of the morning was spent going through, yet again, the boxes of papers for the case. By now I knew many of them off by heart but one or two of them were new since I had last been through them.

At last, after several more threatening requests, the bank had finally produced Millie Barlow's bank statements and I spent quite a while examining these. They did indeed show that Millie had a regular payment into her account over and above her salary from the equine hospital veterinary practice. And Scot's statements showed that the money didn't come from him, or at least it didn't come from his bank account.

The amounts weren't that big, just a few hundred every month, and, from the statements that had been sent by the bank, I was able to tell they had been paid to her for at least a year and a half before she died. But I didn't have any information for before that.

I thought back to when I had met her parents at Scot Barlow's house. Were they likely to have been sending their daughter money? One never knew. Their ill-fitting clothes, their cheap coach travel and their simple ways didn't necessarily mean they had no spare cash. It might just mean they were careful with their money, and there was no crime in that.

Scot, meanwhile, had been doing very well indeed, thank you very much. Almost all his deposits were from Weatherbys, the racing administrators, who paid all the riding fees and win bonuses to owners, trainers and jockeys. There had been a few other minor deposits but nothing that amounted to much. Scot had been at the top of his profession and earning accordingly, but the statements indicated that there was nothing unusual in any of his transactions, at least nothing that I had been able to spot.

I met with Bruce Lygon on Saturday afternoon and we fairly gloomily went through the prosecution case once again. At first glance the evidence seemed overwhelming but, the more I looked at it, the more I began to believe that we had a chance to argue that Mitchell had no case to answer. Everything was circumstantial. There was no proof anywhere in their case that our client had ever been to Honeysuckle Cottage, let alone killed its owner.

'But the evidence does show,' Bruce said, 'that who-ever killed Barlow used Mitchell's pitchfork as the murder

weapon, was wearing Mitchell's boots as he did it, probably drove Mitchell's car from the scene, and,' he empha-
sized, 'also had access to Mitchell's debit card slips.'

'But that doesn't mean it was definitely Mitchell who
did it,' I said.

'What would you think if you were on the jury?' he
said. 'Especially when you add in the fact that Mitchell
hated Barlow. Everyone knew it, and Mitchell had often
been heard to threaten to kill Barlow in exactly the
manner in which he died.'

'That's why we have to argue that there's no case to
answer,' I said. 'If it goes to the jury we are in deep
trouble.'

On Sunday, I went by train to have lunch with my father
in his bungalow in the village of Kings Sutton. He came
down to the village station to collect me in his old Morris
Minor. He had always loved this old car and there was
nothing he adored more than tinkering for hours with the
old engine beneath the bulbous bonnet.

'She's still going well, then?' I said to him as the car
made easy work of the hill up from the station.

'Never better,' he said. 'The odometer has just been
round the clock again.'

I leaned over and saw that it read just twenty-two
miles.

'How many times is that?' I asked.

'Can't remember,' he said. 'Three or four at least.'

This car had been the greatest delight of his life and he had been married to it for far longer, and much more passionately, than he had been to my mother.

It had been the first car I had ever driven. I am sure that the Health and Safety Executive would not have approved of the practice, but I could remember the joy of sitting on my father's lap and steering at an age when my feet wouldn't reach the pedals. Thinking back, it was a surprise that I hadn't wanted to become a racing driver rather than a jockey.

My father's stone-built bungalow sat in a cul-de-sac at the edge of the village with six other similar bungalows, all of them subtly different in design or orientation. He had four bedrooms in a house that looked smaller, but he had converted the smallest bedroom into an office with bookshelves full of law books and Morris Minor manuals.

Just as he had been an infrequent visitor to Barnes since Angela died, I had only been here to Kings Sutton to see him about half a dozen times in the previous three years. My father and I had never been really affectionate towards each other, even when I had been a small child. I suppose we loved each other in the way that parents and children must, and I think I would probably miss him after his days, that is if Julian Trent didn't see me off first. But closeness and a cosy loving relationship between us was something that neither of us had wanted for a very long time, if ever.

However, that Sunday, I had a lovely time with him, sitting at his dining-room table eating a roast beef lunch with Yorkshire puddings and four different vegetables that he had cooked for us.

'I'm very impressed,' I said, laying down my knife and fork. 'I never realized you could cook so well.'

'You should come more often,' he said in response, smiling.

Over lunch we hadn't discussed the Mitchell case, or any other case. I think, in the end, he had been pleased that I had become a barrister, but there had been so many things said between us in those early years, things we probably both would now regret having said, that the whole question of my job and career had never been mentioned again.

'Would you do me a favour?' I asked him as we moved with our coffees into his sitting room.

'Depends what it is,' he said.

'Would you contemplate going away for a couple of weeks?' I said.

'What on earth for?' he said.

How could I explain to him that it might be for his own protection? How could I say that it was so he couldn't be used as a lever to make me do something I didn't want to?

'I'd like to give you a holiday,' I said.

'But why?' he said. 'And where would I go?'

'Wherever you like,' I said.

'But I don't want to go anywhere,' he said. 'If you really want to give me something then give me the money to have my windows and guttering painted.'

'It might be safer for you to go away,' I said.

'Safer?' he said. 'How would it be safer?'

I explained to him just a little about how some people were trying to influence the outcome of a trial by getting me to do things I didn't want to do.

'You ought to go and tell the police,' he said.

'I know,' I replied. 'I will. But for the time being it might be best if the people concerned didn't know where you were.'

'Don't be ridiculous, boy,' he said, putting on his most authoritative voice. 'Why on earth would anyone care where I live?'

I took a photograph out of my pocket and passed it to him. It was the one of him standing outside his front door wearing the green jumper with the hole in the elbow.

He studied it carefully and looked up at my face.

'Are you saying that someone else took this?' he said.

I nodded at him. 'Last November,' I said. 'Do you remember me calling you about that hole in your jumper?'

'Vaguely,' he said, still staring at the picture.

'Well,' I said, 'I just don't want these people coming here to trouble you again, that's all.' I was trying to play down the matter and make light of it so as not to frighten him unnecessarily.

'But why would they want to?' he persisted.

'Because,' I said with a forced laugh, 'I have no intention of doing what they want me to do.'

*

Steve Mitchell's trial started at ten thirty sharp on Monday morning in court number 1 at Oxford Crown Court with a red-robed High Court judge parachuted in from London for the purpose. This was a murder trial with a celebrity, albeit a minor one, in the dock and nothing was to go wrong.

As expected, I had received no call over the weekend from Sir James Horley QC asking me to request an adjournment and had, in fact, been advised by Arthur in an e-mail that Sir James was now doubtful of making it to Oxford at any time before Thursday at the earliest. I thought that he was in danger of being severely reprimanded by the trial judge, but, as they were probably old golfing chums, that wouldn't have amounted to much.

The first hour of any trial is taken up mostly with court procedures. The jury members have to be selected and sworn in, the judge needs to become acquainted with counsel, the clerk of the court has to be happy that the right defendant is in the right court, and so on. Boxes of papers are sorted and everything has to be just right before the judge calls on the prosecution to start proceedings proper by outlining the case for the Crown.

Without exception, all criminal proceedings in the English Crown courts are prosecuted in the name of the reigning monarch. The court papers in this case were headed by *R.* v. *Mitchell*, meaning in this case Regina, the Queen, versus Steve Mitchell.

Criminal cases under English law are adversarial. There are two sides, the prosecution acting for the Crown and the defence acting for the defendant. The two sides argue against each other with the judge sitting like an independent and neutral referee in the middle. The judge is solely responsible for ensuring that the law, and its procedures, are correctly followed. The jury, having heard all the arguments and also having listened to the answers given by the witnesses called by both prosecution and defence, then decide amongst themselves, in secret, what are the facts in the case before pronouncing on the guilt, or otherwise, of the defendant. If the verdict is guilty, then the judge determines the sentence, in theory following guidelines as laid down by the Sentencing Advisory Panel.

The system has operated in this way for hundreds of years and the spread of English-style administration around the world in the sixteenth, seventeenth and eighteenth centuries carried this legal system with it. Consequently it remains the practice in much of the world, including in the United States and in most of the old British Commonwealth.

However, in most of continental Europe the courts follow a different pattern known as the inquisitorial system where the judge, or a panel of judges, investigate the facts in the case, question the witnesses, determine the verdict and then pass sentence, all without the use of a jury. Exponents claim that it may be more precise in finding out the truth, but there is no real evidence to say that one system is more accurate than the other in reaching the correct conclusion.

Number 1 court at Oxford was set out for the adversarial system, as was every other Crown Court in the land, and both the prosecution and the defence teams were laying claim to their space. In our case, the defence consisted solely of Bruce Lygon, his secretary and me. I had asked him to bring his secretary to court so that we didn't, as a line-up, appear too thin on the ground. To be fair, we also had Nikki Payne at our disposal. Nikki was an eager young solicitor's clerk from Bruce's firm, but she wasn't in court at the start of the trial because she was busy in London trying to discover the answers to some questions I had set her the previous evening.

The prosecution, meanwhile, had seven players in situ. A top QC from London was leading, with a local barrister as his junior. These two sat in the front row, to our right, and also slightly to the right of the judge's bench as we looked at it. Two CPS solicitors sat behind them, with two other legal assistants in the row behind that, plus a cross between a secretary and a gofer in row four. If they were trying to impress and intimidate the defence by weight of numbers, it seemed to be succeeding.

'They look very well organized,' Bruce said to me quietly.

'So do we,' I replied. 'So appearances can be deceiving.'

Members of the public and the press were admitted, taking their respective places on the right-hand side of the court. The press were represented in force, both front-page and back-page reporters of the national dailies filling all of the green upholstered seats in the press box. This trial was going to be big news, and the thirty or so seats reserved for the public were mostly full as well.

Mr and Mrs Barlow, Scot's parents, were both seated in the front row of this public area, which, in Oxford, was not an elevated gallery as at the Old Bailey, but on the floor of the courtroom alongside the press.

Next, Steve Mitchell was brought into court from the cells by a prison officer in uniform. Both the prison officer and Steve sat in the glass-fronted dock at the back of the court, behind the barristers' benches. I turned round and gave Steve an encouraging smile. He looked pale and very nervous but was dressed, as I had suggested, in the blazer, white shirt and tie that I had bought for him in Newbury the previous Saturday. Courts are formal places and most of the trial participants were in legal dress or lounge suits. Only juries and the public galleries were casual, and seemingly more so each year.

'All rise,' announced the clerk. Everyone stood and the judge entered the court from his chambers behind. He bowed. We bowed back. And then everyone sat down again. The court was now in session.

The court clerk stood up. 'The defendant will rise,' she said. Steve stood up.

'Are you Stephen Miles Mitchell?' said the clerk.

'Yes, I am,' Steve replied in a strong voice that was partly muffled by the glass front of the dock that ran right to the ceiling of the court.

'You may sit down,' said the clerk, so he did.

'Are you leading for the defence, Mr Mason?' the judge asked loudly, making me jump.

I struggled to my feet. 'Yes, My Lord,' I said.

'Do you not think that your team needs strengthening somewhat?' he asked.

It was his coded way of asking whether I thought that a QC might be more appropriate, as he clearly did.

'My Lord,' I replied. 'Sir James Horley is nominally leading for the defence in this case but is unable to be here today due to another case in which he is acting having run over time.'

'You have not asked for an adjournment,' he said, somewhat accusingly.

'No, My Lord,' I said. 'Sir James and I have made the preparations for the case, and my client is content for the case to proceed today with me acting for him.' I couldn't exactly tell the judge that my client had been ecstatic that Sir James was not here when I'd told him earlier in the cells beneath the court.

'I need to make it clear to you, and to your client, that this will not be grounds for an appeal if the case goes against you.'

'I understand that, My Lord,' I said. 'And so does my client.'

Steve Mitchell nodded his agreement to the judge from the dock.

'Very well,' said the judge. 'I have, in fact, spoken to Sir James this morning when he called me to present his apologies.'

Then why, I thought, did you ask me in the first place, you silly old fart?

The prosecution team were all looking at me and smiling, confidence oozing out of their every pore. I simply smiled back.

'The defendant will rise,' the clerk said again.

Steve stood up in the dock.

'You are charged,' the clerk said to him, 'that on the seventeenth of November 2008, you did murder Hamish Jamie Barlow, also known as Scot Barlow. Do you understand the indictment?'

'Yes,' Steve replied.

'How do you plead?' the clerk asked him.

'Not guilty,' Steve said strongly.

Next came the selection and swearing in of the jury.

Everyone watched as a mixed bag of individuals entered the court and sat on more green-covered seats on the other side. There were eighteen of them in total, drawn randomly from the electoral roll and summoned to attend the court, whether they wanted to or not. Unlike in the United States neither the defence nor the prosecution had any prior knowledge of who they were or where they lived. We were not allowed to ask them any questions and, since 1989, the defence has not been able to object to a juror simply because they didn't like the cut of his coat. Objections to jurors now had to be based on firm grounds and, even then, the judge was most likely to dismiss the objection.

Twelve of the eighteen had their names drawn from a

box by the court clerk and each one, in turn, took their places in the jury box to my left and were sworn in, on oath, promising to try the case according to the evidence.

The six people, four women and two men, who had not been selected looked decidedly disappointed as they were excused by the judge back to the jury rooms upstairs, maybe to get luckier in one of the other courts.

And now we were ready to begin in earnest.

The court clerk stood up and read out the indictment to the jury. 'That on the seventeenth of November 2008, Stephen Miles Mitchell did murder Hamish Jamie Barlow, known as Scot Barlow, contrary to common law.'

'Ladies and gentlemen of the jury,' the prosecution QC was on his feet almost before the clerk had sat down. 'You will hear, in this case, of a bitter feud in the world of horse racing that was so acrimonious that it led to the gruesome killing of one jockey at the hands of another. A story of rivalry and revenge that goes far beyond the accepted limits that exist in any competitive sport.' He paused briefly to draw breath, and also to find a sheet of paper that he picked up from the desk and consulted, not that he probably needed to. It was simply for show. 'Members of the jury, you will hear how the defendant did premeditatively murder the victim by driving a metal-pronged pitchfork deep into his chest, deep into his heart, and how the defendant now claims that he is innocent of the charge and is being framed by person or persons unknown. But the evidence presented to you will convince you, beyond a reasonable doubt, that the defendant is, in fact, culpable of the murder, and that his claims of being framed are meaningless and unfounded, nothing more than the last refuge of a guilty soul.' He replaced the paper onto the desk.

He was good, I thought. Too damned good. He was also far too melodramatic for my taste but it was working. I could see some of the jury members glancing at the dock with distaste.

In all, it took him more than an hour to fully outline, in considerable detail, the case for the prosecution by which time every one of the jury members was eyeing Steve with contempt. As was always the way with the English legal system, the prosecution had first go in the jury persuasion stakes. The defence would have their turn, in time. I just hoped that something would turn up by then that I could use to help me.

The judge adjourned proceedings for lunch. The slow pace of trials, especially murder trials, was becoming clear to both the jury and the defendant. The rest of us knew already.

I went straight down to the cells to see Steve.

'My God,' he said. 'Did you see the way the jury was looking at me? They all think I'm guilty. I've got no bloody chance. I wanted so much to call that lawyer a bloody liar.'

'Calm down, Steve,' I said. 'It's always like that at the beginning of a trial. We'll get our turn later.' I didn't add that it might get worse when they started calling their witnesses. 'Have some lunch. I'll see you in court when we resume, and try to keep calm. Remember what I said to you earlier – don't say anything, ever. It will not look good to the jury, and it will antagonize the judge. Just bite your lip and keep quiet. You will get your turn. Do you understand?'

He nodded. 'It's bloody difficult, though.'

'I know,' I said. 'But it's very important. I'll see you later.'

I went up in the lift and made some calls on my mobile.

There was no reply from Nikki's phone, so I tried Arthur.

'How's it going?' he asked.

'Same as always at the start of a trial,' I said.

'That bad, huh?' he said.

'Worse. Have you heard from Nikki Payne?' I asked him.

'Who?' he said.

'Nikki Payne,' I said again. 'Solicitor's clerk from Bruce Lygon's firm. She said she would pass a message to me through you.'

'Ah yes,' he said. 'Hold on.' I could hear him rustling papers. 'Apparently she's got something from the embassy and she's chasing the lead. Does that make sense?'

'Yes,' I said. 'Good. And thank you for my hotel. Very amusing.'

'Thought you'd feel at home,' he said, laughing.

Arthur had made reservations for me in Oxford at a

hotel conveniently placed just a few hundred yards from the court building. And the reason he amusingly thought that I would feel at home was because the hotel had been created by converting the old Oxford Prison, which had housed a different clientele as recently as 1996. My room was in what had been 'A' wing of the prison, with galleried landings and rows of old cell doorways. It had all been tastefully converted but it still looked just like the interior of an old Victorian prison, except, of course, for the carpets. The hotel had obligingly left one cell as it had been in the prison days so the hotel guests could see how miserably the other half had once lived. I was amused to notice that porridge was on the breakfast menu.

'Tell Nikki to call me later if she calls you again,' I said to him. 'I want to hear how she's doing.'

'Right,' he said. 'I will. Anything else you need?'

'A cast-iron alibi for the defendant would be nice.'

'See what I can do,' he said, laughing, and hung up. Arthur would have to really work a miracle, I thought, to get Mr Mitchell out of this hole.

The afternoon proved to be as frustrating as the morning had been, with the investigating police officer in the witness box for the whole two and a half hours. Only once did the judge briefly adjourn things for a few minutes for us all to stretch our legs and visit the lavatories, and to give me some relief from the damn body shell cutting into my groin. How I wished I could have had my recliner chair from my room in chambers, instead of the upright seats of the court.

The policeman, having consulted his notebooks, went through the whole affair in chronological order, from the moment that the police had first arrived at Barlow's house to discover the body until they had arrested Steve Mitchell at eight fifty-three that evening. He also went on to describe the investigation after the arrest, including the interviewing of the suspect and the forensic tests that the police had performed on Mitchell's boots and car together with his understanding of the results, but, as he said, he was no expert on DNA testing.

We were assured by the prosecution that they would be calling their DNA expert witness in due course, together with a member of the police forensic team that had carried out the tests.

'Inspector,' said the prosecution QC. 'What model of car did the defendant own at the time of the murder?'

'An Audi A4,' he said. 'Silver.'

'Yes,' went on the QC, 'and in the course of your enquiries did you determine if this car was fitted with a security alarm and immobilizer system?'

'Yes,' he said. 'It was.'

'And was the system found to be functioning correctly when the car was examined after the defendant's arrest?'

'Yes,' he said again. 'It was.'

'So would it be accurate to say that the car could only be unlocked and then driven if the correct key had been used for the purpose?'

'That is my understanding, yes,' said the inspector.

'Did you find any keys for the vehicle?' the QC asked him.

'Yes,' he said. 'There were two such keys found in Mr Mitchell's premises when he was arrested. One was on the defendant, in his trouser pocket on a ring with other keys, and the other one,' he consulted his notebook, 'was in the top drawer of Mr Mitchell's desk in his study.'

'And did you approach an Audi dealer and ask them about keys for their cars?'

'Yes,' he said again. 'They informed me that it was normal for two keys to be issued with a new car and also that replacement or additional keys are only provided after strict security checks.'

'And had any additional keys been requested for Mr Mitchell's car?'

'No,' he said. 'They had not.'

'One last thing, Inspector,' the QC said with a flourish. 'Was Mr Mitchell's car locked when you went to his home to arrest him?'

'Yes,' he said. 'It was.'

'Your witness,' the prosecution QC said, turning to me.

I looked at the clock on the courtroom wall. It read twenty past four.

'Would you like to start your cross-examination in the morning, Mr Mason?' asked the judge expectantly.

'If it pleases My Lord,' I said, 'I would like to ask a few questions now.'

The judge looked at the clock.

'Ten minutes, then,' he said.

'Thank you, My Lord.' I turned to the witness and consulted my papers. 'Inspector McNeile, can you please tell the court how it was that the police first became aware that Mr Barlow had been murdered?'

He had left that bit out of his evidence.

'I can't remember how I first heard of it,' he said.

'I asked, Inspector, not how you personally found out, but how the police force in general was informed.'

'I believe it was a call to the police station reporting an intruder at Mr Barlow's residence,' he said.

'Who was this call from?' I asked him.

'I'm sorry, I don't have that information.'

'But surely, Inspector, all emergency calls to the police are logged with the time they are made, and who they are from?'

'That is the usual practice, yes,' he said.

'So how is it that you have no record of who it was that called the police to tell you that an intruder had been seen at Barlow's house?'

He looked slightly uncomfortable. 'The call was taken by the telephone on the desk of a civilian worker in the front office of the police station.'

'Was that not unusual?' I said.

'Yes,' he replied.

'And was the number of that telephone widely available to the public?' I asked him.

'Not that I'm aware of,' he said.

'Do you not think it is strange that the call was taken on a telephone where the number was not widely known, a telephone where no log was taken of incoming calls, and a telephone on which no recording equipment was attached so that the caller and his number would be unknown?'

'Mr Mason,' the judge interjected. 'That's three questions in one.'

'I'm sorry, My Lord,' I said. 'Inspector McNeile, would you agree with me that, until the police arrived at Mr Barlow's house to discover his body, it is likely that the only person or persons who knew that Mr Barlow was dead would be those responsible for his murder?'

'I suppose so, yes,' he said.

'Inspector, how many years in total have you been a detective?' I asked him.

'Fifteen,' he said.

'And how often in those fifteen years,' I said to him, 'have you been telephoned anonymously, on an unrecorded line, to report an intruder in a property so that the police would turn up there and discover a murder victim surrounded by a mass of incriminating evidence?'

'That's enough, Mr Mason,' said the judge.

'My Lord,' I said respectfully, and sat down. It had been a minor victory only, in a day of unremitting bad news.

'Court adjourned until ten o'clock tomorrow morning,' said the judge.

'All rise.'

Eleanor didn't come to Oxford on Monday night. In one way I was relieved, in another, disappointed. When I arrived back at the hotel from court I lay down on the bed, my head aching slightly from all the concentration. This slight headache soon developed into a full-on head-banger.

It was the first such headache I had suffered for some time and I had begun to forget the ferocity of the pain behind my eyes. During the first three weeks immediately after the fall at Cheltenham, I had suffered these on most days and I knew that relaxing horizontally on a bed for a couple of hours was the best and only remedy. A couple of paracetamol tablets took the edge off it, but I had carelessly left my stronger codeine pills at home. They were somewhere in the shambles that had once been my bathroom.

At some point I drifted off to sleep because I was awakened by the phone ringing beside the bed.

'Yes?' I said into it, struggling to sit up because of the shell.

'Mr Mason?' a female voice said.

'Yes,' I replied.

'This is Nikki Payne here,' she said. 'I've been to the Home Office and the South African embassy as you asked and neither of them had any record of a Jacques Rensburg. But they did of someone called Jacques van Rensburg. In fact there are three of them who live in England. Apparently van Rensburg is quite a common name in South Africa.'

It would be.

'Two of the South African Jacques van Rensburgs living here are at university, here on student visas. One is at Durham and the other is a post-graduate at Cambridge and both have been here for the past two years.'

I suppose it was possible that the Jacques we wanted had given up working with horses for a life of academia, but somehow I doubted it.

'What about the third one?' I asked.

'His visa has expired, but it seems he's still here although his right to work has expired too. But, apparently, that's not unusual. That's all I have for the moment.'

'Well done,' I said to her.

'I'm not done yet,' she said. 'A nice chap at the embassy is searching for the third Jacques back in South Africa just in case he went home without telling the Home Office. There aren't any proper records kept when people leave the UK, only when they arrive.'

It was true, I thought. No one from the immigration department checks your passport on the way out, only on the way in. The airlines only check their passengers' passports to ensure they have the same names as on their boarding passes.

'But you did show them the photo?' I asked her.

'Of course I did,' she said. 'My friend at the embassy is trying to get me a copy of this Jacques van Rensburg's passport snap sent from the South African Department of Home Affairs in Pretoria so I can see if it is actually him.'

'Good,' I said. 'Call me tomorrow if you get any-where.'

She hung up and I rested my head back onto the pillow. My headache was only slightly better, so I lay there for a while longer, reclosed my eyes and drifted back off to sleep.

The phone on the bedside cabinet rang once more, waking me again. Damn it, I thought, can't a man have any peace? 'Hello,' I said, irritated. 'Just make sure you lose the case,' said a whispering voice. I was suddenly wide awake. 'Who are you?' I demanded loudly down the line. 'Never mind who,' said the whisperer. 'Just do it.' The line went dead.

CHAPTER SIXTEEN

Detective Inspector McNeile was back in the witness box on Tuesday morning for further cross-examination.

'I remind you that you are still under oath,' the judge said to him.

'Yes, My Lord,' he replied.

I levered myself to my feet, pulling on the lectern on the bench in front of me.

'Inspector McNeile,' I said. 'Yesterday afternoon you told us how the police came to find out about the murder of Mr Barlow from a phone call to a non-recorded, non-emergency number, is that right?'

'Yes,' he replied. There was no harm, I thought, in reminding the jury.

'Yes, thank you,' I said. 'Now I believe that the police also discovered that Mr Barlow had received a text message on his mobile telephone on the day of his death. Is that correct?'

'Yes,' he said again.

'And did this text message say, and I quote,' I picked up a sheet of paper myself and read from it. ' "I'm going to come round and sort you out properly you sneaking little bastard"?' I paused for effect. 'And then the message was signed off with Mr Mitchell's name?'

'I haven't got access to the actual text,' he said, turning to the judge as if for assistance.

'No,' I said. 'But does that sound about right to you?'

'Yes,' he said. 'I believe it said something like that.'

'Thank you,' I said, putting down the paper. 'And were the police able to establish that this text message had indeed been sent to Mr Barlow by Mr Mitchell?'

'No,' he said softly.

'Sorry, Inspector,' I said. 'Could you please speak up, so the jury can hear you?'

'No,' he repeated more strongly.

'And were the police able to establish who was, in fact, responsible for sending that text message to Mr Barlow?' I asked.

'No,' he said. 'We were not.'

'Am I correct in saying that you discovered that the message had been sent anonymously by a free text messaging service available to anyone with access to any computer and the internet anywhere in the world?'

'Yes,' he said. 'That is correct.'

'And is it correct that you were unable to establish which computer had been used to send the message?'

'That is correct,' he replied.

'So, in addition to an anonymous, unrecorded telephone call to the police directing them to a murder scene to discover incriminating evidence against the defendant,'

I glanced at the judge who was looking back at me intently, 'there was also an anonymous text message sent to Mr Barlow's telephone that was made to appear as if it had come from the defendant?'

'I didn't say that it hadn't come from the defendant,' said the inspector. 'I only said that we were unable to establish that it had.'

'Are you claiming now that, in fact, it did come from the defendant?' I asked him with mock astonishment.

'We don't know who it was from,' he said, digging himself further into a hole.

'Thank you,' I said to him. 'No further questions.'

I sat down feeling rather pleased with myself. Bruce Lygon patted me gently on the shoulder. 'Well done,' he whispered.

I turned round to thank him and caught sight of young Julian Trent sitting right next to Mr and Mrs Barlow in the seats reserved for the public. He was watching me. I went quite cold. Damn it, I thought, how much of that cross-examination had he been listening to?

The next witness for the prosecution had been called and there was a lull in proceedings as the court usher went outside the courtroom trying to find the right person. Julian Trent watched me watching him and he clearly decided it was time to leave. He stood up and pushed past the usher as he made his way to the exit. For a moment I thought about going after him, but good sense prevailed so I stayed put. I could hardly chase him on crutches and I am sure the judge wouldn't have taken kindly to me leaving the court in the light of the continued, but unsurprising, absence of Sir James Horley QC.

My cross-examination of Detective Inspector McNeile proved to be the high point of the day for the defence. The three further witnesses called by the prosecution gave us little respite from the damning evidence that implied that the murder had been carried out by the man in the dock.

A specialist DNA witness was followed by a police forensic science expert. Both explained to the jury, in monotonous detail, the method of extracting DNA from blood and hair, and then went on to show beyond any doubt that drops of blood and two hairs from Scot Barlow had been found in the driver's footwell of Steve Mitchell's car and also that more of Barlow's blood and four more of his hairs had been found adhering to the underside of both of Steve Mitchell's wellington boots, subsequently discovered at the Mitchell premises.

They further were able to show that fresh bloody footprints at the scene matched both of Mr Mitchell's wellingtons.

I did manage to extract a small victory for our side by getting the forensic expert to concede that none of Mr Mitchell's DNA had been discovered in Barlow's residence, on the murder weapon, or on the deceased's body. Furthermore, I also got them both to agree that, even though Barlow's DNA had been found on Mr Mitchell's boots and in his car, this did not prove that Mr Mitchell had been wearing his boots at the time, nor driving his car at any point during that afternoon.

In re-examination by the prosecution, however, the first expert did state that traces of Mr Mitchell's DNA had been found inside his own boots, as you might have expected, but that no other person's DNA had also been found there. It didn't exactly further our argument that someone else must have been wearing Mitchell's wellies at the time of the murder, but it didn't destroy it completely either. I managed partly to salvage the situation by getting the second expert to agree that someone could wear a pair of rubber boots without leaving any DNA trace in them, especially someone who was keen not to do so.

The final witness of the day was the pathologist who had done the post-mortem examination of Scot Barlow's body, and his evidence wasn't for the squeamish. The two curved metal prongs of the pitchfork had not, as I had imagined, passed through the rib cage and then into the heart, but had been thrust upwards underneath the ribs, through the diaphragm, one of them entering the heart from below. The five-foot-long double-pronged murder weapon was produced as an exhibit. It looked huge and menacing in the stillness of the courtroom with its ten-inch-long thin, curved, and very sharp metal prongs glinting in the light. The pathologist was invited by the prosecution counsel to demonstrate, on the floor of the court, the upward thrusting action that would have been needed to cause the injuries sustained by Barlow's body. It was a moment of high drama and I noticed some members of the jury shuddering with revulsion. The pathologist explained that a single strike had been sufficient to cause death within just a few minutes with only moderate bleeding from the two wounds, and also a little from the victim's mouth.

The bleeding had not been so moderate, I thought, that both of Mitchell's wellington boots hadn't been able to walk in it.

The pathologist conceded that considerable force would have been needed to cause the fatal injury but, as he said, probably less than that needed to go through the rib cage, where there would have been the risk of one of the fork's prongs hitting and bouncing off a rib. The prosecution counsel then established without difficulty that a fit man of thirty-three, especially one who was a professional sportsman, would have easily had the strength required to deliver the fatal blow, even if he did only stand five foot six inches tall in his socks.

'Had the murder weapon been withdrawn from the victim after death?' I asked him in cross-examination.

'No,' he said. 'When I was first called to the scene, I found the pitchfork still stuck very firmly into Mr Barlow – so firmly, in fact, that it proved impossible to remove at the scene. And I later determined that the puncture wounds to his abdomen, his diaphragm and his heart were all consistent with the weapon having been inserted into the body just once.'

'So anything found on the prongs of the fork between Mr Barlow's body and the fork handle would have had to have been there prior to the fatal blow being struck?'

'Indeed,' he said.

'And was there anything on the prongs?' I prompted him.

'Yes,' he said. 'There were some pieces of paper.'

'Debit card receipts, I believe?' I said.

'I'm not aware of what they were, just that they were present,' he said. 'They were taken away by the police during the postmortem examination at the Royal Berkshire Hospital in Reading, when the murder weapon was finally removed from the body.'

I could only imagine the trouble someone must have had in transporting Barlow's dead body the twenty-six miles from his kitchen floor to the Royal Berkshire Hospital mortuary with a five-foot-long pitchfork firmly embedded in its chest.

The judge adjourned early for the day at four o'clock.

Eleanor didn't come to Oxford on Tuesday night either. There was a message from her on my mobile after the adjournment explaining that one of her colleagues was ill and she had to stay in Lambourn to cover for her. Again, strangely, I was somewhat relieved.

Perhaps it was the expectation, her expectation, that worried me most. It had been a long time since I had slept with anyone, and then it had been Angela, with whom I had been familiar, relaxed and comfortable. Suddenly the prospect of someone new between my sheets filled me with apprehension and worry. Stop being stupid, I said to myself, but the nagging fear of failure and rejection still persisted.

There were, in fact, two messages on my phone.

The other one was from the whisperer.

'Lose the case,' he whispered. 'Or else.'

The message had been left at twelve noon that day. No doubt shortly after Julian Trent had reported back to him on the court proceedings and my determined efforts to undermine the police inspector. How long would it take the whisperer to work out, I wondered, that I became more and more determined to win every time he told me to lose?

I hadn't been outside the court at lunchtime for fear of running into young Mr Trent. Now, at the end of the day, I waited in the courthouse lobby until I saw my taxi pull up close to the doors before I emerged. Most of my boxes remained in the court secure storage overnight but I had one with me in order to prepare for the following day's witnesses.

I clambered into the taxi with my box and crutches and made it safely, unmolested, back to my hotel.

The reception staff thought me a little crazy when I insisted that under no circumstances were they to give my room number to anyone, not even, I said, if they tell you they're my father. And, also, they were not to put any calls through to my room without asking the caller for their name, and telling me that first.

I also asked them how many rooms were free in the hotel for the night.

'Twelve,' one of the female staff said.

'Then could I please change rooms from last night?' I asked.

'Didn't you like your room, sir?' she said.

'It was fine,' I said. 'I would just like to have another one tonight.'

'I will have to check with my manager,' she said. 'The old room would then need to be cleaned and the staff have left for the day.'

'Could it not be left until tomorrow?' I said.

'But then, sir, we couldn't let it tonight, could we?' She was being rather condescending, I thought.

I decided not to mention that, with twelve rooms still unreserved at five o'clock in the afternoon, it was unlikely that they would all be needed.

She went out the back to consult and returned to tell me that it would be fine to move but I would need to pay a late check-out fee on the first room.

'Right, then,' I said to her. 'Can you please arrange a taxi to take me to the Randolph?'

She rapidly disappeared out the back again. A man in a suit, presumably the manager, came out from his office.

'Mr Mason,' he said. 'I'm sorry about the confusion.

Of course you may change rooms if you wish. There will be no extra charge.'

'Fine,' I said. 'Would you please send a porter up for my things?'

'Which room would you like to have?' he said.

'One at the Randolph,' I replied.

'Now Mr Mason,' he said with a smile. 'I am sure we can come to an arrangement.'

We did. I secured a twenty per cent discount on the room rate, backdated to last Friday, together with a complimentary bottle of red wine to be sent up to my new room. It really was useful, sometimes, to be trained in advocacy.

In truth, I didn't really want to move hotels at all. I knew the Randolph, and I liked it, but the converted modern interior of this place made it much easier for me to cope with the crutches even if the room doors were rather narrow as they had been the cell doors of the old prison.

Having settled in to my new room, I lay on the bed with a glass of wine and started reading through the papers for the next day.

The phone rang. I answered it.

'Mr Mason? This is the hotel operator. I have a Miss Clarke on the phone for you. Will you accept the call?'

Miss Clarke? Who was Miss Clarke?

Suddenly I remembered. 'Oh yes, thank you,' I said to the operator.

'What's all that about?' Eleanor asked when she was put through.

'Just my way of screening unwanted calls,' I said cheerfully.

'And have you had any?' she asked me seriously.

'One or two,' I said.

'From Julian Trent?' she said.

'From whoever is behind him,' I said.

'You take care,' she ordered.

'You take care too,' I said. 'Remember, he knows where you live. Don't go anywhere on your own. Not even across to the hospital from your house.'

'Surely I'm safe enough here?' she said.

'Trent attacked me within five yards of the front door of my chambers,' I said. 'Please don't assume anything when it comes to this man. He's very dangerous.'

'Stop it. You're frightening me,' she said.

'Good,' I said. 'Be frightened. Be very frightened. I am.'

'OK, OK,' she said. 'You've made your point.'

'Are you sure you can't come over here?' I said. 'I would be much happier if you were here with me.'

'Now, now, Mister Barrister Man, don't be too eager.' She laughed.

'I really meant for your security,' I said seriously.

'You really do mean it, don't you?' she said.

'Yes. I do. You have no idea how frightening these people are until it's too late. Remember what they did to my house.'

There was a long pause at the other end of the line.

'How are we ever going to be free of them?' she said.

'I'm working on it,' I said. But I didn't know how either.

Detective Constable Hillier, the young policeman I had first met at Barlow's house with Bruce Lygon, was the next witness for the prosecution when the court reconvened at ten thirty on Wednesday morning.

I had kept my eyes open for Julian Trent as I had arrived at the court building but there had been no sign of him. Somewhat perversely, I had rather hoped that he would be there, as it meant he wouldn't have been elsewhere delivering mayhem to my loved ones or their property. Now, I simply worried.

DC Hillier proved to be a model witness for the Crown, stating clearly and persuasively to the jury how the murder weapon was found to be identical to two other pitchforks found at Mitchell's property and how further investigations had discovered a receipt from a Newbury supplier showing that Mitchell had purchased three of the forks the previous year.

He went on to describe how he had ascertained that the debit card receipts, found impaled on the prongs of the fork between Mr Barlow's body and the fork handle, were from a Maestro debit card issued by Lloyds Bank in the name of Mr Stephen Mitchell. Furthermore, the said debit card receipts were from payments made by Mr Mitchell to a licensed bookmaker based in Hungerford.

'Detective Constable Hillier,' I said, starting my cross-examination. 'Do you not think it is strange that a murderer would leave incriminating debit card receipts with his name on them at the scene of the crime?'

'No, not particularly,' he said nonchalantly. 'Many criminals do strange things.'

'But did you not suspect that the receipts had been left on the fork by someone who simply wanted the police to believe that Mr Mitchell had been responsible for the crime?'

'Not really,' he said. 'Perhaps Mitchell put them on the fork to goad Barlow and he hadn't really intended leaving them behind. Maybe he just panicked, or perhaps he couldn't get the murder weapon out of the body to remove them, or indeed to take the fork back home with him.'

'This is conjecture,' interrupted the judge. 'The witness will confine himself to the facts he knows, rather than those he can merely speculate about.'

'Sorry, Your Honour,' said DC Hillier. But the damage had already been done.

I thought of further pointing out that the murderer could surely have ripped the receipts away from the fork without removing it from Barlow's body if, of course, he'd actually wanted to, but this whole line of questioning clearly wasn't helping our case so I let it go.

The next witness was the Hungerford bookmaker who confirmed that the receipts had been issued by the card machine at his premises.

'And are you aware,' the prosecuting counsel said to him, 'that betting on horse racing by a professional jockey is against the Rules of Racing?'

'Yes,' he said. 'I am aware of that.'

'But you took the bets anyway?' the QC asked.

'Yes,' said the bookmaker. 'It was not against either the terms of my permit or the licence of my premises.'

'Was it a regular arrangement with Mr Mitchell?'

'Fairly regular,' the bookmaker replied.

I started to rise but the judge beat me to it.

'Is the regularity of any significance?' he asked the prosecutor.

'Perhaps not, My Lord,' said the QC.

The bookmaker was dismissed. I could have asked him if he regularly took bets from other jockeys but that also wouldn't have been significant, and would probably have antagonized him and the jury unnecessarily, so I didn't. I had no reason to think that he had taken bets from Scot Barlow, so I didn't ask him that either. As for how Steve Mitchell's debit card receipts had found their way onto the pitchfork was anyone's guess. Steve still, unbelievably, refused to comment on the matter, but he wasn't here being tried for gambling in contravention of the Rules of Racing, he was being tried for murder.

'You have one new message,' said my voicemail when I turned my phone on at lunchtime. It was from Nikki Payne.

'Mr Mason,' her disembodied voice said in some excitement. 'I've found your Jacques van Rensburg, or at least I've found out who he is. Call me back when you get this message.'

I called her immediately.

'He was the third one,' she said in a rush. 'They sent his passport photo over from South Africa and there was no mistake.'

'So he's still somewhere here with an expired visa?' I asked.

'Well, no,' she said. 'Not exactly.' She then went on to give me some very interesting information about Mr Jacques van Rensburg, information that explained why the photograph of Millie and the foal had been important. So important that someone had taken it from Scot Barlow's house. Maybe so important, indeed, that Barlow had been murdered to get it.

CHAPTER SEVENTEEN

The afternoon sitting of the court was taken up almost exclusively by witnesses called by the prosecution to testify about the well-known antagonism, even hatred, that had existed between the defendant and the victim for some time.

Any hopes that we, the defence, had of keeping quiet about Barlow's sister Millie were dispelled by the very first on the list, Charles Pickering, a racehorse trainer from Lambourn.

'Mr Pickering,' said the prosecution QC, 'how well did you know Mr Barlow?'

'Very well indeed,' he replied. 'I knew him like my own son. Scot had ridden for me as number one jockey ever since he came down south from Scotland eight years ago. He lived as a member of my family for a while when he first started out.'

'And how well do you know the defendant, Mr Mitchell?'

'Reasonably well,' he said. 'He's ridden my horses a few times, when Scot was unavailable or injured.

And I know him by reputation. He's a top steeplechase jockey.'

'Yes, Mr Pickering,' said the QC. 'But please tell us only what you know personally rather than what you assume from a reputation.'

Charles Pickering nodded.

'Now, Mr Pickering,' the QC went on. 'Did you ever hear Mr Mitchell and Mr Barlow arguing?'

'All the time,' he said. 'Like cat and dog, they were.'

'So there was no love lost between them?'

'I should say not,' replied Pickering with a smile.

'Do you know what they argued about?'

'Scot's sister, mostly,' said Charles Pickering, firing another shot into the defence case.

'Scot Barlow's sister?' the QC said for effect, turning towards the jury.

'Yes,' Pickering said. 'Scot accused Mitchell of as good as killing his sister. Mitchell used to tell him to shut up or he'd kill him too.'

'Were those his exact words?'

'Absolutely,' he said. 'It was the same argument every time. Scot's sister had killed herself about a year ago and he believed that Mitchell's treatment of her had driven her to it.'

'Were Barlow and Mitchell on reasonable terms before Barlow's sister killed herself?' the QC asked, while knowing quite well what the answer would be.

'Oh, no,' said Pickering. 'They've hated each other for

years. Scot didn't like Mitchell seeing his sister at all, right from the start.'

'And when was the start?' the QC asked.

'About three or four years ago, when Barlow's sister came down from Scotland to live in Lambourn.'

'Thank you, Mr Pickering,' said the QC. 'Your witness.' He smiled at me.

'No questions, My Lord,' I said. And Charles Pickering was allowed to depart.

There was nothing I could ask him which would undo the damage he had already done to our case, and I didn't want to inadvertently lead him to reveal more damning details such as Barlow's disclosure of the affair to Mitchell's wife. Now that really would have provided a motive for murder.

However, my hopes of keeping that a secret only lasted as long as it took for the next witness to be sworn in.

'Mr Clemens,' said the QC. 'I believe you are a steeplechase jockey, is that correct?'

'Yes, sir. That's correct,' said Reno Clemens in his Irish accent.

'Are you a successful jockey?' the QC asked.

'I am, sir,' Reno said. 'I am leading the jockeys' table at the moment.'

'So that means you have ridden more winners than anyone else so far this year?'

'This season, yes, sir,' he said.

'So you know the defendant well?'

'Yes, sir.' He glanced briefly at Steve in the dock before returning his eyes to the prosecuting counsel.

'And you knew Mr Barlow well?'

'Yes, sir. I did.'

'Did you ever hear Mr Mitchell and Mr Barlow arguing?' the QC asked.

'Were they ever not?' said Reno. 'Sometimes they would even argue all the way round during a race. The rest of us got fed up listening to them.'

'And what did they argue about?' asked the QC.

'Anything and everything,' said Reno. 'But mostly about Barlow's sister and Mitchell having had an affair with her.'

'And was Mitchell married at the time of the affair?' asked the QC.

Oh no, I thought, here we go.

'He was at the beginning,' said Reno. 'But not at the end.'

'Do you know if Mitchell's wife was aware of his affair with Scot Barlow's sister?' the QC asked almost smugly.

'She was after Barlow told her,' Reno said.

'Is that something you know, Mr Clemens, or just something you have heard from others?'

'I heard it from Mitchell himself,' Reno said. 'He would often shout at Barlow in the jocks' changing room and accuse him of being a Judas for snitching to his wife.'

'You bloody lying bastard,' Steve Mitchell stood up

and shouted at him from the dock, hammering on the glass partition with his fists.

The judge had his gavel banging down almost before the echo in the courtroom had died away.

'Silence,' he ordered. 'Silence in court. Mr Mitchell,' he pointed the gavel at the dock, 'another outburst like that and I will have you taken down to the cells. Do you understand?'

'Yes, My Lord,' said Steve sheepishly. 'I'm sorry.'

Steve sat down again. But more damage had been done to our side.

The prosecution QC had remained standing throughout, and now he had a slight smirk on his face.

'Now, Mr Clemens,' he said, greatly enjoying himself. 'Let me get this straight. Are you telling the court that you had often heard the defendant shouting at Mr Barlow that he, Barlow, had been a Judas for telling Mitchell's wife that Mitchell was having an affair with Barlow's sister?'

'Yes, sir,' said Reno Clemens very distinctly. 'I am.'

A motive for Barlow's murder had just been clearly established by the prosecution.

Two more prosecution witnesses completed the day's proceedings. Both of these gave testimony to reinforce that already given by Charles Pickering and Reno Clemens.

The first was another jockey, Sandy Webster, who did little more than confirm that Mitchell and Barlow argued a lot. When asked what they had argued about he couldn't really say because 'he didn't bother to listen to them ranting on all the time'.

I imagined the prosecution was regretting having called him because he was so nervous that his voice was continuously quivering, and he was hardly giving them the answers they wanted. In my experience, witnesses who were over nervous tended to be discounted by juries, who were inclined to think they were lying.

The second witness was Fred Pleat, a former employee of Mitchell, who had worked as a groom at Mitchell's home soon after the stables were built and when horses were housed there at livery.

'Now, Mr Pleat,' said the prosecution QC in his smarmy manner. 'Were you present at Mr Mitchell's property the day three new pitchforks were delivered?'

'Yes, I was,' he replied.

'And can you recall the actions of Mr Mitchell when he saw that they had been delivered?'

'Yes,' he said again. 'Steve, that's Mr Mitchell, picked one of them up and thrust it forward and said something about sticking that bastard Scot Barlow with it.'

There was a moment of silence in the court.

'Thank you, Mr Pleat,' said the QC. 'Your witness.'

I rose to my foot.

'Mr Pleat,' I said to him. 'Were you frightened by this action you say Mr Mitchell performed?'

'No,' he said.

'Why not?' I asked him.

'I figured Steve was only joking, like,' he said. 'He was laughing. We were both laughing.'

'Thank you, Mr Pleat,' I said. 'No more questions.'

Fred Pleat left the court and, as a bonus to our side, he gave Steve a slight wave as he passed the dock. I hoped the jury had been watching.

'My Lord, that concludes the case for the prosecution,' said their QC.

The judge looked at the clock on the courtroom wall that showed ten past four, then he turned towards the jury.

'Ladies and gentlemen of the jury,' he said. 'You are free to go now until tomorrow morning at ten o'clock. May I remind you not to discuss the case amongst yourselves, nor with anybody else, not even your families. You will get your chance to deliberate in due course.'

The jury was then ushered out of court.

'Mr Mason,' the judge said when the jury door had been closed. I had earlier informed the judge that I wished to make a submission at the conclusion of the prosecution's case, and members of the jury were never present in court during legal argument.

'Yes, My Lord,' I said, struggling upright. 'Thank you.' I collected together some papers in front of me. 'My Lord, the defence wishes to make a submission to the court that the defendant has no case to answer. The prosecution have presented nothing more than circumstantial

335

evidence. There is nothing to show that my client was ever in Mr Barlow's house, let alone being there at the time of the murder.'

I took my time going over each of the witnesses' evidence in some detail.

'In conclusion,' I said. 'The forensic evidence may be able to place my client's pitchfork and wellington boots at the scene, but this does not prove that my client was there with them at the time. The prosecution may also be able to show that hair and blood from the victim were found in my client's car, but they were not able to demonstrate that the car had ever been at Mr Barlow's residence, nor that it had been locked throughout the afternoon and early evening on the day of the murder, while it sat on Mr Mitchell's driveway.

'While the defence readily accepts that our client and Mr Barlow held an ongoing and deep-seated antagonism towards each other, this is not evidence of murder. If it were, then half the nation would be so tainted. The defence further accepts that our client does not have an alibi for the time of the murder, but failure to have an alibi is not evidence of guilt. It is our contention that the prosecution has failed to present *prima facie* evidence of Mr Mitchell's guilt. My Lord, we submit that you should direct the jury to return a not guilty verdict because there is no case for Mr Mitchell to answer.'

I sat down.

'Thank you, Mr Mason,' said the judge. 'I will consider your submission overnight and make a ruling in the morning. Court adjourned until ten o'clock tomorrow.'

'All rise.'

Eleanor finally did come to Oxford on Wednesday night. She was waiting for me in the dimly lit hotel lobby when I returned from court. I hadn't expected her to be so early, and I was worried that there might be a message for me giving yet another good reason why she couldn't make it tonight either. So I was caught unawares as I struggled with both my box of papers and the crutches. She came up behind me and took the box just before it dropped to the floor.

'Oh, thank you,' I said, thinking it had been one of the hotel staff.

Eleanor peeped at me round the side of the box.

'Hello,' I said with a grin from ear to ear. 'How absolutely wonderful. You can catch my boxes any day you like.'

'I thought I'd surprise you,' she said. 'I've been here more than an hour.'

'Blimey,' I said. 'If I'd known that I would have been here more than an hour ago.'

'Why weren't you?' she said in mock annoyance.

'I was busy telling my client what a complete fool he'd been,' I said.

'Why?' she said.

'He shouted at one of the witnesses,' I said. 'What an idiot!'

I had indeed spent the last hour giving Steve a roasting in the holding cells beneath the court.

'I'm sorry,' Steve had whined at me. 'I couldn't help it. I was so mad. That bloody Clemens has been riding all my horses. He'd be delighted if I got convicted. Be laughing all the way to the bloody winner's circle.'

'But you still mustn't do it,' I had urged him again. 'It is the very worst thing you could have done and now the judge has to make a decision about whether we carry on with the trial or if he lets you go, and he will not have been impressed by your actions. You showed him your temper. He might just think that your temper has something to do with the murder.'

'I'm sorry,' he had said again.

'And,' I had said, rubbing salt into his wound, 'Clemens wasn't even lying when you shouted at him. You have often said that Barlow was a Judas. I've heard you myself in the changing rooms.'

Steve had sat on the bare wooden chair in the cell looking very shamefaced. For a change, he'd seemed quite pleased when the prison officer had unlocked the cell door to say that the transport was ready and he had to go. Perhaps I had been a little hard on him but, if the trial were to continue, I needed him to remain sitting calmly and silently in the dock, no matter what the provocation.

Eleanor now leaned forward and gave me a brief kiss on the lips.

'Do you want to go for a drink?' I asked her. 'It's nearly six.'

'No,' she said emphatically. 'I want to go to bed.'

In the end we did both.

I ordered a bottle of champagne and two glasses from the bar to take up to my room.

'I've never made love in a prison before,' said Eleanor excitedly as we came out of the lift onto one of the galleried landings of 'A' wing. 'In fact, I've never even been in a prison before.'

'They're not usually like this,' I said. 'For a start, they always smell dreadful. A mixture of disinfectant and stale BO. Never enough showers.'

'Ugh,' she said.

All my apprehension about this encounter came flooding back with a vengeance and I was shaking like a leaf by the time we had negotiated the long gallery to my room, so much so that I couldn't even get the cork out of the champagne bottle.

'Here,' said Eleanor taking it from my trembling hands. 'Let me do that.' She poured the golden bubbling liquid into the two tall flutes. 'My, we are a nervous boy,' she said as I took the glass with a tremor.

'I'm sorry,' I said.

'Don't be,' she said. 'I'm pretty nervous, too.'

I sat on the edge of the bed, kicked off my shoes and lay down, putting my feet up on the bedcovers. I tapped the hard plastic shell beneath my shirt.

'This damn thing doesn't help either,' I said.

'Let me look after you,' she said, coming over and lying down beside me.

And she did.

All my apprehension drifted away to nothing and all my fears were unfounded. Maybe it really was like riding a bicycle, I thought. Once you had learned the knack you never forgot it.

Eleanor helped ease my itchy body out of the plastic straightjacket and also out of my clothes. I lay naked on the bed as she washed and cooled me using damp towels from the bathroom, and then she herself stripped off and climbed in beside me, between the sheets.

Making love with a broken back is, by necessity, a gentle and tender process. But we discovered it could also be a sensual and passionate one.

Afterwards, we lay entwined together for a while, drifting in and out of light sleep. I would have been so happy to stay like that all night but I needed to do some reading, ready for the morning.

I rolled over gently to look at the digital clock on the bedside cabinet. Seven forty-five. I tried to ease myself up, although it was against my back surgeon's rules. Eleanor stirred as I tried to remove my arm from beneath her waist.

'Hello,' she said, smiling up at me. 'Going somewhere already?'

'Yup,' I said, smiling back. 'Got to get back to my wife.'

She suddenly looked alarmed, but relaxed when she saw I was joking.

'You kidder,' she said, snuggling into my chest.

'But I really do need to get back to my work,' I said. 'I have to be prepared for tomorrow. And, what's more, I'm hungry.'

'I'm hungry for you,' Eleanor said back to me, seductively fluttering her eyelashes.

'Later, dear. Later,' I said. 'Man cannot live by sex alone.'

'But we could try,' she said. Then she sighed and rolled off my arm, releasing me.

She helped me back into my plastic corset and then into a towelling robe.

'Let's have some room service,' I said. 'Then I can work and eat.'

Eleanor called down for the food while I set about looking through the papers that I would need in the event that the judge did not rule in our favour over the defence submission. To be honest, I didn't really expect him to. Even though much of it was circumstantial, there was probably enough evidence to convict, and certainly enough to leave the question to the jury.

If it was in the balance, the judge might simply allow the trial to continue because the decision was then taken out of his hands and passed to the jury. And Steve

Mitchell's conduct during the afternoon had almost certainly not endeared him to the judge – not that that should be a consideration, but it probably would be.

Since the Criminal Justice Act 2003 had come into force, the prosecution had the right to appeal rulings by judges over whether there was a case to answer, and, in my experience, judges had since become less inclined to so rule for fear of having their decision overturned on appeal.

All in all, I wasn't too hopeful, and so I still had to do my homework.

However, over our room-service dinner, eaten in our bathrobes, I told Eleanor about the news I had heard from Nikki at lunchtime.

'What are you going to do about it?' she asked.

I explained to her about the defence submission I had made to the court at the end of the prosecution case.

'If the judge doesn't rule in our favour in the morning,' I said, 'and I don't think he will, I intend calling a couple of witnesses to explore what Nikki found out.'

'Can you call anyone you like as a witness?' she asked.

'Yes and no,' I said.

'Explain,' she said.

'I can call whoever I like as long as their evidence is relevant to the case,' I said. 'But if I'm going to call the defendant as a witness, I have to call him first. I couldn't call someone else first and then go back to Steve. But I don't think I'll be calling him anyway in this case. He's a bit too volatile. And our defence is that he's being framed, so all he could say is that he didn't do it, and he knew nothing about it, and I can say that to the jury anyway.'

I paused to take a mouthful of my dinner.

'I did think about calling character witnesses but I'm not sure that would be a good idea. Steve's character is hardly as pure as the driven snow.'

'You can say that again,' she said. And she should know.

'I asked my solicitor, Bruce Lygon, to contact both my new witnesses this afternoon,' I said. 'I am still waiting to hear what he says but I fully expect that at least one of them won't want to come to court.'

'But what happens then?' Eleanor asked.

'In the end, they don't get any choice in the matter,' I said. 'I can apply to the court for a witness summons which is then served on the potential witnesses and then they have to be there. If they don't turn up, the judge can issue a warrant for their arrest.'

'But surely that doesn't mean they also have to answer your questions.'

'No,' I agreed. 'But if they don't, they have to give a reason not to answer, and the only reason here would be that in doing so they might incriminate themselves. And that should, at least, do some good as it ought to put some doubt into the minds of the jury as to Steve's guilt.' I took another mouthful. 'But what I really need is time. Time to get the witnesses I need to court, but mostly time for more investigating.'

'And what will you do if the judge doesn't give you time?' she asked.

'Probably lose the case,' I said.

At least Julian Trent would then be pleased.

CHAPTER EIGHTEEN

As I had expected, on the Thursday morning at two minutes past ten, and prior to the arrival of the jury in the courtroom, the trial judge rejected the defence submission that there was no case to answer.

'If it then please My Lord,' I said, standing up. 'The defence would like to submit a list of witnesses we wish to be summonsed.'

'And how many witnesses are there on this list, Mr Mason?' the judge asked rather sternly.

'Initially I have two names, My Lord,' I said, picking up a sheet of paper. 'But there may be more, depending on the evidence of these witnesses.'

I passed the paper to the court usher who delivered it to the judge. He looked down at its brief contents.

'Why have these names not been previously submitted to the court, so that summonses might have been issued to them in good time?' he asked me.

'My Lord,' I said. 'Information came to our knowledge only yesterday which indicates that these witnesses are essential to our case.'

'And how is that?' he asked.

'Our case, My Lord,' I said, 'as detailed in the Defence Case Statement, previously submitted to the court, is that the defendant is innocent of the charges and that he is being framed for a crime he did not commit. In the light of fresh information, the defence now wishes to further this argument by calling these witnesses.

'My Lord,' I continued. 'Mr Mitchell's solicitor made an attempt to contact these potential witnesses during yesterday afternoon and evening. One of them indicated verbally to the solicitor that they had no wish, or intention, of attending court to assist the defence in this matter. Consequently, I would like to apply to the court for a witness summons.'

'How about the other?' asked the judge.

'As yet we have been unable to contact the second one, My Lord,' I said. 'But I have every reason to expect the same outcome.'

'Mr Mason,' said the judge. 'Have you shown your list to the prosecution?'

'I have, My Lord,' I said. 'I gave a copy to my learned friend just prior to the court sitting this morning.'

The judge invited the prosecution to respond to the request.

'My Lord,' said the smarmy prosecution QC. 'The prosecution has no objection to the summonsing of these witnesses if it is likely to aid justice. However, the defence has had ample time to prepare for this case and further procrastination should not be tolerated.'

Or in other words, I thought, we don't object but, oh yes, we do after all. Anything to sound reasonable, while not actually being so.

The judge, God bless him, chose to hear only the first part of the QC's statement.

'Very well,' he said. 'As the prosecution have no objection, I will allow a witness summons to be issued for each name. But be warned, Mr Mason, I will take a firm line if I consider that the defence is in any way wasting the court's time. Do I make myself clear?'

'Absolutely, My Lord,' I said.

'Will these witnesses be ready to be examined by this afternoon?' asked the judge.

'My lord,' said the prosecution QC rising rapidly to his feet. 'The prosecution requests more time to consider the names of these witnesses and to prepare for cross-examination.'

It was exactly as I had hoped, because I was not in any position to call my witnesses. Not yet, anyway.

'Would you be ready by tomorrow?' asked the judge.

'We would prefer Monday, My Lord,' said the smarmy QC.

'Any objection, Mr Mason?' asked the judge.

'No, My Lord,' I said, trying hard to keep a grin off my face. 'No objection.'

'Very well,' said the judge. He was probably already looking forward to an extra day on the golf course. 'Court is adjourned until ten o'clock on Monday morning.'

Excellent, I thought. Just what I had wanted, and just what I needed.

I ordered a taxi to take all my papers back to the hotel. I had previously been to the court office to get the witness summonses issued for Monday, and Bruce Lygon had departed eagerly to try and personally deliver them into the correct hands.

As I waited inside the court building lobby, I called Nikki.

'I now have the documentation,' she said excitedly. 'It all came through this morning.'

'Great,' I said. 'Now I have something else for you to do.'

'Fire away,' she said.

'I need you to go to Newbury to ask some more questions,' I said.

'No problem,' she replied.

I explained to her exactly what information I wanted her to find out, and where to get it.

'Right,' she said. 'Call you later.'

She hung up as my taxi arrived.

The taxi took me to the hotel and then waited as the porter carried all the boxes up to my room and I packed a few clothes into one of my new suitcases. Then the taxi took me and my suitcase to Oxford station, where we caught a fast train to London.

*

'What are you doing here?' asked Arthur as I walked into chambers soon after noon.

'The case has been adjourned until Monday,' I said. 'Perhaps Sir James will be ready to take over from me by then.'

'Er,' said Arthur, floundering. 'I believe that his case is still running on.'

'Arthur,' I said sarcastically. 'I pay you to lie *for* me, not *to* me.'

'Sir James pays me more than you do,' he said with a smile.

'Just so long as we know where we stand,' I said.

I had no intention of telling Sir James Horley anything about my new witnesses. The last thing I wanted was for him to now feel that the case wasn't such a lost cause after all, and for him to step back in and hog all the limelight. No way was I going to let that happen.

I went through to my room and set about looking a few things up in my case files and then I telephoned Bob, the driver from the car company. I urgently needed some transportation.

'I'll be there in about half an hour,' he said.

'Fine,' I said. 'I have some more calls to make anyway.'

One of them was to my father on the new mobile phone I had bought him.

'Having a nice time?' I asked him.

'I suppose so,' he said, rather reluctantly. 'But everyone else here is so old.' Just like him, I thought, rather unkindly.

I had sent him to the seaside, to stay in the Victoria Hotel in Sidmouth, Devon, where he could walk along the beach each day and get plenty of healthy fresh air, and where, I hoped, Julian Trent wouldn't think of looking for him.

Next I called Weatherbys, the company that administered British horse racing, the company that had paid Scot Barlow his riding fees as detailed on his bank statements. I needed some different information from them this time and they were most helpful in giving me the answers.

I also called Eleanor and left a message on her mobile phone.

She had left the Oxford hotel early in the morning to get back to work in Lambourn, but not so early that we hadn't had time for a repeat of the previous evening's lovemaking.

She called me back on my mobile as Bob drove me away from chambers.

'I got my time from the judge,' I said to her. 'And the witness summonses, too.'

'Well done you,' she replied.

'I'm in London,' I said. 'The judge adjourned until Monday morning. I've already been to my chambers, and I'm now on my way to Barnes to face the mess. And I'll probably stay there tonight.'

'I won't plan to go to Oxford, then,' she said, laughing.

'No,' I said. 'I won't be back there until Sunday night.'

'Sunday night!' she said. 'Don't I get to see you before then?'

'You could always come to London,' I said.

'I'm on call again,' she said.

'Isn't anyone else ever on call?' I asked.

'It's only for tonight,' she said. 'I could come tomorrow.'

'I have plans for during the day tomorrow,' I said. 'And then I thought I'd come down to you for the night, if that's OK.'

'Great by me,' she said.

The state of my home was worse than I had remembered. The stuff from the fridge that Trent had poured all over the kitchen had started to smell badly. It had been a warm May week with plenty of sunshine having streamed through the large windows into the airless space. The whole place reeked of rotting food.

I was sorry for my downstairs neighbours for having to live beneath it all for the past week, and I hoped for their sake that smells rose upwards like hot air.

I opened all the windows and let some fresh air in, which was a major improvement. Next I found an industrial cleaning company in the Yellow Pages and promised them a huge bonus if they would come round instantly to do an emergency clear-up job. No problem, they said, for a price, a very high price.

While I waited for them I used a whole can of air

freshener that I found, undisturbed, beneath the kitchen sink. The lavender scent did its best to camouflage the stink of decomposing fish and rancid milk, but it was fighting a losing battle.

A team of four arrived from the cleaning company. They didn't seem to be fazed one bit by the mess that, to my eyes, was still appalling.

'Had a teenager's party?' one of them asked in all seriousness.

'No,' I said. 'It was malicious vandalism.'

'Same thing,' he said, laughing. 'Now, is there anything you want to keep from this lot?' He waved a hand around.

'Don't throw out anything that looks unbroken,' I said. 'And keep all the paperwork, whatever condition it's in.'

'Right,' he said. He gave directions to his team and they set to work.

I was amazed at how quickly things began to improve. Two of them set to work with mops, cloths and brooms, while the other two removed the torn and broken furniture and stacked it on the back of their vehicle outside.

Within just a few hours the place was unrecognizable from the disgusting state that I had returned to. Most of the furniture was out, and the carpets and rugs had been pulled up. The kitchen had been transformed from a major health hazard into gleaming chrome and a sparkling floor. Maybe they couldn't mend the cracks in the marble worktops, but they did almost everything else.

'Right, then,' said the team leader finally. 'That wasn't too bad. No rats or anything. And no human remains.'

'Human remains?' I said, surprised.

'Nasty stuff,' he said. 'All too often these jobs involve cleaning places where old people have died and no one notices until the smell gets so bad.'

I shivered. 'What a job,' I said.

'Pays well,' he said.

'Ah, yes,' I said. 'Didn't find my chequebook did you?'

'All your paperwork's over there,' he said, pointing at a couple of large cardboard boxes sitting alone on the floor. Amazingly, my chequebook had survived, and was only slightly stained by the red wine.

I wrote him out a cheque for the agreed exorbitant amount and then they departed, taking with them most of my worldly goods to be delivered to the council dump.

I wandered aimlessly around my house, examining what remained. There was remarkably little. The cleaners had put cardboard boxes in each of the rooms, into which they had placed anything left unbroken. In my bedroom, the box merely contained a few trinkets and some old perfume bottles that had stood on Angela's dressing table. Other than the fitted wardrobe, the dressing table was the only piece of furniture remaining in the room, and that was only because I couldn't bear to see it go. I had asked the men to return it to the bedroom when I had caught sight of them loading it onto their truck.

Angela had sat for hours in front of its now-broken triple mirror every morning, drying her hair and fixing her make-up. She had loved its simplicity and, I discovered, it was too much of a wrench to see it taken away, in spite of the broken mirror on top and the snapped-off leg below.

My bed had gone, Julian Trent's knife having cut not only the mattress to ribbons, but the divan base beneath as well. In the sitting room everything had been swept away to the tip. Only a couple of dining chairs and the chrome kitchen stool had survived intact, although I had also kept back the antique dining-room table in the hope that a French polisher could do something about the myriad of Stanley-knife grooves that had been cut into its polished surface. I had also saved my desk from the dump to see if a furniture restorer could do anything about the green embossed panel that had once been inlaid into its surface but which now was twisted and cut through, the sliced edges of the leather curled upwards like waves in a rough sea.

The trip back to Barnes had been necessary and worthwhile. Not only had I managed to bring some semblance of order to my remaining belongings, but my hatred and contempt for Julian Trent had been rekindled. There was fire in my belly and I aimed to consume him with it.

I decided not to spend the night at Ranelagh Avenue as there was nothing left for me to sleep on, other than the floor, and I didn't fancy that. At about six o'clock I ordered a taxi and booked myself into the West London Novotel, overlooking Hammersmith flyover.

I lay on the bed in the room for a while idly watching the continuous stream of aircraft on their approach into London's Heathrow airport. One every minute or so, non-stop, like a conveyor belt, each aluminium tube in turn full of people with lives to lead, places to go, each of them with families and friends, wives and husbands, lovers and admirers.

I thought about other eyes that might also have been watching the same aircraft. Some of my past clients, plus a few that I had prosecuted, were housed at Her Majesty's expense in Wormwood Scrubs Prison, just up the road from the hotel.

At least I was able, if I wished, to join the throng in the air, coming or going on holiday to anywhere in the world I liked. Depriving someone of their liberty by sending them to prison may rob them of their self-respect, but, mostly, it deprives them of choice. The choice to go where and when they please, and the choice to do what they want when they get there. To lose that is the price one pays for wrongdoing, and for getting caught.

As I watched those aircraft, and their apparent freedom from the bounds of earth, I resolved once more to release Steve Mitchell from the threat of a lifetime spent watching the world pass him by through the bars of a prison window.

*

Bob collected me in the silver Mercedes at eight-thirty on Friday morning, and we set off northwards from Hammersmith to Golders Green.

Josef Hughes was waiting for us when we arrived at 845 Finchley Road. I hadn't been very confident that he would be there, firstly because I'd had to leave a message for him with someone else in the house using the payphone in the hallway, and secondly because I had real doubts that he would be prepared to help me. But, thankfully, my fears were unfounded as he came quickly across the pavement and climbed into the back seat of the car.

'Morning, Josef,' I said to him, turning round as best I could and smiling.

He continued to peer all around him, sweeping his eyes and head from side to side. It was the frightened look that I had come to know so well.

'Morning,' he said to me only after we had driven away. He turned to glance a few more times through the rear window and then finally settled into his seat.

'This is Bob,' I said, pointing at our driver. 'Bob is most definitely on our side.' Bob looked at me somewhat strangely but I ignored him.

'Where to now?' Bob asked me.

'Hendon,' I said.

We picked up George Barnett from outside the Hendon bus station as he had requested. He didn't want me going near his home, he'd said, in case anyone was watching. He, too, looked all around him as he climbed into the car.

I introduced him to Bob, and also to Josef.

'Where now?' asked Bob. I purposely hadn't told any of them where we were going.

'Weybridge,' I said to him.

Josef visibly tensed. He didn't like it, and the closer we came to Weybridge the more agitated he became.

'Josef,' I said calmly. 'All I want is for you to point out where you were told to go and tell the solicitor about approaching the members of the jury in the first Trent trial. We will just drive past. I don't expect you to go back in there yourself.'

He mumbled something about wishing he hadn't come. The long finger of fear extended by Julian Trent and his allies was difficult to ignore. I knew, I'd been trying to do so now for weeks.

As we went slowly along the High Street Josef sank lower and lower in the seat until he was almost kneeling on the floor of the car.

'There,' he said breathlessly, pointing above a Chinese takeaway. COULSTON AND BLACK, SOLICITORS AT LAW was painted onto the glass across three of the windows on the first floor.

Bob stopped the car in a side street and then he helped me out with the crutches. I closed the door and asked Bob to try and ensure that neither of his remaining passengers lost their nerve and ran off while I was away. I also asked him to get Josef out of the car in precisely three minutes and walk him to the corner and stay there until I waved from the window. Then I walked back to the High Street and slowly climbed the stairs to the offices of Coulston and Black, Solicitors at Law.

A middle-aged woman in a grey skirt and tight maroon jumper was seated at a cream-painted desk in the small reception office.

'Can I help you?' she said, looking up as I opened the door.

'Is Mr Coulston or Mr Black in, please?' I asked her.

'I'm afraid they're both dead,' she said with a smile.

'Dead?' I said.

'For many years now,' she said, still smiling. This was obviously a regular turn of hers, but one that clearly still amused her. 'Mr Hamilton is the only solicitor we now have in the firm. I am his secretary. Would you like to see him?'

'Yes please,' I said. 'I would.'

'Accident, was it?' she said, indicating towards the crutches. 'Personal injury case is it?'

'Something like that,' I replied.

'What name shall I say?' she asked, standing up and moving as if to go through the door behind her.

'Trent,' I said boldly. 'Julian Trent.'

The effect on her was startling. She went into near collapse and lunged at the door, which opened wide and sent her sprawling onto the floor inside the other room.

There I could see a smartly dressed man sitting behind a rather nicer desk than he provided for his secretary.

'Patrick,' the woman managed to say. 'This man says he's Julian Trent.'

There was a tightening around the eyes but Patrick Hamilton was more in control.

'It's all right, Audrey,' said Mr Hamilton. 'This isn't Julian Trent. Julian Trent is only in his early twenties.' He looked from Audrey up to my face 'Who are you?' he said. 'And what do you want from me?'

'Tell me what you know about Julian Trent,' I said to him, walking across to his desk and sitting down on the chair in front of it.

'Why should I?' he said.

'Because otherwise,' I said, 'I might go straight to the Law Society and report you for aiding and abetting a known offender. I might tell them about your role in getting Julian Trent off an attempted murder conviction.'

'You can't,' he said. 'You don't have the evidence.'

'Ah,' I said. 'There you might be wrong. I assume you've heard of Josef Hughes?'

He went a little pale. I stood up and went to the window. Bob and Josef were both standing on the corner opposite.

'Would you like me to ask him to come up and identify you?' I said to Hamilton.

He stood up and looked out of the window. Then he sat down again, heavily, into his chair. I waved at Bob.

'Now, Mr Hamilton,' I said. 'What do you know of Julian Trent?'

In all, I spent forty-five minutes in Patrick Hamilton's office listening to another sorry tale of petty greed gone wrong. As before, the chance of a quick buck had been the carrot dangled in front of his nose. Just a small thing had been asked for, to start with. Just to collect a statement from someone who would deliver it with no questions asked and to notarize it as a sworn affidavit. Then had come the further demands to attend at the High Court and, if necessary, commit perjury in order to convince the appeal judges as to the truth of the statement. There was no risk, he'd been told by his persuasive visitor. Josef Hughes would never tell anyone, the visitor had guaranteed it. Fortunately for him, he hadn't needed to testify, so technically he was in the clear. That was, until the next time.

I showed him the pictures of my house.

'This is what happens to those who stand up and fight,' I said. 'Unless we all do it together.'

I showed him another photo and he seemed to visibly shrink before my eyes. I didn't need to ask him if the photo was of the visitor. I could tell it was.

I stood up to go.

'Just one last question,' I said. 'Why you?'

I didn't really expect an answer, but what he said was very revealing.

'I've been the Trent family solicitor for years,' he said. 'Drawn up their wills and done the conveyancing of their properties. Michael and Barbara Trent have now moved to Walton-on-Thames, but they lived in Weybridge for years.'

'But your visitor wasn't Julian Trent's father?' I said to him.

'No, it was his godfather.'

CHAPTER NINETEEN

I took Josef Hughes and George Barnett to lunch at the Runnymede Hotel, in the restaurant there overlooking the Thames. Nikki Payne, the solicitor's clerk from Bruce's firm, came to join us. I had chosen the venue with care. I wanted somewhere peaceful and quiet, somewhere stress free and calming. I wanted somewhere to tell Josef and George what I had discovered and what I needed them to do to help me.

The four of us sat at a table in the window, with Nikki next to me and Josef and George opposite us. For a while we made small talk and chatted about the weather as we watched the pleasure boats moving up and down through the lock, and we laughed at a duck and her brood waddling in a line along the river bank. Everyone relaxed a little, and a glass of cool Chablis further eased their anxieties.

Finally, after we had eaten lunch from the buffet, we sat over our coffee while I told them about the murder of Scot Barlow. I told them how Steve Mitchell had been arrested for it, and how he was currently on trial at Oxford Crown Court.

'I've seen reports in the papers,' George said, nodding. 'Doesn't seem to be much doubt he did it, if you believe what you read there.'

'Never believe anything you read in the papers,' I said seriously. 'I have no doubt whatsoever that Steve Mitchell is innocent, and he is being framed.'

Both Josef and George looked at me with that same expression of incredulity that people have when a politician says that he really cares about drug addicts, or illegal immigrants.

'It's true,' I said. 'And I believe he's being framed by this man.' I placed a copy of the photograph I had shown to Patrick Hamilton on the table in front of them.

The effect was immediate. Both Josef and George shied away from the image as if it could somehow jump up and hit them. Josef began to take fast, shallow breaths, and I feared he was in danger of passing out, while George just sat there grinding his teeth together, never once taking his eyes off the man in the picture.

'It's all right, guys,' I said, trying to lighten the moment. 'He isn't here. And he doesn't know we're here, or even that I know either of you.'

Neither of them was much mollified by my assurances. They went on looking scared and uncertain.

'With your help,' I said. 'I can put this man behind bars where he can't get at you.'

'Julian Trent was behind bars,' said Josef quickly. 'But . . .' He tailed off, perhaps not wanting to say that it had been he who had helped get him out. 'Who says he can't still get at us from there? Where's the guarantee?'

'I agree with Josef,' said George with a furrowed brow. 'Julian Trent would simply repay the favour and get him out, and then where would we be?'

I felt that I was losing them.

'Let me first explain to you what I want to do,' I said. 'And then you can decide if you'll help. But, I'll tell you, I'm going to try and get this man, whether you help me or not. And it will be easier with your backing.'

Between us, Nikki and I told them everything we had discovered.

'But why do you need us?' said Josef. 'Why don't you just take all this to the police and let them deal with it?'

'I could,' I said. 'But, for a start, in this sort of case the police would take ages to do their investigating and, in the meantime, Steve Mitchell would be convicted of murder. And, as you both well know, it is easier to get someone acquitted at the first trial than to have to wait for an appeal.'

'So what do you intend to do?' asked George.

I told them.

I had to trust them all, including Nikki, not to tell anyone of my plans. So I didn't tell them quite everything. I did think about showing them the other photos, the ones of the wreckage of my house, which were still in my jacket pocket. Then Josef and George would understand that I was in the same position as they were. But it would also mean telling Nikki the inconvenient truth that I was being intimidated to influence the outcome of a trial, and that might put her under an obligation to tell the court, or, at least, to tell Bruce, who was her immediate superior. I didn't want to have to ask her to keep more confidences than I already had, and certainly not to do so when it would be so blatantly against the law.

When I had finished, the three of them sat silently for quite a while, as if digesting what I had said.

Eventually it was George who broke the spell.

'Do you really think it will work?' he said.

'It's worth a try,' I said. 'And I think it might if you two play your part.'

'I don't know,' said Josef, all his unease returning in full measure. 'I've got to think of Bridget and Rory.'

'Well, I'm game,' said George, smiling. 'If only to see his face.'

'Good,' I said, standing up. 'Come on. Let's go. There's something I want to show you.'

Bob drove us the half a mile or so to the far end of Runnymede Meadow and then waited in the car while the rest of us went for a walk. It was a bright sunny spring day but there was still a chill in the air, so the open space was largely deserted as we made our way briskly across the few hundred yards of grass to a small round classical-temple-style structure set on a plinth at the base of Cooper's Hill, on the south side of the meadow.

It had been no accident that we had come to lunch at Runnymede. This was where King John had been forced to sign the Magna Carta, the Great Charter of 15 June 1215. The Magna Carta remained the basis of much of our common law, including the right to be tried by a panel of one's peers, the right to trial by jury.

The Magna Carta Memorial had been built in 1957 and paid for by voluntary donations from more than nine thousand lawyers, members of the American Bar Association, in recognition of the importance of the ancient document in shaping laws in their country, and throughout Western civilization. The memorial itself is of strikingly simple design with eight slim pillars supporting an unfussy, flattish, two-step dome about fifteen feet or so in diameter. Under the dome, in the centre of the memorial, stands a seven-foot-high pillar of English granite with the inscription: TO COMMEMORATE MAGNA CARTA, SYMBOL OF FREEDOM UNDER LAW.

Every lawyer, myself included, knew that most of the clauses were now either obsolete, or had been repealed or replaced by new legislation. However, four crucial clauses of the original charter were still valid in English courts, nearly eight hundred years after they were first sealed into law, at this place, by King John. One such clause concerns the freedom of the Church from royal interference, another with the ancient liberties and free customs of the City of London and elsewhere, while the remaining two clauses were about the freedom of the individual. As translated from the original Latin, with the 'we' meaning 'the Crown', these two ran:

> *No freeman shall be seized, or imprisoned, or dispossessed, or outlawed, or in any way destroyed; nor will we condemn him, nor will we commit him to prison, excepting by the legal judgement of his peers, or by the laws of the land.*

and

> *To none will we sell, to none will we deny, to none will we delay right or justice.*

These clauses provided for freedoms that most of us took for granted. Only when the likes of Julian Trent or his godfather came along, acting above and beyond the law, did we understand what it meant to have our rights and justice denied, to be destroyed and dispossessed without proper process of the laws of the land.

I had spent the time we had been walking telling the others about the great meeting that had taken place so long ago on this very spot between King John and the English barons, and how the king had been forced to sign away his autocratic powers. And how, in return, the barons, together with the king, had agreed to be governed by the rule of law, and to provide basic freedoms to their subjects.

Now, I leaned against the granite pillar and its succinct inscription.

'So will you help me?' I said to Josef. 'Will you help me get justice and allow us freedom under law?'

'Yes,' he said, looking me straight in the eye. 'I will.'

Bob took Josef and George back to their respective homes in north London, while Nikki drove me to the railway station at Slough.

'Mr Mason?' Nikki said on the way.

'Yes?' I replied.

'Is what you're doing entirely legal?' she asked.

I sat silently for a moment. 'I'm not sure,' I said. 'In England, I know that it's not against the law *not* to tell the police about a crime, provided that you didn't stand idly by and let it happen, when informing the police might have prevented it. Other than where stolen goods are involved, and also for some terrorism offences, members of the public are not under any legal obligation to report something that other people have done just because they know it was unlawful.' She sat silently concentrating on her driving, and probably trying to make some sense of what I had said. 'Does any of that help?' I said.

'Yes,' she said. 'That's fine.'

'Is there a problem?' I asked her.

'No,' she said uncertainly. 'I don't think so. I just don't want to get into any sort of trouble.'

'You won't,' I said. 'I promise.' It was me, not her,

who might get into trouble for not having told the court about the intimidation.

She dropped me at the station and gave me a small wave as she drove off. I wondered if she might go and talk to Bruce after all. I looked at my watch. It was quarter past four on Friday afternoon and the case would resume at ten on Monday morning. Even if she called Bruce now, would it stop me on Monday? Maybe. I would just have to take my chances. I had needed to tell Nikki my plans. I still wanted more help from her.

As I waited on the platform at Slough my phone rang in my pocket.

'Hello,' I said.

'What does it take to get you to do as you're told?' said the whispering voice.

'More than you could ever know,' I said, and hung up.

What he probably didn't realize was how frightened I had been at what he might do. In fact, I still was.

I called Eleanor.

'Are you free from now on for the night?' I asked.

'All weekend,' she said happily.

'Good,' I said. 'Please will you pack a bag now. Put everything from your room that you absolutely couldn't bear to lose in your car and go to Newbury station and wait for me there.'

'Geoffrey,' she sounded worried. 'You're frightening me again.'

'Eleanor, please,' I said. 'Do it now and quickly. Get

away from the hospital and the house and then call me.'
I was thinking fast. 'Are you in your room or in the
hospital?'

'In my room,' she said.

'Is there anyone else with you?'

'No. But there are still a few in the hospital.'

'Call them,' I said. 'Get as many as you can to come
over to the house and be with you while you pack. Ask
someone to get your car to the door and then go. Do it.
Go now.'

'Right,' she said. 'I'm on my way.' The urgency of
my voice had clearly cut through her reservations.

'And make sure you're not followed,' I said. 'Go
round roundabouts twice and stop often to see if anyone
stops behind you.'

'Right,' she said again.

'I'll be at Newbury in forty-five minutes,' I said. 'Try
and keep on the move until then and don't take lonely
lanes. Main roads only.'

'OK,' she said. 'I get the message.'

Good girl, I thought.

I sat restlessly on the train until Eleanor called to say
she was safely away from Lambourn and she was now on
the M4, travelling eastwards between junctions fourteen
and thirteen.

'Is anyone following you?' I asked her.

'Not that I can see,' she said.

'Good,' I said. 'I'll see you at Newbury station.'

'Right,' she said. 'There are two exits at Newbury.

Come out of the station on the same side as the platform you get off the train. I'll be there.'

She pulled up outside the red-brick station building as I struggled through the narrow doorway with my suitcase and the crutches. I tossed the suitcase onto the back seat of her car and climbed into the passenger seat. Eleanor leaned over and gave me a kiss.

'Where to?' she said, driving away.

'Oxford,' I said.

One of the good things about having a room in an ex-prison was that it was just as difficult to break into as it had once been to break out of. My room at the hotel was as safe a place as I could think of to spend the weekend, especially as the cell-door locks were now controlled by the person on the inside.

I made Eleanor drive twice round the roundabout where the A34 crosses the M4 but, if there was someone tailing us, I couldn't see them.

'Do you really think that someone would have come to Lambourn looking for me?' asked Eleanor.

'Yes,' I said. 'I do. I think these people will stop at nothing. It's no longer about Steve Mitchell any more, it's to do with them not getting convicted for the murder of Scot Barlow. Once you've killed one person, it's much easier to kill again.'

I'd once been assured by one cold-bloodied client, following his well-deserved conviction for a string of murders, that, after the first couple, it had been as easy as stepping on a spider.

For the rest of the journey Eleanor spent almost as much time looking in the rear-view mirror as she did watching the road in front, but we made it to the hotel safely without hitting anything, and also without seeing anyone tailing us.

As we pulled up at the hotel entrance, Eleanor's phone rang.

'Hello,' she said, pushing the button. She listened for a few moments. 'Suzie, hold on a minute.' She put her hand over the microphone and turned to me. 'It's Suzie, one of the other vets at the hospital. Seems a young man has turned up there asking for me, says he's my younger brother.'

'And is he?' I asked her.

'I'm an only child,' she said.

'Does the young man know that Suzie is making this call?' I asked.

Eleanor spoke into the phone, asked the question and listened for a moment.

'No,' she said. 'The young man has talked his way up into my room and is waiting there. Suzie is downstairs.'

'Let me talk to her,' I said.

Eleanor spoke again into the phone and then handed it to me. I tossed my own phone at Eleanor. 'Call the police,' I said to her. 'Tell them there's an intruder in the house there with a girl on her own.' That should bring them coming with the sirens blazing.

'Suzie,' I said into Eleanor's phone. 'This is Geoffrey Mason, I'm a friend of Eleanor's.'

'I know,' she said, laughing. 'She's talked of nothing else for weeks.'

'Are you there on your own?' I asked her, cutting off her laughter.

'Yes,' she said. 'Except for him upstairs. The others have gone down the pub, but I didn't feel up to it.'

'Suzie, this is a serious situation,' I said. 'I don't want to alarm you too much, but the young man is not Eleanor's younger brother. She doesn't have any brothers. And I fear he could be dangerous.'

There was silence from the other end of the line.

I went on. 'Eleanor is talking to the police now.'

'Oh God!' she said shakily.

'Suzie,' I said urgently, not wanting her to go into a complete panic. 'As he's asked for Eleanor, go and tell him that she's gone to stay with her boyfriend in London. He might then go away.'

'I'm not going up there again,' she said with real fear in her voice.

'All right,' I said calmly. 'If you can leave the house without him seeing you, then go straight away. Go round to the pub, and stay there with the others.'

'OK,' she said rapidly. 'I'm going now.'

'Good. But go quickly and quietly,' I said. 'Are you talking on a mobile phone?'

'Yes,' she said.

'Then keep talking to me as you leave the house. Do it now.'

I could hear her breathing and also the squeak of a door being opened, and then it slammed shut.

'Bugger,' she said to the world in general.

'Quietly,' I hissed into the phone, but I don't think she heard me.

There was the sound of her feet crunching on the gravel as she ran down the path.

'Oh my God,' she screamed. 'He's coming after me.'

'Run,' I said.

I didn't need to say it. I could hear Suzie running. Then the running stopped and I heard a car door slam.

'I'm in my car,' she said breathlessly. 'But I haven't got the damn keys.' She was crying. 'Help me,' she shouted down the phone. 'Oh my God,' she said, her voice again in rising panic. 'He's walking down the path.'

'Can you lock the doors?' I said to her.

'Yes,' she said. I heard the central locking go click.

'Good,' I said. 'Does the horn work?'

I could hear her bashing at the button but there was no noise.

'It won't work,' she cried, still bashing. It obviously needed the key in the ignition.

'Where's Eleanor Clarke?' I could hear Julian Trent shouting, his voice muffled by the car doors and windows.

'Go away,' screamed Suzie. 'Leave me alone.'

It was like listening to a radio drama – all sound and no pictures. The noise of Trent banging on the windows of the car was plainly audible and I could clearly visualize the scene in my mind's eye.

'Go away,' Suzie screamed at him again. 'I've called the police.'

'Where's Eleanor?' Trent shouted again.

'With her boyfriend,' shouted Suzie back at him. 'In London.'

Well done her, I thought. It went quiet, save for the sound of Suzie's rapid shallow breathing.

'Suzie?' I asked. 'What's happening?'

'He's run off,' she said. 'He's disappeared round the corner of the hospital. Do you really think he's gone?'

'I don't know,' I said. 'But stay in the car. We've called the police. They are on their way. Stay in the car until they come.' I hoped that Trent hadn't disappeared round the corner of the hospital simply to get his trusty baseball bat, so he could smash his way into Suzie's car.

'Who the hell was it?' she asked me.

'I don't know,' I lied. 'But he definitely wasn't Eleanor's brother. I think he may have been someone on the lookout for women.'

'Oh my God,' she said again, but without the urgency of before. 'He might have raped me.'

'Suzie,' I said as calmly as possible. 'Be happy he didn't. You're fine. Describe him to the police and they will look after you. Ask them to get the others back from the pub to stay with you.'

'But I don't think I want to stay here,' she said.

'OK, OK,' I said. 'You can do whatever you please.'

By now she had calmed down a lot. Vets were obviously made of stern stuff.

'The police are here.' She sounded so relieved.

'Good,' I said. 'Give Eleanor a call later, after you've spoken to them.'

'OK,' she said. 'I will.' She sounded quite normal, almost as if she was now rather enjoying the situation. It must be due to the release of tension, I thought.

I hung up and passed the phone back to Eleanor.

'Why didn't you tell her that it was Julian Trent?' she said, almost accusingly.

'We don't absolutely know for certain that it was him, even if we are pretty sure that it was. The police are bound to be in touch with us soon because it was my phone you used to call them, so they'll have the number, and you must have had to give them your name.'

She nodded.

'If we want, we can give them Trent's name then as a possible suspect,' I said. 'But I certainly will not be telling them that I think he went there intending to threaten you so that I would purposely lose the Mitchell case.'

'No,' she said with conviction. 'Nor will I.'

Good girl, I thought, again.

Next, I called my father.

'Hello,' he said.

'Hi, Dad,' I said to him. 'How are things in sunny Devon?'

'Boring,' he said. 'When can I go home?'

'Soon,' I said. 'I'll let you know when. But please stay there for a bit longer.'

'Why?' he said. 'Why do I have to stay here?'

I hadn't explained everything to him about Julian Trent. Perhaps I should have, but I hadn't wanted to worry him. These days he tended to live in a more gentle world of pottering about in his garden and playing bridge with his neighbours. Baseball-bat wielding maniacs were not his typical concerns.

'I'll tell you everything next week,' I said. 'In the meantime, can't you go off on a drive somewhere? Go and visit Dartmoor or something.'

'I've been there before,' he said unhelpfully. 'Why would I want to go again?'

I gave up. 'Just stay in Sidmouth for a few more days,' I said sharply.

'Don't you tell me what to do,' he said with irritation.

'Please, Dad,' I said more gently.

'You're a strange boy,' he said. It was his usual answer for everything.

'Maybe,' I said. 'But please, Dad, stay there. It's important. Please just do as I ask.'

'All right,' he said reluctantly. 'At least you're paying.'

Indeed I was, and the Victoria Hotel in Sidmouth wasn't cheap. I'd had to give them my credit-card details over the phone, and send them a signed fax guaranteeing the full amount.

*

With the knowledge that Julian Trent had been in Lambourn only fifteen minutes previously, Eleanor and I felt quite relaxed as we made our way into the hotel with the stuff from her car, which was then taken away to the hotel car park.

I closed and locked the room/cell door with us securely on the inside, and felt safe for the first time in hours. Then I called down to the front desk and ordered a bottle of red wine and some glasses. Eleanor and I may need to be locked up in a prison cell for the weekend, but it didn't mean we couldn't have a few of life's little pleasures to while away the time.

When the room-service waiter delivered the wine, we ordered some food as well. I then asked the receptionist to ensure that I wasn't disturbed and that no calls were put through. 'Certainly sir,' she said.

'So tell me,' said Eleanor finally. 'Why do you suddenly think that I am now in danger from Julian Trent when I wasn't before?'

'Because since the witness summonses were delivered, he now knows for sure that I won't do what he wants. I think he would try to use you as a lever rather than as just an implied threat.'

'And it seems you are right,' she said. 'So now what?'

I glanced around our prison-secure room. It had been created out of three old cells knocked together, complete with the high-up barred windows that had been intended to give the prisoners only light rather than a view. Thankfully, a modern bathroom had been added during the conversion so 'slopping out' was no longer required.

'Eleanor,' I said, turning to look at her face. 'No one, not even you, has really understood what sort of people we are dealing with here, although I think you might now be beginning to. We are not living here in some television drama where the blood is fake and the characters mostly behave in a fairly decent manner. This is a story of blackmail and murder, where seriously nasty people would as easily kill you as they would a fly.' She stared at me with wide eyes. 'But I don't intend to let them do either.'

'But how?' she said.

I told her. Some of it she knew, and some she didn't. I spoke for more than an hour with her listening intently to what I said.

Only after I stopped did she ask me the big question. 'Why don't you just take all this to the police?' she said.

'Because I want my day in court,' I said. And I didn't want to have to admit that I had been intimidated for so long without saying anything. I valued my career.

I told her what I proposed to do on Monday morning when the trial resumed.

'Just as long as we are both still alive on Monday morning,' she said.

Now, for a change, she was frightening me.

CHAPTER TWENTY

'All rise,' called the court clerk.

The judge entered from his chambers, bowed slightly towards us and took his seat behind the bench. Everyone else then sat down. The court was now in session.

'Mr Mason,' said the judge.

'Yes, My Lord,' I said, rising.

'Still no sign of Sir James Horley?' he asked with raised eyebrows.

'No, My Lord,' I said.

'And you, and your client, are happy to continue with the case for the defence with you acting alone?' he said.

'Yes, My Lord,' I said. Steve nodded at the judge from the dock.

'I don't need to remind you of what I said about that not being grounds for an appeal,' said the judge.

'I understand, My Lord,' I said.

He nodded, as if to himself, and consulted a sheet of paper on the bench in front of him.

'Are your witnesses present?' he asked.

'As far as I am aware, My Lord,' I replied. I hadn't

actually been outside into the waiting area to check, but Bruce Lygon seemed happy they were ready.

In fact, I hadn't been outside at all since last Friday.

At ten thirty on Friday evening the telephone in the hotel room had rung. 'I thought I said no calls,' I had complained to the hotel operator when I'd answered it.

'Yes, Mr Mason, we are very sorry to disturb you,' she had said. 'But we have your nephew on the telephone, and he's frantic to get in touch with you. I'm very sorry, but he tells me your elderly father has had a fall and that he's been taken to hospital.'

'Did you confirm to my nephew that I was here?' I'd asked her.

'Of course,' she'd said. 'Shall I put him through?'

'Thank you,' I'd said. There had been a click or two, but no one had been on the line. Trent had already gained the information he had wanted. Thereafter Eleanor and I had not left the room for the whole weekend, not even for an exercise period in the old prison yard, although we had made up for it with plenty of exercise in bed. We had ordered room service for every meal and had instructed the staff to ensure that they were completely alone when it was delivered. They had probably thought we were totally mad, but they had been too polite to say so, to us at least.

I had called Bruce to discuss the question of how to get safely to court on Monday morning. Without telling him exactly why I was concerned, I explained to him that I really didn't want to run into either of my two witnesses before they were called and I needed some secure transport from the hotel to the court buildings. He had come up with the ingenious idea of getting one of the private security companies to collect me in a prison transfer van. It transpired that Bruce was a friend of the managing director, and he had thought the idea was a great hoot and had been happy to oblige, for a fee of course.

So, at nine o'clock on Monday morning, Eleanor and I had moved as quickly as my crutches would allow along the hanging gallery of 'A' wing, down in the lift and out through the hotel lobby. We had gone from the front door of the hotel, across six feet of paving, straight into the waiting white box-like vehicle with its high dark-tinted square windows, while Bruce had stood by on guard. Some of the hotel staff had watched this piece of theatre with wide eyes. I was sure that they must believe we were either escaped lunatics or convicts, or both.

Needless to say, Julian Trent had been nowhere to be seen, but it was better to be safe than dead.

Our prison van had then delivered us right into the court complex through the security gates round the back, just as it would have done if we had been defendants on remand. We had emerged into court number 1 along the cell corridor beneath, and then via the steps up to the dock. Eleanor, who had called the equine hospital to say she wasn't coming in to work, now sat right behind me in court, next to Bruce.

'Very well,' said the judge. He nodded at the court

usher, who went to fetch the jury. As we waited for them, I looked around the courtroom with its grand paintings of past High Sheriffs of Oxfordshire. On the wall above the judge there was the royal crest with its motto, HONI SOIT QUI MAL Y PENSE, written around the central crest. *Evil to him who evil thinks* was a translation from Old French, the medieval language of the Norman and Plantagenet kings of England. How about 'Evil to him that evil does', I thought. That would be much more appropriate in this place.

The press box was busy but not quite so full as it had been at the start of the trial the week before. Public interest had waned a little as well, and only about half of the thirty or so of the public seats were occupied, with Mr and Mrs Barlow senior sitting together in the front row, as ever.

The five men and seven women of the jury filed into the court and took their seats to my left in the jury box. They all looked quite normal. Mothers and fathers, brothers and sisters, professional people and manual workers, all of them thrown together into a panel by simple chance. There was nothing unusual or extraordinary about any one of them, but collectively they had to perform the extraordinary task of determining the facts, and deciding if the defendant was guilty or not. They'd had no training for the task, and they had no instruction manual to follow. Our whole legal system was reliant on such groups of people, who had never met one another prior to the trial, doing the 'right' thing and together making exceptional decisions on questions far beyond their regular daily experiences. It was one of the greatest strengths of our system, but also, on occasion, one of its major weaknesses, especially in some fraud trials where the evidence was complex and intricate, often beyond the understanding of the common man.

I looked at the members of this jury one by one, and hoped they had been well rested by four days away from the court. They might need to be alert and on the ball to follow what would happen here today, and to understand its significance.

'Mr Mason,' said the judge, looking down at me from the bench.

It was now time.

'Thank you, My Lord,' I said, rising. 'The defence calls . . .' Suddenly my mouth was dry and my tongue felt enormous. I took a sip from my glass of water. 'The defence calls Mr Roger Radcliffe.'

Roger Radcliffe was shown into court by the usher, who directed him to the witness box. He was asked to give his full name. 'Roger Kimble Radcliffe,' he said confidently. He was then given a New Testament to hold in his left hand and asked to read out loud from a card. 'I swear by almighty God that the evidence I shall give shall be the truth, the whole truth, and nothing but the truth.'

One could but hope, I thought.

I stood up but, before I had a chance to say anything, Radcliffe turned to the judge.

'Your Honour,' he said. 'I have no idea why I have been asked to come here today. I knew Scot Barlow only by reputation. I have never spoken to him and he has never ridden any of my horses. Your honour, I'm a very busy man running my own company and I resent having to waste my time coming to court.'

He stood bolt upright in the witness box looking at the judge with an air of someone who had been greatly inconvenienced for no good reason. His body language was clearly asking the judge to allow him to get back to his business.

'Mr Radcliffe,' the judge replied. 'The defence have every right to call whomsoever they wish, provided that their evidence is relevant to the trial. As yet, I cannot tell if that is the case here because I haven't yet heard any of the questions that Mr Mason wishes to ask. But rest assured,' he went on, 'if I consider that your presence is a waste of your time, or of the court's time, then I shall say so. But that decision shall be mine, not yours. Do you understand?'

'Yes, Your Honour,' Radcliffe said.

'Mr Mason,' invited the judge.

'Thank you, My Lord,' I said.

I had been thinking of nothing else all weekend except how to conduct this examination of my witness and now, when I had to start, I felt completely at sea. I had intended opening by asking him how well he knew Scot Barlow, but that point seemed to have been covered already.

I took another sip of water. The silence in the court-room was almost tangible and every eye was on me, waiting for me to begin.

'Mr Radcliffe,' I said. 'Could you please tell the jury what it is your company does?'

It was not what he had expected and he seemed to relax a little, the stress-lines around his eyes loosened a fraction and his furrowed brow flattened slightly.

'My main business,' he said, 'is the running of the Radcliffe Foaling Centre.'

'And could you please explain to the jury what that involves?' I asked him.

Roger Radcliffe looked imploringly at the bench.

'Is this relevant?' the judge asked me, getting the message.

'Yes, My Lord,' I said. 'I will show the relevance as my examination proceeds.'

'Very well,' said the judge. He turned to the witness box. 'Please answer the question, Mr Radcliffe.'

Roger Radcliffe blew down his nose with irritation. 'It involves exactly what the name implies.'

I waited in silence.

He finally continued without further prompting. 'We have about two hundred mares come to us each year. The foals are delivered in special conditions with proper veterinary care on hand and a team of specially trained grooms. The whole set-up has proved very popular with owners of mares as they feel more comfortable with the care their animals receive.'

Two hundred was about double the number of mares that Larry Clayton had claimed ten days previously while he had been resting his cowboy boots on his desk, but I was hardly going to accuse Roger Radcliffe of perjury over a minor exaggeration of the size of his business.

'And how long has your business been in operation?' I asked him.

'About seven or eight years,' he said. 'But it has become much bigger recently, and it continues to expand.'

'And are there specific reasons for that expansion?' I asked.

'We are doing well,' he said. 'And over the last twelve months I have been able to inject a substantial investment into the business.'

'Would that investment have been possible due to the success of your horse Peninsula?' I asked.

'Yes,' he said. 'Exactly so.'

'Mr Radcliffe,' I said. 'Some members of the jury may not be familiar with horse racing so perhaps you could tell them about Peninsula.'

I glanced at the judge. He was looking at me intently and raised his eyebrows so that they seemed to disappear under the horsehair of his wig.

'Technically, Peninsula is no longer my horse,' said Roger Radcliffe. 'He was syndicated for stud at the end of last year and is now part owned by a number of individuals or organizations. I have retained only two shares in him out of sixty.'

'But you did own him throughout his racing career?' I asked.

'Yes, I did.' He smiled at the memory. 'And I bred him. I owned his mare and he was foaled at my place. I decided to keep him rather than sending him to the sales, and now I am so glad I did.'

'So he was a success on the racecourse?' I asked.

'Yes, indeed he was,' said Radcliffe. 'He was both the Champion two-year-old and he was named Horse of the Year in 2007. But that was nothing compared with last year.' Radcliffe was enjoying himself now and was totally relaxed. 'He won the Two Thousand Guineas at Newmarket in May, the Derby at Epsom in June and the Breeders' Cup Classic in California last October. It was quite a year.' He smiled at the jury and many of them smiled back at him.

Nikki came into the courtroom and sat down next to Eleanor.

'All set,' she said quietly to my back.

I turned around and leaned down to her.

'Good,' I said quietly. 'Keep watch from the door, I'll give you the signal. Go back out now.'

She stood up, bowed slightly to the bench, and departed.

'Mr Mason,' said the judge. 'I am sure the jury and I have enjoyed our little lesson in Thoroughbred racing, but could you please show us the relevance of your questions, or else I shall release Mr Radcliffe back to his busy business schedule.'

'Yes, My Lord,' I said rather sheepishly.

Roger Radcliffe continued to stand ramrod stiff in the witness box. He was enjoying my discomfort. Now, I thought, it was time to rub that smirk off his face.

'Mr Radcliffe,' I said to him. 'We have heard already that you hardly knew the victim of this murder, but how well do you know the defendant, Mr Mitchell?'

'About the same as Barlow,' he said. 'Mitchell has been champion jockey over the jumps. I personally don't have jump horses but I know him by reputation. We may have met a few times at events. I really can't remember.'

'And how about Miss Millie Barlow, Scot Barlow's sister. Did you know her?'

I noticed a very slight tightening of the skin around his eyes. He was getting a little worried.

'I don't believe I did,' he said calmly.

It was his first lie.

'Are you sure?' I asked him.

'Quite sure,' he said.

'She was an equine veterinary surgeon,' I said. 'Sadly, she died last June. Does that jog your memory?'

'I know that a vet died during a party last year,' he said. 'Was that her?'

'Yes,' I said. 'It was. An inquest jury in January

concluded that she had taken her own life by injecting herself with a substantial dose of the barbiturate anaesthetic thiopental.'

'Very sad,' he said, rather condescendingly. 'But I can't see the relevance.'

'Mr Radcliffe,' I said, ignoring his comment. 'Were you having an affair with Millie Barlow?'

'No I was not,' he almost shouted. 'How dare you suggest such a thing?'

He glanced across at his wife, Deborah. She had come into the court with him when he had been called, and she was now sitting in the public seats behind Mr and Mrs Barlow. I turned to look at her but I couldn't see the expression on her face.

'Mr Radcliffe, did you attend the party where Millie Barlow died?'

'Yes,' he said. 'As a matter of fact, I did.'

'And can you recall if there was a reason for the party?'

'Yes, there was,' he said. 'It was a party given jointly by me and Simon Dacey, at Simon's house, to celebrate Peninsula winning the Derby.'

'Simon Dacey being the trainer of the horse?' I said.

'Yes,' Radcliffe replied.

'Can you recall why Millie Barlow was also a guest at this party?' I asked him.

'Mr Mason,' said the judge. 'Are these questions really relevant to the case before this court?'

'My Lord,' I said. 'The prosecution has previously

made it clear that the relationship that existed between the defendant and Miss Barlow was a major cause of the antagonism between the defendant and the victim, and hence, they claim, it ultimately provided the motive for murder. It is my intention to explore this relationship further by reference to Miss Barlow's untimely death last June.'

'Very well,' he said. 'You may continue.'

'Thank you, My Lord.' I turned back to the witness box. 'Now, Mr Radcliffe,' I said. 'I was asking you if you knew why Millie Barlow was invited to the party.'

'I have no idea,' he said. 'I told you I didn't know her.'

'Then why,' I said, picking up a piece of paper from the table, 'did you purchase a brand-new sports car and give it to her as a gift?'

He was initially flustered, but he recovered fast. 'I have no idea what you are talking about.'

'I'm talking about a bright red Mazda MX-5 Roadster purchased in September 2007 from the Mazda dealership in Newbury,' I referred to the piece of paper in front of me that Nikki had obtained from the dealership the previous Friday, 'at a cost of fifteen thousand, seven hundred and fifty pounds.'

He stood silently in the witness box staring at me.

'Come now, Mr Radcliffe,' I said. 'Are you telling the court that you did not know the person to whom you gave a brand-new car worth more than fifteen thousand pounds?'

'I still have no idea what you are talking about,' he said. 'I've never been to any Mazda dealer.'

'Mr Radcliffe,' I said. 'Last Friday my solicitor's clerk visited the dealership and they told her they remembered this car being bought. They remembered because it was paid for, in full, with a banker's draft, which is most unusual. The draft did not have the name of the purchaser on it. However, the sales representative remembered the purchaser, and he was able to positively identify you from this photograph.'

I held up the large glossy brochure that I had taken from the foaling centre on my first visit there, the brochure with the photograph on the front of a smiling Roger and Deborah Radcliffe standing in a paddock with some mares and foals. The same brochure I had showed first to Patrick Hamilton in his office, and then to Josef Hughes and George Barnett at Runnymede the previous Friday.

'I can call the Mazda sales representative as a witness if you want me to.' I paused. He said nothing. 'Now, Mr Radcliffe, please can you tell the jury why you gave a brand-new car worth over fifteen thousand pounds to Miss Millie Barlow in September 2007?'

'It's none of your business,' said Radcliffe defiantly.

'Mr Radcliffe,' the judge intervened. 'You will answer the question, unless, that is, you wish to claim that, in doing so, you might incriminate yourself. And if that is the case, then, one can assume, the question may be of interest to the police.'

Radcliffe stood silent for a moment and then he smiled.

'It was a gift to her for doing a fine job when Peninsula was foaled. She was the attending vet. I didn't want to say so, or to give my name when I purchased the car as I didn't want there to be a tax implication for her. I didn't want the Inland Revenue to consider it as a payment for services and require her to pay income tax on its value, or require me to pay the National Insurance contributions.'

He stood relaxed in the witness box smiling at the jury. 'I am sorry I tried to avoid a little tax,' he said with a laugh. 'We all try it occasionally, don't we? I will pay the back tax right away.'

He had done well, I thought. Quick thinking, in the circumstances.

'Was it not payment to her because she was black-mailing you?' I asked him.

The smile disappeared from his face. 'Blackmail?' he said.

'Yes, Mr Radcliffe, blackmail.'

'That's nonsense,' he said with an air of confidence.

I turned and waved at Nikki, who was watching me through the glass panel in the courtroom door.

She entered the court followed by two other people.

All three of them bowed slightly to the bench and then came and sat behind Eleanor and Bruce.

I watched the colour drain out of Roger Radcliffe's face as he stared at the newcomers. He gripped the sides of the witness box as if to prevent himself falling over.

Both Josef Hughes and George Barnett sat quite still and stared back at him.

'Mr Radcliffe,' I said calmly. 'Do you know someone called Julian Trent?'

Roger Radcliffe was more than flustered this time. He was in a panic. I could tell from the way the skin had tightened over his face and there was a slight tic in the corner of his left eye. He stood quite still in the witness box. But I was sure that, behind those steely eyes, his brain was moving fast.

'Julian Trent is your godson, isn't he?' I asked him.

'Yes,' he said quietly.

'I'm sorry, Mr Radcliffe,' I said. 'Would you please speak up. The jury can't hear you if you whisper.'

The irony of the comment was not lost on him. He positively glared at me.

I noticed that the press box had filled considerably since the start of the day. Word had clearly been passed outside that something was afoot and more reporters had been dispatched to the court. The public seats had also noticeably filled, and two court security officers now stood either side of the door. Detective Inspector McNeile, his evidence completed, was sat in a row of seats positioned in front of the press box, and he too was taking a keen interest in the proceedings.

I poured myself more water from the carafe on my table, and then slowly drank some of it.

'Now, Mr Radcliffe,' I said finally. 'Can we return to the question of blackmail?'

'I don't know what you mean,' he said, but the confidence had gone out of his performance.

'We have heard that you bought a new car and then gave it to Millie Barlow,' I said. 'Is that correct?'

'Yes,' he said quietly.

'Speak up,' said the judge.

'Yes,' Radcliffe repeated louder.

'I repeat my question,' I said. 'Was that car given by you to Millie Barlow as a payment for blackmail?'

'No. That's utter rubbish,' he said.

I collected some more papers together in my hands.

'These are bank statements,' I said. 'Millie Barlow's bank statements. They show that she received regular payments into her account over and above her salary from the equine hospital. Can you explain these payments?'

'Of course not,' Radcliffe said.

'Were these also blackmail payments, Mr Radcliffe, and did they come from your bank account?'

'No,' he said. But he didn't convince me, and some of the jury looked sceptical as well.

'Mr Radcliffe,' I said, changing direction. 'Do you ever have need for anaesthetics at your equine maternity unit?'

'No,' he said firmly. 'Why should we?'

'Perhaps for a Caesarean birth if a foal cannot be born naturally?' I asked.

'No,' he said, suddenly back on surer ground. 'The mare would be transferred to one of the local equine hospitals and anaesthetized there.'

'And what would happen if a foal was born grossly deformed, or blind?'

'That is very rare,' he said.

'But it must have happened at least once or twice in your experience.'

'A few times, yes,' he said.

'And would the foal be immediately put down?'

He could see where I was going, and he didn't like it.

'I suppose so,' he said.

'And isn't a very large dose of a barbiturate anaesthetic used for that purpose, a barbiturate anaesthetic like thiopental for example?' I asked.

'I wouldn't know,' he said.

'Mr Radcliffe,' I said, changing tack again. 'Do you know of someone called Jacques van Rensburg?

'I don't think so,' he said. But he started to sweat.

'You may have known of him simply as Jack Rensburg,' I said. 'He used to work for you as a groom.'

'We have lots of grooms during the foaling season,' he said. 'And they come and go regularly. I tend to use their first names only. We've had quite a few Jacks.'

'Perhaps I can help you,' I said. 'I have a photograph of him.'

I took a stack of the Millie and foal pictures out of one of my boxes and passed them to the court usher, who passed one to the judge, one to the prosecution, six to the jury and, finally, one to Radcliffe in the witness box.

Some of the colour had returned to his face but now it drained away again and he swayed back and forth. Unfortunately both the judge and the jury had been looking at the photograph and had missed it.

SILKS

'Members of the jury,' I said, 'you will see that the photograph is of a new-born foal. The woman in the picture is Millie Barlow, the veterinary surgeon who had been present at the birth, and the man standing behind her, who you can clearly see in spite of the slightly blurred image, is Jacques van Rensburg, a South African citizen. Isn't that right, Mr Radcliffe?'

'If you say so,' he said.

'I do. And the foal is Peninsula, the horse that went on to be such a champion,' I said. 'Isn't that right?'

'It might be,' he said. 'Or it could be another foal. I can't tell. Many foals look alike.'

'Of course,' I said. 'But I assure you that the foal in this picture is Peninsula. He was the very first foal that Millie Barlow had delivered on her own. She was so proud of that horse and her part in its life that she kept a copy of that picture in a silver frame. It was her most prized possession. Isn't that right, Mr Radcliffe?'

'I have no idea,' he said.

'After his sister's death, Scot Barlow asked for the picture in the silver frame to keep in his home as a lasting reminder of her. But the photo was removed from its frame and taken away from Scot Barlow's house on the night he was killed. Why do you think that was?'

'I have no idea,' he said again.

'I put it to you, Mr Radcliffe, that the picture was removed because it was being used by Scot Barlow to blackmail you in the same way that his sister had done previously. Isn't that right?'

397

'No,' he said. 'That's nonsense. I don't know what you're talking about. Why would anyone blackmail me?'

'Does Jacques van Rensburg still work for you?' I asked him.

'No,' he said. 'I don't believe he does.'

'No,' I said. 'He couldn't, could he? Because he's dead. Isn't that right, Mr Radcliffe?'

'I have no idea,' he said yet again.

'Oh yes, I think you do,' I said. 'Jacques van Rensburg went on holiday to Thailand, didn't he?'

'If you say so,' Radcliffe replied.

'Not if I say so, Mr Radcliffe,' I said, taking yet another sheet of paper from my stack and holding it up. 'The South African Department of Home Affairs in Pretoria says so. He went to Thailand on holiday and he never came back, isn't that right?'

Roger Radcliffe stood silently in the witness box.

'Do you know why he didn't come back, Mr Radcliffe?' I asked.

Again he was silent.

'He didn't come back because, as the South African government records show, he was drowned on Phuket beach by the Great Asian Tsunami. Isn't that right?'

Radcliffe still said nothing.

'And, Mr Radcliffe, do you know when the Great Asian Tsunami disaster occurred?'

Radcliffe shook his head and looked down.

'It is sometimes known as the Boxing Day Tsunami, is

it not, Mr Radcliffe?' I said. 'Because it took place on December the twenty-sixth. Isn't that right?'

He made no move to answer.

I continued. 'Which means that, as Jacques van Rensburg was drowned in Thailand by the Great Asian Tsunami on the twenty-sixth of December 2004, this picture had to have been taken before Christmas that year. Which also means, does it not, Mr Radcliffe, that, even though the record of the birth submitted by you to Weatherbys shows otherwise, Peninsula had to have been foaled prior to the first of January 2005 and was therefore, in fact, officially a four-year-old horse when he won the Two Thousand Guineas and the Derby last year and not a three-year-old as demanded by the Rules of Racing?'

For what seemed like an age, the silence in the court was broken only by the sound of fast-moving pencils on notebooks in the press box, and by a slight sob from Deborah Radcliffe in the public seats.

The judge looked intently at Roger Radcliffe, who was standing silently in the witness box with his head down, his previous ramrod appearance now nothing but a distant memory.

'Well?' said the judge to him. 'The witness will please answer the question. Was Peninsula a four-year-old horse when he ran in the Derby?'

Radcliffe lifted his head a fraction. 'I refuse to answer on the grounds that I might incriminate myself.'

It was as close to a confession as we were likely to get.

But I hadn't finished with him yet.

'Mr Radcliffe,' I said. 'Did you murder Millie Barlow?'

His head came up sharply and he looked at me. 'No,' he said, but without much conviction.

I pressed on. 'Did you murder Millie Barlow because she made further blackmail demands on you after Peninsula had won the Derby?'

'No,' he said again.

'And did you then murder Scot Barlow when he took over the blackmail demands from his dead sister?'

'No,' he said once more.

'Or was it your godson, Julian Trent, who actually carried out that second murder, on your instructions, after you had used intimidation of these innocent people in order to secure his release from prison for that very purpose?' I waved my right hand towards Josef Hughes and George Barnett behind me.

Radcliffe's demeanour finally broke completely.

'You bastard,' he shouted at me. 'You fucking bastard. I'll kill you too.'

He tried to leave the witness box, but he had made just two steps towards me before he was surrounded by court security guards, and the police. The judge banged his gavel and silence was briefly restored. 'The defence rests, My Lord,' I said, and sat down. Perry Mason himself would have been proud of me.

CHAPTER TWENTY-ONE

The judge adjourned the case for lunch while Roger Radcliffe was arrested by Inspector McNeile. Radcliffe was cautioned and made aware that he had the right to remain silent, but that advice was obviously a bit late. The man I had come to know as 'the whisperer' was finally led away, still spouting obscenities in my direction.

The smarmy prosecution QC came across and firmly shook my hand. 'Well done,' he said with obvious warmth. 'We don't often get to see the likes of that in an English court.'

'Thank you,' I said. 'I intend to make another "no case" application and request an acquittal.'

'Up to the judge, old boy,' he said, 'I'll seek instruction from the CPS, but I don't think there will be any objection from our side. This jury would never convict Mitchell after hearing that lot.' He laughed. 'Best fun I've had in years. I don't even mind losing this one.'

Eleanor, behind me, rubbed my shoulders.

'You were brilliant,' she said. 'Absolutely brilliant.'

I turned and smiled at her. Josef Hughes and George

Barnett sat behind her, beaming away as if smiles could go out of fashion.

'You two can have your self-respect back,' I said. 'Without you here I think he might have bluffed his way out.'

If it was possible, they smiled even wider, and then shook me and each other by the hand. I thought it unlikely that the Law Society would give Josef back his right to practise, but he was still a young man and he was bright. I was confident that, without the fear that had consumed them over the past fifteen months, he and Bridget and baby Rory would now be fine.

'How about a coffee?' I said to them.

As we made our way out of court I bumped into Scot Barlow's parents. Mr Barlow senior was a big man and he stood full-square in front of me, blocking my path to the door. He was also considerably taller than I, and now he stood quite still and silent, looking down at me. I wondered if he was pleased or not. He had just discovered the truth about who had killed his children and why, but he had also discovered that they had both been blackmailers. Perhaps he might have preferred it if Steve Mitchell had been convicted of the murder of his son. That would have brought finality. Now he would have to endure another trial, and some unpleasant revelations.

He went on staring at me while I stood waiting in front of him, staring back. Eventually he nodded just once, and then turned aside to let me pass.

Eleanor, Josef, George, Bruce, Nikki and I sat at one

of the tables in the small self-service cafeteria area in the main court corridor, drinking vending-machine coffee from thin brown plastic cups, toasting our success.

'But why was it so important?' asked Bruce.

'Why was what so important?' I said.

'About the horse's age,' he said. 'So what if the horse was a year older than it was supposed to be when it ran in the Derby? I know that it was cheating and all that, but was it really worth murdering someone over? It was only a race.'

'Bruce,' I said. 'It may have been "only a race", but horse racing is very big business indeed. That horse, Peninsula, was sold to stud for sixty million US dollars. And mainly because it won that race.'

His eyebrows rose a notch or two.

'But it was because he won it as a three-year-old running against other three-year-olds that he was worth all that money. Three is young for a horse, but only horses of that age are allowed to run in the "classic" races held in England, and also the Triple Crown races in America.'

'I never realized,' said Bruce.

'Peninsula was syndicated into sixty shares,' I said. 'That means that he was sold in sixty different parts. Radcliffe says that he kept two for himself, so there are fifty-eight other shareholders who each paid Radcliffe a million dollars for their share. I suspect that most of those will soon be wanting their money back. I'd like to bet there are now going to be a whole bunch of law suits. It will all get very nasty.'

'But why didn't Radcliffe just register the horse with the right age and run him the year before?' Josef asked.

'Most racehorse foals are born between the first of February and the end of April, certainly by the middle of May,' I said. 'The gestation period for a horse is eleven months and mares need to be mated with the stallion at the right time so that the foals arrive on cue. The trick is to get the foals born as soon as possible after the turn of the year so that they are as old as possible, without them actually being officially a year older. In Peninsula's case, either someone messed up with the date of his mare's covering or, more likely, he was simply born a couple of weeks prematurely when he was due to be a very early foal anyway. Radcliffe must have decided to keep his birth secret until January. If he had registered it correctly in December then Peninsula would have been officially a yearling when he was biologically less than a month old. Then he would have been at a great disadvantage against the other horses born nearly a whole year before him but classified as being the same age. He would most likely still have been a good horse, but not a great one. Not sixty million dollars great. To say nothing of the prize money that Radcliffe will now have to give back for all of those races. The Epsom Derby alone was worth over seven hundred thousand pounds to the winner, and the Breeders' Cup Classic had a total purse of more than five million dollars.' I had looked them both up on the internet. It was going to be a real mess.

'But Millie knew the truth because she'd been there when Peninsula was foaled,' said Eleanor.

'Exactly,' I said. 'Radcliffe had probably paid her off. But maybe she was greedy, and that cost her her life. It was our good fortune that you were able to find an image of that picture of Millie and Peninsula as a foal.' I smiled at her. 'But the silly thing is that, if Radcliffe hadn't taken that photo from the silver frame in Scot Barlow's house, I would never have realized that it was important. He'd have literally got away with murder, and the racing fraud. I suppose, to Radcliffe, it must have shone bright as a lighthouse, advertising his guilt, but no one else would have thought so, certainly not this long after the event.'

'But how did you know about Millie's car?' Eleanor said.

'I became suspicious when I couldn't find any regular payments to any car-finance companies on Millie's bank statements,' I said. 'And there was no one-off large payment around the date you told me she had bought it. And Scot's statements didn't show that he had bought it for her, so I sent Nikki to the dealer in Newbury to ask some questions.'

Nikki smiled. 'But you were a bit naughty telling Radcliffe that they definitely recognized him from the photo,' she said. 'They only said that it might have been him, but they weren't at all sure.'

I looked at their shocked faces and laughed. 'It was a bit of a risk, I know. But I was pretty sure by then that I was right, and Radcliffe couldn't take the chance of me calling the Mazda chap.'

'How about Julian Trent?' asked George. 'What will happen to him?'

'I hope the police will now be looking for him in connection with Barlow's murder,' I said. 'In the meantime, I intend to keep well clear of him.'

'So do we all,' said George seriously. He was clearly worried and still frightened by the prospect of coming face to face with young Mr Trent. And with good reason.

'What about the second witness?' Bruce asked, indicating towards a man sitting alone reading a newspaper at one of the other tables. 'Aren't you going to call him?'

'No,' I replied. 'I always intended calling only one of them, but last Thursday when we got the witness summonses, I didn't know which of them it would be. I only found out on Friday when I showed the picture of Radcliffe to Josef and George and saw their reaction.'

I'd had a second picture in my pocket on Friday. A picture of my second witness, cut out from the *Racing Post*, but it hadn't been needed.

Now I stood up and walked over to him on my crutches.

'Hello,' I said. 'Thank you so much for coming. But I'm afraid I don't think I'll be needing you any more.'

Simon Dacey turned in his chair and faced me. 'This has all been a waste of time, then,' he said with slight irritation. He folded his newspaper and stood up.

'Yes,' I said. 'I'm sorry.'

'What's been going on in there?' he asked, nodding his head towards the door of number 1 court. 'There seems to have been lots of excitement.'

'You could call it that, I suppose,' I said. 'Roger Radcliffe seems to be in a spot of bother.'

There was a slightly awkward moment of silence while he waited for me to explain further, but I didn't. The trial was not yet technically over, and he was still, in theory, a potential witness.

'No doubt I'll find out why in due course,' Dacey said with a little more irritation.

Indeed he would, I thought. For a start, he would also be losing his win percentage from all those Peninsula race victories. He might even lose his training licence, but I rather hoped not. I suspected that he knew nothing about the fraud, or the murders, just as he knew nothing about his wife's affair with Steve Mitchell.

Francesca Dacey's affair had been a bit of a red herring in my thinking. At one point I had wondered if Mitchell had been framed by her husband simply to get him out of the way. But the truth was that Steve had been nothing more than a convenient fall guy.

Radcliffe had clearly been determined that Mitchell should be convicted so as to close the police file on the case, to ensure that no further investigations were made, investigations that might uncover the blackmail, and the true reason for Barlow's murder. Radcliffe's whispering intervention with me, the belt and braces of his frame-up plot, had ultimately led to his downfall. Without it, I was quite certain, Steve Mitchell would, even now, be starting a life sentence behind bars, and I would have been one of the prosecution witnesses, describing in detail my encounter with Scot Barlow in the showers at Sandown Park racecourse.

Ironically, the very attempt to pervert the cause of justice had ultimately been responsible for justice being done.

When the court resumed at two o'clock, I hardly had to make my submission. The judge immediately asked the prosecution for the Crown's position and their QC indicated that he had been instructed not to oppose the application. The judge then instructed the jury to return a not-guilty verdict and Steve Mitchell was allowed to walk free from the dock.

The story had travelled fast and there was a mass of reporters and television cameras outside the court building when Bruce and I emerged with Steve Mitchell at about three o'clock, into a wall of flash photography. Sir James Horley QC, I thought while smiling at the cameras, would be absolutely livid when he watched the evening news. He had missed out completely on the number one story of the day.

As we were engulfed by the sea of reporters, Eleanor shouted that she would go and fetch her car. There would be no chance of finding a taxi with all this lot about.

'Be careful,' I shouted back at her, thinking of Julian Trent, but she was gone.

Steve and Bruce answered questions until they were nearly hoarse from having to talk loudly over the traffic noise and the general hubbub, and even I was cajoled by some of the reporters into a rash comment or two. I was careful not to say things that would find me in hot water for giving out privileged or sensitive information, things that might be pertinent to the future trial. However, Steve Mitchell had no such qualms. He eagerly laid into the now-ruined reputation of Roger Radcliffe, and also managed to include some pretty derogatory remarks about his old adversary, Scot Barlow, as if it had somehow been all Barlow's fault that Radcliffe had framed him. I thought that it was a good job that, under English law, the dead couldn't sue for slander.

Finally, with deadlines approaching and their copy to file, the reporters began to drift away and eventually to leave us in peace.

'Bloody marvellous, Perry,' Steve said to me while pumping my hand up and down. 'Almost as good as winning the National. Thank you so much.'

I decided not to mention my fee – not just yet, anyway.

Bruce and Steve departed together on foot, while I stepped back inside the court building to wait for Eleanor and the car.

I decided to call my father.

'Hello, Dad,' I said when he answered. 'How are things?'

'It's good to be home,' he said.

Alarm bells suddenly started ringing in my head.

'What do you mean, it's good to be home?' I said.

'Got back here about ten minutes ago,' he said. 'I left the hotel as soon as I got your message.'

'But I didn't give anyone a message,' I said.

'Yes you did,' he said with certainty. 'On this phone. One of those damned text things. Hold on. I could hear him pushing the buttons. Here it is. "Hi Dad, Everything fine. Please go home as quickly as possible. Love Geoffrey".'

'What time did you get it?' I asked him.

'About half past ten this morning,' he said. 'My old Morris is quite slow on the motorway these days.'

Radcliffe had already been in the witness box at half past ten. The message had to have been sent by Julian Trent.

'I thought I told you not to tell anyone where you were.'

'I didn't,' he said, sounding pained. 'No one knew where I was other than you, but I still don't see why it was so important.'

'But who else knew the number of that phone?' I asked.

'Oh, I called and gave it to Beryl and Tony on Saturday,' he said. 'They're my neighbours. Just in case anything happened to the house.'

I could just imagine Julian Trent turning up to find the place deserted and asking the neighbours, in his most charming manner, if they knew where Mr Mason had gone. He probably told them he was Mr Mason's grandson, come to surprise him. Of course they would have given him the phone number.

'Dad,' I said quite urgently. 'Please go back out and get in the car and drive anywhere, but get away from your house. Or go next door to Beryl and Tony's. Just please get away from the house.'

'What on earth for?' he said, annoyed. 'I've only just got back.'

'Dad, please just do it, and do it right now.'

'Oh, all right,' he said. 'I'll just make my cup of tea. I've put the kettle on.'

'Please, Dad,' I said more urgently. 'Leave the tea. Go now.'

'All right,' he said, his annoyance showing again. 'You're a strange boy.'

'Dad, take the phone with you. I'll call you back in a few minutes.'

Eleanor pulled up in the car outside the court buildings, and I hobbled out to her as quickly as I could.

'Drive,' I said urgently as I struggled in. 'Straight on.'

'I can't,' she said pointing at the sign. 'Buses and taxis only.'

'Ignore it,' I said. 'I think Julian Trent is somewhere around my father's bungalow.'

She looked at me, then back to the road. 'But surely your dad is still in Devon.'

'I wish,' I said. 'He's gone home. Trent sent him a text message this morning as if it had come from me, telling him to go back home as soon as possible.'

'Oh my God,' she said, putting her foot down on the accelerator.

'I'm calling the police,' I said.

I dialled 999 and the emergency operator answered almost immediately.

'Which service?' she said.

'Police,' I replied.

Eleanor dodged a few shiny metal bollards and then drove straight down Cornmarket Street, which was usually reserved for pedestrians, but it was the best short cut through the city. A few people looked at us rather strangely, and some shouted, but no one actually stopped us and we were soon racing down St Giles and away from the city centre northwards.

I heard the police come on the line and the telephone operator gave them my phone number. 'Yes,' said a policeman finally. 'How can we help?'

I tried to explain that my father was alone in his house and that he was in danger from a potential intruder. I should have lied to them but, stupidly, I told them the truth.

'So there isn't actually an intruder in the house at the moment?' the policeman said.

'No,' I replied. 'But I think that he might be outside, watching and waiting.'

'And why is that, sir?' he said.

What could I say? 'I just do,' I said unconvincingly.

'We can't send police cars as an emergency all over

the country just because people think they may be troubled at some time in the future. Now can we, sir?'

'Look,' I said. 'I am a barrister and I have been acting
at the Crown Court in Oxford and I'm telling you that I
have very good reason to believe that my father may be
in great danger. I am on my way to his house right now,
but I will be at least another twenty minutes getting there.
Will you please send a patrol car immediately?'

'I'll do what I can, sir,' he said. 'I'll record the incident
as a priority, but it will take some time to get a car to that
part of Northamptonshire.' It was his way of saying that
the police wouldn't actually be there for quite a long
while. 'Perhaps you could give us another call when you
arrive, sir.'

'Hopeless,' I said to Eleanor, hanging up. 'Mind the
speed camera!'

She slammed on the brakes and we crawled past the
yellow box at exactly thirty miles an hour. Then we were
off again, considerably faster.

I dialled my father's mobile number again.

'Are you out of the house?' I said when he answered.

'Nearly,' he said.

'What have you been doing?' I asked him in exasperation. It had been at least ten minutes since I had first
called him. I wondered if everyone's parents became so
cantankerous and obstinate as they neared their eightieth
birthdays.

'I've been looking for the little present I bought Beryl

413

and Tony in Sidmouth,' he said. 'I know it's in my suitcase somewhere.'

'Dad, please,' I almost shouted at him. 'Just get yourself out of the house right now. Get the present for them later.'

'Ah,' he said triumphantly. 'I've found it.'

'Good,' I said. 'Now get out of the house and stay out.'

'Hold on a minute,' he said. 'There's someone at the door.'

'Don't answer it,' I shouted urgently into the phone, but he obviously didn't hear me.

I hoped that it might have been Beryl and Tony coming round from next door to welcome him home, but, of course, it wasn't. The phone was still connected in his hand and I could faintly hear the exchange taking place on my father's front doorstep.

'What do you want?' I heard my father say rather bossily. There was something that I didn't catch from his visitor, and then I could hear my father again, his voice now full of concern. 'No,' he said. 'I don't want any. Please go away.'

Suddenly there was a crash and the phone line went dead.

I quickly called the house landline number, but it simply rang and rang until, eventually, someone picked it up. But it went dead again before I had a chance to say anything. I tried it again, but this time there was nothing but the engaged tone.

'Oh my God,' I said. 'I think Julian Trent has just arrived, and my father is still there.'

Eleanor floored the accelerator as we swept onto the A34 dual carriageway north. Fortunately, the rush hour had yet to get into full swing and we hurtled up to the motorway junction and onto the M40 at breakneck speed.

I tried my father's landline once more, but it was still engaged.

'Call the police again,' said Eleanor.

This time I was connected to a different policeman and he now recorded the incident as an emergency. He promised to dispatch a patrol car immediately.

'How long will it take?' I said.

'About twenty minutes,' he said. 'At best. Maybe longer.'

'Twenty minutes!' I said incredulously. 'Can't you get someone there sooner than that?'

'Kings Sutton is right on the edge of the county,' he said. 'The patrol car has to come from Towcester.'

'How about Banbury?' I said. 'That's got to be closer.'

'Banbury is Thames Valley,' he said. 'Kings Sutton is Northamptonshire Constabulary.'

'I don't believe it,' I said. 'Just get someone there as soon as you can.'

Throughout the call, Eleanor had been driving like a woman possessed, overtaking a lorry around the outside of a roundabout when turning right, and then causing a group of mothers and toddlers crossing the road to leap for their lives. But we made it safely to Kings Sutton in record time and she pulled up where I told her, round the corner and just out of sight of my father's bungalow.

'Wait here,' I said, climbing out of the car and struggling with the crutches.

'Why don't you wait for the police?' she said. She came round the car and took my hand. 'Please will you wait?'

It had only been about seven or eight minutes since I had last spoken to them. And they wouldn't be here for ages yet.

'Eleanor, my darling, my father's in there on his own with Julian Trent,' I said. 'Would you wait?'

'I'll come with you, then,' she said.

'No,' I said. 'You must wait here and speak to the police when they arrive. Show them which is the right house.'

Eleanor grabbed me and hugged me hard. 'Be careful, my Barrister Man,' she said. 'I love you.'

'I love you more,' I said, but then I pushed her away. I had things to do.

I made my way gingerly through an herbaceous border and along the side of the bungalow to my father's front door. It was standing wide open. I peeped inside but could see nothing unusual, save for the mobile phone, which lay on the floor with its back off, the battery lying close by. I reckoned my father must have dropped it as Trent had forced his way in.

I stepped through the doorway into the hall, rather wishing that the crutches didn't make so much of a clink

when I put them down on the hard wood-block floor. But
I needn't have worried about the noise. As I moved across
the hallway I could clearly hear Julian Trent and his
baseball bat systematically doing to my father's home
what he had previously done to mine. He was down the
far end of the corridor causing mayhem in the bedrooms.

I looked into the sitting room. My father lay face down
on the carpet, with blood oozing from his head. I quickly
went over to him and bent down, using one end of the
light blue sofa for support. He was not in great shape, not
at all. I turned him over slightly and saw that he had been
struck severely at least once across his face, and also that
there was a nasty wound behind his right ear. I couldn't
really tell if he was breathing or not, and I tried unsuc-
cessfully to find a pulse in his neck. However, the cuts on
his head were still bleeding slightly, which gave me some
hope. I checked that his mouth and airway were open by
tilting his head back a bit and laying him more on his
side.

Where were those damn police? I thought.

The noise of destruction in the bedrooms suddenly
ceased and I could hear Trent's footsteps coming back
along the corridor. I struggled up and hid behind the open
sitting-room door. Perhaps he would go past me. Perhaps
he would go away.

My father groaned.

In truth, it was not much more than a sigh, but Trent
heard it and he stopped in the doorway.

I looked down at my father on the floor and realized

with horror that I'd left one of my crutches lying right next to him on the carpet.

It was too late to retrieve it now.

Trent came into the sitting room. I pressed myself back tight against the wall behind the door and sensed rather than saw him, but there was no doubt he was there. I could see the end of the baseball bat as he held it out in front of him. From where he stood, he would be clearly able to see my father, and the crutch.

'OK,' he said loudly into the silence, making me jump. 'I know you're here. Show yourself.'

Oh shit, I thought. I was hardly in any shape to fight a twelve-year-old cripple, let alone someone twice that age who was very fit and healthy, and who was holding a baseball bat to boot. I stayed exactly where I was.

The door was pulled away from me, exposing my hiding place. And there he was, in blue denim jeans and a short-sleeved dark green polo shirt, swinging his base-ball bat back and forth. And, once again, he was smiling.

'Time to complete some unfinished business,' he said with relish.

'It won't do you any good,' I said defiantly. 'Your godfather was arrested in court this morning and the police are on their way here to arrest you.'

He hardly seemed to care. I glanced out of the window. Where were those wretched police?

'I'd better make it quick, then,' he said nonchalantly. 'That's a shame. I was planning to take my time and enjoy killing you.'

'No handy pitchfork for you to use this time,' I said.

'No,' he said, still smiling. 'That is a pity, but this will do instead.'

He swung the baseball bat at my head so fast that he almost caught me unawares.

At the last moment I ducked down and the wooden bat thumped into the wall, right where my head had been only a fraction of a second before. I dived away from him, hopping madly on one leg. I would just have to put the other foot down, I thought, and hope my knee would carry my weight. I tried it as I made my way across the room and without too much of a problem. But I was too slow, and Trent had time to turn and swing the bat again, landing a glancing blow on my left biceps, just above the elbow. It wasn't a direct hit but it was enough to cause my arm to go completely dead, numb and useless.

I leaned up against the wall by the window, breathing heavily. Two months of inactivity since the races at Cheltenham had left me hopelessly unfit. This battle was going to be over much too soon for my liking.

The feeling and movement in my left arm began to return slightly, but I feared it was too little, too late. Trent advanced towards me, grinning broadly, and he raised the bat for another strike. I stood stock still and stared at him. If he was going to kill me he would have to do it with me watching him. I wasn't going to cower down and let him hit me over the back of the head, as he had clearly done to my father.

I dived down to my left at the last instant and the bat

thumped again into the wall above my right shoulder. I grabbed it with my good right hand, and also with my nearly useless left. I clung on to the bat for dear life. I gripped it so tight that my fingers felt as if they were digging into the wood.

With both hands up above my shoulders, my body was completely unprotected by my arms. Trent took his right hand off the bat and punched me as hard as he could in the stomach.

It was a fatal error on his part.

While, to him, my abdomen may have appeared to be defenceless, he clearly didn't know, or perhaps he had forgotten, about the hard plastic body shell that I still wore out of sight beneath my starched white shirt.

He screamed. Along, loud, agonizing scream.

It must have been like punching a brick wall. The bones in his hand would have cracked and splintered from the impact.

He dropped the baseball bat from his other hand and went down on his knees in obvious agony, clutching at his right wrist.

But I wasn't going to let him get off that easily.

I picked up the bat and hit him with it, audibly breaking his jaw and sending him sprawling on to the floor, seemingly unconscious.

I sat down on the arm of the sofa and looked out of the window. There was still no sign of the boys in blue, but now I wasn't so worried, I was even a little bit pleased.

I leaned down to the telephone, picked up the dangling handset and used it to call for an ambulance. Then I went across to my father. He was definitely alive, but only just. His breathing was perceptible but shallow, and I still couldn't find a pulse in his neck but there was a faint one in his wrist. I moved him properly into the recovery position and he obligingly groaned again. I stroked his blood-matted hair. I may have been a strange boy, and he was definitely a strange and stubborn father, but I still loved him.

Julian Trent moaned a little, so I went back and sat on the arm of the sofa and looked down at him lying on the carpet in front of me, the young man who had brought so much misery to so many innocent people.

He began to stir, pulling his knees up under him so he was kneeling on the floor facing away from me. He cradled his right hand in his left, and his head was bowed down in front. As I watched him, his head came up a fraction and he tried to slowly reach out with his left hand towards the baseball bat that I had put down on the sofa beside him.

Would he ever give up? I asked myself.

I leaned down quickly and picked up the bat before he could reach it. Instead, he used his left hand to push down on the blue upholstery, as if he were about to try and stand.

No, I suddenly realized. He would never give up, not ever.

Eleanor and I might make our life together but there

would always be three of us in the relationship, the spectre of Julian Trent hovering nearby in the darkness, forever waiting for the chance to settle the score in his favour. Even if he was convicted of Scot Barlow's murder, and past form gave no guarantee of that, I was under no illusion that a lengthy term of imprisonment would reform or rehabilitate him. He would simply spend the time planning the completion of what he thought of as his 'unfinished business'.

Just like Josef Hughes and George Barnett, we would never be free of the fear. Not for as long as Julian Trent was alive.

In common law, self-defence is called an 'absolute defence', that is, it doesn't just mitigate a crime, it means that no crime exists in the first place. But in order for a justification of self-defence to succeed, certain conditions needed to apply. I knew this because I had recently defended someone accused of causing grievous bodily harm to a would-be mugger.

The conditions were a two-stage test, one of which was subjective and the other objective. First, did the accused genuinely believe that force was necessary to protect himself? And, secondly, if he did have that belief, then was the degree of force reasonable to meet the threat as he saw it?

The degree of force used was always the key. The law demanded that the force used should not have been excessive or, if it had been, then the perpetrator was making an honest, even if over zealous, attempt to uphold the law rather than taking the law into his own hands for the purposes of revenge or retribution.

In a landmark case in 1971 Lord Morris, the Lord of Appeal, stated, 'If there has been an attack so that self-defence is reasonably necessary, it will be recognized that a person defending himself cannot weigh to a nicety the exact measure of his defensive action. If the jury thought that, in a moment of unexpected anguish, the person attacked had only done what he honestly and instinctively thought was necessary, that would be the most potent evidence that only reasonable defensive action had been taken.'

I glanced briefly out of the window. There was still no sign of the police, nor of the arrival of an ambulance.

Julian Trent drew his left leg forward beneath him and slowly began to rise.

It had to be now or never.

I stood up, lifted my arms high over my head and hit him again, bringing the bat down hard and catching him at the base of the skull where the neck joins the head. I hit him with the very end of the bat in order to gain maximum leverage. There was a terrible crunching noise and he went flat down again onto the carpet, and lay still.

I wasn't certain whether it had been a lethal blow or not, but it would have to be enough. I felt sick.

All the frustration and fear of the past six months had gone into that strike, together with the anger at losing my possessions, the rage I had for him having torn to shreds the photograph of my Angela, the resentment I bore for having to dance to his tune for so long, and the fury at what he had done to my father.

I sat down again calmly on the arm of the sofa.

It was finally over. I had done only what I honestly and instinctively thought had been necessary to meet the threat as I saw it, and I would have to take my chances in court.

I glanced out of the window once more.

At long last, I could see two policemen coming down the driveway.

But now I needed help of a different kind.

I picked up the telephone and called Arthur.

www.panmacmillan.com